A SPARK IN THE CINDERS

Also by Jenny Elder Moke

Hood
Curse of the Specter Queen
Rise of the Snake Goddess

A SPARK IN THE CINDERS

JENNY ELDER MOKE

HYPERION
Los Angeles   New York

First Edition, June 2023
10 9 8 7 6 5 4 3 2 1
FAC-004510-23111
Printed in the United States of America

This book is set in Fairfield LT Std.
Designed by Phil T. Buchanan

Library of Congress Cataloging-in-Publication Data
Names: Moke, Jenny Elder, author.
Title: A spark in the cinders / by Jenny Elder Moke.
Description: First edition. • Los Angeles : Hyperion, 2023. • Audience:
  Ages 12–18. • Audience: Grades 7–12. • Summary: "In a kingdom on the
  brink of ruin, one wicked stepsister will use her wits, cunning, and
  fortitude (plus a little help from her fairy godparent) to embark on a
  dangerous quest for a magical relic that will save her people"
  —Provided by publisher.
Identifiers: LCCN 2022026802 (print) • LCCN 2022026803 (ebook) •
  ISBN 9781368039918 (hardcover) • ISBN 9781368046169 (ebook)
Subjects: CYAC: Magic—Fiction. • Stepsisters—Fiction. •
  Fairy godmothers—Fiction. • Fantasy. • LCGFT: Fantasy fiction. • Novels.
Classification: LCC PZ7.1.M639 Sp 2023 (print) • LCC PZ7.1.M639 (ebook) •
  DDC [Fic]—dc23
LC record available at https://lccn.loc.gov/2022026802
LC ebook record available at https://lccn.loc.gov/2022026803

Reinforced binding
Visit www.HyperionTeens.com

SUSTAINABLE FORESTRY INITIATIVE

Certified Sourcing
www.sfiprogram.org
SFI-01681

Logo Applies to Text Stock Only

To all the girls
who found themselves late

PROLOGUE

MOTHER IS AS ANGRY AS I HAVE EVER SEEN HER, which is truly saying something.

"That feckless, empty-headed, backstabbing, gold-digging little harlot," she seethes, snatching up the glass shoe the duke has thoughtlessly left behind and aiming it squarely at the door he's just disappeared through, taking Cinderella and our hopes for the future along with him. The delicate slipper shatters against the ragged wood, little shards tinkling onto the worn flagstones of the entrance. I guess her fairy godmother didn't think to bespell it against a stepmother's rage.

"After all I have done for her!" Mother storms around the room, tearing down curtains, revealing the rotted wooden sill and the grimy glass. The parts Cinderella didn't have time to clean before the duke's arrival. The whorls of ancient dust bend the late-afternoon sunlight to their will, scattering beams at haphazard angles around the room. The light catches Mother across the eyes, glowing gold in her rage, and she narrows them at me.

"You," she says, her voice so still and quiet it chills me far more than her anger. I wish she would scream, or throw a glass shoe at me. Anything but that bone-deep look of disappointment. "All you had to do was fit into the shoe."

"It was far too small," I say, even though I know speaking up now will only get me in deeper trouble. I look helplessly at Divya, who is trying to blend into the peeling wallpaper. She didn't fit into the shoe, either, but I won't put her in Mother's path to say so. "What could I have done?"

"You could have *made* it fit," Mother says, advancing on me. She pulls her silk gloves loose and tosses them at the nearest chair, one we had to forage from the carriage house. It was the only one the moths had not completely destroyed. "What are a few little toes against the balance of our future?"

"What good would the self-mutilation have done me?" I ask, knowing she doesn't mean it. Hoping she doesn't mean it. "It wasn't me who danced with the prince at that ball and he knows it. This whole business of searching the kingdom for the girl with the glass slipper has been a sham from the beginning. It's a shoe. It could have fit hundreds of girls. Only Cinderella had the matching slipper."

"I should have locked that girl up," Mother fumes, already back to the favorite target of her ire. "Somewhere even that vile fairy godmother of hers couldn't reach her. It's the high chancellor who should have her locked up, playing about with magic like that. It's dangerous, consorting with the fey. Unnatural. What if she bespelled people? It's the only explanation for the hold she seems to have on Prince Fael. We should report her, before this goes too far."

"But Cinderella will be queen," Divya pipes up unwisely. "What if she tries to throw *us* in the dungeons?"

"She will never make it to queen," Mother says with so much assurance it makes me shiver. "The prince will grow tired of her long before that and toss her for some other pretty-faced idiot the moment she does not deliver him a male heir. Let her expend herself on childbirth and see whose attention she steals thereafter. I was the most radiant beauty in Novador before you girls. If I'd been such a fool as to rely on my looks alone, we would be destitute by now."

It takes all my years of training to keep a neutral expression, because even though her eyes are not directly on me, I'm not so much a fool as to think my mother is not observing me. I know what Divya does not—why Mother had her gloves cut from her night-gown, why we had our shoes dyed instead of purchasing new ones, why this was the only room the duke was permitted to enter. We *are* destitute, or nearly so. All the wealth of Cinderella's father and his once-sprawling estate, now whittled down into a few gold pieces and a stack of threatening letters from bill collectors.

Collectors I was meant to rescue us from.

"There is still the suit from Lord Calveron," I say, doing my best not to wince at the thought of the old man who had to eat his roasted beef with a soup spoon.

"Calveron is betrothed to that yellow-haired, bucktoothed dis-grace," Mother says with a dismissive wave of her hand. "They announced it last week."

She means Lucy Theronwood, who does have unfortunately pro-nounced front teeth. I have a moment of pity for the girl, betrothed to a man who went to school with her grandfather, before remem-bering that she has a future now and we still do not.

"What about Captain Ramsey?" I ask, mirroring Mother's move-ments as she paces about the small receiving room. It's a dance we often do, when Mother is in a high dudgeon, but I have none of the usual tools at my disposal. I can no longer promise her new ball gowns or cut-crystal glassware. The best I can hope for is food in the larder and wood for the fireplace.

"Captain Ramsey doesn't even have a title," Mother says, stopping to glare at me. "You were meant to marry the prince, Aralyn. You were meant to be a queen! And now you would debase yourself as some shipman's wife?"

I wouldn't debase myself as anyone's wife, if it were up to me. But it's not up to me, it never has been. Not since we learned of the debts Cinderella's father acquired during his lengthy illness. Not since I learned that for all of Mother's social maneuvering, she never had a head for money or how to keep it.

"We are not without options," I say, soothingly, holding out my hands to Mother. Willing her to take them, to look into my eyes and let me calm her, so she can calm me. Mother has always had a plan, all my life. "There are others, as eligible as the prince and far wealthier. Fael is a lovesick idiot, anyhow."

"He shall reap what he sows," Mother says, her gaze going hard. "And we shall sow new seeds."

"Yes, of course we will," I say, relief flooding through me. "I shall fetch the roster."

"You shall do no such thing," Mother says, her voice staying me at the door. It turns sickly sweet, like a rich dessert that turns your stomach after two bites. "Divya, darling, would you be so good as to run up to my room and get the roster of eligible bachelors in Novador?"

"Me?" Divya says in surprise, glancing between the two of us. "Really?"

"Yes, darling, really," Mother says, letting her annoyance seep into her tone. But she gathers herself, turning a radiant smile on my younger sister. It's like staring directly into the sun, being the recipient of that smile. It blinds you. "You will need to acquaint yourself with every aspect of their lives if we are to pick the most eligible among them."

Something heavy settles in the pit of my stomach, like the world has moved several degrees off-kilter and I'm still standing in the wrong place. "Why would Divya need to acquaint herself with the roster?"

Mother's expression is pure satisfaction as she turns back to me. "Because, Aralyn, it appears Divya must accomplish what you and all the years of training I wasted on you cannot."

I suck in a soft breath. "Mother, I know our plans did not work out for the prince, but that doesn't mean I cannot—"

Mother holds up a hand, silencing me. "What you cannot do could fill a tome, Ary. I only regret putting all our eggs in your basket, my darling. It's not your fault, you have too much of your father in you. Those oversize feet, that pointed nose. Your lack of conversational wit. I should have known you wouldn't turn the prince's head. You're far too ordinary."

"Mother," I breathe, shock drawing the inappropriate emotional display out of me. She couldn't have driven the spike deeper if she'd told me I was horse-faced and empty-headed.

"And since Cinderella took what was meant for you, you will take what was meant for her." She points her hand in the direction of the kitchens like it's a death sentence. "You will sleep in Cinderella's place."

"Surely you cannot be serious," I say, my voice an agonizing tremble. Oh, if Mistress Clara could hear me now, she would snap her stick across my knuckles. A lady never betrays her emotions in public. Of course, I am not the lady I was meant to be.

"Someone must wash the dresses and prepare the meals now that Cinderella is off on her little fairy tale," Mother says, her tone so reasonable. As if I am the one acting outrageously. "And Divya must keep her hands clean for the gentlemen to kiss them. It wouldn't do to have dirty fingernails when one is courting. She'll need that dress you're wearing as well, for her trousseau. See that it's cleaned and put away in her trunk by morning."

"Courting?" Divya squeals, caught up in Mother's glamour as I once was. The look she gives me is positively gloating.

"Mother, I'm sorry," I say, but she is already looping her arm through Divya's.

"Don't embarrass yourself any more than you already have this evening, Ary," she says over her shoulder. She pats Divya's hand affectionately. "Now come along, darling, and let's discuss what to do with that hair of yours."

The house has grown dark, the sunlight escaping the tragedy it witnessed here. The halls beyond the receiving room are cold and empty, all the better to hide the ugly things welling up in my eyes. It's only because I am so exhausted that my body can get away with such weakness. I'm nearly blind by the time I stumble through a doorway and my shin finds the unforgiving edge of a cast-iron stove. Gowns were not designed to be contained in cramped kitchens, and more than once I hear the soul-crushing rip of delicate lace as it catches on various equipment. There are no windows in the kitchen, no lanterns to guide me or roaring hearth to warm me. I can dance a complicated Ballorean waltz, pair a delicate whitefish with a sweet red wine or a hearty roast with a bold white, and negotiate trade relations with hostile nations, but I don't know how to start a fire.

The best I can manage is the stub of a candle left beside the fireplace, next to one of the last precious books Cinderella was able to keep from my mother's enterprising grasp. Her pallet is just as she left it, a meager bundle of hay and a blanket more threadbare than our pocketbooks. Hardly good enough for a wayward calf, much less an inconvenient stepsister. I lift up the blanket to inspect it for mites and a wave of Cinderella's soft, sweet scent tickles its way up my nose. She always smelled faintly of lavender and sugar, even when we had long since run dry of both in the garden and the larder.

And perhaps it's because I'm so tired—or because Mother's dismissal still drives its stinger into my heart—that the rage Mistress Clara always tried to beat out of me comes crashing in like a runaway horse bent on destruction. Little Ella, always covered in soot and cinder, has stolen *everything* from me. My future, my chance at rescuing us from criminal poverty, my mother's approval. Her and that fairy godmother of hers, waving her magic wand and erasing years of hard work and training. As if all it really takes in this world is a glittering dress and a simpering smile.

I will have my revenge on Cinderella, no matter how many hems I have to mend or hearths I have to scrub.

ONE

THE CLOTH MERCHANT IS TRYING TO CHEAT ME
again. He insults the gifted needle of Monsieur Lisseu by offering
a paltry thirty silver pieces for one of his finest ball gowns, a deep
blue skirt with waves of soft white chiffon that make it look like the
undulation of the sea when you dance. It's my most favorite dress,
and I have managed to keep it hidden from Mother through several
rounds of purges, but we'll starve if I don't sell it.

"This was six hundred silver pieces, brand-new, and has been kept
in pristine condition," I say, lifting the skirt to show him the hem.
"Hand embroidered by Monsieur Lisseu, the most celebrated dress-
maker in all the kingdom. Imported silk from the mountain region of
Torneau. The Lady of Canenberg herself envied its slimming bodice
and rippling skirt at her opening ball last year."

The cloth merchant, a sweaty man with a nose the size of a garlic
bulb, shrugs his shoulders inside his poorly cut jacket. "Go sell it to
her, then. I keep telling you, miss, we don't have need for a flouncy
ball gown. You got sturdy cotton underthings or a good pair of trousers, we'll take them. But this kind of thing ain't much use out in
the fields."

I ball my fists up in the dress fabric, crumpling the soft silk while trying to contain an anger that has writhed within me for months, ever since Cinderella and that ridiculous shoe of hers stomped all over my plans. Once upon a time I could dispatch a heathen like this merchant with a well-placed barb, but now I find myself swallowing down a scream.

"Sixty silver pieces at least," I say, my voice breathy from the effort to maintain a polite veneer. "That's a tenth of the cost, and more than a bargain for you."

The cloth merchant tilts his head at the skirt, sucking in air through his teeth and leaving a fine ridge of spittle along his upper lip. It should be a crime to hand over Lisseu's work to such a man.

"I could maybe do forty, though it's a real stretch, it is." He lifts his brows suggestively to me. "Maybe you could put it on for me, show me how it looks."

We are both saved the indignity and inconvenience of my slapping his impertinent face by the blast of a trumpet from the entry to the town square. For a brief, ludicrous moment I fear it's the horns of war, but then a shining white carriage trundles through the narrow entry between stalls and I actually wish it were the horns of war. I'd prefer an invading army to the solitary coach doing its best to pass through the crowded pedestrian streets with six knights in full armor on horseback surrounding it. The gathered crowds grumble and shift their heavy burdens to drop to one knee in the filthy trenches of dirt, heads lowered. I press back against the cloth merchant's stall, hoping I will blend in with the trousers and leather aprons hanging above me. But even when I wish to go unnoticed, Monsieur Lisseu's creation could never.

"You will kneel when your sovereign passes," calls out one of the knights.

"If I kneel, my dress will get dirty," I call back, lifting the froth of chiffon as evidence. "This is a Monsieur Lisseu creation."

"Have you stolen it?" the knight demands, drawing the horse to the side to face me directly. Glinting green eyes challenge me from two long slits in the metal, a finely honed nose just showing through the front. Something about the tone sparks my irritation anew.

"What use would I have for a stolen ball gown?" I ask. "Better to take the silver, or the food. What good is a ball gown? I cannot wear it. I cannot sell it. What a foolish question."

"Did you call me foolish?" the knight demands.

"Better just to kneel, girlie," mutters the cloth merchant from behind me.

"Easy for you to say with your stout trousers and their reinforced knees," I mutter back.

"You will kneel, or I will make you kneel," the knight says, dismounting and pulling off the slitted helmet to tuck it beneath one arm.

"You're a girl," I say, taking in her sparkling green eyes and finely hewn features. Now I sound like the foolish one.

"What a keen observation of unerring intelligence," the girl says dryly. She's tall, much taller than I am, and broad through the shoulders and hips. Her hair is short, like a man's, and a deep golden brown in the warm sun. "Now you will kneel, or I will have you put in the dungeons for dishonoring the princess."

"That's not actually a crime," I say, shaking my head. Though I hear the dungeons have porridge, at least. But the rest of her statement catches up with me, and I frown hard at the carriage, my stomach twisting in dread. "Whom did you say was in the carriage?"

"Vee, have we arrived?" Cinderella's powder-blue eyes appear at the half-opened window, landing on me and flicking left and right before widening. "Oh, Vee, by the starry skies, we're *in* the town square."

"Of course we are, Your Majesty," Vee says. "I would not have you walk through town and muddy your hems in these unkempt streets."

I roll my eyes. "But it's good enough for the rest of us?"

The girl cuts her glance at me. "And yet still, you do not kneel. Clearly you need assistance."

Before I realize what she intends to do, she hooks her foot behind my knee and jerks forward, dropping me to the ground with a hard thud. The dress spills out of my arms into a muddy divot where the carriage has stopped.

"There," Vee says, self-satisfied.

"Vee, I asked you to leave the carriage at the edge of town so we would not make such a spectacle as this one," Cinderella whispers. She presses her eyes closed. "It is done now, I suppose, and you have found her."

Vee glances at me in surprise. "This is her? Your stepsister? The one meant to marry my cousin? She looks like a commoner."

"I am not a commoner," I snap, fighting back tears at the state of Monsieur Lisseu's dress. How will we eat now?

"And yet there you are, kneeling in the mud like one." Vee's lips quirk like they want to smile, but her knight's training won't allow it. If I could, I'd slap her and the cloth merchant in one go. But instead I struggle to rise, gathering the dress in my arms like a dying child.

"If you're quite through playing queen of the hill, I have business to attend to," I say.

"Aralyn, wait," Cinderella says, the door to the carriage sweeping open as she steps out. The collected crowd gives a gasp and spontaneously starts clapping. I don't know who they thought was in the carriage before now, but I suppose Cinderella inspires their feeble minds. She wears a soft pink dress with puffed sleeves and a full skirt that goes against fashion. They'll probably bring it back and rename it in her honor. "Vee, would you take the carriage and meet us back at the manor?"

Vee stiffens. "I'm sworn to protect you. I cannot do that by abandoning you here alone."

"I won't be alone," Cinderella says, waving in my direction. "I'll be with my stepsister."

Vee lands another heavy gaze on me. "Yes. I'm aware of your familial history."

I don't miss the implication in her tone, and I don't care for it. I bare my teeth at her and she steps toward me, her gauntlet creaking into a fist. Cinderella puts a hand on Vee's arm.

"We don't threaten our subjects, Vee," Cinderella says in a patient voice that tells me this isn't the first time she's had to call off her watchdog. "I'll be fine. Please take the carriage to the main house and wait for us there. I wish to speak with my stepsister."

Vee looks like she would rather ride into the thick of battle than turn her back on me, but her sovereign has spoken, and we're all subservient to our masters. So she nods, taking her time getting back on her horse to leave. I follow in their wake, eager to avoid the stares of the villagers, and Cinderella has the nerve to give me a smile as she falls in step beside me.

"I apologize for her. She's a magnificent fighter but a tad eager at times."

"A tad eager? You make her sound like a puppy, and not the wolf I suspect she is."

Cinderella tilts her head in concession. "Perhaps more than a tad eager."

"What do you want?" I snap, the viciousness of my question undercut by the froth of dress still filling my arms.

Cinderella reaches forward, smoothing out the skirt and carefully folding the dress into a manageable square, lifting it out of my arms and pressing it against her chest as we clear the market square and walk through the outskirts of town. Beggar children gather like flies and Cinderella pauses, reaching into a pocket in her dress to produce sweets and coins for each one. As if any of that will save them from starvation. "I've come to ask your help, Aralyn."

I jerk back. "What could you possibly need my help with?"

She hesitates only a moment, her expression turning shadowed. "With saving the kingdom."

"Saving the kingdom from what?" I ask, leaving off the insult of *Your ineptitude?* in favor of my curiosity.

Cinderella begins walking slowly toward the manor, her shoulders slumping forward and her back curling over as it always did when she walked home from the market with her arms full of goods. It's as if her body carries a phantom burden from all those years of chores. I scoff at the peasantly posture before realizing I'm doing the exact same thing. By the fairies, do I look like that? Mistress Clara would lay her switch across my shoulders if she could see me now. I pull my shoulders back, following along in the ruts beside my stepsister.

"Do you know how I envied you, all these years?" Cinderella asks, running her fingertips unconsciously over the smooth silk underskirt. "After Father died, I tried to learn to care for those of the manor who still remained. When your mother began bringing tutors to the house, I had hoped to build my own knowledge of how to run a successful holding."

But those tutors weren't schooled in the domestic affairs of a minor landowner; they were foreign affairs experts and diplomatic consorts and military strategists. And they weren't meant for Cinderella; they were meant for me.

"I taught myself what I could from Papa's dwindling library, and then I eavesdropped on your lessons when I wasn't so tired that I fell asleep in my soup," she continues. She shakes her head. "But the reality of running a kingdom as wide and diverse as Novador has proven far greater a challenge than running a manor."

I grit my teeth at the audacity of this servant girl thinking she should have the run of an entire country with no training. Of course it takes work to run a kingdom, and of course this daft little buttercup would think she could waltz into the role as easily as she waltzed into the prince's arms. But I *have* received diplomatic training, so I let none of those thoughts show.

"It's the king's duty to run the country, is it not?" I ask, even though I know the answer as clearly as birds know how to fly.

Cinderella gives a hesitant nod. "It is. When he will do it."

This is a far more intriguing turn. If empty-headed little Ella can see there's something wrong with the king's rule, then there must be something *very* wrong.

"I think the king has grown weary," she says, treading the line between concern and treason carefully. "From what I've gathered in my short stay at the castle, the king spends a great deal of his time on the royal hunt, or sequestered in his chambers. Even Fael rarely sees him. My husband worries for his father, and I worry for our kingdom."

Husband. So there was a wedding. I was too busy scrubbing pots to notice. "The king doesn't rule alone. He has the king's council. Can your prince not appeal to their reasoning?"

She glances at me, the struggle playing out across her face like the worst of chess players. What a life it must be, to have all your emotions so transparent. No wonder Mother ate her alive like a swarm of biting flies.

"High Chancellor Cordo has the run of the council," she says.

Ah, Cordo, the king's younger brother, outsize in his ambitions. Shoehorned into the role of high chancellor as a pacifying measure for his ambitious greed. There are even rumors of an attempted coup many years ago, when the king first took the throne. But those rumors are fanatically suppressed, probably by Cordo himself.

Cinderella lets out a sigh. "Our people are starving. Fael has done what he can, but his uncle is more interested in building up our military and throwing lavish balls in his honor. And since his uncle owns the high council—"

"He owns the kingdom," I finish. We stop just outside the manor gates, her guards lined up along the front of the house like menacing decorations. Vee stands at their head, her emerald gaze boring into me. I give her a little wave, which doesn't seem to ingratiate me with her.

"So, what is it you think I can do about any of this?" I ask, crossing my arms. "If you want to replace the high chancellor, you'll have to go through the council. If he owns the council, then you'll have to convince the king to do his duty long enough to have the prince appointed head of the council. Which, frankly, he should have done ages ago."

Cinderella chews at her bottom lip and cuts a glance at her guards. "That's the very problem I face. I don't know what we *can* do. Cordo has kept Fael from assuming any roles within the council that will give him real power. I've tried every way I know to gain confidences within the castle, and I've made some small inroads, but I fear that the kingdom is in far worse state than we even know. You've trained for this your entire life. You know more about diplomacy and the inner workings of the court than I ever could. You were the only person I could think of to ask for help, and I wouldn't have done so were we not desperate."

I'd rather scrub every last hearth in Novador than give Cinderella the benefit of all my years of education and training. Let her fail and learn the true depth of what she lacks. But . . . Mistress Clara's training wraps up my rage in a brutal cage of logic, and I stuff it deep down where all emotions belong. Cinderella has offered me an opportunity she couldn't have envisioned. If circumstances at the castle really are as dire as she fears, then there could be fortunes made on the changing of the guard. If I can better understand the shifting alliances and High Chancellor Cordo's intentions, I can better wield them to our benefit. Possibly even hand Mother an advisory seat on the council if a prince-shaped one opens up. And I wouldn't have to marry the hay-brained man to do it.

"I'll need access to the royal library," I say, my tired mind rejuvenated by the promise of fulfillment and revenge. "Specifically, the bylaws of the king's obligations to the council and the rules of succession."

"Thank you, Aralyn," Cinderella says, relief washing over her features as she takes my hand. My nails leave little crescents of black against her white suede gloves, which brings me satisfaction. "I'm grateful for whatever help you can provide."

I don't intend to be any help to *her*, but she doesn't need to know that. "I'll also need a servant for the day, to do the chores at the manor I won't be able to do because I'm helping you."

She nods again. "Of course. I'll send to the castle right away."

I allow myself a most delicious smile as I turn to the guards standing before the main house and the tall girl at their head. "That would take too long. I have someone better in mind."

TWO

I'VE NEVER BEEN TO THE CASTLE FOR ANYTHING other than balls, banquets, and coronations, so it's rather a shock how dreary it is in the full light of day without the typical trappings of a royal celebration. Everything is so gray, the stones of the outer wall pockmarked with green lichen and the trees shaggy and unkempt. Even the gate guards slouch in their positions. They straighten to salute as we pass, and I see that one has had the audacity to bring a stool.

"I'd have him drawn and quartered for that," I murmur.

"Gerald?" says Cinderella with warm affection in her tone. "He has a terrible case of gout that pains him in his left leg. I had the head of the guard bring him out that stool so he could rest it while he was on duty."

Of course she did; it's no wonder the kingdom is falling apart with a muffin like her in charge. "What is your official story for bringing me to the castle? It's not as if the animosity within our family is unknown to the rest of the court. We did not even receive an invitation to your wedding, I hardly think they'll accept that you're inviting me to a friendly tea."

Cinderella raises her brows at me in surprise. "Of course I invited you to our wedding. Why would I exclude you?"

I could think of a thousand reasons, all of them mundane household chores. "I never saw such an invite."

Cinderella folds her hands primly in her lap. "Well, your mother certainly sent her . . . regrets."

I can well imagine what kinds of *regrets* Mother might have sent. The kinds of backhanded insults Cinderella would be used to receiving. The kind meant to put your lessers in their place, regardless of whatever station they'd managed to crawl their way up to.

"I didn't know," I say, for lack of anything else to say. It's not as if I would have attended had I known; but Cinderella seems oddly disappointed that we were not there, which I cannot begin to fathom. I would never have invited us, and certainly not *her* if the situations had been reversed and all of Mother's plans had come to fruition.

"It's neither here nor there," Cinderella says in a voice that is far too chipper to be real. "Ah, we've arrived."

The coachman opens the door and hands us both down, and it's not until I've righted the skirts of the dress I retrieved from Divya's armoire that I notice we're not at the main entrance to the palace. In fact, we are nowhere near it. I'm not even sure where we are.

"This is not the main entrance," I say.

"No, I prefer a more discreet entrance," Cinderella says, blushing. "If I enter through the main doors, the servants must line up and make formal announcements and bow as I enter. It's awfully disruptive, and entirely unnecessary, but I can't seem to make them stop. So I enter through here, where the groomers access the stables."

Of *course* Cinderella would enter through the groomers' entrance. By the fairies, what an embarrassment. Taking the council seat from her and that simpering prince of hers will be a mercy, both for them and for the kingdom.

"Where is the library?" I ask.

The interior of the castle isn't much more inviting than the exterior, the hallways bare of any decorations and filled with unseemly drafts. Was this truly the same castle I visited not six months ago for the prince's ill-fated ball, lit up with colorful fires and teeming with so many guests they had to build a second dance floor out in the gardens?

"Did someone die?" I ask Cinderella as yet another servant scuttles past with eyes downcast, avoiding our gazes.

She looks to me in shock. "Why? What have you heard?"

I had only asked it in jest, but now I fear I might not have been too far off the mark. "Everyone is scurrying about like there is a funerary march to prepare for. Is it really so bad as all that? I knew the king was withdrawn, but this is . . ."

"Now you see the reason for my urgency" is her only response.

It has been rumored throughout the kingdom for months now— longer than the prince's desperate ball to secure a wife—that King Soteo has been on the decline. And Cinderella admitted as much to me herself not a few hours ago when she came begging for my help. But the mood in the castle implies that things are far worse off than a king who simply hunts too much, or withdraws from his people for too long. It is as if the sovereign has already crossed the veil, and left nothing but uncertainty and fear in his passing. This is . . . something else.

What would Mother do with such information?

"Here we are," Cinderella says in a hushed tone as we reach a tall set of wooden doors with an engraving in the language of the fey

21

above it. I cannot read Feyrish—no one but the fey can—but I'm sure it's something pompous and unnecessary about how education will deliver us from our lower selves. Because the fey are pompous about such things.

Cinderella pushes the doors open and the smell of leather hide and inkpots assaults me, the ceiling vaulting another two or three stories overhead as we enter this hallowed, empty ground. I have never been one much for libraries—books have only ever been used as weapons against me, intellectually and once physically when Divya lost her temper—but as Cinderella's face softens and her eyes gleam I remember that she holds a fondness for them.

Her father kept an entire wing of the manor stocked with them, all for her, until Mother sold them off one by one to pay for dresses and lessons. She was always careful to choose the ones that would wound Cinderella most deeply, the ones she cherished most dearly. I had thought it a kindness at the time—what good were books to a girl like Cinderella?—but now I wonder if perhaps Mother might have left the girl something of her father. I know I would love something more than the oblique insults about my own. A name, perhaps.

But he abandoned us, according to Mother, as soon as he learned she had made the mistake of getting herself with child again when Divya was born. All the better for us, she had said. All we needed in the world was her, and she had been right. We survived those cold winters, and we would survive the one before us. Together.

"Ah, Princess," comes a voice as dusty as the surrounding tomes, creaking with a well-worn exasperation. A tiny old man with white hair and hands like tree roots emerges from behind a stack of books and hobbles toward us. "To what do I owe the . . . *pleasure* of your company today? More gardening advice?"

"Ah, Pagemaester Givien," Cinderella says, oddly hesitant. I would assume these two would be fast friends, building book caves and sequestering themselves away in them. But she folds her hands in front of her and clears her throat, obviously stalling. "I believe I should like to peruse the stacks on my own accord today."

"Nonsense," the old man snaps, before realizing he is talking to *his* master. He attempts a smile with abysmal results. "Please, Your Royal Highness, keeping the books is *my* duty. You need only tell me which topics you seek, and I will provide. The cataloging system is intricate and takes many years to learn, and we would not want our collection out of order, would we?"

"Er, no," Cinderella hedges, glancing at me. "In that case, we are looking for—"

"A recipe," I say, giving him a smile. "The prince is hosting a banquet this evening for Maroian dignitaries and he would like to prepare a traditional Maro soufflé to welcome them."

His scraggly eyebrows crawl up his face, the longer hairs disappearing in the folds of his forehead. "Maroian? Why, they have not visited the kingdom since I was a boy!"

"Exactly," I say with a nod. "Which is why it's crucial to Prince Fael that we honor their long overdue visit properly. Though I suppose this library might not contain such records as Maro traditions."

"Of course it does," the old man says, banging one fist against a nearby chair. "I shall consult the index and have the results sent to the kitchens immediately."

"Oh, that's all right," I say, sweeping my skirts around another one of the chairs and plopping myself down. "We'll wait. Cind—er, Princess Ellarose will have tea brought for us. Won't you, Your Royal Highness?"

"Yes," Cinderella says, taking up the chair beside me. She turns a sweet smile on the old man. "We eagerly await your results, Pagemaester."

The old man grunts, glaring at us suspiciously, but he can hardly eject the princess. "And you won't touch anything while I'm gone?" he asks, unable to help himself.

"Wouldn't dream of it," I say. "I'm allergic to books."

He grunts again, but hobbles off in what I assume is the direction of his precious index, disappearing around one of the enormous bookshelves. Cinderella leans over the arm of her chair, watching his retreat, before turning back to me.

"Why did you tell him to find a recipe?" she whispers to me.

"Because it doesn't exist," I say, standing up and righting my skirts. "Maroians don't eat soufflés. They have a strict raw diet. But he'll be searching for that recipe for hours, which should leave us plenty of time to review the council bylaws."

"Ah," Cinderella says, standing beside me with a smile. "How clever of you."

"Of course it is," I say flatly, not wishing to acknowledge the prickle of pride her compliment gives me. She probably hands them out like those candies she gave the village children. "Now I assume you know where the king's decrees are stored?"

"Yes, right this way," Cinderella says, leading me into the library in the opposite direction of the pagemaester. "Sometimes I sneak into the library late at night, when the pagemaester is asleep, so I can learn the stacks for myself."

"Of course you do," I mutter.

We find the appropriate stacks and begin reading, my eyes tiring quickly from the scrawling, overly florid font. Why do scribes insist on such pomp in their writing? It's as if they wish to have their own language apart from the rest of us. The legal documents are far worse, and soon my head is pounding. I wish Cinderella had sent for that tea after all. I cannot remember the last full meal I ate.

"Oh," Cinderella says softly, her light blond eyebrows rising as her mouth draws into a perfect O. She's sitting cross-legged on the floor like an absolute commoner, a massive leather book with loose parchment papers collected within lying open on her lap.

"What did you find?" I ask, setting aside an account of taxes levied on agricultural production for the last fifty years. The rates have gone up a staggering amount, most notably in the last ten years. Ever since Cordo assumed the high chancellor position.

"Oh no," Cinderella says, looking up at me in surprise as a dusky pink splashes over her cheeks. "Nothing of note. I was just reading the account of a visit from Queen Myra of Banomal when Gryndor the Magnificent was king. It was quite . . . eventful."

"Ah, you mean the affair," I say, nodding.

Cinderella's back straightens in surprise. "Yes! How do you know?"

"I was trained to know all events of historical significance in Novador," I say, leaving the obvious bit silent. "It was a terribly messy affair. By all accounts, the king fell madly in love with Myra, which sat none too well with his wife, Queen Alrene. She had Myra poisoned."

"No," Cinderella gasps, leaning forward with the same expression that she used to have when her father would regale her with tales of Novador's past. "Did Myra die?"

"No, luckily for all of Novador," I say, turning away and pulling another book off the shelf to avoid Cinderella's rapt face. "She fell deathly ill and the king never left her bedside, and when she finally recovered he had his queen exiled and married Myra instead. It united the two lands for several centuries, until the War of the Valley."

"My father fought in that war," she says, a mixture of fondness and sadness. "It was how he was granted the land to create the manor. A gift for his service."

"The scuffle over the Valley could have easily been settled were King Soteo's father not such a stubborn old mule," I say. "They could have made arrangements to share the water sources, but he couldn't stand the idea of sharing land he considered his birthright. Three thousand young men died fruitlessly for it, and to this day our relations with Banomal have been strained at best, and outright hostile at worst."

Cinderella is quiet for several minutes, and I assume she's fallen under the spell of Gryndor and Myra's ridiculous love affair until she speaks again. "You would have made a better princess than I have."

Her voice is so quiet and resigned, I would have missed the statement were we not sitting in an absolute mausoleum of solitude. I glance down at her, my hand trailing over the open page before me. "What do you mean?"

Cinderella spreads her hands wide over the book in her lap. "You know more about the political machinations of the court than I ever will. I love Fael with my whole heart, and I accept that he is the prince, but this all feels so far over my head. I want what is best for the people, but I have no idea what that actually is, or how to achieve it."

I tap my finger against the page, weighing my options. Were Mother here, she would encourage me to psychologically sabotage Cinderella into giving up the throne here and now. I could tell her to convince the prince to abdicate his position and they could happily live out their days on a little farm at the edge of Novador without the pesky worry of starvation and taxation. She'd be so busy raising beets and babies she would hardly notice who took over.

But I don't. I don't know why I don't, which I find supremely irritating. Cinderella is right; I *am* far more qualified to be princess than she is. I know more about Novador politics and foreign affairs than she could ever possibly hope to learn, and what's more, I *understand* them. I'm not so full of hope and magic and good cheer that anyone will walk right over me.

"Stop wasting your time on old tales and choose another book," I snap, because it is far easier to turn my anger on Cinderella than on myself. "That old fool will figure out my deception any minute."

"You're right." Cinderella sighs, and the moment is past.

"Of course I am," I mutter, turning back to my own research. Only, the page is smeared where I've let my hand trail over it. I frown, checking my fingers for any more lingering soot from my morning spent sweeping the chimney at the manor, but my fingernails are clean. I made sure of that before we left Vee to do the rest of the scrubbing.

It's not my fingers that have smudged the page. It's the ink.

"Someone has been writing in this book," I say, forgoing all my training in manners to sink to the floor beside Cinderella. I hold my fingers out. "Look, the ink is still wet in places. But this book is nearly a hundred years old. Why would anyone bother with it now?"

"What does it say?" Cinderella asks, leaning over my shoulders and filling my nose with her sugary-sweet scent.

I shake my head, scanning the smeared words. "I can't make it all out because of the smudging, but it just seems to be . . ."

"To be what?" Cinderella prompts when I don't finish my sentence.

"The bylaws," I whisper, looking up at the shelf from where I pulled them down. "But that's not where they belong. That's the registry of taxes and crop production."

Cinderella shakes her head. "I can't imagine Pagemaester Givien getting that wrong, despite his squinty stare. He's obsessive about his cataloging system."

"This wasn't him," I say, leaning in to examine the cramped writing. "Someone stashed this here to make their changes in secret, where the pagemaester wouldn't find out. No doubt they meant to return it to its rightful place once they were done."

"Someone is changing the bylaws in secret?" Cinderella asks, aghast. "Who? Why?"

I read the last line of the new entry. "I believe you have a coup on your hands, Your Royal Highness."

THREE

I TAP MY FINGER ON THE SECTION, READING ALOUD.
"'And wherefore the king is rendered incapacitated whether by ailment physical or mental, so the high chancellor of the king's council will effectively assume all his sovereign duties until such time as the king can be restored to full health. In the event of permanent incapacitation, the high chancellor will assume such duties in perpetuity by the blessing of the king's council.' He's attempting to circumvent the inheritance laws and replace the prince as sovereign."

"But that's not . . . That's impossible!" Cinderella exclaims, looking to me in concern. "Isn't it?"

I shrug. "Laws are only as strong as those willing to enforce them. My guess is, Cordo has been planning this for quite a while. And if he's rewriting the bylaws to put himself into power based on the blessing of the king's council, he must be fairly confident that he has the council in hand. Which means he must have the generals as well. And where the military goes . . ."

"The might follows," Cinderella whispers, pressing her hands to her cheeks. "I think I must be feeling faint. I should have called for that tea after all."

"It's not too late," I muse, my own stomach rumbling. I catch her look of hope. "I meant for the tea. I do believe Cordo has your prince in a bind here."

"But we cannot just give in. He is breaking our laws!" Cinderella exclaims. "Mustn't he be punished for such transgressions against the crown?"

I give her a wry look. "And who will do the punishing when he has the council and the army at his command?" I shake my head. "Better to get on his good side now. Maybe he'll bequeath your prince a small parcel of land on the outskirts of the kingdom. It'll be better than the alternative."

Cinderella goes pale as morning mist, swaying back into the nearest shelf. Her eyes flutter closed and she goes completely still, and for a moment I worry that she truly has fainted. But then a deep crease forms in her brow, her lips compressing into a thin line. When she finally cracks her eyes open again, she looks around like she's expecting to be somewhere else. She blows out a breath that sounds irritated, stirring the soft blond curls that frame her face.

"What are you doing?" I ask in bewilderment.

"Nothing," she says, turning a deep scarlet. I worry for her blood flow if she experiences such drastic swings so often. "Nothing, apparently," she mutters again, knotting her fingers in her lap.

What a deeply odd girl.

"What are we going to do now?" Cinderella asks, her voice small and tired and already resigned.

Yes, what are *we* going to do? I return my attention to the hidden bylaws. High Chancellor Cordo planning an outright coup is not exactly the gift I would have hoped for. A subtle shifting of alliances? Sure. Those are easy to manage if you ingratiate yourself with the right people. But an outright coup could turn violent and bloody, and people like us always get trampled underfoot when the soldiers start mucking about.

I'll need to discuss this with Mother, get her perspective. She'll know how to turn the circumstances in our favor, I'm sure of it.

"I need to return to the manor," I say, snapping the book shut and sliding it back on the shelf where it belongs. "Mother will be returning soon and she'll worry if I am gone."

"Is that all?" Cinderella says, attempting to raise herself from the floor while burdened with two delicate books and an unseemly flounce of skirt. "Will you not help me to stop Cordo and right the course of the kingdom?"

"What is it you think I could do?" I ask, bewildered. "We have no money, no social standing since you married the prince, and everyone knows of the animosity between us. Even that guard dog of yours. If I am seen suddenly whiling away the hours with you, everyone will grow suspicious. You wouldn't want that, would you?"

"No, I suppose not," Cinderella says, knotting her fingers together so tightly I fear she'll break a knuckle. I make for the center aisle, but she snags my sleeve and I still, terrified she'll rip it and ruin another desperately needed dress. "What if I could help you, too?"

"How do you mean?" I ask suspiciously.

"High Chancellor Cordo knows you and your family from nothing. If he seizes control of the kingdom, there's nothing to stop him from calling your mother's debts in. And I know those debts are significant. He's proven he cares far more for coin than he does for anything else your mother thinks she could offer. But if Fael were to secure the throne, I could guarantee your mother's debts would be forgiven, and promise a generous endowment for your aid besides. You could get back in your mother's good graces."

"*You* would help my mother?" I ask, my voice drier than a Corovian red wine.

She takes a deep breath, smoothing out her skirts as she releases it. "Yes, if it means saving the kingdom."

Hmm. Perhaps little Cinderella is not so bad at negotiations after all. I certainly have no desire to return to the manor and resume my backbreaking chores, but the truth is I'm not really sure what recourse Cinderella and her prince have to stop Cordo at this point. I haven't returned to court since the humiliating night of the prince's "find a bride" ball, and most of my contacts shunned me the moment Mother stuffed me in a work dress. I might know the laws and traditions of Novador, but knowledge will only get you so far. Cinderella needs allies, and it's clear she doesn't have them. And I'd rather not be perceived as an ally to the losing side of this royal skirmish.

"I will ponder on it," I say, extracting myself from her grasp. "It's all I can do at the moment."

"Thank you, Aralyn," Cinderella says, seizing me in a hug. I freeze, unfamiliar with the intimacy, but she doesn't seem to mind.

We return to the main section of the library only moments before the pagemaester comes stumping in from the back.

"Your Royal Highness!" he declares sharply. "I've some bad news. Apparently Maroians only eat raw foods! Whatever made your prince think they had a traditional soufflé recipe?"

I give him a bland smile. "Must have been a misunderstanding. Thanks so much for your dedicated search, Pagemaester. We'll be taking our leave now."

"Only raw foods," he mutters, resuming his post at the desk. "What a strange people."

Cinderella disappears to fetch an unmarked carriage while I wait outside the servants' entrance. Someone comes stalking out of the stables nearby, armor glinting, streaks of soot peeking out from underneath the glimmering helmet as Vee stomps to a halt before me.

"You people," she manages, shaking her head, "live worse than wild dogs."

I look her up and down, taking in the thick black half-moons of her nails and the scratches along her wrists, probably from reaching into the mice nests that have collected in the various fireplaces around the manor since Cinderella stopped singing to the creatures. "How did you manage to get down on your hands and knees to scrub the floors in that ridiculous getup?"

"If anyone looks ridiculous, it's you in that cake topper you call a dress," Vee shoots back. "That looks more suited to a child's playdate than the royal grounds."

I'm inclined to agree with her, as Divya's taste has always run more toward the outrageous, but I won't give her the satisfaction of showing it. "I see some honest hard work did little to improve your disposition, as the high chancellor is often claiming about the peasant class."

Her face goes white, and I assume she's planning to lob another retort at me in our game of insult badminton, but instead she shoves past me toward the castle entrance. She pauses in the doorway, her face like a marble bust.

"May our paths never cross again," she says primly, before disappearing through the door with a clang.

"On that, we can agree," I call back to the closed door.

FOUR

I AM UPSTAIRS REARRANGING THE LAST TWO LOGS OF firewood in Mother's room when the front door slams open and Mother's voice fills the manor, more cheerful than I've heard it in years. It's clipped and rapid-fire, almost frantic, the same as when she was planning my entire trousseau when she believed Prince Fael would choose me at his ball.

"We shall have to make do with our current wardrobe since that scoundrel Monsieur Lisseu has refused us entry in his shop." Her voice floats up the stairs. "But I believe with the prince's influence we could make our connections with the modiste de style in the capital there. We will, after all, want to be à la mode in their court."

"What of transportation?" Divya asks in her flat, nasally tone. "They cannot think to make us take a hired hack all the way to the border!"

The border? The border of what? And what could they possibly use Prince Fael's influence to achieve, besides a dank cell in a dungeon somewhere?

"Your mother is not nearly so foolish or desperate as others would have you believe," Mother replies, her voice drawing closer.

"I have made arrangements, and we shall arrive for your beau in the style we des— Aralyn, there you are. Oh, darling, your *posture*. You look as if you should be ringing bells in a tower somewhere. Chin up!"

If I look so hunched, it is only because I have spent the last several hours scrubbing the far corners of the hearths where Vee did not bother to reach with her long wingspan while Mother and Divya were out taking tea with whichever lords will still allow them to call. I believe it was Lord Yaren this time, a doddering old man with more gaps than teeth and a stash of coins even the prince would envy. It's said he's gone mad from the tea he drinks, so I can't imagine why Mother would be in such a good mood after a visit with him.

"Good afternoon, Mother," I say, muscles aching and joints cracking as I right myself. But I force my shoulders back until the bones touch. "How was your visit with Lord Yaren?"

"Lord Yaren is dead." Mother sighs, though I know the regret is not for a life lost but rather an opportunity. "Finally exhaled his last fetid breath last night. Left everything to his hunting dogs—they'll be sorting that mess for ages. But Yaren is no longer of concern to us."

"Why not?" I ask, glancing at Divya, who is positively glowing with the effort of keeping in whatever secret they share. It pains me to be so out of touch. I've been a ghost these past months as Mother and Divya spend the coin we don't have, haunting a home that isn't even mine. "What has happened?"

Mother takes me by the shoulders, her expression radiant, chasing away the chill of the room. "Your sister has made a match."

"Truly?" I say in astonishment, looking to Divya, whose expression sours immediately.

"Of course I have," she says sharply. "And why shouldn't I?"

"Div, I did not mean it as such," I say, tired of these missteps with my sister. "Only I am . . . well, I *am* surprised. Did you happen upon an eligible lord on the road to Yaren's estate?"

"Of course not, darling, don't be so daft," Mother says, sweeping away from me toward her armoire and the paltry stash of dresses still packed within. "I am not such a fool as to put all our eggs in that rotted-out basket. What have I always told you girls about men?"

"They're feckless, inconsistent, and easily distracted by an ample bosom?" Divya offers.

"They're like garden tools," I say, knowing what Mother truly means. "If you want to eat, you need more than one."

Mother gives me an approving look, the first of such I've received in so long it fills me up like no tea service ever could. "I see not all of my training has gone to waste. Now, while you girls have been lazing about these past few months, bemoaning our fates, I have been hard at work. Securing our future. And I have finally done so. Divya will very soon be betrothed to—"

"I'm going to marry Prince Pever!" Divya bursts out, unable to contain such a choice reveal any longer. Frankly, I'm amazed she held out as long as she did.

"Darling, do learn to hold your tongue." Mother sighs at Divya, irritated that her thunder has been stolen. "Honestly, you are like a cow in the meadow sometimes."

My jaw goes soft in surprise. "Prince Pever of Banomal? Novador's sworn enemy? But how did you— *When* did y— Why?"

"Eight years of elocution lessons gone to waste," Mother tuts. "When that little urchin Cinderella stole our chance at the throne, I could not resign myself to such a fate. I had to think of you girls,

after all. What future could I provide in a kingdom run by an imbe-
cile and his mouse-talking wife? Look at the squalor they have
reduced us to! Everyone is suffering, and soon that suffering will
rise up like a wave to drown us all. So, I made other arrangements."

"For Divya to marry Prince Pever?" I ask, my voice cracking on its
way up. "Mother, we will be considered traitors in Novador! We'll
never be allowed to set foot on this soil again."

Mother looks around the room in disdain. "What is there to wish
for here? We are outcasts at court, nearly penniless from the pitiful
stipend Cinderella's father left us, and selling off our wardrobe to
finance our dinners. This is not a life, Aralyn. It is a punishment,
and we have committed no crime. But in Valley Banomal, we can
live as we were truly meant to, in a luxury that Novador can only
dream of. This country is a carcass-filled swamp compared to what
Queen Marsola has done in the Valley."

She reaches for my cheek and I flinch, but she doesn't slap me.
Instead she runs her perfectly manicured nails down my cheek
softly, her gaze looking right through me. "We will be like we once
were, long before Cinderella's father yoked us with this deathtrap of
a manor house. Do you remember, darling?"

Of course I remember. Endless parties, streams of guests, Mother
at their center, bright as the sun. There were champagne towers.
Tiny, perfect cake squares frosted in sugar and magic. Warm beds—
real beds, with sheets that did not scratch and padding that did
not bite. Late mornings, sunshine and light. When Mother had a
paramour, we lived like kings.

But I remember the long stretches between the light, too. When
Mother was on the hunt again, and Divya and I were baggage she
couldn't afford to ship along with the rest of her things. When she

would leave us with the potter's wife for months on end, who made us work until our nails grew so brittle they would crack in the winter. Divya was too young to really understand, and I did my best to protect her from the loneliness and the woman's quick hand. But when you make yourself a shield for someone else, you take the brunt of the blow.

"Novador is our home," I say, looking between Mother and Divya. "Is it not?"

"Novador will not be much of anything for long if Queen Marsola has anything to say about it," Mother says.

"What does that mean?" I gasp.

Mother huffs, flopping down a gown of red wine silk and black lace on the bed. "Enough chattering, darling, fetch me a trunk from the carriage house! Divya and I have a great many miles to make up, and Sir Reginald will be here any moment to assess the manor for sale."

My head is spinning; I can't keep up with Mother's casual destruction of everything I've known for the last eight years. "You're selling the manor? How?"

"We need the money to reach Banomal," Mother says, as if it were the most obvious thing in the world. She pops back up from the bed, already in motion again. "Divya, we will need a full assessment of your trousseau. Aralyn, fetch the sewing kit. No doubt there will be alterations and repairs to be made. I don't know how you manage it, Divya darling. Even when there is no food on the table, you grow soft around the middle."

She disappears into the hallway, her commands trailing along behind her, but Divya doesn't hop along in her shadow as usual. Instead she stares at me, her expression twisted.

"Why can you not just be happy for me?" she asks in a quiet, plaintive voice. "Does your envy run so deep, now that Mother actually pays me attention?"

"That is not my concern, Divya," I say, crossing the room to take her hands. I hesitate, unsure what information I can trust her with. "You are still so young. Fifteen! And there is a great deal you do not know yet. Marrying the prince of a hostile neighbor—it is a great burden to put on you. I have seen firsthand what becomes of a sovereign who is not adequately prepared to rule."

Divya snatches her hands from mine, sneering. "Oh, and I suppose you think you would be the better match for the prince, with all your lessons and training? You cannot help but center yourself, even when you are the reason I am being parceled off to the prince in the first place! Mother is right to leave you behind. No doubt you will attempt some form of sabotage to sway the prince your way."

"Leave me behind?" I ask, breathless. Mother sweeps back into the room, a line of irritation forming between her brows.

"Why are the two of you still standing about? Come along! There is work to be done."

"Mother." I look to Divya, who refuses to return my gaze. "Do you intend to leave me behind?"

Mother lets out a sharp sigh. "I told you not to speak to her about it until I could discuss it with her first, you cotton-brained little fool."

"Apologies, Mother," Divya says, though she doesn't sound sorry at all.

"Mother, please." I drag my leaden feet across the room, collapsing half against the side of the door and half against her. I take her hand and squeeze it. "You can't abandon me."

"I'm not abandoning you, child, pull yourself together," she says, pulling her hand free. "It is only temporary. We cannot have anything distracting Prince Pever in his suit for Divya. We shall send for you when Divya and the prince are settled."

She means when I can no longer ruin her plans. But I know what it means when Mother leaves—the long cold nights, the unbearable loneliness. The terror that she may never come back. Only this time there is no potter's wife to feed me, no Divya to play games with on hot summer afternoons. No home, no family, and certainly no friends.

"But what will I do?" I beg. "Where will I go? Mother, I have no one if you are gone!"

The look Mother gives me is like waking up in the middle of the night to find a snowstorm has swept in and the fire has gone out. I feel the dead chill of it down in my bones.

"I have spent my entire life with no one and nothing," she says, her voice soft. "My father died when I was seven and my mother sent me to the workhouse to pay off his drinking debts. I fought, tooth and nail, for every scrap I ever had in this life. I did not bring myself up out of the gutter and fashion myself a lady to let anyone sink us right back down into the muck. Everything I do is for you girls. Now stand up, compose yourself, and *fetch our trunk.*"

I hardly know how I find my way out of the room, much less to the carriage house, but I am suddenly confronted with its looming shape. The manor may be in shambles, but the carriage house is downright haunted. It lists to the side, the ground cracked beneath it, with broken-out windows and a door we've had to chain because it slams open during storms. I fumble with the chain, my hands shaking, until it slithers loose and lands on my toes. I let forth a deeply satisfying curse as I slam the door open, alerting all the creeping crawlers within that something far more dangerous has arrived.

The interior is a worse mess, loaded with decrepit old furniture and moth-eaten blankets. Spiders lurk between every beam overhead, surveilling me with their gleaming eyes. And far more sinister things lurk in the dark patches between broken chair legs, plucking out heart-stopping melodies within a rotted piano. I take no care with the damaged furniture, shoving over cabinets and smashing chairs, leaving a wake of splintered boards behind me. But the yawning void in my chest where a mother's love belongs is still hungry, and only violence will feed it.

It feels good, putting my fist through a rotted weaving loom, the raw edges raising trails of blood along my knuckles. The elaborate tapestries that Cinderella's father was always commissioning to support the local artists don't rip as easily, but the weave has been subjected to the elements out here and eventually frays when I set my teeth to it. It tastes of filth and neglect, a flavor I know all too well. What does anything in here matter, really? What were we saving all of this for? Firewood? Crude weaponry to fight off the creditors? This place means nothing. When I scream into a tapestry, it fills my lungs with mold spores.

"I wish I knew how to get out of this," I whisper.

There's a pressure at the base of my neck, an over-awareness crawling across my skin as something crashes through the furniture behind me. I've disturbed something bigger than a mouse, and it's not happy. I reach for the nearest blunt object I can find, a broken chair leg.

I'm expecting a wild dog, maybe, or some large nesting bird. What I am definitely *not* expecting is a person-shaped female wielding what looks suspiciously like a turkey leg. She might be person-shaped, but she is most definitely *not* a person. Her skin is a deep gray, bordering on purple, and her full figure is outfitted in a variety of leathers and furs. Her nose is triangular—wide and flat and coming down to points at the side and another small point in the middle—and her ears curl at the top, disappearing into wavy black hair. We square off, me with my broken chair leg and her with her wild fowl leg looking as shocked as I feel.

"Who in blazes are you?" I demand, when it seems like we'll be legging off forever.

"Bury me in the fields of Silveritl and ring the gong of Threpnar, you're Aralyn," the creature says in surprise. Suddenly she throws her arms wide, a grin splitting her face and showing four rows of sharp silver teeth. "Finally! I'd thought you'd died! Come here, you great lump of mortal flesh!"

She throws her arms around me and lifts me clear off the ground, her arms thick and rippling with muscles that I'm positive Cinderella's lady knight would envy. With all those furs I assume she'd smell of stinking animal meat, but an intoxicating waft of something sweet and flowery rises off her skin. I might have tried to take a deep breath of it if she weren't currently crushing the air from my lungs.

"Put me down," I manage to wheeze, my toes bumping her shins.

"Arg, tickle me tinsel, I forget how pliable your human bones are," she says, dropping me so suddenly I stumble back into the piano with an inglorious plunking sound. "I'm just so damned pleased to finally *meet* you! I've been petitioning the guild for *ages* to assign me a new human, thinking you'd been killed or maimed or had your tongue cut out or some such."

"Why in the starry skies would you think that?" I ask, bewildered.

"Because you never called for me!" she says, throwing her arms wide.

"I don't even know who you *are*," I say, accidentally wielding my chair leg in her face.

She swats it away with a friendly hand the size of a large dinner plate. "I'm Lyra. Your fairy godmother!"

FIVE

"My fairy . . ." I take a deep breath, sure that the mold spores from the tapestry have now made their way to my brain. "I don't have a fairy godmother. You must have gotten lost on your way to Cinderella."

"What's a Cinderella?" the creature asks—for I refuse to think of her as a fairy godmother, and most certainly not my fairy godmother. I don't talk to birds or let mice sew my clothing. Unnatural. But the creature doesn't seem to mind, for she slaps her hands together excitedly while looking around. "Now, what are we getting out of today? I'm assuming this abandoned building that has collapsed on you?"

"What are you talking about?" I ask, exasperated. As far as spore-induced hallucinations go, this one is rather annoying.

The creature looks at me in the manner one would use on a dog they were housebreaking. "You called for me and said 'I wish I knew how to get out of this.'"

"Well, yes, I said that, but I wasn't calling for you. I was trying . . . It doesn't matter what I was trying to do. I had no intention of call-ing for you. I didn't even know you were you. And I don't need your help, getting out of here or otherwise. It was a mistake, calling you. I'm sorry."

"No, no, no, no, no, no," the creature says, moving to block my exit. She holds out her hands in supplication, and only from this close can I see that instead of eyebrows she has twin ridges of armored skin above her silvered eyes. "Just wait, please? Listen, it's been ages since I've been to the human realm, much less been called on for celestial aid. Can't you let me do something for you? If you send me back now, I'll never live it down in Eventide."

I frown. "What is Eventide?"

"The Court of Eventide? Most powerful court in the fey realm? Sagitta the Venerable? You've not heard of any of that?"

I shake my head. "Frankly, I always thought Cinderella was making up her fairy godmother business. I just assumed she stole that dress from somewhere. And who gives a girl a pair of glass slippers? One wrong step and you're wounded for life."

"That's just . . . well, plunkers," Lyra says, dropping down on Mother's traveling trunk that I came to fetch. It gives an ominous creak, its wood as weakened as the rest of these decrepit pieces of furniture. "Mother won't be pleased to know we've faded from human awareness so much. No wonder the crystals have grown dim."

"If I wish for just one thing you say to make sense, will you leave me be?" I ask, leaning against the part of the piano that is missing all its keys.

Lyra leans forward with her arms on her knees, sighing heavily and testing the limits of the traveling trunk. "The fey realm is powered by human belief. The more wishes you lot make, the greater our power. And fey magic powers everything in our realm—the light, the water, the nutrients in the earth, even the air we breathe. All of it needs human wishes to survive."

"So if humans stop asking you for things, you . . . suffocate? Starve?" I shiver. "That sounds—"

"Horrifying?" Lyra gives a humorless chuckle. "That's the balance of power between the human realm and the fey. We have magic beyond your ken, but only you can power it."

"It's rather humiliating to rely on someone else so completely for your entire existence, isn't it?" I say, deflating a bit.

"See? You understand!" She pops up, and the trunk blessedly retains its proper shape. "So, what are we getting out of? That potato sack you're pretending is a dress? I'll warn you, I'm not so keen a designer as Galandrel, but I'll do my right best. Any color combinations I should stay away from? You people are daft concerned with colors that compliment your flesh sack."

There is far too much to address in that statement, but couture is the least of my concerns presently. "I need far more than a dress. I'm not seeking to win a prince, I'm seeking to save a kingdom."

"Oooh, what a line," Lyra says, sitting back down on the trunk, her silver eyes unnaturally wide and round. "Do tell."

"I'd rather not, and could you remove your person from that trunk before you make it a pallet? My mother will eviscerate me if I don't return it all in one piece."

"Oh, this thing?" she asks, standing and looking back behind her. "Where's it need to go? That haunted mansion over there?"

"It's not haunted," I say, annoyed. "And yes."

"No problem," she says, snapping her fingers. The trunk was there, and then suddenly it's . . . not. She grins at me with those teeth, and I wonder why they need to be so sharp. "See? I can be a help."

"That's— How—" It is one thing to have heard of magic, and another thing entirely to witness it with one's own eyes. It's as if someone has cut a slice out of my memory, the part where someone surely walked in, lifted that trunk, and hauled it out of the carriage house. "How did you do that?"

"What, teletransportation? Oh, that's the easiest of them. I'd move a thousand empty trunks before I'd try to bead a single ball gown. Go on, then, what else have you got?"

Perhaps she could be the answer to my problems. I could simply . . . wish Divya's potential engagement away. Or better yet, wish Mother's debts away. I could wish away Cordo, or wish for prosperity for Novador. But if it were that simple, why had Cinderella not already done so with her fairy godmother?

"What can you actually do?" I ask curiously.

"Ah, well," says Lyra, scratching at the rough of her neck with a sheepish look. "I'm not really supposed to reveal the extent of our powers to the likes of you, but I suppose you did get me out of a bind, wishing me here after all this time. Well, we can move objects with our minds, of course, but there's a limit to that. Small things over short distances is our motto. And we can command light and bend it to our will, but only for short periods of time. Oh, and the dress bit, though that's more of a Stomur faction business. That's Galandrel's faction, your . . . what did you call her? Cinderella? That's her fairy godmother. Though Galandrel's been a bit of an empire waist, if you catch my meaning. High and mighty and then suddenly disappearing. Oh! My specialty, though, is food. Conjuring it, manipulating it, changing the flavors of things. Human food is a right mess, honestly, and fascinating to no end. Look at soup. What a strange invention! Who thought 'Let's take these solid things and liquefy them'? You silly humans."

"Is that it?" I ask, spreading my hands wide. "Flashes of light and turkey legs? Parlor tricks meant to appease the young and infirm of mind?"

"I wouldn't put it quite like that," Lyra says, sounding offended. "Have you ever held a ball of light in your hand that you submitted to your will?"

I growl in frustration. "Those do me no good. I need real magic. Something to put the fear of the fey and the human who commands them into people. Not a bloody fireworks show. It's no wonder Cinderella was so easily won over by your Galandrel."

"You know, I don't think I care for your tone," Lyra says, rising to her full height and reminding me that it is a good foot over mine. She balls her prodigious hands into fists, setting them on her hips. "I can see why Fornax calls you the ugly sister."

"Who in blazes is Fornax?" I ask.

"Your sister's fairy godfather."

My jaw could sweep Mother's floor right now. "Divya has a fairy godfather? That lying, conniving . . . Oh, it's all coming together now! No wonder her sour disposition is suddenly so appealing to someone like Prince Pever. She probably magicked him into wanting to marry her."

"Prince Pever?" Lyra echoes, her ears twitching and tossing her hair around. "From Valley Banomal?"

"Yes, how do you know him?" I ask in surprise.

"Because Valley Banomal is served by the Court of Vespers," says Lyra, suddenly serious. She takes me by the shoulders, the span of her fingers covering my entire upper arm from shoulder to elbow. Her eyes gleam silver in the half-light, reflecting my startled expression back to me. "Whatever happens, you can't let your sister marry that human."

SIX

"WHAT?" I ASK, STARTLED BY THE SEVERITY OF HER expression. "What do you expect me to do? You just said you didn't have the power to help me stop it. And it's not as if my mother or sister would heed any warning I gave them these days. What does it matter to you if my sister marries Prince Pever?"

But Lyra is still shaking her head, the tops of her ears uncurling before rolling down into a tight ball. "No, you don't understand. The Court of Vespers, they're . . . Something very strange is going on over there, ever since the queen of Banomal called forth her fairy godfather. They've shrouded themselves in the mists of the ancient ones, and no other court has been able to visit or figure out what they're up to over there."

I raise my eyebrows, my curiosity piqued with this flood of new information. "Valley Banomal has known unprecedented wealth and prosperity since Queen Marola took the throne. If it is because they have access to forbidden fey magic, then Novador is worse off than I imagined."

"What do you mean?" Lyra asks. "What's wrong in Novador?"

I snort. "Only everything. People are starving, crops are failing, there's a coup in the castle, and I've just learned Queen Marola intends to invade Novador after my sister marries her son."

"Well, we have to stop that!" Lyra says, swinging an arm like she's in a bloody bard's tale.

"With what?" I say sarcastically. "A fireworks show? Or shall we play hide-and-seek with their weaponry? What is it you think we can actually *do*?"

"That's . . . a good question," she says, tearing into her turkey leg thoughtfully. She points it at me, bits of gristle hanging down and turning my stomach. "I could make their weapons disappear, if I had some help. Do you think your sister can call on Fornax? He's a snob about teletransportation, considers it beneath him, but it's better than being subjugated by the Court of Vespers."

"There are no weapons to disappear as of yet," I say. "I don't know what they're planning. But I know that Novador itself is on the verge of revolt, and will be primed for invasion if we don't sort out the issues here at home. Cinderella and her daft prince couldn't scheme their way out of an open door, and while I might have the knowledge we need, I have none of the power. Without a real protector for Novador, I fear the whole kingdom is doomed."

"The Protector!" Lyra declares in a spray of turkey carcass. A large piece lands on the bodice of my dress, so I suppose I'll have to burn it now. She knocks herself on the head with the bone. "Novador's Protector, of course! You daft bungerbee, why didn't you think of that before!"

"What is Novador's Protector?" I ask, wishing I had a map for the journey this conversation has taken me on.

"Oh, ahhhh . . . I'm not supposed to tell you lot," Lyra says, her purple skin flushing a deep brown. I think it's her version of blushing.

"We're long past the point of your maintaining the secret allure of the fey, aren't we?" I counter. "And to your point, if you don't help me stop the invasion by Valley Banomal, you'll have no fey court to lord over us, will you?"

"A compelling counterpoint," Lyra concedes. She sticks out her lower jaw, the sharp teeth there more pronounced with the movement. "All right, fine. But don't tell anyone I told you. I don't want to get sanctioned. They'll take my cave away and I just moved out of the lower caves, took me ages. You don't know how hard those exams are to pass."

"The Protector," I say loudly.

"Right, right, untwist your knickers. Once upon a time—"

I groan. "I don't need a bedtime story. Get to the point!"

"Plunkers, but you are impatient," Lyra says, sniffing. It makes her nose bend at odd angles, rounding it out. "The story *is* the point. Once upon a time, when the founding fairies of Eventide first bridged the divide between our world and yours and made contact with the humans here, they learned that human belief could fuel their magic. Truth be told, it had been a rather exhausting process up to that point. It's no small thing, bending the laws of nature to your will. The Mother is a fickle, twisting provider. If you weren't careful, it would eat you right up. You lot were like a great buffet table of energy, filling us right up with your awe."

"Yes, I believe I can feel such awe coursing through me at the moment," I say flatly. "Where does the Protector come into play here?"

"Oh, right, that," Lyra says with a grin. "Felt a bit of my grandmother spinning the tales through me just now. Well, once the fey knew of this great source of power, there was a sudden rush to cross the veil and make contact. And some courts—like Vespers—were not so nice about it. We often came to war because of territorial claims. Wars that spilled over into your realm and cost both sides a great many lives."

Cinderella's enraptured reading earlier that day comes back to me. "The affair between the mortal King Gryndor and Queen Myra of Banomal?"

Lyra has the nerve to look sheepish. "Bit of a property dispute, that one. Someone enchanted the waters, the queen went swimming in them, and the king happened upon her during a hunt, and, well . . ." She spreads her hands wide as if to say *these things happen*.

But these things very much do *not* happen. "Did Cinderella's godmother do the same for her? Did she enchant the dress Cinderella wore the night of the ball? Is that how she ensnared the prince?"

"Oh, no, no, no, we're not allowed that kind of magic anymore," Lyra says, shaking her head emphatically. "In fact, that's what the Peace Accords were meant to address, if you'd let me finish my story."

"Oh," I say, deflating back onto the piano. I can't believe I let myself be disappointed by Lyra's answer. After all, if I had managed to secure the prince's proposal, it would be me combing through the castle library right now, trying to find a way to keep my head attached to my neck. Still, it would have been nice to have a neat, tidy answer for why Cinderella succeeded where I failed.

"As I was saying," Lyra pronounces, giving me a baleful look, "things got messy on both sides of the veil. Courts needed a way to protect their human claims from other factions of the fey. And so the Protector was created."

She says it very dramatically, holding her arms out wide and giving me a look. When she doesn't continue on right away, I sigh. "You'll recall we're having this conversation because I have no idea what the Protector is."

"Ah, right," she says, dropping her arms in disappointment. "The Protector was a single fey chosen to stay on the human side of the veil, tattooed all over with spells by every single member of their court to strengthen their power. And they were given an enchanted weapon through which they could channel that power in protection of their human kingdom. Every human kingdom that had a Protector would be safe from the attacks of other fey courts, and those kingdoms in turn grew prosperous, their faith feeding a Protector's power."

I shake my head. "But I've never heard of a Protector anywhere. What happened?"

"I told you, the Peace Accords. Things got so bloody on our side, they nearly wiped out the ancient ones in their feuds. The Protector protected their human kingdom, but at the cost of the fey courts. It weakened them, putting so much power into one member of the court, and opened them to attack on our side. Which is pretty ironic, if you think about it."

"So they just . . . stopped protecting the humans?" I ask.

"Not quite," Lyra says. "They came to an agreement. Fey courts that had already struck their claims on the human side would officially be recognized and magically bound to those kingdoms. They outlawed the forbidden magic as part of those Accords as well.

They brought balance back to the fey realm and stopped the constant warfare on the human side."

"And what of the Protectors? Where are they now?"

Lyra fidgets with a strand of leather hanging down from a band around her arm, her sharp nails shredding the tough ends. "The Protectors had to be . . . destroyed."

I suck in a breath. "You mean killed? You killed your own people?"

"I didn't do it!" Lyra protests, flattening a hand across her chest. "I wasn't even manifested back then! But my mother was, and she was part of the tribunal that decreed the Protectors would have to be unspelled. They had too much power, and if any one of them decided to go rogue, well . . . it could undo everything the Accords had worked to resolve. But unspelling a fey who's been marked like that, it was . . . certain death. Even those fey who unspelled them were marked, the knowledge of the Protectors locked away within them. They couldn't tell you how to make another Protector even if they wanted to."

"If Novador's Protector is dead, then why are you even telling me this ridiculous fairy tale?" I demand. "You're only wasting my time."

"You haven't let me finish," Lyra says defensively, gnawing on her turkey bone and grunting in disappointment when she realizes all the meat is gone. "Novador's Protector was a fairy named Kaung, and from the way my mother tells it, he was none too happy to give up his post, much less his life. Can't say as how I blame him, but he argued that we were fools for trusting the other courts to uphold the Accords forever. He said Novador would need a Protector again one day, but by the time they called for one the fey courts would be so weakened they wouldn't be able to bring one forth. So he went a bit . . . rogue."

I raise my eyebrows. "What does that mean? Like he ran away?"

Lyra shakes her head. "Oh, no, that wouldn't have been possible. But according to legend—legend in this case being my mother—before the court unspelled him, he put a blessing on his weapon. He put his powers—the power of the Protector—into his blade, and then he tore it into three pieces and cast each piece to the farthest-flung corners of Novador where no one could ever find them. My mother was the last one to un-ink her spell, and she said as he died, he told her where the pieces were hidden."

I straighten up, every nerve ending in my body quivering to attention. "Where are they?"

Lyra leans forward, silver eyes glassy. "I . . . have . . . no idea."

I could howl, if I weren't afraid of drawing Mother's and Divya's attention. "Is it possible for me to wish you out of my presence forever?"

"My mother never told me!" Lyra protests. "I told you, those fey who un-inked the Protector were marked, the knowledge locked away. She knows that she knows, but she doesn't know what she knows. You know?"

"I can't possibly imagine how you think I could know anything from that," I say. "Isn't there anything we can do to unlock the knowledge within your mother? Some spell you could cast, or a magical key to unlock it? Shall I say something silly like 'I wish you would tell me where the bloody Protector weapon is'?"

Lyra goes stiff, her eyes staring off in the middle distance, a humming vibrating out of the back of her throat like someone's hit the edge of a large copper pot. I suck in a breath, waiting for the answer to all of my problems.

Lyra speaks out in a low, singsong voice. "It doesn't work like that."

Her face splits into a grin again, and if she weren't nearly twice my size I would put my fist square in her triangular nose.

"You're a terrible fairy godmother," I accuse, which does nothing to lessen her grin.

"This is my first go-round, so actually I think I'm doing a pretty decent job considering my ward," Lyra counters. "Magic isn't a lock-and-key business. It's like the shifting of the plates in the earth. A fundamental change. It creates something new, something different. That's why the Protector told her where the pieces were, because he knew once she un-inked him she couldn't speak of it. Mother and Kaung were, ah . . . they didn't get along so well. I think it was his final way of saying 'Eat the poison mushroom' to my mother."

I draw on the memory of every single time Mistress Clara snapped her switch between my shoulders because I wasn't the picture of comportment, taking a deep breath and centering myself to regain some semblance of composure. I've spent too many months slouched over hearths like a common servant and I've forgotten the regal bearing she beat into me.

"So what good is any of this if your mother can't tell us where to find the pieces?" I ask, my words careful and measured.

"Because," Lyra says, drawing out the second syllable, "she gave me a clue."

"What clue?" I ask, leaning forward.

"She said the power of the Protector, it was always going to be cursed. A single fey can't hold that kind of power without repercussions. Which means if Kaung put his cursed power into those pieces, wherever they landed here on the mortal side—"

"Must be cursed, too," I say, sucking in a breath.

"Exactly," Lyra grins. "That much power would have changed the earth, wherever it landed. It might have created a crater where there hadn't been one the day before, or torn a valley through the land. Or it could have created—"

"A mountain range," I cut in, delving into my own knowledge of Novadorian history. "There is a legend here in Novador, about the Mortel Mountains that border Banomal. It's foolish and confusing, like most legends, but the gist of it is that the people of the Mortel Plains awoke in the middle of the night to a quake that was so powerful they felt it all the way to the capital. And when they emerged from their homes, the sky was a deeper black than they had ever seen. Half the stars were suddenly gone. They feared that the stars had fallen to the earth and the world was ending, but by morning they saw what had happened. A mountain range—the Mortel Mountains—had risen out of the earth overnight and blocked out the sky."

Lyra claps her hands together triumphantly. "There's your clue! That must be where the first piece is hidden. So now you just go and retrieve it."

"Sure, I'll just trek through the mountains of madness and pluck an ancient weapon imbued with the power of all the Court of Eventide," I say. "I'm sure it'll be that simple."

Lyra grins. "That's the spirit. So, when do we depart?"

I sigh, forcing myself off the piano. "I'll need to make preparations and secure provisions. And I'll need to be sure my mother and sister don't suspect anything before they depart for Banomal."

Lyra shivers. "They'd be better off accompanying you to the Mortel Mountains."

I pause by the door of the carriage house, looking back to where Lyra is sniffing around a cabinet. "Can I simply . . . call on you? Whenever I need you?"

"That's the general idea of it," Lyra agrees, pulling open the door and slamming it quickly after a series of squeaks. "These critters don't smell as good alive as they do roasted with a bit of salt and garlic, do they?"

"Here's hoping I never have to call on you, then," I mutter, leaving the carriage house and heading back to the manor. There's a flicker of movement from one of the upstairs windows, and I swear I catch the silhouettes of someone standing behind the curtains, with a tall, thin figure looming over their shoulder. But by the time my eyes adjust, the window is dark and cold, as if it had never been occupied at all.

SEVEN

THE MANOR IS EMPTY BY THE TIME I AWAKEN THE next morning, and while I didn't exactly expect a tearful send-off, it still needles my heart that Mother left without so much as a goodbye. She hasn't left me a scrap of clothing besides the work dress I've fallen asleep in, which means I'll have to call on Cinderella in this state. I halfway consider wishing for Lyra's help to at least give me a decent dress fashioned from silk instead of filthy wool, but she admitted the fashionable arts were not her forte; and besides, I'd be more likely to end up in leather and furs, based on her own choice of attire. The work dress it will have to be, but I give it a good scrubbing before I leave the manor and make the long trip to the castle.

I have plenty of time on the walk to reconsider my choices. Mother and Divya can't be that far away—Divya couldn't rouse herself before sunrise if the house were burning down around her. There's only one main traveling road between here and the border with Banomal; I could try to catch up with them and tell Mother what I learned from Lyra the previous evening. But without actual proof of the Protector's weapon, all I really have to offer her at this point is a fairy tale.

No, I can't tell Mother. Not yet. Not until I can hand her a victory.

Which only leaves Cinderella. The thought of it—needing Cinderella's help, of all people—lies thick and bitter on my tongue. Or perhaps that's only the acid from my stomach eating its way up my throat in hunger. I can't think of the last time I've had a decent tea cake, much less an entire meal. I should have called upon that useless fairy godmother of mine this morning. Lyra said she was fascinated with food, after all. She could have laid a buffet for me to fuel this interminable walk.

I've cataloged in delicious detail every feast I've ever attended by the time the castle comes into view, my vision spotting black and starry in places. I haven't even thought to bring water with me, and my tongue has now shriveled up and stuck to the roof of my mouth so that when the soldiers call at me to halt I cannot unstick it from its place to tell them who I am.

"No begging round here, peasant," one of the boys on the gate calls, his voice filled with disgust. I'm absolutely positive he's the one who gazed after me with a soft jaw when I came through here for the prince's ball. How easily they are swayed by a swath of silk.

"I'm not a peasant, you buffoon," I say, my tongue coming unstuck by the force of my annoyance. "I'm here to see the princess."

That gives them a good laugh, even the fellows up on the walk above the gate. I wonder if Lyra could blind them if I called to her now. Fireworks right in their pocked faces.

"I've got a dinner invite with the king later," says the other guard on the gate. "Maybe you could be my guest and meet the princess then."

"I am not jesting," I grind out, a breeze coming through and making me sway. Which rather undercuts my attempts at dignity. "Please tell Cin—er, Princess Ellarose that her stepsister is here to see here. Aralyn, of House Teramina."

"Oh, you hear that, lads?" calls the first boy. "She's got herself a house. Better snap to attention!"

All of them fall into a salute, which quickly dissolves into another round of laughter. I really don't have time for this, and I certainly don't have the blood flow to spare in the flush that heats my face. It makes my knees go weak, and I swear that if I pass out before these complete morons, just let me cross the veil to the wandering fields of the dead and be done with it.

"If you are all quite finished proving why you are on gate watch and not part of the king's personal retinue, could you deliver my message to the princess?" I say, my words sharp.

"I don't know, Eris, she sure do sound like one of them daughters of a lord," says the second boy on the gate. "A lot of words to say a little."

The first boy looks me up and down. "If she is, she's one of the ones who can't afford their taxes no more."

I'm going to do it. I'm going to call on Lyra and ask her to shoot one of her parlor tricks right into their eyes. Let them comment on my appearance from the infirmary where their feeble brains belong. I open my mouth to say as much when there's a clattering behind me, drawing their attention off me to a horse approaching the gate.

"What is going on here?" asks a voice I recognize immediately, much to my complete humiliation. "Why are you torturing this peasant woman? Give her some bread and let her be on her way."

That gives the boys another bellyful, and while I wish I could set this place aflame with the heat boiling my blood right now, I have to remember there are more important things to be accomplished. So I do the bravest thing I have ever done and turn my face up to the rider.

"Hello, Vee," I say, each syllable deepening my mortification.

Her green eyes widen in surprise, before narrowing to slits. "Aralyn."

I grit my teeth to get through the next part. "I need to see the princess. But these idiots won't let me pass."

"Ah," Vee says, glancing at the guards. "No."

"What do you mean, no?" I ask, startled.

"I mean, visiting you was a complete waste of Princess Ellarose's time, as well as mine. And I won't have you filling her head with whatever nonsense you've brought this time. The princess might believe you are an ally, but I know a rat when I see one."

I clench my fists and close my eyes, the force of my fury threatening to knock me off my feet. Calm. I need to stay calm.

"I have important information for the princess, regarding the subject she came to see me about yesterday," I say, keeping my voice low so the guards don't hear me. I give Vee a meaningful look. "Do you really want to be the one to stand in the way of delivering that information?"

Vee looks as if she would like to stand in the way, very much, but she must have some idea of what Cinderella came to speak to me about, because she gives a growling sigh and nudges her horse forward. "Open the gates!" she commands.

The first boy looks at her doubtfully. "What about the peasant girl?"

Vee lets the question stretch out as she huffs a sigh. "She is with me. Let her pass."

But neither one of the gate guards moves. "We'll have to alert the captain first. You know your father's rule. No unannounced guests on castle grounds."

"I am aware of the rules, Eris; I helped draft them," Vee snaps. "I also know that any guest accompanying a royal or a member of the court is allowed to pass without inspection by the captain of the guard. So open the damn gate and let me pass!"

The boy shakes his head, but he gives a signal to the guards on the wall above and the gate cranks to life, squealing from disuse as the rusted chains pull the heavy wooden door open. Vee clicks her tongue and urges her horse forward, and I follow after, feeling like a rescued street dog. The boy, Eris, mutters to himself as I pass.

"Don't let me be the one catching her father's hand if he don't like it," he says.

I wait until we've cleared the gate and headed toward the stables— and Cinderella's favored entrance—to interrogate Vee. "Who is your father?" I ask.

"It doesn't matter," she grinds out.

Which means it very much does. Could her father be the captain of the guard? Was it his rule that all guests be inspected? But no, I vaguely remember the man, and he's far too young to have a daughter Vee's age. And then it strikes me. She said any member of the royal court should be allowed to pass without inspection.

"Of course," I breathe, shaking my head. "You're a bloody *royal*."

"Who told you that?" she asks, drawing her horse to an abrupt halt and giving me a face full of tail hair.

"You did, just now," I say, grinning. "It all makes sense now."

"What does?" she asks suspiciously.

"Why they let you become a knight."

She swings her leg over and jumps down, her face flaming red. "They didn't *let* me become anything. I earned my spurs."

"Oh, sure. I'll bet you were the best squire among the bunch."

"I was," she grinds out, using her height advantage to tower over me. "I knew it was a mistake, letting you in. You'll never so much as lay eyes on Princess Ellarose as long as I am around to protect her. Maybe I will bring you up before the captain, let him decide what to do with you. He doesn't look kindly on traitors."

"Vee, what's wrong?" comes Cinderella's jasmine-scented voice. She appears around the horse's head, holding out a small apple as a treat for the beast. I bet she goes about with her pockets filled with food for all the various animals in the castle. "Aralyn! What are you doing here?"

I give myself the luxury of one triumphant look in Vee's direction before addressing Cinderella. "I've got news you'll want to hear. Urgently."

"Of course," Cinderella says, patting the horse on the nose before signaling for the door. "Follow me. Vee, you can find your way to us after stabling Thundermere?"

"Thundermere? You named your horse Thundermere?" I say.

"I can call one of the stable boys to do it," Vee says, pointedly ignoring me. "I don't want to leave you alone."

"Oh, Vee, you worry too much," Cinderella says, waving her hand. "Aralyn would never harm me. Come along, you must be starving."

I am, actually, not that I would admit as much in front of either of them. Vee glares at me so hard I'm sure she's wishing *she* had a fairy godmother to light me up with fireworks. She steps closer, grabbing my arm in a grip that will leave marks.

"If she gets so much as a splinter in your presence—"

"You'll bring down the wrath of the kingdom on me, I'm sure," I say, peeling off her fingers to free myself. "Unclench your jaw. If I wanted Cinderella harmed, it would have happened long before the prince chose her. I need her help."

"That much is obvious," Vee says, looking down at my work dress meaningfully. "Do not play about her with her emotions. She still cares for you, same as she cares for the rats who come to sing her songs every morning."

I raise my eyebrows at her. "Did you learn such manners in your finishing lessons here at the castle?"

Vee snarls, but she releases me and grabs her horse by the reins, stomping off to return him to the stables. I press my lips together to suppress the smile of triumph that wants to break free.

"They're mice, actually," I can't help but call after her.

"What have you discovered?" Cinderella asks as soon as we are comfortably ensconced in her quarters with a small feast sent up from the kitchens. The furnishings are sparse—far too sparse for the future queen—but I suppose Cinderella wouldn't notice after spending the last decade sleeping on a pallet near the kitchen fire.

"Something that might help us stop Cordo," I say carefully, throwing my finishing training to the wind and devouring a tea cake in a single bite. I've debated how much to reveal to her—how much she needs to know to agree to help me versus how much would allow her to undertake the journey on her own and leave me out entirely. "An old fairy myth, if it's to be believed."

Cinderella looks to me in surprise, a splash of tea landing on the table beside the cup she was in the middle of pouring. She doesn't even have her serving girl pour the tea. Honestly, it's a wonder she doesn't sweep her own hearth.

"Where did you learn of an old fairy myth?" she asks.

"Er," I say around a mouthful of cake number three. "That bit is hardly important. The important thing is that it's a rather perilous journey to retrieve it. I'll need supplies and a retinue of guards to protect me along the way. A carriage, a full complement of clothes, food, and coin for lodgings. It shouldn't be difficult for your prince to provide such accommodations, unless Cordo has seized control of his purse strings as well."

"No, Fael still has a healthy monthly stipend, but . . ." Cinderella passes me the teacup, a tremor going through her hand. "The fairies are forbidden from revealing their stories to humankind. How could you have learned of such a legend? And what *is* the legend?"

I was really hoping Cinderella would keep these kinds of questions to a minimum, but I can see I underestimated her curiosity. "Have you heard of Novador's Protector?"

Cinderella gives me a blank look. "What is that?"

"An ancient fey weapon that was used to protect the kingdom from invading forces, including other fey," I say, moving on to the cheese plate. It's been *months* since I've had a decently aged cheese, and every bite is a tangy, sharp benediction. "It was supposed to be destroyed, but the fey who wielded it tore it in three pieces instead, and cast them to the far corners of the kingdom. If all the pieces are assembled once again, it could be used to bring power and prosperity back to Novador."

Cinderella sits forward eagerly, forgetting the tea in her lap and knocking a milky brown stain over the powder blue of her skirts. "That's it! That's exactly what we need! Where are the pieces?"

"That's the tricky bit," I hedge. "The locations are hidden by magic. But I have a clue of where to begin looking. Still, it could take some time to track it down."

She stands up, dumping the entire cup of tea on the carpet. This girl tests the very limits of my patience. "Then we had better leave now."

"Leave where?" asks Vee from the doorway of Cinderella's quarters, tracking in bits of hay that got stuck in her spurs. "Where are we going?"

"*We* are not going anywhere," I say emphatically, setting down my cup of tea. "As I said, the trip could take some time, and you cannot afford to be gone from the palace for that long, Ci—er, Ellarose. Certain people would take notice, and not in a good way. You'll need to stay here with Fael to attend to court matters. I will go."

"And Vee will go with you," Cinderella says, clapping her hands together.

"NO," Vee and I chorus, in agreement for the first and only time ever to be recorded.

"I am not going anywhere that you are not," Vee continues to Cinderella before giving me a suspicious look. "And certainly not with her."

"And I need to move quickly and quietly without drawing much attention," I add, giving the look right back. "None of which I believe your guard dog here is capable of."

"See how quickly and quietly I move to escort you to the dungeons," Vee says, taking a menacing step toward me.

Cinderella swishes in between both of us, putting a light hand on my shoulder and another on Vee's breastplate. "Both of you, that is enough." Her voice is soft but commanding, kind but exasperated. She almost—*almost*—sounds like a royal. It's infuriating. "Listen to me. Aralyn has been helping me investigate a way to restore prosperity to Novador and to help the prince and me guide the kingdom. And she believes she has found a solution, but the journey will be long and perilous. She will need someone along to protect her—"

"I don't require *her* protection," I interject, but Cinderella silences me with a glare. A pretty good one, actually.

"She will need someone along to protect her," Cinderella continues emphatically, "and I require someone I trust to do it. And you know better than anyone, Vee, that I can count on one hand how many guards are loyal to Fael or me in this castle."

She holds up her index finger for emphasis, pointing it once more at Vee. But Vee is not so easily swayed, her armor creaking as she crosses her arms and glares at me.

"How do you know she's even telling the truth?" Vee demands. "What is this supposed solution she had supposedly discovered?"

"It's a fey weapon that once protected the entire kingdom of Novador," I snipe.

Vee snorts. "Sounds like your invention of one of their outlandish tales."

"It's not," I say hotly. "I heard it from a fairy godmother myself."

Cinderella turns on me. "Whose fairy godmother?"

"My fairy godmother," I say, still glaring at Vee.

Cinderella's mouth drops open. "*You* have a fairy godmother? And she actually came when you called?"

"Yes," I spit sarcastically. "Even I, a lowly woman with no prince to woo me, have a fairy godmother. And so does Divya, apparently. Sorry to burst your fairy-tale bubble, but they're everywhere. And utterly useless."

"No, I didn't mean . . ." Cinderella shakes her head, though her complexion has gone pale. I never took her for an egotistical girl, but her complete shock at my also having a fairy godmother really rankles. She doesn't have the market on them.

"Never mind that," Cinderella says sternly—though I can't tell if she's saying it to me or herself. "We need the Protector's weapon. At this point, it's our only hope. And you two will have to go together, regardless of your feelings toward each other. Novador needs this. I need this. And frankly, you two need this as well. You will do as we all must do and set aside your personal feelings for the greater good of Novador. Are we clear?"

She looks to Vee, who mumbles something that sounds like begrudging assent, and then to me. I'm oddly compelled by her little speech, a stirring in my chest I've never felt before at the mention of Novador. She's right, though she can't imagine *how* she's right; I do need this. If it means dragging a deadweight like Vee along, I'll just have to accommodate. There are a thousand places to lose a self-righteous do-gooder like her between here and the Mortel Mountains.

"Very well," I say, looking at Vee with determination. "We'll leave first thing tomorrow. I hope you will be prepared."

"I am always prepared," Vee says.

EIGHT

"WHO TAUGHT YOU TO RIDE A HORSE, A SENTIENT SACK of potatoes?" Vee says as soon as we've cleared the city walls of the capital. They're the first words she's said to me since we agreed to this ill-fated journey together yesterday, and they're as unwelcome as her presence.

"We didn't all have the luxury of the royal horse breeders to teach us," I shoot back. I sit up straighter, realizing I had within my reach a way to pass the endless miles of riding with a new entertainment. "Is that your father? Sir Galanthrop?"

Vee looks at me sourly. "No."

I look over her profile, her nose strong and distinct, her brow wide and dusted with fine golden hairs cut short. "No, I suppose not, he's far too dark-skinned and hairy to have bred you. Ah, the queen's old champion, then. Sir Bundag? He was said to be a great golden lion of a man. Condolences on his loss, if it was."

"Sir Bundag died ten years ago, and he was aged seventy-five," Vee says, irritated. "Of course he wasn't my father."

"Hmm, did he have a son?"

"I do not wish to discuss my parentage with you!" Vee says, far too sharply.

I only respond with a mild lift of my eyebrows. "Rather sensitive about it, aren't you?"

She spears me with a look. "Shall we discuss your parentage instead?"

That's possibly a fair hit, and a direct one. I sniff, giving my horse a little kick and trotting out ahead of her. "Silence it is, then. I was already beginning to tire of the grate of your voice against my ears."

But with no conversation to engage me, I was forced to turn my attention to the passing countryside as we traveled. I've walked the road to Sebanthorn often enough over the past few months to try and sell our dresses to their tailor there, and the view does not improve from atop a mount. The earth is cracked and pockmarked from wells half dug by the locals searching for water as the rains have eluded us, the grass bleached to a lifeless yellow that crackles under our horses' hooves. The meager huts that make up the outskirts of Sebanthorn haven't fared much better—many of their roofs have fallen in and their walls lean heavily in one direction, a result of the dry ground shifting beneath them. Animals roam free, skin hanging loose over the rough ridges of their ribs and backbones, small children in tattered clothes running and whooping around them. They spot Vee first, like a shining beacon of comfortable ignorance.

"No more than a copper each, and don't let them get behind you," I murmur to her as they start for us in a dash.

"What?" she asks, bewildered.

I can't help a small grin. "You'll see."

They crowd the horses, their nails caked black and their arms lined with scratches and cuts as they beg for anything that enters their head—a meal, a coin, a wish bestowed from the fey. I take a few coppers I've tucked into a small pocket at my waist for exactly this occasion, flashing the coins over their heads before tossing them into the dirt along the pathway. The children scatter, shoving each other over in their pursuit of the money and leaving my horse free.

I can't say Vee is enjoying the same freedom, as the remaining children have overwhelmed her to the point that she's had to stop her horse. While she fumbles about with the coin bag tied to her waist, two of the smaller children slip behind her and sneak their hands into her saddlebags. They're there and gone so fast no one would ever notice the gesture had I not been watching them. One snags an apple, red as a jewel, and tucks it down their shirt with a grin filled with rotted, crooked teeth.

"By the fairies, Vee, shoo them away," I say loudly, when she's still trying to appease them with more coins. She's taken out a gold piece, like an absolute idiot. "Not the gold, Vee! I told you, stick to copper."

She glances at me, helpless, and for once I feel a twinge of pity. She's so completely out of her element here among the down-trodden masses. I send a sigh up to the heavens, promising that I'll raid her coin satchel myself the first chance I get. I draw another silver piece out of my pocket, holding it up and waving it at the other children.

"Hey! You lot! Who can run the fastest?" I call out.

"Me!" one shouts, only to be crowded and shoved by the rest of them.

"Let's see!" I say, chucking the silver coin far into the grass.

The children take off at a sprint, and I dig my heels hard into my horse's flanks. "Come on, Vee! Before they swarm again."

Vee catches up and passes me quickly, as if pursued by a wild, woolly forest creature and not a gaggle of small children. I laugh, letting the wind carry the sound to her as she leans over her horse's neck and spurs him on faster.

"Ride, Thundermere!" I call out, followed by another full-bellied laugh.

We run the horses until we can no longer see Sebanthorn, until the lands open up flat and dead, only the occasional hut breaking up the empty landscape. There are plenty more towns to pass through, each poorer than the last, until we reach our stop for the evening. But the farther out we go, the more hungry the children are and the more glassy-eyed and listless they become, until even I lose my grin. After we pass just such a town, where the sheep do not even stir from their tiny patches of shade as we pass, Vee slows her horse to a crawl, allowing me to catch up.

"I had no idea," she says, her voice soft with horror. "I mean, I knew this year has been harder than the last, and that one harder than the one that came before. But I had no idea it had gotten this bad."

"When was the last time you actually left the city walls?" I ask, my voice sharp.

But Vee is staring out at the broken land, too consumed by its barren expanse to rise to my bait. "How can they live like this? With . . . with nothing?"

"They don't," I say succinctly.

She looks to me, so completely lost I can hardly be mad, which only incites a greater fury. Of course she would know none of this, a child of some royal father who gets to play knight and protect a princess who wears fairy-spun glass slippers while the rest of the kingdom slips into misery. Completely useless, the lot of them.

"I had no idea," she whispers again, shaking her head.

"And yet it does not make you any less culpable," I say, though I'm not even sure if I mean it unkindly.

We ride on in silence, Vee steeped in her misery and me steeped in my resolve. It was easy to get distracted by Cinderella and her fancy, jasmine-scented speeches. But out here, amid the ravaged land and its frail inhabitants, I know I'm right. None of them deserve to guide this country. Not the king, hiding like a coward in his quarters; not Cordo, with his stores of coin and wheat and greed; and certainly not starry-eyed Cinderella and her ineffectual prince. This country does not need fairy godmothers fulfilling pandering wishes; it needs a strong hand and a clear vision of the future. A strong hand I can deliver, as soon as I have the Protector's weapon.

NINE

THE JOURNEY TAKES THE GREATER PART OF A WEEK,
and by the time the distant horizon shimmers and cracks and raises
itself into jagged peaks, Vee has given away the bulk of her coin
satchel and it's been left to me to provide for our food and accommodations. Luckily, I stole a few silver pieces from her pouch the
first night, otherwise we would starve altogether. The only thing
worse than her ignorance is her guilt.

"I must speak with the king's council immediately upon our
return," she states as a chill wind cuts down from the mountains
and across the plain, bringing with it the scent of snow. "They need
to know the wretched state of affairs plaguing our people."

"Plaguing," I say, rolling my eyes, as if this were a blight that happened upon the people and not one orchestrated and executed by
the council itself. "You think they truly do not know the state of
affairs? You think their tax collectors do not bring back half-filled
sacks and tales of the starving masses? They know, Vee. They simply
do not care."

"How could they not?" she asks, truly bewildered. Her expression
shifts into determination. "Then they must be made to care. No one

could travel these townships as we have the past several days and not be moved to pity."

"You must not have met the high chancellor, then," I mutter.

Vee blanches. "High Chancellor Cordo might be . . . rigid in his beliefs, but he wouldn't allow Novador to come to *this*. What good does it do him if his people are starving and on the verge of revolt? A kingdom cannot prosper if its people suffer."

I rein in my horse and twist in the saddle to face her. "Do you not understand that the suffering is precisely the point? Men like Cordo—born into royalty, begetting royalty—they see themselves as greater than. They do not view themselves as stewards entrusted with protecting the country, but rather as pampered toddlers who expect their every demand to be fulfilled. They do not care what happens to their people because they do not see them as people. They see them as servants, existing to meet their needs. If one faints away dead in the fields from hunger or exhaustion, they have another ten children to take their place and reap the harvest and pay their taxes. Cordo does not see the poverty of our nation as a personal blight, but rather a symptom of a lazy working class. He, very simply put, is incapable of human feeling."

Vee has gone white and trembling, and I think it must be from rage until her voice comes out in anguish. "That is not true. He is not as you say. I cannot believe it. I refuse to believe it. He is not beyond compassion. He is not incapable of love."

"I never said anything about love," I snort, but then I finally put it all together. "Oh, plunkers. High Chancellor Cordo is your father, isn't he?"

"I do not wish to speak on this any longer, or to you at all," Vee says, suddenly spurring her horse forward. But not before I catch a glimpse of shimmering tracks staining her cheeks, furiously brushed away by her gloved hands. The stain stays on the fingertips of the delicate tan hide of her glove, leaving it dark.

Well, I've stepped in it, haven't I.

Vee keeps up a backside-bruising pace toward the base of the Mortel Mountains, far too quick and jarring for me to even catch up, much less attempt a conversation. Which, I suspect, is the point. So instead of discussing the matter with her, I debate it with myself. Perhaps I had been a bit harsh on her father; after all, I knew what it was like to have an ambitious parent with murky morals. The only difference between Cordo and my mother was that he had suc-ceeded where she still struggled. Who was I to judge, truly?

But still, the facts remained. High Chancellor Cordo presumably had control of the king's council, and in lieu of the actual king to direct matters, had effective control of the country. And what had he done with it? Run it into the ground. I had never met the man directly, but I'd seen him at enough royal functions at the castle. He did not eschew luxury. He always wore the finest wools, the smoothest silks, the richest furs. He claimed they were a necessity, a representation of Novador's power and wealth. Rumor had it he even installed a tub made of gold and inlaid with Mortel granite in his private bathing facilities.

In short, he was as corrupt as they came. But that did not make Vee responsible for his actions, nor did it condemn her desire for him to prove himself a better man.

Once, long ago, when Cinderella's father was still alive and the manor still prospered, a young serving girl became my friend before I learned what a liability friends could be in the manor. She asked me how I could ever love such a monster, after Mother went on a tear about the wrong type of flowers being brought in to decorate the house before a ball. I hadn't understood her question. The flowers were wrong; why would Mother not have cause to be so upset? It never occurred to me that my mother could be perceived as anything other than just and right, because she was my moral compass to the world. The question troubled me so much I asked my mother, and the serving girl was gone the next day. I never saw her again.

How do you love a monster? The simple, complicated answer is that you love them the same as anyone else. It just hurts more.

The temperature drops sharply as we ride into the long shadow of the mountains, the sun falling away so suddenly my eyes hardly have time to adjust to the darkness. There are no gradual, rose-tinted sunsets around here, I suppose. Just light, and dark. I had thought we would reach the mountains by nightfall, but the farther we ride the more distant they seem. I can hardly keep track of Vee ahead of me, the gallop of her horse's hooves lost among mine. I would have appreciated a lantern—or better yet, a carriage—and I lean forward and squint to keep my eyes on the road that has grown rocky and pockmarked the farther along we've gone.

Something looms in the distance, and I can only hope it is a roadside inn with a more decent stew than the last place we stayed, but as I draw near I realize it's Vee, her horse stopped in the middle of the road. I slow my own mount, grateful for the break for my trembling thighs and rattling teeth, but the more her outline takes shape, the slower my pace. Her back is ramrod straight, tension radiating out from her plated shoulders and calves.

"Vee?" I call cautiously.

"Don't come any closer, Aralyn," Vee calls back, her voice strange and tight.

"Why would I not—"

But then I see the man as I draw even with Vee, his armor dented and rusted through in patches, his beard so thick and matted it seems fused to the blanket he has wrapped around his shoulders. He's got a sword, the edge of it pointing at the armor plating covering Vee's midsection.

"Are you all right?" I ask her, checking the exposed bit of her tunic for any sign of blood.

"He came out from behind that boulder and was on me before I could dodge him," Vee says quietly, barely daring to draw in a breath. "He put his sword in my gut and called me a demon. I do not think he is well."

"I didn't kill her!" the man says in a shrill voice, his eyes shining too bright. He's crying, but his eyes are bloodshot and he seems to barely register the tears pooling in the corners of his mouth. I think he's been crying for some time, his skin leathery from dehydration. "It wasn't my fault! She fell!"

"Sir, I don't know who you think we are," Vee says, loudly and calmly. "But we are only looking to pass into the Mortel Mountains."

"Slipped on the edge!" the man continues, still crying. Still holding Vee at the end of his sword. "I told her not to get so close, but she was such a carefree, curious lass. Wanted to know how far down it went. Those satin slippers were useless!"

"Who is he talking about?" I ask.

"I have no idea," Vee says quietly. "But he's been talking about her ever since he jumped out at me. I'm not even sure he *sees* me."

"Can you not back up?" I whisper.

"Not without risking my innards," Vee says. "His sword might be rusty, but I can confirm it's quite sharp."

"Sir," I say, as loudly and authoritatively as I can manage under the circumstances, "please remove your sword from my companion's midsection. We are strangers to you, and have done you no harm. Stand down."

"I tried to grab her hand," he sobs, as if I haven't spoken at all. "Nearly went over myself. I was too late. Always too late!"

"Sir!" I say, sharply, and though his tears still track rivers down his face, my words seem to draw his attention to me. He turns and Vee sucks in a breath sharply.

"Aralyn," she hisses.

"Sorry," I mutter. But when the man turns toward me, I get a better view of the blanket wrapped around his shoulders, and I see that it's not a blanket at all. "Vee, is that the standard of House Goldren?"

"I'm not exactly in the position to test my knowledge of house standards," Vee whispers harshly, sucking in her breath again as the man's sword presses in on her tender belly.

"I think this man is Sir Kenna of House Goldren," I whisper.

Vee's eyes go wide and round. "The Missing Knight? It cannot be."

It's an old tale around the capital, one that children would tell in dark corners to test the mettle of one another. The story of a knight so brave and true, the king sent him off to the wilds of the Mortel Mountains to tame the dark creatures said to reside there. Many months the king awaited his return, sending a contingent of royal soldiers to inquire after him. The people along the way remembered him riding proudly through their villages, but no one reported ever seeing him return. The soldiers ventured as close as they dared to the Mortel Mountains, but the calls of the creatures that lived there so curdled their blood that they fled for the safety of the capital without ever setting foot on the mountain range.

"I thought that was just a legend," Vee whispers.

"I thought so as well, but this man is very much alive," I say. "And who else would have the standard of House Goldren with him?"

"But . . . what has become of him?" Vee asks.

"Sir Kenna?" I say tentatively, watching his expression for any flicker of recognition. "Sir Kenna of House Goldren, first of his name and beloved protector of King Soteo?"

The man blinks rapidly, several times in a row, taking some of the shine off his dark eyes. "I . . . I have not heard that name in so long."

"Is it you, truly, Sir Kenna of House Goldren?" Vee asks.

The man looks up at her, blinking once again in surprise at the sword pointed at Vee's midsection and gripped tightly in his hand. His fingers flex open, the sword clattering to the ground. "My word, young knight, what have I done? Are you injured? I cannot imagine why I would have . . . I am not . . . Please, could you tell me where I am?"

"You are at the base of the Mortel Mountains," Vee says gently, nodding toward the darker patches of sky before us. The mountains are no more than an outline now, but still distinct against the pulpy blue sky. "Sir Kenna, what do you know? What do you remember?"

"I . . . The king, he sent me on a quest," says Sir Kenna, his voice smoothing out and taking on definition with each word. "To retrieve . . . To retrieve . . . To retrieve . . ."

"A treasure?" I ask.

"What treasure?" asks the man, his expression completely blank.

I look to Vee, unsure how to proceed. Whatever has afflicted him seems to have cleared at the mention of his name, but it seems to have also cleared out his memory.

"Sir Kenna, you have been gone a great many years," Vee says softly, kindly. "The king mourned you for dead."

"Dead? Mourned? I have only just departed!" Sir Kenna declares. "Why would he mourn me?"

"Oh dear," I murmur. "Sir Kenna, would you happen to recall whether or not there is a township anywhere nearby? The hour has grown late and we require accommodations for the night. I believe you do as well."

"Why, there is one just up the road," says Sir Kenna, waving behind him. "I shall simply fetch my mount and guide you there."

"Take mine," Vee says hastily, swinging down from her horse. "I could do with a good, brisk walk."

"I would never take another knight's mount," says Sir Kenna, sounding offended.

"Please, I insist," Vee says, holding out the reins. "You've suffered a perilous journey. It is the least I can do to honor a knight of your reputation."

"Very well," Sir Kenna says, though he still sounds hesitant. He takes the reins and swings up onto Vee's mount, earning a snort from the horse. But he takes Thundermere well in hand, obviously no stranger to riding. "Keep up, if you would!"

I sigh, scooting as far forward on my saddle as the pommel will allow. "Get on," I growl at Vee.

She looks up at me in confusion, going scarlet around the tips of her ears. "Why in the world would I do that?"

"Because you'll never make it on foot in that getup, and if there are any other mad questers lurking about these boulders, your clattering will draw them down right on us. Now get up and stop making this so awkward."

"I am not making it awkward," Vee says stiffly, though she does set her foot into the stirrup and haul herself up behind me.

My horse is considerably less accommodating of the bulk of her armor than Thundermere, and gives a little sideways prance trying to dislodge the both of us. Vee tips to the side, scrabbling at my waist to keep from getting launched. Her fingers are strong and sure against the slight span of my waist, the intimacy of the contact shocking. I don't believe anyone has ever touched me like this, with the exception of Monsieur Lisseu when taking measurements for a new dress. And even then, his touch was often light and quick, almost clinical. Vee's hands on my hips, her breath in my ear, the metal of her armor digging into the backs of my knees, make my heart pound and my palms sweat.

"Are you all right?" Vee asks, her voice so close.

"Fine," I say, too loudly, before giving my horse a sharp kick that nearly bucks us both off again. I almost wish it would.

TEN

CALLING THE ENCAMPMENT AT THE BASE OF THE
Mortel Mountains a township seems an exaggeration, if not an outright lie. There are barely half a dozen houses, all of them squat and
low and covered over by moss and tree branches like enormous fairy
houses. The effect might be quaint in full sunlight, but here in the
dark they stagger up from the landscape like bloodthirsty creatures.
One of their mouths yawns open as our horses clomp closer, and a
man roughly the size and shape of the round door exits, preceded
by a wicked looking curved tool.

"No closer, old man!" he calls in a rumbling voice. His eyes are
squinty behind a snow-white beard, his clothes well layered against
the cold that seems to sift down from the sky and rise up from the
ground at the same time. "We told you what would happen if you
crossed our town lines again. We don't want to cause you harm, but
we have to protect our homestead."

"I do not understand," Sir Kenna says, truly confused. He raises
his voice. "Sir, I do not understand your cold welcome. The last our
paths crossed was not a week past. You were stoic but hospitable,

offering your very own home for me to rest my head before continuing my journey up into the mountain pass. Have I offended you in some way?"

The man snorts. "You have haunted our borders for years, scaring the women at their washing and snatching up our wee ones and attempting to carry them off with you, promising to rescue them from the cliffside as you could not rescue your Claudette."

The blood drains from Sir Kenna's ruddy, weathered cheeks. "How do you know of my daughter? What foul magic is this?"

"His daughter," I whisper, my heart opening a bit. "It was your daughter who fell."

Sir Kenna looks to me, startled. "You know the tale of my tragedy as well? Has the kingdom been overrun with it?"

I shake my head, turning to the man with the white beard and holding up my hands to show we are unarmed and uninclined to snatch wee ones. "Sir, my name is Aralyn of House Teramina and this is my travel companion, Vee, knight of the royal court. If you would allow us shelter for the evening, we would pay you handsomely. I can promise Sir Kenna is no longer a threat to you or your family. I believe he was bewitched."

"He's more than bewitched," growls the man. "He's cursed, same as they all are. Same as every questing fool who sets foot in the hills of Mortel."

I glance warily at Sir Kenna. "There are more like him?"

The man snorts again. "As many as there are rocks on the hillside. They roam the mountains like feral things, attacking anyone foolhardy enough to seek it. They've driven off everyone in our township save myself and my wife."

Vee leans forward, pressing against me and driving the pommel of my saddle into my hip, her eyes bright. "So there is something in the mountains."

"Oh, sure," the man says expansively, before his expression goes flat again. "Madness and death."

"Well, that's a cheery introduction," I mutter. "Please, sir, could we trouble you for accommodations? The hour grows late and our bellies have long grown empty."

"A trouble it is," the man mutters, but he lowers his strange weapon and disappears through the door. "Come on, if you're coming, then. You're letting all the good heat out. Name's Cliod. And have a care tying up those horses of yours; they're likely to spook and bolt on you if you don't."

"Thundermere would never," Vee says indignantly behind me.

It takes a good while to find adequate shelter for the horses, and in that time the weather turns vicious, a howling wind blowing down like vengeance from the mountains and bringing gusts of fat, white flakes that settle on our shoulders like a mantle before swirling off again on the next cut. By the time we return to Cliod's house we're driven within by a gust that feels like a pair of hands at our backs, swinging the door closed behind us with a clap that shakes the drifts of snow off our clothes.

"It'll rage like that all night long," says a woman with a cloud of gray hair and sharp eyes. She stands over a fire in the middle of their home, a large cauldron bubbling over with something that smells odd but looks thick and hearty. She looks to me, and then Vee, clucking her tongue. "Not much use round these parts, that tin getup of yours."

Vee stiffens at the insult to her armor, and I can feel the protest forming in the back of her throat.

"Your home is lovely and spacious," I say, falling back on Mistress Clara's etiquette lessons. "Quite inviting."

"Don't get too comfortable," the woman says flatly, but she ladles a bowlful of the stew for both of us, which is the only hospitality I really care about. "I'm Thana, wife of Cliod. He's gathering more wood for the fire before the storm truly settles."

Sir Kenna occupies a round wooden table toward the back of the hut, waving cheerily to us over a mostly empty bowl. His eyes still glisten too much, and he could do with a shave and a good scrubbing, but whatever curse had driven him to almost put a sword in Vee's gut seems to have lifted. We sit beside him, going to work on the stew. It's thick and earthy, filled with woody mushrooms and small green bulbs that explode with vinegary flavor when you bite into them. It's strange, nothing like the meat and cream dishes preferred in the capital, but I'm sipping the dregs before I realize it.

"It's quite filling, is it not?" Sir Kenna says with a genial smile. At least he's still got all his teeth. "A local staple, I've been made to understand. The mushrooms grow around the base of the mountains, and those little podful delights are apparently called capers."

"We brine them ourselves," says Thana, dropping onto the bench beside me and rocking the thick slats of wood. "So, you lot are questers."

"We are . . . travelers," I say, glancing at Vee with a warning.

"Travelers, right," harrumphs Thana, and in that moment I can see what a pair she and Cliod make. "Whatever excuse you have for traveling up that pass, you'll end up as cursed as the rest of them. As empty-handed as well."

"Who are these questers you speak of?" Vee asks.

"All types," says Thana shortly. "Knights like your man here, poor fellows from the coast of Maro, tree men from the forests of Fenn. All thinking they'll be the ones to break the curse."

"But what is it they seek?" I ask, trying my best to sound casually curious and landing somewhere around overly intent.

Thana shrugs. "I don't bother myself asking. Anyone who wants to keep their mind knows better than to venture into those mountains. Even down here you can hear it."

Vee looks startled. "Hear what?"

Thana flashes a glare at her. "If you ever stopped talking, you'd hear it."

We fall silent at that, straining our ears to hear anything above the howling wind outside. There is the bubbling of the remaining stew in the pot, the crackle of the pile of thin sticks beneath it. The gentle wheeze of Thana's breath as she slurps at her soup. A faint creak of Vee's armor as she adjusts her seat. All of it a gentle symphony, but not out of the ordinary.

But then there's just the faintest whisper of . . . something. Not quite words, not quite distinct, but the feel of it brushing against my consciousness tightens my stomach like a fist. I close my eyes, trying to turn the hazy wisps of sound into distinct words, when Sir Kenna gives a hiccuping sob beside me.

"Oh, my darling Claudette," he says in a soft wail.

The door to the hut bangs open, startling me up off the bench. Thana grumbles her annoyance at the disruption, scooting to the center of the bench to continue eating her stew as Cliod bustles in with an armload of sticks. The wind is blowing so fiercely now he's got to put his shoulder against the door to get it closed again, the fire guttering low and peeking out of the smoldering sticks as he shakes off the snow like a beast.

"It's a rager out there, it is," he grouses, leaving trails of snow between the door and the fireplace. The fire sizzles in protest as he dumps more snow on the meager flames along with his haul of sticks. "She'll be going all night long and well into the morn. Mountains are angry."

"Why would the mountains be angry?" Vee asks.

Cliod gives her a discerning once-over, bringing up a flush of red along her cheekbones. "Maybe they know you're coming."

We finish our stews and Thana grumbles some more as she fixes up sleeping pallets for the three of us, a damp collection of straw with a rough wool blanket thrown over each one. It's not much worse than the moldy stretches of mattress we've suffered on at our various stops along the way, and at least now as the fire gutters low and Sir Kenna settles into a muffled snore, I don't have to contend with the boisterous drinking and shouting of a tavern below us. I might have a decent night's sleep for once.

Except that, when I close my eyes, I swear I hear my mother's voice. It's impossible, I know—she should be well ensconced in the bosom of Valley Banomal by now—but the harder I try to ignore it, the more distinct it grows until it feels as if she's lying on the bed beside me as she used to do when I was a young girl. My forehead tickles where she used to stroke back my unfortunate overhang of fringe, slipping behind my ear with a soft scrape of her perfectly shaped nails.

"I need to travel again, Ary," she had said, her voice thick and raspy as if she'd been arguing.

"But what about the duke?" I had asked in alarm. It had been a duke that time, a count before him, an earl the time before. The duke had lasted the longest, nearly three years. I thought we might finally have a home. He'd bought her this apartment where we lay down, and for once Divya and I had our own beds. She still crawled into mine most nights, though, when the revelry just outside our door got too loud and dangerous.

"The duke is feckless, inconsistent, and easily distracted by an opera singer's bosom," Mother spat. But then her voice gentled, her fingers curling through my hair again. "You'll have to look after Divya, darling. She's old enough that she'll ask questions now."

"Are we . . . are we leaving?" I asked, my heart racing. *Please don't let her say the potter's wife.* I still had scars.

"This is no longer our apartment," Mother said, and I could hear the hard lines her face fell into when she said it. "I'll need to find another patron."

She meant *paramour.* I was old enough, and the walls were thin enough.

"Let us come with you this time," I whispered, taking her hand. "I can look after Divya while you . . . search. We'll stay out of sight, I promise. We won't make any trouble. Just don't . . . please don't leave us again."

"I can't do that, Ary darling, and you know it." Her hands ghosted through my hair again, already pulling away. Taking the sun and leaving us the dark. "Men must be harvested delicately, like the spring flowers they are. You cannot give them any reason to wilt on you before you've planted them in your pot. Another man's children are like a pestilence to them. They must be built up nice and strong before you can introduce them. And this time, I swear to find one who will last. No more of this hiding and scrabbling for us. We'll never starve again, no matter what I must do. You must be strong while I am gone. And smart. You will learn the lessons I failed to learn myself. No brats to ruin your figure, no extra mouths to feed. Don't let anyone in. It is you, Divya, and me. We are all that matters in this world. Do you understand?"

"But, Mama," I said, "I'm scared."

"Aralyn?"

I gasp awake, not realizing I had ever fallen asleep. Vee is propped up on her elbow, holding a small book in her hands by the light of a candle stub. She's read that infernal thing—some simpering book of poetry—every night of our travels. She'll likely run out of that candle before we reach the Protector's weapon.

"I was dreaming," I say, still caught in the sticky web of Mother's ambitions.

"You said you were scared," Vee says, frowning. "If you are afraid to venture into the Mortel Mountains—"

"I am not scared of the mountain," I say firmly. "It was only a dream. I shall be ready as soon as the storm passes."

"I can travel up the mountain alone and return to you here," Vee says.

Not a chance, I think, but to her I only say, "I'll be ready."

I turn my back to her, curling up and bringing my knees into my chest for warmth. The wind rages outside, rustling the mud walls of Cliod and Thana's home, but it is a long while before I risk closing my eyes and losing myself to sleep again.

ELEVEN

I USE THE LAST OF OUR SILVER TO BUY FUR WRAPPINGS
from Thana and to pay Cliod to mind the horses while we're up the
mountain. I'm only a little worried he'll try to sell them the second
we disappear up the pass, but Vee threatens the very marrow in his
bones if anything untoward happens to Thundermere. She can use
that height of hers to good advantage, especially on a man Cliod's
size, and he seems to get the message well enough, even though he
stomps about the hut the rest of the time we're there.

"I shall accompany you ladies up the mountain to serve as protection against the creatures that dwell there," Sir Kenna declares
chivalrously as we load our packs.

"No, no, no," Vee says hastily, holding up her hands in horror. Sir
Kenna's mouth sags, his beard drooping down to his waist.

"What my companion means is that we need someone down here,
to watch over our horses and protect the pass from other questers," I
say before Vee can attempt to extract her foot from her mouth. "We
are well equipped for what lies ahead, but only if we know we have
someone brave and loyal guarding our backs down here."

Sir Kenna's eyes have gone misty again, and I'm worried he'll start calling again for his lost daughter. But he looks right at me as he speaks, his gaze so intense it raises goose bumps on my arms. "You have no idea what waits for you up those mountains. The trials, the horrors . . . Greater men than I have tried and failed. I was only lucky to make it back down, before . . ."

He trails off, his eyes drifting away from me as a trail of tears gleams down his cheeks. I glance at Vee, who gives me a faint shrug.

"Before what, Sir Kenna?" I prompt.

His gaze snaps back to me. "Before what?"

"You said you were only lucky to make it back down the mountain, before . . ."

His eyes cloud for a moment, before he gives me a full-toothed grin. "Before dinner, of course! Doesn't Thana make a delicious stew? Hearty enough for the farthest-flung travelers."

I sigh, doing my best to shake off the spell as easily as he has. "She truly does. Thank you, Sir Kenna. Do take care, won't you?"

"And mind Thundermere," Vee adds. "He'll want a good neck-stretching at least twice a day, or he's likely to chew through his restraints and take it on himself."

"Of course, of course," Sir Kenna says as Thana hands us a fragrant bundle of food.

"You'll only come back mad like the rest of that lot," she says frankly. "If you come back at all."

I give her a wan smile. "A well-heeded warning to begin our travels," I say. "Thank you for your hospitality."

It takes the five of us a good half hour to dig out the front door enough that Vee and I can emerge into the blinding landscape outside. It's astonishing, the way the snow has hidden the earth and blanketed the boulders. It's as if we went into one hut and emerged from another on the far side of the country. We don't have much snow in the capital, and what little we get turns to black mush as soon as the farmers haul their crops in to the market.

But here it's like one of Lyra's parlor tricks, as if a fairy godmother snapped her fingers and dressed the land in white. It adorns the peaks overhead, lending their craggy faces an air of whimsy. It's quite lovely, actually, until one puts a foot into it and sinks up to one's waist in cold, wet snow.

"We'll never make it up the mountain like this," I say, having only trudged a few feet into the white.

"You'll need these," says Cliod, holding up what looks for all the world like fishing net stretched between two archery bows. "They're snow walkers. They'll help you stay above the drift."

They look as if I should be scooping fish out of a river with them, but Vee seems to be familiar with their construction because she takes them from Cliod and ties them to the bottom of her feet, clambering her way up the piles of snow to reach the fresh powder. She's eschewed her armor, leaving it to Sir Kenna's care, and standing triumphantly atop a mountain of snow with her feet braced apart to allow space for the snow walkers; she looks as if she were born to scale these ranges. She grins at me, a challenge in her bright eyes.

"Are you coming?"

The thinner, colder atmosphere here has done something to my lungs, pressed all the air out of them, or shrunk them, or made it harder to breathe. That can be the only explanation for why my chest feels so heavy when I look up at her, at that grin still painting her wide mouth, the wan light of morning streaking her hair gold. It makes my feet clumsy in the snow walkers, and I nearly faceplant into the first drift I attempt to climb. Vee laughs—a husky, rumbling sound.

"Having trouble?" she asks.

"I'm pushing you over the first cliff face we reach," I grumble, my lungs working just fine now. I shove past her, tromping my way across the snow toward the mountain pass.

The week in the saddle has bowed my legs sufficiently that I can manage the strange waddle required to tromp through the snow with the walkers on, but my sore thighs and backside from the unforgiving leather of the saddle take their toll on my pace. Vee seems to have no trouble, of course, and she happily larks through the snow like a fox in deep winter. She seems so at home, actually, that it makes me wonder when she's seen snow, and what she loves about it, and what her memories are of it. The picture she makes reminds me of the serving girl, the only true friend I've ever known, the friendship my mother cut short by sacking her. But to have such . . . friendly feelings for Vee is unacceptable. I am sleep-deprived; it's the madness of the mountain creeping up on me; I've been eating mysteriously meated stews for the past week. Such a combination would drive anyone to the edge of their sanity, for that is surely where I must be to wonder over anything about Vee.

"You are lagging," Vee calls from ahead, ruddy cheeked and grinning as she glances back at me. The sun graces her with a crown of gold, blazing like a holy figure. "Shall I carry you on my back like a baby?"

"Please do," I huff, glad for the rough cut of wind across

my face to hide my blush. "It will give me easy access to your neck."

After the howling wind of the storm the previous evening, the snow dampens all the sound around us, the crunch of the snow underfoot and our labored breathing the only accompaniment. Everything is so silenced out here, buried under the snow, that it makes me twitchy. It's strange—I didn't realize how used to the sounds of birdsong and work animals and the rustling of trees I'd gotten, waking up early every morning to attend to the chores at the manor.

So easily adjusted to the labors of common man—what a disappointment.

"What?" I ask, sharply and loudly, my stomach tightening into a fist. "What did you say to me?"

Vee looks back in surprise. "What did who say to you?"

"You, it must have been you. There's no one else within range."

She shakes her head. "I said nothing. Perhaps it was the snow, or a bird."

Ah yes, a bird that can execute the best-placed barb, I'm sure. Vee still stands there, looking so genuinely confused that it infuriates me. I know it was she who said it; why is she hiding from her insults now, blaming them on the snow?

"Never mind," I mutter, scaling the snow once again. "Just keep your conversations to a minimum. We don't want to draw attention to ourselves. And if you have something to say to me, say it directly, not with your back turned."

"All right," Vee says, looking at me as if I've lost my mind.

You have lost your mind, to be out here with this disgraceful girl in service of weak little Cinderella. Such a horrible disappointment you are.

"No!" I say, rounding on Vee. "I heard that clear as day, and you'll answer for it now. I'll not risk my head out here seeking some lost fairy tale to have you question my motives every step of the way."

"Aralyn, what in the name of the fey are you talking about?" Vee says, for once at a height disadvantage because she's sunk farther down into the snow. We're nearly eye level. "I haven't said a word since I asked if you needed me to carry you on my back. Which, I admit, was meant in jest. But I didn't intend it as an insult, and if it upsets you this much I will apologize."

"No, you went far beyond that," I say, shoving a finger in the furs wreathing her shoulders. "You called me a horrible disappointment."

Vee draws back in shock, nearly falling over when the snow shifts beneath her walkers. "I would never say such a thing! How cruel. I'll admit I have my suspicions about you, but I have seen how you are with the village children. You show them kindness and generosity, even when you did not know I was looking. You are, perhaps, not entirely unredeemable."

I shake my head, looking about the sparkling white landscape. "No, no. I heard it. I heard . . . *you*. Didn't I?"

Kindness and generosity to the peasant brats—what comes next? Shall you use the Protector's weapon to restore Cinderella and her mealymouthed prince to the throne? Give them the weapon with which to slit your throat to repay your trust and weakness? You truly are the lesser daughter.

I gasp, drawing back and losing my balance entirely. I circle my arms desperately, but there is nothing out here to catch me save more snow. At least when I land it is soft, the powder cradling me as I sink several feet down. The shock as it hits my neck, cold and wet, draws a sob out of me.

"Aralyn!" Vee calls, her hands reaching down and drawing me up out of my makeshift snow grave. "What's happened to you?"

"It was . . . I heard . . . How is it possible? How could she do it?"

For I know, beyond certainty, that the voice I thought belonged to Vee is actually my mother's.

TWELVE

"It must be Divya," I mutter as I work ungracefully to regain my balance on the snow walkers. "Her and that fairy godfather she connived into serving her. That is the only answer."

"The only answer for what?" Vee asks, far beyond bewildered at this point.

I shake my head. "Nothing. We shall continue on, no more disruptions."

For I would rather bury myself in snow all over again than admit to Vee that my sister had somehow found a way to project such pathetic fears into my mind. Of anyone, Divya knew the pain of Mother's disfavor better than even I could. The exact right tone to strike when mimicking Mother's voice as she tells you what a life she could have lived had you not come along and ruined it for her. I don't know why she would attack me like this now, when she is poised to have everything she wants, but perhaps Lyra let slip our plan to her fairy godfather. It seems the type of thing Lyra would do.

"Should we stop and rest?" Vee calls, slowly following along in my tracks.

"No," I growl, my well fully refilled by spite. "We're going to find that missing piece of the Protector's blade even if I have to start a fairy war to do it."

The insults continue on the higher we climb, soft and subtle and steeped in loving disappointment. I try my best to ignore them, to push them aside, to remind myself these are not coming from Mother herself, but from Divya's pathetic attempts at manipulation. Still, my eyes grow hot the farther we go, the tears freezing immediately on my cheeks.

I will not let her get to me. I will not let her win.

But it sounds so awfully like Mother.

"Aralyn, wait!" Vee cries behind me, so harshly I freeze with one leg stretched far in front of the other. It's an awkward position, and I hold my arms out to keep my balance.

"What is it?" I whisper over my shoulder, trying to catch a glimpse of her without getting a face full of snow.

"There is . . . I heard something," she says, her voice fraught. "Someone. I thought . . . No, that is impossible. He couldn't know! I said nothing, and Cinderella was meant to . . ."

She gasps, and I really am losing my mind because my first instinct is to come to her aid. Which is easier said than done from my lunging position, but I manage to free my legs with minimal fuss and clomp back toward her. She's got her hands pressed over her mouth, her eyes gleaming.

"What?" I take her by the shoulders, the fur tickling the backs of my hands, and give her a little shake. "Vee, what is it? What did you hear? Another quester?"

Vee shakes her head in horror, her eyes searching for mine but not quite focusing. "No, I . . . It was . . . No, Father. Please don't. *Please.*"

She gasps again, a half sob, half hiccup, a single trail of tears leaking down the side of her nose. I look around, suddenly on guard, expecting half the castle guard to come swarming our position and arrest us for sedition or treason. But there is nothing save the snow and our messy tracks behind us, and the unforgiving mountain face ahead.

And then it all clicks into place.

"It's the mountain," I whisper. I raise my voice, shaking Vee harder. "Vee, listen to me. Don't listen to the voice of your father. It's *not* your father, do you hear me? Do you understand? It's the mountain. The curse! This is the curse of the mountain, it must be! It plays upon our fears and weaknesses. Our greatest failures. That's what plagued Sir Kenna, and what tries to poison us now. We must shut it out, Vee."

But now there are twin tracks of tears freezing on her cheeks, and she is not looking at me at all. "Father, please, please do not do this. It is my one desire in life. Please do not marry me off to Banomal. I wish only to become a knight. I swear on our house flagstone I would never embarrass you. I will be the greatest knight this country has ever seen. Please."

Well, that is a surprising bit of knowledge, but not one I have much use for at this point. I need a sane Vee, focused on retrieving the Protector's weapon. What had we done to release Sir Kenna from the mountain's spell?

I grip Vee's shoulders more firmly. "Listen to me. You are Vee-Lira of House Doerr, lady knight and sworn protector to Princess Ellarose. Now snap out of it."

I give her a little slap on the cheek for good measure—just in case and certainly not for personal reasons—and her eyes widen slightly before narrowing.

"How dare you strike me," she says, indignant. "I told you, it was not me who spoke such an insult to you."

"No, I know, Vee, I know," I assure her, holding up my other hand in surrender. "It's the mountain. You were hearing your father."

Vee's face flames a deep red. "What would you know of my father?"

A lot more than I did a few moments ago, but this is hardly the place to dig into that. "Vee, listen to me. The curse of the mountain— it plays on our fears and weaknesses. That's what drove Sir Kenna mad, what you and I were hearing just now. It seeks to drive us to madness with our own fears. We must not let it."

"But how do we stop it?" Vee asks.

"If I begin to cry inconsolably, or whine some nonsense about my mother, say to me, 'You are Aralyn of House Teramina, and you will not be bested by a bloody pile of rock.' And I shall do the same for you. We must . . . we must work together, Vee. It is the only way to survive the mountain. It's why every quester before us has failed. They sought the Protector's weapon alone. We must save each other instead."

Vee nods, her expression growing determined. "All right. Let's continue on, Aralyn of House Teramina."

We get barely five more steps before the voices start in on us again, louder and clearer than the last time as if the mountain has had a taste of our madness and gone feral with it. I can feel my mother's fingers digging into my shoulder, practically shoving me toward the prince. *It will be the workhouse for us all if you don't.*

"You are Aralyn of House Teramina" comes Vee's voice, loud and confident and blasting away Mother's chiding like a fresh burst of snow. "And you will not be bested by a bloody pile of rocks."

I laugh, ending on a sob, and wipe at my cheeks. "Thank you."

We continue on in such a manner, trekking higher as the terrain grows rockier and less sure, the path dropping off a sheer cliff on our right side and overgrown with stubborn mountain trees on the left. The snow gathers above the trees in drifts so high they form towers and spires. It reminds me of the more fanciful sections of the castle back in the capital, beautifully decorated and utterly useless. *Like little Ella, covered in cinders. Beautifully decorated and utterly useless. When you are queen, you will have those useless spires converted to a brewery, or an additional kitchen bakehouse.*

I'm not even sure whose voice that was, Mother's or my own.

"Papa, no," Vee whispers, drawing my attention.

"You are Vee-Lira of House Doerr," I say loudly, giving her a little shove with my shoulder. "You will not be bested by a—"

"Pile of bloody rock," Vee gasps, taking in a deep breath. "Thank you."

"If we keep thanking each other, we really will go mad."

Even as we work in tandem, saving each other from the madness, the sheer weight of so much fear and sadness presses down on us, as if the mountain has absorbed the nightmares of all the questers who came before us. Eventually I can hear other voices, farther off and keening like the wind, cries of anguish and sobs of pleading and screams of horror. Once, I even believe I hear Sir Kenna's voice mixed in, a child's plaintive *Papa* woven through his cries of pain.

Somehow the pain of others is almost worse to bear; I have had a lifetime to grow accustomed to my own fears and failings, but hearing the tortured cries of dozens of nightmares is oppressive. It bleaches the blue from the sky, steals the green from the scrubby trees that mark our path, and shrouds the brilliant white snow in heavy swaths of gray. It drags my feet through the snow, so that large piles collect on the front of my snow walkers, slowing my progress. It bows Vee's back, her proud shoulders hunching and curling into themselves, her face gone pale and ashy.

"You are Vee-Lira," I begin, but she waves me off.

"I am not . . . I am fine," she huffs, her voice monotone. "It is only that I am hearing . . ."

"The fears of others," I finish.

She glances at me, her eyes dull and glassy. "Yes. That."

"It is what I have felt these past months since Cinderella took the throne. Since I was made to shoulder her chores. Walking through the markets of neighboring villages, seeing how the people suffer . . ."

Vee glances at me again, her eyes slightly clearer. "Why do you call the princess Cinderella?"

The question surprises me, so much so that I blurt out the first thing that comes to mind. "Because it's her name."

"But it's not," Vee insists. "Her name is Ellarose. Her father named her after her mother, who died when she was born, and his favorite flower."

I didn't know that, about her mother or the flower. I suppose there are many things I don't know about her, things I never bothered to learn because Mother made me think they weren't worth knowing. That *she* wasn't worth knowing.

"And why were you made to take over Princess Ellarose's chores?" Vee presses. "Why was she made to do them in the first place? Did you not have serving girls to keep the house?"

I snort. "Serving girls were a luxury that died with Cinderella's father. The hearths still had to be scrubbed. Mother said Divya needed to keep her nails clean for courting."

"Your mother sounds a very cruel sort," Vee says casually, as if she's thought on the topic before.

"Your father sounds worse," I say sharply, because whatever I have to say about my mother, she is still my mother. The only thing standing between me and oblivion. I will not hear slander against her from the likes of Vee.

Vee raises her brows in surprise at me. "I did not mean to upset you. Only . . . to commiserate. I know what it is to labor under the heavy expectations of an ambitious parent."

"Yes, so I've heard," I mutter.

Vee's face flames red. "What is it you have heard?"

I don't know why I bothered bringing any of this up, only that speaking aloud seems to stave off some of the misery poisoning the air. But the more we speak, the more quarrelsome our conversation becomes, as if this is yet another aspect of the mountain's curse. To turn questers against one another. And perhaps it is; or perhaps this is only the great divide that separates me from Vee, our perceptions of our shared circumstances. She views her father as ambitious; I see him as despotic. I view my mother as calculating; Vee sees her only as cruel.

"Never mind," I mutter, kicking up more snow with my clumsy walking. "Let's just keep going. I do not want to find myself still on this mountain come nightfall."

I'm worried what it will do to me in my sleep.

"I had thought you something more, perhaps something kinder than your family's reputation," Vee calls out, her voice growing hot. "But you are the same spoiled brat who flounced about in petticoats she could not afford while ignoring her stepsister's enslavement in her dead father's own home. Calling her dreadful names like

Cinderella. And what good did all those lessons do you? What have you really become?"

A failure. A complete and utter disappointment.

My own internal voice layers over my mother's, and this time I know the mountain is only half my madness. I want to get as angry as Vee, I want to feed myself with fury and spite as I have these past few months, let them be my driving force since Cinderella stole mine in her glass-slippered feet. But the mountain has done its job wearing down my defenses, polishing all my sharp edges to dull curves. I breathe out a sigh, staring up at the impossible peak before us. What hubris led us to believe we could do this? After so many failed before us, men of unimpeachable honor and strength. If the mountain could best Sir Kenna, what hope did a failed belle and an errant lady knight have?

"No, Papa, please," Vee sobs behind me. "Please, I don't want to marry the prince from Banomal. I do not love him. I love only the order. Please, Papa, do not make me do this."

The air slips farther from my lungs, and I sink down into the snow despite my walkers. We were fools to try, and now we'll be fools who die. Better to give in now.

"You are . . . Vee . . ." The words come out stiff from my frozen lips, the work to form them almost impossible. I turn slowly, digging a deeper trench in the snow as I try to focus on Vee. "You are Vee-Lira of . . . something . . . a house . . . oh, Vee, snap out of it, would you?"

Vee stares at a blank space beyond me, her eyes red and her cheeks splotchy with rashes from the wind and her tears. "Papa, don't say such things. I am still your daughter."

I suck in breath, trying to collect some semblance of concern. "You are Vee—"

A screeching sound cuts across my words, an anguished cry that I assume is some new tactic of the mountain until the trees just off the path rattle and shake, spitting out a wild man. His hair hangs in snarls, his teeth jagged as he bares them at us, his feet bare and his toes black against the white of the snow where the frost has claimed them. His face is streaked with tears, his eyes so red there's hardly any white left to them. His roving gaze lands on Vee, eyes unnaturally bright.

"You will not best me this time, foul beast," he growls in a low-country accent, before launching himself directly at Vee and sending both of them tumbling over the cliff's edge.

THIRTEEN

"VEE," I GASP, CLAWING MY WAY ACROSS THE CUMBER-some snow in my search for the cliff's edge. A scream of horror so bright and sharp it could only be from imminent danger and not the mountain cuts across the wind, close enough that I hold out hope she's not fallen to her death already. Snow gathers on the tops of my walkers, clumping and freezing and turning to heavy ice that knocks me to my knees once, then twice, then a third time as I make precious little progress toward the cliff. "Vee, are you there?"

"Aralyn!" Vee screams, all the disdain sliced out of her tone. Now there is only desperation. "Aralyn, help me!"

"I'm coming," I pant, risking my fingers to scoop away the ice and snow. They seize almost immediately, the cold turning them to claws. But I manage to clear away enough of the debris that I can free my walkers to attempt the uneven trail the quester left when he made his mad dash for Vee.

"Aralyn, it won't hold!" Vee screams. "There is a branch, I am caught, but it's bowing. It won't hold. Please!"

"I am . . . I will . . ." I can't walk and give petty assurances at the same time, and the effort punishes me by catching the edge of my snow walker on a hidden rock, sending me face-first into the drifts. Snow fills my mouth, packs into my ears, crawls up the edges of my neck to slide down my back in clawing fingers, drawing me farther into its embrace. I breathe and it swirls into my lungs, shrinking them to rocks in my chest. By the fairies, I've never been so cold in my life. If only I had a blanket, or a fire, or even a hot meal in my belly.

You will have all those things, and more, when you are queen of Novador. Mother strokes my neck, her fingers like ice. It is only her will that makes them bend against the unrelenting cold that first winter after Cinderella's father died. When we learned just how destitute his extended illness had left the estate. *We will have fires roaring in every room. They will keep a forest just for the firewood to sustain us alone. We will have everything we could ever want, and we would have only to raise a hand to send someone scurrying to fetch it. Can you imagine it, Aralyn? Let it warm you, let it feed you. Let that be what sustains you when others turn their backs on you. When they cast you out and withdraw their favor. And they will, my darling. Everyone will let you down, except for me. To put your trust in others is to give them the rope with which to hang you. It is a lesson best learned now, before you are queen and they come for you from all sides. Never let yourself become reliant on others, for they will only betray you in the end.*

Could I not even trust the prince? I ask, wishing Mother would use her hands to embrace me instead, that we might share our meager warmth. *Am I not meant to love him?*

Mother's laugh is bright and loud and slashes my eardrums in punishment for such a naive question. *Do not give your love to unworthy men, Ary. Use it to further your own ambitions, but never give it away.*

Never make yourself vulnerable. If you do not use it against him, he will use it against you. Love is the legacy of fools.

"Love is the legacy of fools," I repeat, the mantra locking around my neck like a jewel.

"Aralyn!" Mother's voice is strange, too young and frantic. I frown, but she digs her fingers into my neck, forcing me to pay attention.

Aralyn, she says, her voice like a barb, hooking me back. *Never forget your purpose in life. To further our ambitions. Do not let yourself be sidetracked by foolish, unnecessary quests.*

"Quests?" I say, shaking my head. What quests?

"Aralyn! Aralyn of House Teramina—"

You must serve the House of Teramina, the only loyalty that matters in this life. Mother's hands are around my throat now, pressing down. *Do not let anyone else distract you from your obligation to our family. Cease this foolishness and return to me immediately.*

"What foolish . . . Mother, what are you talking about?"

"You are Aralyn of House Teramina! By the fairies, do not let yourself be bested by a—"

"Bloody pile of rock," I gasp as the ghost of Mother's fingers claw into my neck. There is a growl in my ear, inhuman and unmotherly, and suddenly I am no longer curled against her in that frigid apartment but lying facedown in snow on a mountainside. I startle up, batting away the snow from my face and neck. I can barely breathe, my chest aches from the cold, but I force myself to move.

You will never be more than a disappointment and a failure, Mother says.

"I am Aralyn of House Teramina," I say, wishing I sounded far more confident. But I glare at the snow as I toss it on the ground, crushing it under my walkers. "And I will not be bested by a bloody pile of bloody rock. I was raised by the best in the business, and you are only a pale comparison. Torture someone else."

I swear the mountain rumbles beneath my feet, gnashing its rocky teeth in rage as I reach the cliff's edge to peer over. I don't know what I am expecting to find, but it's not the bottom end of one of Vee's snow walkers, wedged into a scraggly tree root sticking out from the side of the cliff. There is no sign of the quester who ran into her, lost to the clouded depths of the rocks below, no doubt. But Vee hangs there, plastered against the side of the mountain, furs hanging in her face. It's such an unexpected, upended picture that my body can't help itself. A laugh bubbles up out of me, round and shiny.

"Are you— Is that laughter?" Vee screeches, batting the furred edges of her coat from her face in an attempt to peer up at me. Her face is bright as a pomegranate seed. "Are you laughing at me? While I hang in mortal peril!"

"You cannot imagine how you look right now," I gasp as more laughter bubbles up. It sweeps away the gray like a broom across a hearth, and the more I laugh the more I can breathe. "You are . . . Look at you . . . Your foot, it's . . . You look exactly like a rabbit caught in a snare. Hanging by one large back paw."

"I am so pleased that you could find *humor* in my demise," Vee hisses. "I'm sure it will bring me great comfort when these bloody branches crack and send me to my death on the rocks below."

"They're roots, actually," I say, which only makes me laugh harder.

"Get me up!" Vee yells, and the small bit she moves shakes dirt loose to rain down her pant leg.

"Right, rescue first, amusement after," I say, slinging my pack off my shoulder and digging through the provisions Cliod and Thana provided us before we left their hut what feels ages ago now. Bless those fore-thinking mountain dwellers, there is a coil of rope and an ice pick among them.

"I'm lowering a rope," I say, taking the ice pick and swinging it into the packed snow that has already formed a hard layer of ice. I secure the rope around my waist, gripping the pick with one hand as I lower the other end of the rope to Vee in her upside-down position. "Can you reach it?"

"I've got it," Vee calls, and then there is a sharp pull on my midsection. It jerks the air out of me, and I grab the pick with both hands and hunker down as Vee begins her agonizing climb.

If I had breath to speak, I'd tell her that even without her armor she must weigh as much as a small pony. My arms shake with the effort to keep hold of the ice pick, our only tether to this life. It must be all that knight's training, packing her thighs with unrelenting muscle. The rope rubs against my hip bones, reminding me of how little padding they've had in the past few months. I am sure I will have burn marks from the friction by the time she makes her way up the cliff face.

The rope gives a sharp tug and my hands slip on the ice pick; the only thing saving me from losing my grip entirely is the flared base of the handle. I will my fingers to hold tighter, then beg them as the rope jerks once again. If Vee cannot free herself and get up this bloody cliff side, we'll both be keeping the lost quester company in a moment.

You see, this is what comes of putting your trust in others. You allow them to bring about your own demise.

"Oh, shut up," I grunt, as much at my mother as at the mountain. The rope cuts off any other retorts I might have, pulling excruciatingly tight before going slack so suddenly that I pitch forward into the snow again. But before it can claim me with its icy fingers, something hauls me out.

"Aralyn, what in the starry skies were you thinking?" Vee asks, her face still red and her short golden hair flying around her face. "You tied the rope to *yourself*?"

"What else was I supposed to tie it to?" I gasp, struggling with the knots at my waist. The tension has tightened them so that I cannot get them loose, the binds still cutting into my stomach and making it hard to breathe. I pant in small, short breaths as I try to work my frozen fingers into the knots.

"Stop that, let me," Vee snaps, grabbing them in her callused hands and digging in. The cords on the back of her hands stand out as she forces her fingers into the crevices of the knot, working it loose until the rope falls away.

I take a deep breath, nearly collapsing as I let it back out. "Thank you. I couldn't breathe."

"The lack of air must have been what led to your ridiculous idea to tie the rope to yourself in the first place," Vee says. "I had no idea! I had to pull my foot free of the roots, I must have been pulling on the rope quite hard."

"Yes, you were," I say, testing the tender areas above my hip bones. Bruises, to be sure.

"Why . . . why would you do that? You could have been pulled to your death along with me!"

"I would have been dead if not for you," I say without thinking, still distracted by the damage to my midsection. I'll probably have a ring around my waist, like an ugly belt.

"What does that mean?" Vee asks.

"The second you went over the cliff's edge, the mountain did its best to claim me as well," I say. "It was only your intervention, speaking my name, that allowed me to break free. I told you, neither one of us will make it to that summit alive without the other."

"But you could have let me die," Vee insists, though I can't fathom why she's pursuing this line of protest. "You certainly did not have to risk your own life to save mine, even for the Protector's weapon."

"But I didn't let you die," I say with a shrug. "We need each other."

"But you *could* have let me die," Vee says.

"But I *didn't*. What is your point?"

"Your mother would have let me die."

"What has that to do with anything?" I ask, bewildered.

"Everything," Vee says, and she sounds uncomfortable to say it, as if she's only just realizing something for herself. I do wish she'd stop being so ambiguous and tell me what it is so I can realize it along with her.

"What is your point?" I demand again, irritated already that I have saved her life. Perhaps I should have let her dangle a bit longer, for her head clearly needs the excess blood flow.

Vee stares at the snow, torn up from our efforts, and blinks several times before shaking her head. "I don't know my point. We should continue on."

"Vee!" I say, throwing my arms wide in annoyance, but she hikes back to where our trail was interrupted with determination, leaving me behind. "You are impossible!"

"I know," she calls back. "It's what makes me a good knight."

And it's only after I clamber along behind her, huffing in annoyance, that I realize what I unwittingly admitted. Vee was right—Mother never would have endangered her own life to save Vee. She would have left her to die there on the side of the mountain. She tried to make me do the same, even if only through the mountain's influence. I have accidentally defied my mother for the first time in my life. And I did it to save Vee, of all people.

"Oh, plunkers," I mutter, crushing the snow underfoot with unnecessary viciousness.

FOURTEEN

I HAD THOUGHT WE'D SEEN THE WORST OF THE mountain from Vee's disadvantage point hanging upside down from the edge of it, but the going does not improve as we climb. The air grows intolerable, my chest aching with the effort of dragging each breath in and shoving it back out. The wind howls from without, tearing at our clothes and frosting us with snow, while the mountain howls from within, filling our minds with the terrors it has collected from all the questers past. At some point the path disappears, overgrown with rocks and boulders that continue dauntingly into the clouds above.

Vee secures the rope around her waist and then ties it around mine, the fur of her hood brushing against my cheek as she passes the rope behind my back. Her face is red when she pulls back, but so is mine. I don't care for this uneasy tension between us, this knowledge that I have saved her life, and she has saved mine, and we've done it for possibly unselfish reasons. Somewhere between the bottom of the mountain and this close to the summit, the dynamics have shifted. She has seen my darkest fears, and I have seen hers. I cannot continue to despise her properly with such precious knowledge, and I find I resent the mountain most of all for this.

"We'll need to climb from here," Vee shouts over the howling wind. She undoes the straps on her snow walkers, stashing them in her pack and pulling out the ice pick from mine. She hands it to me, as if I know what in the starry skies to do with it.

"Just follow my lead," she says, presumably catching the panic in my gaze. She tugs on the rope between us. "If you slip, I'll be able to catch you. Same as you did for me."

"But if I fall, you'll fall along with me." And the same goes if she falls, though I don't say that bit out loud.

Vee huffs a breath, white and puffy and obscuring her face. "I won't fall. And you won't, either. We're close, Aralyn, can't you hear it? Can't you feel it?"

I 've been so fixated on the wind and the impassable boulders that I haven't paid much attention to the mountain, but as I let silence fall between us, I do hear it. Or feel it, rather. The mountain is growing desperate. The cries of pain in my mind's ear have pitched to a fevered intensity, clawing at the edges of my sanity, making the rocky path before us stretch and distend and seem impossible to traverse. In the silence, I witness questers slipping and plunging into the abyss; or falling and cracking in half on a sharp edge before tumbling over as Vee had. I see *Vee* tumbling over the edge, over and over, until I fear my stomach will riot from the sensation.

"You are Aralyn of House Teramina," Vee says, loud and sure. "And the mountain is afraid."

The boulders shrink and squat and round out to their usual size, no less daunting but somehow—the smallest of maybes—passable.

"Are you ready?" she asks, her eyes boring into mine.

I nod. "Let's climb."

Vee scales the first few boulders with ease, finding cracks in the rock and fitting her fingers to them, or small ledges where she can set the spiky ends of her shoes. Patches of ice where she can drive her pick in to help leverage her upward. She moves with an ease that tells me she's done this before, though maybe not with a mountain trying to drive her to madness.

"How do you know how to do this?" I shout after I've scrambled along in her wake and reached the top of the first boulder.

"Training," Vee calls back, tilting her head up to survey the next slide of rock before us. "We were taught to scale enemy fortifications. I used to climb the outer castle walls every morning before my runs."

The highest I have ever climbed was up a rickety old ladder in the abandoned barn behind the manor to deal with a pesky family of badgers that laid waste to our food stores. And even that had been a bit nauseating. This climb is far more arduous, and each time my foot slips or my hand comes away with only a crumble of rock, my heart stops in my chest. I can barely concentrate on my own movements, much less watch Vee and try to mimic hers. The higher we go, the steeper the tilt of the rock face, until we scramble up onto a ledge and meet with a faceful of plain gray rock.

"What now?" I huff, shaking my head at the straight line upward.

"We keep climbing," Vee says with a shrug.

"Has the mountain finally conquered your sanity?" I ask. "Where are we to go? There is nothing but rock here. No handholds, nowhere to stop."

"There are if you know where to look," Vee says, patting an area that I swear to the starry skies looks flat and smooth. "This is a foot-hold right here, if you know how to set your toes just right."

"And if you do not, what then? A quick plunge to a long death? That's not . . . Vee, what you are suggesting is sheer insanity. We cannot climb this wall. There must be another way. We have to find another way."

And then, I make the most naive, most ill-informed choice of anyone who has climbed to a high position without realizing it.

I look down.

We must be up three hundred feet. Four hundred. A thousand, maybe, for how far the rocks stretch and fall away to the ground so very . . . *very* far below. The trees look like playthings below, no taller than my thumbnail as I hold it up. Climbing up the rocks, they'd seemed pitched forward at an angle; but from up here, they look flat and impassable. I don't even know how we managed to get this far.

My stomach rises, hard and fast, and I can only lean forward before our pathetic breakfast comes rushing up in a hot surge of bile. Vee gives a shout, scrabbling with the rope to hold me steady as my stomach muscles clench and rebel and try to make their escape through the only means available, up my throat. I could pitch for-ward right now, with nothing but wind to catch me, and the thought makes my head swim.

"I can't," I gasp, shaking my head and dropping back against the wall while my legs shake with a violence that threatens to pitch me over the edge in reality. My mouth is slick with acid, my nose clogged from bits of my breakfast that make me want to heave again. How had I ever compared this to the loft in the barn back at the manor? That was child's play, like climbing a potentially rotted tree. The worst I would have faced then was a sore backside. Here it is—

"I can't do it," I say again, pushing back until I am flush against the rock wall. I cradle into it, a sick child to an unfeeling mother. "I can't climb that, Vee."

"Yes, you can," Vee says, squatting down beside me. I sense something in her tone, the beginnings of a rousing speech she probably once heard on the edge of a battlefield, or before a jousting tournament, or some other such nonsense. The kind of valiance one chooses, rides headfirst into. "You are Aralyn—"

"I know who I am," I snap. "This is not the mountain's madness. I was not raised scaling castle walls, Vee! I do not approach everything with a broadsword in my grip. My armor is fashioned of wits and tulle, not your incessantly clanking metal contraption. I am not a warrior, nor am I an idiot. I will not charge at death with a happy cry and an empty head."

Vee draws back sharply. "I am not an idiot, either. Nor am I charging at anything with a happy cry. We simply have no other options. The way is up, or down. Or do you plan to starve on this ledge instead while the mountain eats away at your sanity?"

"There must be another way!"

"There is not!" Vee's voice rings loud and clear, sharp and rebuking. "I had not taken you for a coward, Aralyn."

"A coward?" I sputter. "Is that what we are calling common sense now? Cowardly? If it weren't for me, you would be haunting these mountains begging for your father's love as Sir Kenna cried out for his dead daughter. A thing long gone, if it ever existed at all."

Vee's face goes pale as the snow that surrounds us, but her eyes are bright as fire, warming the frigid depths of my being. She stands tall, pulling at the knots around her waist with viciously deft fingers.

"Wait, what . . . what are you doing?" I ask, my anger evaporating into fear once again. "Vee, why are you—"

"Someone needs to scale this mountain and find the Protector's weapon," Vee says, her voice as cold and distant as the peak she intends to reach. "And since you are unable, I will shoulder the burden for both of us."

"The mountain will take you before you scale the next rock face," I say, the words petty and mean and instantly regrettable.

Vee's smile is full of the disdain she held for me the first day we met, and it strikes me in the same way. Right in the gut. "You are out of your element here, Aralyn of House Teramina. Leave the heroics to the true heroes."

"Vee, no! Please don't leave me!" I can barely move—the mountain seems to have fused to me, its grip unrelenting—but I catch the back of her heel as she sets her foot to the toehold and levers herself upward. Without my deadweight tied to her from below, she scales the cliff face with astonishing speed. She'd been holding herself back for me.

"Vee! Don't leave me!" I scream, but the wind screams louder. It could be seconds, or minutes, or a dozen lifetimes strung together, but regardless of the passage of time, she's gone. I am alone, abandoned on the dizzying ledge of a mountain.

Well, aren't you my greatest disappointment.

"Not now, Mother," I moan, pressing my face to the rock. It numbs my forehead, but does little to fix my aching soul.

I told you what would come of trusting others. You allowed her to bring about your own demise.

"*I* brought about my own demise! I was the one who would not climb! I was the one with this . . . stupidly inconvenient fear."

And yet you did not ask yourself if there might not be another way. You allowed her to choose, and she chose the route that immobilized you and allowed her to claim my weapon as her own.

I shake my head. "There was no other way."

There is always a way for the one worthy of walking it! But you have proven yourself as unworthy as all the others who sought it before you. It should have been you who tumbled over that cliff.

My cheeks freeze as soon as the tears hit them and my voice is no more than a rough whisper. "I wish it had been."

There is a disturbance in the air beside me, a shimmering and solidifying, and then Lyra stands there with a mug the size of a large cat gripped in her hand. "A rematch it is, then, Gillyn . . . what in Elvnar's graces? Whoa!"

Her wide, round eyes go wider and rounder, and she leans over the edge of the cliff to look at the steep drop below. "That'll curdle your milk cakes, won't it? Aralyn! What in the starry skies are you doing up here?"

"Lyra," I grind out, feeling the rocks beneath me as I sink to a new low. This is what it means to be at literal rock bottom. But then an idea takes hold, and I swallow back my bile and self-loathing. "Lyra, I need your help."

"Finally!" Lyra roars, tossing off some foam from her mug. "Let's do this. What is it? Somebody need blinding? Or you need a new layering of fur? It's damn chilly up here, isn't it?"

"I need you to get me up that mountain," I say, my teeth chattering as I point up to the peak.

Lyra glances upward. "Huh? Where?"

"There! Up there!" I am short on words and patience.

Lyra shades her eyes with one hand, squinting into the gray distance. "How are we going to get up there?"

"That's for you to solve, isn't it?" I growl. "Can't you fly, or magically transport us? Or at least climb and carry me on your back?"

"Oh," Lyra says, nodding and looking back down at me. "Now I get it."

"Good," I say, forcing myself to an upright position. My stomach rebels, the world tilting at a dangerous angle, and I quickly fall back to my knees. "I prefer to be unconscious for this bit, if you don't mind."

"Oh, no, no, sorry, you misunderstood," Lyra says. "I can't get you up there."

I glance up in despair. "What?"

She wiggles her fingers at me, little sparks dancing out from them. "Parlor tricks, remember? We're not the flying fairies, that's the Court of Turbus. You should see them all try to stand next to one another and not get their wings tangled up. It's a real gas." She chuckles, the sound like someone clawing my eardrums.

"Can't you, I don't know, disappear from here and reappear up there? Just with me in tow?"

The scaly ridges over her eyes raise in wonder. "Do you have any idea what would happen to you if I tried to move you through the fabric between worlds, you daft bungerbee? Fairies spend eons of mortal time learning the passage, and even then if we're not careful we're liable to lose a toe or an ear during the crossing. It literally tears you apart, and you've got to have the magic and knowledge to put yourself back together. Unless you want to reach the summit as a pile of goop and gizzards, I don't recommend it."

"Then carry me on your back!" I snap. "Or cradle me like a baby, I don't care, I just need to get to that summit. We've almost reached the Protector's weapon, Lyra, I can feel it, I just . . . I couldn't . . . "

You couldn't execute when our lives most depended on it, Mother says, her form shimmering behind Lyra. We truly must be close, if the mountain is willing to attempt to manifest her in physical form. Still, seeing even the basic outline of her makes me want to crawl over sharp rocks on my bare hands and knees to beg her forgiveness.

"No, I won't let you down," I say, shaking my head to rid it of her voice. But her form only solidifies, right down to the cutting sneer she executes so well.

"You want me to get you down?" Lyra says, tipping forward and glancing at the rocks below. "I can try, but I don't know. That looks like a pretty steep drop. You might end up goop and gizzards anyway."

"No," I say, irritated. "I wasn't talking— Never mind. Figure out how to get me up there, before Vee."

Lyra looks at me in confusion. "Before V? What is that? Are you mortals measuring time in letters now?"

"No, Vee is a person."

Lyra looks around the narrow ledge. "Another mortal? Where are they?"

I point upward, careful not to actually tilt my gaze in that direction. "Climbing."

"Oh, well, why don't you just do that?"

I briefly consider latching on to Lyra and hurtling us both to oblivion to end this conversation. "If I could have done that, I would have already."

"Oh," Lyra says, sounding disappointed. Then she peers at me more closely, the ridges on her face rising up her forehead. "Ohhhhh. Are you afraid of heights?"

"Apparently so," I say through clenched teeth.

"Oh boy, this must be terrible for you, then."

I'm going to do it. I'm going to throw us both over the edge. "Lyra. I wish for you to get me to the summit. Now do it!"

Lyra spreads her hands wide. "I don't know how. Sorry."

I exhale everything in me, folding back into the cruel embrace of the mountain and my mother. "You are . . . *truly* . . . the worst fairy godmother I have ever met."

"Have you met a great many of us?" Lyra asks.

"I have not," I say, pressing my forehead to the rock. "But that does not change my opinion of you."

"Huh," Lyra grunts, sounding less offended than I would have preferred. "Well, why do you think I got assigned to you?"

"I . . ." The point is a valid, if stinging, one. Mother lays her icy hand on the back of my neck, freezing me in place.

You failed once again, my darling, but it's all right. I forgive you. I should never have expected so much from you anyway.

"No, Mother, I can still save us," I whisper, rubbing my cheek against the cold rock. The skin catches and tugs, the tears fusing me to the wall. "Please, give me another chance."

A lifetime of chances would change nothing. You are simply not strong enough. You are not enough.

"No, that's not true," I whisper.

"Aralyn?" comes Lyra's voice from a great distance. "Who are you talking to?"

Don't mind her, she doesn't matter now. Nothing matters now. What matters is that I am here now, with you. You belong to me now. Come along. Come with your mother.

"Where are we going?" I ask, and I am once again seven years old, cold and scared, my mother's hand the only tether to the world.

Somewhere where no one will hurt us ever again. Where I will care for you always. Where I will never leave you.

"Mother," I whisper, her hand tugging me along.

"Ara . . . Hey, Aralyn! What are you doing! You're going to walk right off the edge! Stop that!"

"What?" I ask, the word sluggish and unfocused.

Don't listen to her. Listen to your mother. Come with me. I'll keep you safe forever.

"Aralyn!"

The wind kicks up sharply, burning my eyes as Mother's form turns blurry and indistinct before me. I pause, rubbing at them, but when I open them she is there, solid and fully formed, her expression furious.

Do not attempt to defy me, Aralyn. You were nothing before I brought you into being, and I can make you nothing again. Come with me now.

"But I . . ." Something is wrong, but I can't figure out what it is. I tug against her hand, but her grip is like ice. Like rock.

Now!

"Aralyn!" says another voice, one I should recognize, one I feel like I recognized only a moment ago. But Mother is digging her claws into me, leaving streaks of blood behind.

Do not dare to defy me.

The wind is a maelstrom around me, shoving me forward as Mother drags me along, all of it screaming in my head. I try my best to resist, but the pull is so strong. Mother is so furious. I have failed her once again. I will always fail her. I will always be a failure.

How did I ever think differently? She is right. I should go with her. I would be nothing without her. I take another step forward, but then Mother's form blurs, distending her sharp features into a garish mask of fury.

NO! DO NOT TOUCH THE BLADE!

"I didn't—"

But there is a gust of wind so hard it screams past me, and then Mother is gone. I am left standing on the very edge of the cliff, one foot hanging over the abyss. I gasp, windmilling my arms backward, my body in full panic as I scramble to keep my foothold. Lyra grabs me, dragging me back.

"What in the name of us were you doing?" she asks. "You tried to walk right off the edge of the cliff!"

"I heard . . . I thought . . . Where did she go?"

I look around, expecting to find Mother, but I am met with only stillness. The wind is quiet; my mind is quiet. The mountain has gone silent.

"She did it," I whisper, a mixture of desperation and relief. "She really did it."

"Who did what?" Lyra asks.

But a shadow falls over us from above, and I know who it is and what she holds without having to look up. Vee drops to the ledge behind Lyra, holding a blade the length of her arm engraved on both sides with beautiful script. When she raises it, her eyes burning, my entire being withers away. Finally, I see her as she is. A warrior knight, stronger than I could ever hope to be.

"The Protector's blade," Lyra says, dropping to one knee before her.

Vee's eyes meet mine, still blazing. "I found it."

I catch her subtext as loud as a shout. She succeeded, and I failed.

FIFTEEN

NIGHT FALLS FAST ON THE MOUNTAIN, AND WE ONLY
make it down to the lower reaches of the cliffs before we're forced to
seek shelter for the night. At least in this manner Lyra proves useful,
lighting the way with her parlor tricks until we find a shallow cave
that gives us enough protection from the elements to catch some
rest before the sun comes back up and we follow the path down to
the bottom of the mountain. Vee collects wood and starts a fire, and
we pull the last rations from Cliod and Thana from our packs to eat
for our nightly meal.

It's unbearably quiet without the mountain infecting our minds,
and while I don't miss its particular brand of Mother's needling
insults, it does leave me in the unenviable position of having to
make conversation with Vee instead. Not that Vee seems much
interested in conversation with me. She guards the blade jealously,
as if I might try to snatch it from her the moment she glances away.
Whatever progress we thought we made toward some kind of truce
was abandoned on that ledge the moment Vee undid the knots binding us together. Now the tension simmers between us once again,
and Vee refuses to meet my gaze across the flickering firelight.

All of which Lyra seems blissfully unattuned to.

"The Protector's blade!" she crows, leaning into Vee's personal space to inspect the writing along one side of the weapon. "In High Feyrish, too. I tell you, Fornax would give up his gift of sight to take a look at that. Not that he could actually read it, though he'd pretend he could."

"Do you know what it says?" Vee asks, reluctantly, like speaking to even my fairy godmother is a surrender she doesn't want to give.

Lyra shakes her head. "Not a clue. High Feyrish was outlawed when they stripped the Protectors of their powers. Mother knows a few phrases, the ones we still use to guard the borders of the courts. They'll only get passed on to me when I assume control of the court, not that I'm in any hurry."

"*You* are meant to inherit your court?" I say incredulously. I hadn't meant to speak at all, but the idea of Lyra being in charge of anything is so ludicrous.

"Yes," Lyra says, but she sighs as she says it. "By the laws of inheritance, it's my duty."

"You don't sound particularly pleased with the task," Vee says.

"I ought to be, oughtn't I?" Lyra says, pondering the fire. "My mother thinks I'll be ready, when the time comes. The Sky Watchers know she's done all she can to prepare me. But . . . it's a lot to take on, isn't it? The weight of your people's needs, their expectations. I'm always mucking things up, ruining simple spells. Some of the more gifted members of the court like Fornax call me halfling, as if I didn't manifest in the same manner as them. Sometimes it feels like human food is the only thing I can do right."

I shake my head, poking at my side of the fire. "Sometimes the best thing you can do for your people is to choose someone else to lead them," I mutter.

"What would you know of the requirements of governing?" Vee asks, her voice sharp. "You are so quick to pass judgment on the choices of others, yet you yourself have never wielded so much as the command of a ball."

The insult lands as squarely as she intends it, and I stiffen in response. "I couldn't do much worse than your uncle, your buffoon of a cousin, or his insipid wife."

Vee stiffens. "The prince and Princess Ellarose are upstanding peers of the realm whose characters are beyond reproach, certainly from someone of your low breeding."

I sneer at her. "Is that what you told little Cinderella on her wedding night?"

Her jaw unhinges slightly, a sure sign of my victory. "There it is again, that name. Cinderella. You must think yourself clever. Yet your envy turns you cold and ugly inside. You failed where Ellarose succeeded in securing the prince's affection."

"Oh please," I scoff. "I never wanted to *marry* the prince."

"Then what is it you wanted?" Vee challenges.

I speak without thinking, which never works in my favor. "I wanted to *be* the prince."

Vee's expression grows suspicious, her gaze darting between me and Lyra. "You mean to take over his position, in some sort of magical body swap? Is that why she is here?"

"What?" I say, incredulous, as Lyra holds her hands up.

"That's not something we're allowed to do, even if we could," she says hastily, before tilting her head in consideration. "Wait, do you humans think we can do that?"

"Of course not," I say, shaking my head. "Honestly, they let you carry a *sword*, Vee? I don't mean I want to physically become the prince, I mean I want to be in charge of the kingdom. Well, more in charge than Prince Fael has ever truly been."

"So that is your aim after all." Vee practically gloats. "You want to steal the blade and use its power to steal the throne along with the kingdom. I knew it. I knew you were not to be trusted."

"I don't want to steal it," I gripe, far too annoyed by how close to the truth she has landed. "I want to *fix* it."

Vee frowns. "What does that mean, fix it?"

I lean back against the cave wall, already tired of this conversation. "Your prince may be an upstanding peer of the realm, as you say, but he's an utter simpleton when it comes to political machinations."

"That is my cousin you speak of," Vee says in a warning tone, her grip on the blade tightening.

"And if your loyalty to blood allows you to turn a blind eye to his mistakes at the cost of the kingdom, then you are a buffoon as well. Or perhaps your loyalty lies with your traitorous father instead."

Vee's breath is a like a storm gale as she draws it in. "My father is not a traitor."

I snort. "The king's council bylaws say otherwise."

"What do you know of the bylaws?" she asks, not nearly so confident now.

"More than you, apparently. Why do you think Cinderella sent us on this ridiculous mission in the first place?"

Vee's gaze darkens, cutting to Lyra and back to me. "She sent us to retrieve a weapon that can restore peace and prosperity to the kingdom. To stop the blight."

"What a gift it must be, to move through the world so ignorantly,"

I say, shaking my head. "Is that what you've let yourself be led to believe? That there's some kind of unpredictable blight on the kingdom? Probably magical of some sort, since I'd guess High Chancellor Cordo's power rests in bringing doubt upon Cinderella and her fairy godmother."

Vee's gaze flicks once again to Lyra. "The way of the fey is not well-known within the court. We had thought them a . . . well, a fairy tale. A relic of the simple beliefs of the ancestors. Until Ellarose appeared at Prince Fael's betrothal ball, we did not know they truly existed."

"Of course we exist," Lyra says, affronted. "It's you mortals who have forgotten the old ways. We used to work in harmony with the humans, to the betterment of both our realms. Until good old-fashioned greed got in the way."

"What did you mean about the council bylaws?" Vee asks, and it's clear she's struggling. Like she needs to know the answer, but doesn't want to ask the question.

I debate what to tell her; how much, and how truthful. I don't really owe her anything, do I? She's clearly as much a part of the problem as her father, for she's let herself be led down this path. Playing at the noble lady knight while her country starves. She might not be the one trying to steal her uncle's throne, but she'll certainly benefit from it, and tell herself there was nothing she could have done.

But I suppose I was like her, once upon a time. A not-so-long-ago time. And am I really so much better than Cordo? Was I also not planning to use the Protector's blade for my own gain? Did I not consider myself a better fit for the throne than Fael or Cinderella? I don't care for the comparison, and I shift against the cave wall to let the rock dig into my spine, keeping me sharp.

"That day Cinderella came to the manor—"

"Ellarose," Vee says mechanically. "Princess Ellarose."

"Cinderella," I say, for no other reason than to annoy her. "She came to visit me because she needed my help. She could see clearly enough that the kingdom was failing, but she couldn't see a way clear to help save it. With King Soteo playing the recluse and High Chancellor Cordo strangling the king's council, Fael had effectively been shut out of any real position of power. Cinderella and her new husband wanted so desperately to help, but she didn't have the knowledge on how to do so."

"And I suppose you think you did, with your years of ambitious training," Vee says sarcastically.

She intends it as an insult, but it hardly hits as one. I simply smirk. "Cinderella certainly seemed to think so. We turned to the kingdom archives for answers, but we found far more than we bargained for. She suspected that Cordo—your father in this scenario, you'll recall—was trying to keep Fael from assuming his rightful position at the head of the king's council. What she couldn't possibly know is how far he'd gone to secure his own position."

"What are you talking about?" Vee asks, looking as if she doesn't truly want the answer.

"Someone had rewritten the bylaws to change the order of inheritance," I say. I hold up my fingers, even though the ink has long since washed away. "The ink was still fresh enough to smear. *Someone* had hidden the bylaws in a different section of the library. And that same *someone* changed the law so that in the event of a king's death, the king's council could vote to select their new sovereign rather than inherit by blood."

Vee takes in a sharp breath. "But that is—"

"Treason?" I suggest. "Only if someone is willing to call it so, and enforce it by the blade. But when you own the council seats and the military, who is to say it's so?"

Vee shakes her head, her skin bleached to a deathly pallor. "But King Soteo is in fine form, is he not? There is no talk of failing health."

"Not yet," I say, raising an eyebrow. "At least not until the ink dries. But the machinations are already in place. How long do you think your father will let those loose threads dangle?"

"He couldn't," Vee whispers, staring into the fire in horror. "He wouldn't. He simply could not. It is . . . No."

The rock at my back is like the teeth of a wolf, eating away at my spine. "If I could impart any wisdom from my own familial tensions, it would be that who you wish a person to be is your own burden to bear. If you cannot face who they truly are, you are only deluding yourself. You cannot wish your father to be different from who he is, any more than I can wish . . ."

Wish for my mother to love me. Lyra's silvered gaze is unbearable, and I clamp my lips shut before I do something so foolish as to say my feelings aloud. For all I know, she might try to make good on such a wish, and what a disaster that would prove to be. No, I am perfectly capable of fulfilling my own wishes. Beginning with the Protector's blade, and ending when I have all three pieces in my possession.

"Why would he do such a thing?" Vee whispers, her eyes gleaming in the firelight. Tears spill over the edges of her golden lashes, streaking new paths down her face.

But the mountain has already wrung all the tears from my body, and I won't give it the satisfaction of any more. I am done being soft.

"He would do it for the same reason we would," I say, the words heavy and slow as I slip closer to sleep. "The power to change the kingdom. But our task is far from complete. We need to find the other two pieces, Lyra."

Lyra nods. "Right. Which means you need to know where to find them. I'll get right on that."

I give a soft grunt, finally letting my eyes drift closed. "It would be excellent if you could finally make yourself useful."

There is an odd pressure before a sharp pop, and then Lyra is gone. Leaving me to Vee and the fire between us. I want nothing more than to sink into the oblivion of a mountainless sleep, but Vee's grief is like a living thing, occupying the remaining space in the cave. I crack one eye open, watching her cry silently. It's disturbing, how silent she can truly be while her face contorts from the effort.

"Why do you care for him so much?" I ask suddenly, when I can't stand the portrait any longer.

Vee looks at me across the fire, too upset to bother with her usual disdain. "He is my father. What else can I do?"

"You can choose," I say, not sure where the sentiment comes from. "You can choose different. You can choose to *be* different. He doesn't define you, Vee. Or he doesn't have to anymore."

Vee shakes her head. "He is the foundation upon which I am built. How do you change such a thing without bringing your entire house down?"

I let go of a deep breath, my eyes drifting closed again. "Maybe you have to let it come down if you ever hope to rebuild it better and stronger than before. Some houses deserve to fall."

"Like House Teramina?" Vee asks, but there's no malice in the question.

I don't know the answer to that. I don't know if I want to know the answer to that. So instead I let my breathing go soft and slow, pretending that I have fallen asleep. It's the coward's way out, I know. But I'm a coward after all, aren't I?

SIXTEEN

"GOOD NEWS!" COMES LYRA'S VOICE LIKE A CANNON-ball through my starboard side, ricocheting around the small confines of the cave and nearly stopping my heart.

I startle up, gasping for breath, a terrible pain in my neck where I've let it rest at an odd angle against the cave wall while I slept. My only comfort is that Vee looks as discombobulated as I feel, her short hair sticking up in shock waves. I have the most ridiculous urge to smooth them down, to run my fingers through her hair and tame those wild waves. I wonder if it's soft or coarse, if it will wrap itself around my fingers or slip away like a sigh.

"Have you no sense of circumstance?" I snap at Lyra, as much in irritation at having been awoken so abruptly as I am at the unguarded thoughts that followed. I avoid Vee's gaze as she smooths down her own hair. "Or is it that you operate at no other volume save full?"

"Ooo, aye, my mother says when I was born there was no need to sound the Bell of Manifestation because my lungs did all the announcing," Lyra says happily. "But I promise this is news worth waking up for. I think I know where the second piece of the Protector's weapon resides."

Such a proclamation is enough to iron the wrinkles out of my disposition, and Vee's hair ends up in tangled waves as she forcefully jerks her fingers away from her scalp. "You found it?" she asks. "So soon? How?"

Lyra pokes through the dregs of stew we'd left over the fire from our dinner the previous evening, her nostrils flaring as she sniffs the contents. "Not bad. Let me see what I've got here."

She rifles around in her furs, pulling out various fragrant sprigs and tubers from her person until she's halfway refilled the pot. She takes a stick and rearranges the logs beneath the pot, blowing on the glowing embers. They spring to life, invigorated by her magical breath, and almost immediately a savory, earthy fragrance fills the cave, eliciting grumbles from our collective stomachs.

"Lyra," I say, too hungry and tired to even bother with being annoyed.

"Hmm?" she says, watching as bubbles rise in the pot. "Say, Aralyn, fetch me a few scoops of snow, would you? This needs moisture."

"Lyra," I say, louder, and this time I let myself be annoyed.

"What?" She looks at me, then Vee. "What is it?"

"The second piece of the Protector's blade?" Vee prompts. When Lyra doesn't immediately respond, her eyes widen and then narrow. "You said you found it?"

"Oh, right. That's because I think I did."

"Where?" I ask loudly.

"Sorry. Got distracted. What do you think about putting some smoked razorfish in here? It's a gamble, I know the flavor is a touch fishy, but I really think it could elevate the whole pot. I'm pretty sure I've got some—"

"Lyra!" Vee and I shout simultaneously.

"Yeesh, all right, keep your tails untwisted," Lyra mutters, but I catch her rooting around in her furs again, presumably for the smoked razorfish. "Right, so. I was doing some thinking last night after the two of you knocked out like a couple of fainting goats. We figured the first piece of the Protector's weapon was up here in the Mortel Mountains on account of the legends about them being cursed, and the mountains springing up overnight, right?"

"Yes," I say with a nod. "Is there another mountain range somewhere in the realm with the same reputation?"

Lyra shakes her head, her silver eyes gleaming in the cooking fire light. "Not a mountain. The opposite of a mountain."

Vee frowns. "What's the opposite of a mountain?"

Lyra grins with her pointed teeth. "A sinkhole."

I suck in a breath, my stomach feeling rather like a sinkhole. "The Impassable Sea."

"Exactly," Lyra says with a nod.

But Vee looks incredulous. "The Impassable Sea? Are you joking? That's been under the purview of pirate crews for nearly a hundred years despite the king's best attempts to rout them. They've dragged every sandy inch of that beach. There isn't so much as a stray gold coin buried under a crab there, and everyone knows to steer clear of the bay. If there was a piece of magical fey weaponry in the depths there, it's long since gone. Purloined in some seedy tavern exchange."

On this one occasion I'm inclined to agree with Vee, except . . .

"There have been rumors," I say, slowly, looking over the fire at her. "La Sirena."

She snorts. "La Sirena is a myth."

I wave a hand at the mountain beyond our cave opening. "So was the madness of the Mortel Mountains."

"This is different. La Sirena is just an old pirate ghost story meant to scare other crews away from the gold-laden shores of the Impassable Sea after the hundred-year storm."

Lyra's brow ridges go up, and she tosses something out of her coat into the boiling pot that I pray is smoked fish and not a chunk of fur. "Oooo, I love a good pirate ghost story. How does this one go?"

I cross my arms, squaring off with Vee across the fire and daring her to cast doubt on my version of events as I relay them. "As you might expect, the Impassable Sea was not always so impassable. It was once a regular sea, centuries ago, the hub of commerce between Novador and the Hundilions from the far shores. The Salty Sea, it was called, because the merchants carried so much black salt from the barrens of the Hundilion Pass. But then tragedy struck, in the form of a raging storm that seemed to span the entire sea and made trade impossible. It raged for over a hundred years, ravaging the coastline and driving the fishing villages farther and farther inland until they had to turn to other trade to survive. The sea was considered impassable, a lost route, scrubbed from maps of the kingdom."

Lyra's eyes are luminous, and for the first time I wonder how old she really is. In mortal years, or fey years, or emotional temperament. She looks exactly like the beggar children in the markets when one of the older children tells them about the butcher who lost a hand to a feral pig. "Hence the name, huh?" she says. "The Impassable Sea."

I tilt my head in concession. "For many generations, it had no name. Some called it the Stormlands, others called it a tear in the veil between the fey realm and ours. Some thought it was blood magic, others thought it was a sign of the land's discontent. The fish rising up in rebellion. The span of ridiculous theories lasted as long as the storm."

"But then what?" Lyra asks, leaping over the last of my words. "There's always a 'but then.'"

"But then," I say, rolling my eyes, "the storm stopped. Not gradually, not gently. Just one morning, the storm was gone. But the sea was . . . different. The waters were darker, colder. Deeper than any of the old-timers could remember. There were pockets that seemed to go on forever, so black you could dip your hand under the surface and not see your fingers. And the fish they pulled up with their nets were different as well. Larger, wilder, some with long, sharp teeth. And then, of course, there was La Sirena."

"Oooo, what is that?" Lyra asks, plopping herself down beside the fire and tucking both fists up under her chin.

"Depends on whom you ask. To some, she appears as a woman, drawing them out to sea with the promise of a lost treasure greater than all the other treasures ever discovered on the shores. To others, she is the figurehead of a ship that sails the waters like a ghost, never pulling into port and never picking up new crew members. However she comes to you, she's the last thing you'll ever see. No one who's gone in search of La Sirena has ever returned. There are those who say the waters of the Impassable Sea are cursed and refuse to put their boats out along its waves ever again. But for those willing to brave the impassable expanse after the storms disappeared, there were riches across the waters in Hundilion."

"Warriors," Lyra says reverently.

Vee snorts. "She means pirates. Immoral knaves with no loyalty to country or kind. Willing to fill their ships with ill-gotten goods and ill-mannered sailors."

"Should they have toiled away in the fields instead, burning their skins and breaking their backs to give up their harvest for pennies?" I counter sarcastically. "I suppose that is the only way for Novadorians to gain your respect."

"Of course not," Vee scoffs. "But the pirate crews of the Impassable Sea are brigands and thieves, murderers and plunderers. We've had envoys from Hundilion begging the king's council to stop their coastal marauding. King Soteo has done his best to clear their ranks, but they've a stronghold on an island just out to sea. Sandtrap Island, they call it. Because if you try to sail past, they've piled sand all around to stop any other boats from getting near. Only the pirates who live there know where to navigate through the mazes."

"Then that's where we need to go," Lyra says, ladling a bowlful of her stew and passing it to me. "We'll leave after breakfast."

"Did you not just hear the part where the island is unreachable?" I ask. "And the sea is literally named the Impassable Sea? How would we even begin to attempt to reach Sandtrap?"

"Same way you navigated the cliffs of the Mortel Mountains to retrieve the Protector's blade," Lyra says, offhand, as if it were a casual stroll through the lower countryside and not the crippling emotional and nearly physical defeat it was.

"The Sender Coast is at least two weeks' ride from here," Vee says, more practically. "And that is with fresh horses and a full retinue of soldiers. Just the two of us on our travel-weary horses? It could take up to a month. I'll not risk going any faster and having Thundermere come up lame. Unless you, fey one, could somehow aid us in our travel?"

"No, no," I say hastily, remembering Lyra's vivid description of being passed across the veil. "But we'll cut our travel time in half if we go through the Silent Forest."

Both Vee and Lyra go still, looking at me as if I've sprouted fey wings. I spread my hands wide at their incredulity, trying my best to look confident and casual.

"What?" I ask.

"The Silent Forest," Vee says, her voice doubtful. "So named because the birds will not perch in its trees? Because not even the feral hogs of the plains will risk rooting through its underbrush? Where the trees supposedly watch you and those who leave the path never return? Where those few who have foolishly attempted the route and managed to return are stricken of their ability to speak until death? That's the route you want to take, that haunted reach?"

I point out the cave entrance. "More haunted than the Mortel Mountains? For all we know, the third and final piece of the Protector's blade could be hidden beneath its canopy. Perhaps we'll pick it up on our way to the Impassable Sea. Which is also allegedly cursed, you'll recall. We did not undertake this journey as an idle reprieve from the pressures of the capital city, now did we?"

"The Silent Forest is different," Lyra says, surprising me. She chews at one sharp claw. "Even the fey are afraid of it. It's the one piece of the kingdom where we don't dare to travel, not since the time of the Protector. It's too wild, too lawless. Our magic doesn't even work the same there. I'm not sure I could be of any help if you needed it."

"As opposed to all the other times where it's been vital to our survival?" I say dryly. "Whatever the legends, it's our only option if we want to reach the Impassable Sea quickly. We cannot let superstition overcome logic."

Vee chews at one corner of her lip in doubt, though she does not immediately leap in with more arguments to the contrary. "Thundermere won't like it."

I laugh. "Do you run everything by your horse?"

"Of course," Vee says, as if I am the mad one. "But it will save us time, you're right. We could reach the outer bands of the Sender Coast in a week. *If* we survive the forest."

"Which we will," I say emphatically, feeling little to none of the confidence I profess. I'm no more keen to brave the cursed canopy of the Silent Forest, but surely Mother and Divya have reached Banomal by now. We may not have a month to spare.

"We'll need to restock, whatever Cliod and Thana can spare," Vee says, her tone resigned. "I don't want to need so much as a drop of water from the forest."

We shall need a great deal more than a drop of water from the forest, but this is hardly the time to point that out. I take a fortifying bite of Lyra's stew, the flavors exploding in my mouth with surprising pungency. I grunt in appreciation, which earns me a grin from my fairy godmother.

"We'll leave as soon as breakfast is done," I say, already eyeing the pot in search of the second bowl I know I'll want. As Lyra watches me eat, satisfied, I grimace at her. "It's only because I have the hunger of nearly dying yesterday. Don't flatter yourself."

"Oh, I won't," Lyra says, still grinning.

I spend the majority of our descent from the Mortel Mountains considering bargaining tactics to convince Cliod and Thana to give up their winter stores to fuel our journey through the forest. But it turns out I had no reason to worry about their stalwart refusal, because the moment we come down out of the pass they're waiting for us, tears in their eyes.

"You have done what no quester could do before you," Cliod says, his voice thick with surprising emotion as he drags us into an embrace. "You have stopped the voices."

"We knew it the moment you ended the curse," says Thana, more reserved but no less moved. "I awoke to birdsong for the first time in my life. My garden bloomed with long-dormant growth. Our lives are forever changed, and we have you two to thank for it."

"I thought you were meat for the mountain for sure," says Cliod. "But damn the rocks, if you two weren't scrappier than I gave you credit for."

"Thank you," Vee says hesitantly, looking about. "Where is—"

"Here," comes a strong, bounding voice. Sir Kenna appears from behind a mud hut a moment later, leading Thundermere and my horse, and both Vee and I gasp.

"Sir Kenna, look at you," Vee says, her eyes wide and round. "You're—"

"Healed," he says, inclining his head. He has shaved his beard and scrubbed the filth from his clothes, and though the colors are still faded and his skin still deeply lined and blistered from the sun, he stands straight as an arrow, his eyes clear. He looks every inch the knight, and I can feel Vee suppressing the urge to kneel before him. "And I owe it all to you two. The true heroes."

"Oh, no," Vee says, flushing a bright red. "We are not heroes, we simply . . ."

"Succeeded where generations of others had failed?" I offer dryly.

"You are far more than you realize, the two of you together," Sir

Kenna says, gracing me with a small smile. "But I sense your journey is far from over."

"We must travel to the Impassable Sea," Vee says. "By way of the Silent Forest."

Sir Kenna gives a shudder, not the most encouraging of reactions from a seasoned knight who survived the madness of the Mortel Mountains. "The tales of that forest are chilling in their absence. I knew a knight once, a brave man of such courage that he would ride into battle where others would flee. He made it his quest to tame the wilds of the Silent Forest, but some wilderness runs too deep to ever be tamed."

"Did he make it back to the capital?" Vee asked in a hushed tone.

"He did, though I'm not sure whether that was a blessing or a curse," Sir Kenna says gravely. "When he returned, he had aged so much he looked more like my grandfather than my peer. And he never spoke again, though sometimes I would find him weeping in the castle gardens. He never held a sword again, either. His hands trembled too badly."

"That's . . . encouraging," I say faintly. "But the trip is a necessary one. The sooner we can leave, the sooner we can have it over with."

"I will pledge you my sword," Sir Kenna says bravely. But then his facade cracks. "As soon I relocate it."

"Your services are needed far more in the capital, Sir Kenna," Vee says hastily. "We will need someone there to guard Princess Ellarose and Prince Fael until we can return from our quests. I have had many sleepless nights worrying about leaving my post there, but I know you will keep them safe in my stead until I can return."

"Of course," Sir Kenna says, clapping a fist to his chest and looking a little relieved. "I shall prepare your triumphant way home.

Besides which, I believe you both have all the skills you need to succeed in your tasks. You conquered the Mortel Mountains, and you shall tame the wilderness of the Silent Forest and the depths of the Impassable Sea besides."

"Be careful, Sir Kenna," I say. "The kingdom is not the same one you left to pursue your quest so many years ago."

Sir Kenna nods, his expression grave. "Yes, I sensed that as well. I can only imagine what dire straits it must be in, to send the two of you on such a quest as this. But someone must be there to welcome you both back when you return. I will make sure the capital is safe for both of you."

"Thank you," I say quietly, knowing he means it. "Grace speed you on your journey and keep you safe along the way."

"The same to you," he says. And then he does what I could never do no matter how outrageously I behaved. He renders Vee speechless by dropping to one knee before her. "The order of Novador and all her servants past protect you on your journey, great knight."

Vee's mouth drops open slightly, her eyes wet, but no sound comes from her mouth. It's a painfully endearing moment, and I find even I don't have the lack of heart to interrupt it. But Vee's mount has no respect, because he nudges her shoulder and snuffles into her hair, a reprimand for having gone so long without giving him a scratch behind the ears. Vee laughs, the sound of it like honeyed wine, and my heart clenches.

"Thank you, Sir Kenna," she says, the words thick.

He straightens, towering over her, and I can see why the order chose both of them. Not that I would ever admit as much to Vee. "Thank *you*, Sir Vee-Lira. You do the order proud."

Cliod and Thana come bustling out of their hut, packs laden and overflowing with what I hope is not their entire store of goods for the season. I try to protest so much excess, but they insist on it, promising me that their garden is now returning more than even they can handle. And Vee had a point up on the mountain; we don't want to find ourselves at the mercy of what the forest is willing to provide. So I take the pack, suppressing my groan as the weight settles on my shoulders, and grab the reins of my mare.

"Careful, wherever you're off to," says Thana. "Not every corner of the kingdom is as welcoming as ours."

We thank her and Cliod again, Vee doing a half curtsy, half bow to Sir Kenna before Thundermere headbutts her again. And then we are mounted up, well supplied, and on our way to the Silent Forest and the Impassable Sea beyond.

SEVENTEEN

THE SILENT FOREST RISES UP GRADUALLY AROUND us over the next three days of traveling. The rocky passages of the Mortel Mountains give way to the flat plains, which in turn rise and shift from low, scrubby trees to towering monoliths that block out the sun and silence the wind. We meet no more towns or villages, not even so much as a lone hut like the one Cliod and Thana inhabited. It's clear before we ever spot the first tree that the people of eastern Novador give the Silent Forest a wide, empty berth.

But there is a path through the thickening tree line, one obviously cut and laid many generations before us. The bushes encroach on the dirt path, but they don't overrun it.

"What do you suppose keeps the path from being overgrown?" I ask Vee, when I can no longer stand the silence and the loud clomp of our horses' hooves on the hard-packed earth. At least Vee has left her armor in the care of Sir Kenna and I don't have to hear the creak of metal joints driving me mad.

"Perhaps they used fire to burn out the roots," Vee says, her eyes darting back and forth like a pendulum, watching the tree line as if a feral creature could burst through at any moment.

"It's magic," says a small, squeaky voice in my left ear. I gasp, glancing to the side, expecting to see something in the trees. The forest is clear, but there is something perched on my shoulder, the size of a bird. I scream, swatting at it, and it goes flying with a cry before disappearing into thin air with a distinct pop. My horse rears up, threatening to dislodge me, and it's only Vee snatching my reins at the last moment that keeps the mare from taking off at a run.

"Whoa, girl, whoa," Vee says, remarkably calm considering some talking beast was just nestled on my shoulder like a pet. She smooths one hand down the mare's nose, and I wish someone would do the same for me. I can't get my heart to come back down out of my throat. Vee gives me a severe look. "What in the starry skies was that?"

"There was . . . *something* . . . on my shoulder," I say, swatting at the empty line of fabric as if it might come back. "I didn't even see it land. It was just *there*."

"That's because it was me, you daft bungerbee" comes the squeaky voice again, this time from the right.

I scream, ready to swat anew, but the creature has taken hold of the collar on my coat and given it a surprisingly strong shake, making me pause just long enough that I focus on its features. I squint, trying to make sense of what I'm seeing. *"Lyra?"*

"Yes!" says bird-size Lyra, grinning with teeth like pebbles. She leans over, still hanging on to my collar, and gives Vee a wave. "Hello there."

Vee's eyes have grown wide and disbelieving. "Lyra? Is that you? You're . . . tiny."

"I know! Isn't it impressive?" Lyra says, releasing my collar to step back and sweep her arms down her frame and out with a flourish.

Her steps are like someone tapping me politely on the shoulder, almost ticklish. "Nobody's ever manifested this compact on a first try, my mother says."

"Lyra, *how* are you tiny?" I ask, resisting the urge to flick her off my shoulder like the pest she is. "And *why* are you on my shoulder scaring the heart out of me?"

"Oh, I'm practicing," says Lyra, as if this were the most reasonable and complete explanation in the world. When we give no sign of understanding, she huffs a little. "I told you, the way we manifest in your realm is a bit messy. But some fey can use that rearranging process to change their form. You know, gather excess material and make themselves larger, shed material to make themselves smaller. Some of the most highly skilled fey in our court can alter their appearance entirely, though my mother has outlawed that particular manifestation. She says it is our duty not to, and I quote, 'scare the squishy insides out of the humans.'"

"Well, you certainly failed on that front, didn't you?" I mutter, taking a deep breath to fully restore my equilibrium. I squint at Lyra sideways, which is starting to give me a headache. "Although I think I vastly prefer you in this form."

Lyra perks up. "Really?"

"Yes. So much more flickable," I say, before doing just that. Lyra gives a squeak, flying off my shoulder and disappearing again with a pop.

"That was hardly kind of you," Vee admonishes.

"Like most shoulder-size pests, I am sure she will be back."

Sure enough, there's a glimmer to my left and Lyra is there, standing on my shoulder as if nothing has happened. "I ought to bite you for that."

"It's only what you deserved, for scaring the squishy insides out of me in the first place," I reason. "Besides, if you bite me, I'll flick you again. We could waste our time on this all day, or you could let Vee and me continue our perilous journey through the possibly haunted forest."

Lyra grunts, which is considerably cuter in bird size. "Fine. But keep your posture upright. It's daft hard popping out and back in this form."

I consider rolling my shoulder down just to make a point as we set our horses to a walk again, but it would only set us farther behind. And as delightful as the distraction has been, the oppression of the stillness around us soon settles on the road like a blanket soaked in frigid water and weighted down with stones. I never much cared for birdsong in the way that Cinderella did, flouncing about the manor with her bristle broom humming along to their chirping, but it provided a soothing background chatter that is loud in its absence. It's part of the natural ornamentation of the outdoors, and not having it is like walking inside a house with no walls.

"You said it was magic," Vee says quietly, as if the act of speaking aloud in so much silence takes effort. She glances not quite at me, and I realize she's talking to Lyra. "The path. Why the trees do not overgrow it. What manner of magic?"

"The Protector," Lyra squeaks, happily munching on something the size of a crumb. I don't even know where she got it from, but she waves it toward me. "Want some? Made it fresh myself this morning. Bit of rosemary and goat cheese is the secret."

"No thank you," I say, though I get a small whiff of it and it does smell quite enticing. "The Protector made this road?"

"He made all the roads in Novador," Lyra says, spraying minuscule crumbs on my shoulder. "Though I've heard tell this was the hardest of them all to carve. According to my mother—who was quite suspicious of why I was asking in the first place—whatever inhabits the Silent Forest was here long ago, long before even the Protector came to Novador. The trees did not take kindly to his efforts to tame their expanse, and they fought him most viciously. That's why there is only this single path that cuts through. He spelled it, to protect any travelers from coming to harm while on its length. But step off the path . . ."

"That won't be necessary," Vee says hastily.

"Did you say he fought the *trees*?" I ask.

"Perhaps it is best to save such questions for when we are not currently deep within their hold," Vee says.

I raise my brows at her. "You are not afraid, are you, good lady knight?"

Vee cuts a wicked glare at me. "I am, and you would be, too, if you had any sense underneath those mahogany locks."

"Mahogany?" I say in surprise. I glance at the simple braid hanging down my shoulder, which Lyra is currently employed in trying to climb. "Is it mahogany? I had always thought it a rather dull brown."

"Yes, well," Vee says, her gaze sliding away. I swear her cheeks flush pink, but she is slightly ahead of me and refuses to turn back in my direction, so I cannot tell.

Mahogany. No one has ever said a word about my hair, except my mother. And only then to criticize when it was not shiny enough.

"My mother knows naught of the trees," Lyra says, swinging from the bottom end of my braid. She looks like a tiny pirate caught in the rigging of a ship. "Neither does any living fey. The Protector never spoke of his time among them, except to warn away any other fey from attempting to tame their wilderness. But the path should be safe, so long as you do not stray from its borders."

"Please stop saying that," I mutter, glancing warily at the impenetrable line the trees looming on either side of the path. They had seemed like ordinary trees before, but now they seem menacing, as if they have pressed against the very edges of the road to test its hold. There are even places where the needles of the branches look flattened, as if they are squashed against some kind of invisible barrier. I shudder, wondering what they might try to do if they ever broke through, and Lyra squeaks in protest at the sudden movement.

"How many days are we on this path again?" I ask, doing my best to sound casual and not terrified by the prospect of sentient, angry trees.

"Four days," Vee says, already sounding weary. "We have food enough for the journey, if we ration. But we'll need to find fresh water sources by tomorrow."

"But Lyra said not to leave the path," I say, suddenly panicking. "If I am to be killed prematurely, I would prefer it not be death by tree."

"We'll have to watch for water that comes close to the path, so that we can quickly cross over and cross back," Vee says. She glances back at me, and her voice cannot hide the lines of worry crinkling the edges of her mouth. "It will be a risk, but one we must make. The horses cannot survive without water. It was too heavy and cumbersome to have brought the entire supply with us."

I look to the press of trees on either side of the path, and I swear they seem to have doubled in the few feet we've traveled. As if they have heard our conversation and are eager to prove what a foolish risk crossing the border would be. Something tells me there would be no crossing back if we were ever foolish enough to pass that border. But Vee is right; we can't let the horses die of thirst. Already I feel the need for water scratching at the back of my throat, like an itch from the most persistent of insect bites. A panicked need, settling in for the duration.

"I think I preferred the cliffs of the Mortel Mountains," I say, swallowing hard as if that might eliminate some of the itch. "At least there was snow to melt and drink."

"You only say that because you were not the one caught upside down hanging off the side of those cliffs," Vee says. "I shall take my dangers head-on, where I can see them coming and face them in full preparation."

"I don't know about that," I murmur, looking up at the nearest tree. The entire side of it is pressed flat against the barrier, needles straining to stab through. The knots in the trunk look like eyes, staggered at odd intervals throughout the wood, the lines around them, dark slashes forming dramatic angles. It's as if the forest has a thousand eyes, all of them watching our passage. Watching and waiting.

EIGHTEEN

WE MAKE CAMP ALONG THE PATH ONCE THE SUN IS down, the loss of light so sudden and complete that we have to finish our setup by Lyra's magic light. Vee attempts to start a fire, but with the first meager tongue of flame a great hissing fills the air around us. We crouch together, Lyra nestling in the weave of my braid, looking about in terror at the stretch of barrier around the path. It's nearly impossible to see anything, and Lyra has to send up a large ball of light for us to face whatever is making that noise.

Under the pale gleam of blue light, though, it's immediately obvious where it's coming from. The trees are shaking, their branches knocking together, their leaves rubbing against one another to make that great hissing noise. There is a thump, loud as a solid wood trunk being dropped from the top of the castle wall, and then another. The trees are slamming against the barrier, shedding leaves and cracking branches, the booming now like cannons. A single needle-shaped leaf drifts down on the path before me, landing point down in the dirt.

"Put out the fire," I say, my voice a rusty croak.

"What?" Vee asks, shuddering with each strike against the barrier.

"Put out the fire!" I shout, reaching for the unlit sticks and scattering them across the path, away from the growing tongue of flame. "Now!"

Vee leaps to her feet and stamps through the fire, extinguishing it under the heel of her boot. The hissing continues for several more minutes, but at least the thumping stops.

"I guess we'll be eating cold meat tonight," Vee says, her voice uneven. "Not such a silent forest after all, is it?"

I huff humorlessly. "Perhaps it is our silence they reference. The trees themselves seem to be quite talkative when they wish to be."

Sleep proves even more unsatisfactory than our meal of hardened lumps of meat and stale rolls of bread, and we are all red-eyed and dragging by the time wan sunlight touches the path. We break camp quickly, shoving our sleeping pallets into packs and hastily mounting our horses before pulling up the stake Vee set to keep them tethered the night before. The lone tree needle remains embedded in the dirt, a marker of our passage. I shudder, happy to leave it behind, as the eyes of the gathered trees watch us pass.

"Lyra," I say, after we are past the site of our attempted ambush and well on our way again. "Now seems like an excellent time to inquire after your specific magical abilities. With particular attention to any protective skills you might have."

"Protective skills?" Lyra says, gazing musingly into the sky as she makes her way through the hunk of sheep's meat I gave her for breakfast. "Would you consider a blinding burst of light in someone's face protective?"

I glance at the eyes of the watching trees. "I don't think their eyes work that way. Can your light act as fire?"

Lyra shakes her head. "No, you would need a fire fey. Our magic is in the ability to manipulate nature. There are some elements that all fey can command—light, air, earth. But other elements require greater specialties, like fire or water. Slippery element, water is. It's the nature of the trickster fey, like the Court of Nmurna."

"You said you can manipulate earth," I say. "What does that mean, specifically? Could you, I don't know, uproot a bunch of angry trees?"

"That would take an enormous amount of magic," Lyra says. "You would need a circle. Multiple fey combining their magic together, along with their mortal counterparts. I've only ever managed small, localized quakes. It's harder than you think, convincing the earth to move. It's heavy and slow, filled with roots and rocks and things. It doesn't like changing its routine."

"The earth has feelings?" Vee asks in surprise.

"Oh sure, all the elements do," says Lyra. "Water is fickle, always slipping in and out of moods. Earth is steady, but dreadfully cranky. Fire is actually calmer than you'd think, but it's relentless as well. Arrogant. Light is fast, but dumb as a drunk sprite. Air is expansive, blustery. Likes to pick fights if you're not careful. In my early days of learning magic I accidentally offended a patch of air and it blew me two kingdoms away. You have to be respectful of all the elements, for they can all turn on you if they so choose."

"Oh good, more things to worry about on this journey," I say, blinking several times, as if that would carry away the gritty feeling coating my eyeballs. I cannot imagine another three days of this. Already the barriers on either side of the path are crowded with trees, pressed against the invisible field and staring with menace in their carved eyes. Even Lyra seems jumpier than usual, popping in and out of manifestations on my shoulders, in my lap, hanging from my braid, and once on the horse's head. The mare had flicked her ears in distress, shearing toward the barrier, and I had to jerk the reins back the other way to keep from crossing over.

"We'll need to find water soon," Vee says, distress layered through her tone like creme through a rich dessert. The kind that turns your stomach after you eat it.

"Are you sure we can't just die of thirst instead?" I ask, only partially kidding.

"I couldn't do that to Thundermere," Vee says severely. In any other situation I would assume she was irritated with me, but her grip on the leather reins is too tight, her jaw too tense.

"I'll scout ahead," Lyra says, her boisterous tone fooling none of us. "I can manifest in and out faster than a tree can sprout new leaves. I'll find us some water that's safe to drink."

"I'm not sure that's—" I begin, but there's a pop, a release of pressure, and she's gone. I sigh. "Here's hoping she returns in one manifestation."

Vee's gaze slides to me. "I can cross the barrier on my own. Bring water back for all of us. There's no need to put both of us in danger and jeopardize our entire quest."

I jerk back in surprise. "Why would you do that? Is this some knight's code of self-sacrifice? Should I be impressed and insist on immortalizing you in verse?"

"Do not jest," Vee says, turning away, her jaw still sharp. "I owe that much to Princess Ellarose. If what you said is true about my father, about his . . . plans."

"Ah," I say, understanding dawning. "You are trying to assuage your guilt."

"I am not!" Vee protests, and the trees shiver in warning. Thundermere jerks at his bit, sidestepping closer to my mare.

"You needn't worry about my opinion of you," I say. "I know you're not your father. The only thing you are guilty of is perhaps an excess of naïveté, or ignorance. Or both."

Vee shakes her head in annoyance. "How can you say something meant to comfort and somehow make it worse?"

I tilt my head to the side in consideration. "Would you rather I coddle you? Is your ego so fragile that you cannot accurately take stock of your own shortcomings?"

"My ego is not fragile," Vee says through gritted teeth. "Nor do I need coddling. I only wish, as I always do in your presence, for silence."

I sigh. "Suit yourself. But I am not wrong. You have nothing to feel guilty about, and you shouldn't risk yourself unnecessarily to prove otherwise."

"I wasn't doing it to risk myself," Vee says, exasperated. "Or, that was not my only reasoning. I also meant—"

"Good news!" Lyra appears before us on the path in her full-size form, arms spread wide and teeth bared in a grin. The horses snort and stomp at the ground, unsettled by her sudden appearance. "I found water!"

"Where?" Vee asks, running a hand through Thundermere's mane to soothe him. I do the same to my mare while idly wondering if I should grace her with her own ridiculous name. Lightning Strike, or Rolling Thunder. Her coat is a lovely gray, like a late-afternoon rainstorm. Perhaps I'll call her that. Rainstorm.

"About a quarter of a mile ahead, and here's the best part," Lyra says, drawing out the suspense before clapping her hands together and startling the horses all over again. "It's on the path!"

"What?" Vee and I intone simultaneously.

"How is that possible?" I ask.

"Can we ford it with the horses?" Vee asks.

"It's a small creek that runs across the path, and it only comes up to my waist," Lyra says. "The horses can drink their fill, you can refill your canteens, and no one has to risk tree murder. It's brilliant!"

I glance at Vee nervously. Could it really be our luck that we could locate water so easily?

"There's only one way to find out," Vee says, as if divining my thoughts.

We nudge the horses forward, their pace picking up as if they can smell the water ahead. True to Lyra's instructions, we spot the small stream crossing the path ahead. The water bubbles and moves at a brisk pace, fresh and clear. My mouth aches just thinking of fresh, cool water that does not taste of the animal skin it has stewed in for the past few days. I nudge Rainstorm to move a hair faster, but Vee calls out to me in caution.

"Let Thundermere smell it first," she says, edging ahead of me. "He'll know if it's safe to drink."

I lift both brows at her. "You trust your horse that much?"

"I trust Thundermere with my life," Vee says, letting him slow to a stop as he dips his head over the water. He snuffles at it, blowing his warm breath across the surface in a way that makes steam rise. He dips his nose in, tossing the water about, before dipping once again to drink deeply. Rainstorm is only a beat behind him, and she doesn't so much as blink an eye before plunging her whole head in.

We dismount, kneeling beside the water's edge to scoop handfuls of water to our lips. It's cold and delicious, so clear I can see every tiny pebble at the bottom. Lyra was right; it's only waist-high at the most, and I resist the urge to plunge into its depths and scrub the days of travel from my skin. The trees have gone awfully quiet.

"Well, at least I know you can trust something, even if it is just a horse," I say, dipping the mouth of my canteen into the water to refill it.

"Thundermere is not just a horse," Vee scoffs. "He is a warhorse. He is *my* horse. I've trained with him since he was birthed, and he's known no other rider."

"Fancy," I say, stung by her haughty tone. "Was that a special dispensation from your father?"

Vee's face burns red. "It is the way of all knights. The bond between a rider and their warhorse must be unspoken and unbreakable. There can be no doubt, no room for error when you ride into battle. Our lives literally depend on it."

"Oh," I mutter, properly chastised. I don't know why it bothered me so much in the first place, Vee's unbreakable trust in a work beast. "It's just . . . you held a great deal of mistrust for me before you ever met me. And still, it feels as if—I know there are plenty of rumors about my family at court, especially since Cinder—er, my stepsister married your cousin, but why do you hate us so much? Why does it feel so personal from you?"

Vee sits back on her heels, blowing out a stream of breath. "I knew Princess Ellarose's father, the earl, long before your mother married him. He was a great gardener, his gardens at the manor renowned throughout the capital. It was said he could coax even the most fickle, reluctant plants to blossom. He often brought his more exotic blooms to the castle for the late queen. He was a kind man, gentle and generous, indulgent to his only daughter. When I told my father I wanted to become a knight, he . . . I . . ."

Her voice cracks, and something in me instinctively wants to reach out and take hold of her hand. But I don't, and she clears her throat and continues on.

"I needed a nobleman to agree to accept me as a squire, to sponsor my pursuit of knighthood. My father had made it known that he didn't want my *flight of fancy*, as he called it, indulged. And no one at court would dare to cross my father, even back then. Lord Chancemoor found me one afternoon, crying in the garden. Because every single lord I had approached rejected my application. He said he could not bring me on as a squire, since he had no formal training himself. But he told me he would do what he could to find a position. The very next week, Lord Bruto accepted my application after initially declining. He never said why he changed his mind, but I knew it must have been Lord Chancemoor."

My memories of Cinderella's father are hazy and distant, like the edge of a field at the peak of a summer's day, but I do remember his kindness and generosity. At least before the illness and my mother's needs clawed it out of him.

"I watched him wither away," Vee whispers, shaking her head, her eyes shining. "Such a big, lovely, generous man, worn down by Lady Teramina's poison, and then by the poison of his own body turning against him. He deserved better. Princess Ellarose deserved better. When I met you, I could not look at you without seeing what of your mother lay within you. Her cruelty, her capricious nature, her self-serving impulses. I thought you were the same, especially the way you spoke to the princess. But now . . ."

My hands are still in the water, my canteen forgotten, my joints aching from the cold, but I cannot make them move. I am riveted to Vee's voice, to whatever will come next. I want her to look at me, and yet I don't think I could bear it.

"But now, what?" I ask, my voice cracking.

She looks at me, her eyes so full it makes my heart ache. But then it's not me she's looking at, it's something just beyond my shoulder, terror rolling off her in waves.

"Aralyn," she says, but I don't hear the rest because my hands are like stones, sinking to the bottom of the creek, as something takes hold and drags me under the water.

NINETEEN

I DON'T HAVE TIME TO TAKE SO MUCH AS A GASP OF
breath before the water closes over my head, but my mouth opens
anyway as a reflex and sucks in a mouthful of liquid. My chest
spasms, fighting against the influx, the water thrashing and dragging me swiftly away from Vee's terrified face above me. I kick and
thrash back, fighting against whatever has a hold on me, struggling
to catch just a glimpse of it. But there is nothing there, nothing I can
see, nothing I can hold on to. It's as if the water itself has dragged
me under.

My chest hurts so badly and I gulp again, desperate for air but taking in only water, more and more of it until I'm vomiting it back out.
It's in my stomach, my lungs, my eyes, threading its fingers through
my hair and tugging me farther down, until the light is gone and I
want to die from the panic and the pain. I should have known better than to trust a horse and this damn enchanted water. It's only as
my legs stop kicking and my arms do little more than twitch in their
final throes that I have what I expect to be my last coherent thought:
No one will even mourn my passing.

Then I am suddenly spat back onto the creek's edge, heaving out water and gasping for air, fingers clawing into the damp earth. It's rough and fragrant, stabbing into my fingers with biting intention. I can't open my eyes without them filling with streaming tears, but even as I bless the air filling my lungs, I know something is wrong. The ground is wrong, the light is wrong, the very smell that drags through my nostrils is wrong. I have escaped one death, only to be ejected into another.

I'm on the wrong side of the barrier.

I only have time to glance up and see a spray of needles as a branch swoops down from the nearest tree toward me. I roll out of the way, slamming into the trunk of the tree, and the leaves shake violently and hiss at me. I scramble to get upright, but my skirts are tangled around my legs and my arms are still weak from fighting against the water. Great clods of earth shower down on me as the tree rips its roots from the ground, lashing them across my legs and torso, shoving me into the earth with enough force that my chest makes a cracking noise.

"Aralyn!" Vee screams from the other side of the barrier, but she doesn't seem able to pass. I can only see her in snatches, the branches tearing at my face and shoulders, but I can tell she's been driven back by an invisible force. In the same way the barrier kept the trees on this side, it traps her over there. Leaving me alone.

"No!" I gasp as dirt rains into my mouth and eyes and the roots tighten around my thighs until I feel my bones bending, cracking. I claw at the bark, my nails ripping and tearing and bleeding, but I don't stop. I can't, even as I know I could never hope to stop a single tree, much less an entire angry forest of them.

There's a splashing sound, and then a sharp cry, and then the trees are screaming. It's the only way I can characterize the sound of their branches slapping against one another, their leafy arms flailing about wildly as something hacks away at the roots pressing down on me. The earth itself shudders, the dirt loosening enough that I can turn my head side to side and clear my vision.

Vee stands over me like an avenging spirit, her eyes spitting fire and the battle cry that rips from her throat enough to stop the heart of a full-grown man. The trees shriek in reply, and she swings her sword down into the root binding my legs, the blade chipping away at the wood and drawing up thick beads of sap.

"Aralyn!" she cries, soaking wet, and I realize how she's gotten across the barrier. She jumped into the creek and swam underneath it. That must have been how I was able to cross to this side in the first place. She holds out a hand to me, her other waving her sword with menace. "Take my hand!"

"I can't," I gasp, shoving at the roots entombing me, kicking with my heels for purchase. She's gained me a few inches, but the tree's rage at her interference runs as deep as its feet. "I'm still trapped. My feet. I need the tree to let me go."

Another nearby tree swings low, a branch the size of a pillar swiping at Vee. She leaps up on it, using the momentum to jump back down and bring her sword down hard onto my tree's root. It screams, covering us in needles that prickle like fire, its dark, sticky sap smeared across the blade of her sword. But still the trees keep coming, and Vee can only dive and twist and swipe for so long.

"Vee, your left foot!" I shout as a root rises out of the ground just behind her heel.

She jerks around, the root biting back into the earth in fury.

"There are too many of them!" I shout, futilely tugging at the roots binding me. "You can't do it, Vee. You have to leave me."

"Never," Vee says fiercely, pivoting to face me.

The tree behind her screams and shivers back, and in the half-light of the late sun something flashes over her shoulder. I gasp, struggling against the tree roots anew.

"The Protector's blade!" I call, pounding my fists against the tree. "They're afraid of the Protector's blade!"

Vee needs no more explanation, reaching over her shoulder to draw the weapon from the harness in which she has carried it the past several days. The trees shriek once again, leaves flying everywhere until they nearly blot out the sun. But they draw back from Vee as she swings the bare blade in an arc. She makes a full pivot before rounding on the tree trapping me, the blade lending her an ethereal light.

"Let her go," she growls.

The tree shivers violently, the roots pressing down hard on my chest, and I fear it would rather squeeze the life out of me before relenting to Vee's demands. But then the earth shifts again, and suddenly my arms are free and my legs can move enough that I crawl out from under the tree, dragging myself toward Vee and our only meager protection against the forest.

"What do we do?" I whisper, the pain in my chest so sharp that every breath is an agony.

"We'll have to swim under the barrier again," Vee says, not taking her eyes off the tree.

"I can't," I say, half a sob. "I can't go back in there."

"It's the only way," Vee says, reaching down her hand to grip mine. "I'll be with you the whole time, all right? I won't let you go. You can do this, Aralyn. I won't leave you, I swear it on Thundermere's life. It's the only way back across the barrier. Will you trust me?"

There is no more time for second-guessing, because if the trees were angry before, they are *furious* now. Screaming so loud it makes me clap my free hand over my ear. The Protector's blade won't keep them at bay forever.

"Yes," I gasp, though I can't even hear myself speak. "I trust you."

Vee nods at me once, catching my intention, and then we're running the few steps toward the creek and diving into its cold rush once more. It fights us, pushing back, wanting to drive us farther into the forest. But Vee is far more determined, slicing the Protector's blade through the water with each stroke, pushing off the shallow bottom to drive us back across the barrier. We break the surface along the path and there are hands hauling me up, and I swear to the fey Lyra is crying. Sobbing.

"Aralyn, I'm so sorry," she says, hugging me tighter than the tree's roots. "I'm so, so sorry. I had no idea. I didn't know the water ran beneath the barrier. I thought it would be safe. But then that *thing* just came out of the water, or maybe it *was* the water. I don't know. It was so fast, like a wave, and you were gone before we could . . . and then we couldn't get across the barrier. I didn't even think about going in the water after you! If Vee hadn't gone, I don't . . . My magic wouldn't work, I couldn't do anything. I failed you. I completely failed you. You were my charge and I *failed* you."

"Lyra!" I say, loudly enough that I hope it interrupts her self-castigation. The effort bends me in half, my chest warning me against making any such rash decisions again. "Lyra, it's all right. You didn't know. You couldn't have. But I'm alive. I made it back."

My eyes travel over Lyra's shoulder to find Vee, kneeling beside the creek, panting but still determined. She wields the Protector's bare blade in one hand, the edge of it pressing into her palm. It hadn't even occurred to me that it might cut her when she held it, since it has no hilt.

"You saved me," I whisper, because anything more hurts too much.

"If it's all the same to you, I'd rather you not give me any more opportunities to do so," Vee says, though she smiles at me as she says it.

"But *why*?"

She cocks her head to the side. "Well, I think it would slow us down quite a bit if I had to keep rescuing you from things like angry trees."

"No," I say, shaking my head. "I mean, *why* did you save me?"

"Oh." Her cheeks flush pink, either from the exertion of her rescue or something else. I can't tell. She pauses, as if weighing her words. "Because we're in this together. However we started, I do believe we've only made it this far by relying on each other. By trusting each other."

"But you were right," I blurt out. "You've been right all along. I only wanted the Protector's blade for my own gain. I never intended to hand it over to Cin—to Ellarose."

She tilts her head in consideration. "Perhaps you think you started out that way. But someone very annoying once told me I could choose something different for myself. That I am not defined by my father's choices. You were taught to call the princess Cinderella, but just now, you chose to call her Ellarose. And if you can choose that small kindness, here where it doesn't matter, imagine what you can choose when it does."

She stands up, gathering the horses and reaching her hand to me. "We should move. I don't want to find out what happens when these trees decide to test the boundary here."

I force myself to climb on my horse's back even though it feels like vital things are tearing apart inside me with every stretch. It gets worse as the horses begin to move, their hoofbeats the only sound in the eerie stillness as the trees settle back into their silence. But none of it distracts me from the rising tide of feelings within me, scattered and chaotic and untethered. Mistress Clara would be horrified at my lack of comportment.

I watch Vee lead the way, her posture relaxed yet alert, perfectly in tune with her horse. I should feel resentment, or wariness. I should be planning my next move, to steal the blade when she is sleeping. To abandon her on Sandtrap, if we ever make it there. We've reached some new understanding, some tentative alliance, that I should be turning in my favor. But all I can feel is a profound, unsettling gratitude. A deep, distressing sense of trust. We are nothing to each other—not blood, not bone, not kin. And yet she risked her life to save mine in a way I know my own kin never would. And it's entirely possible I would do the same for her.

Who could I be, if I chose for myself?

TWENTY

WE TAKE NO MORE CHANCES DURING THE REMAINING
days of our journey through the Silent Forest, risking death from
thirst or starvation before ever attempting to deviate from the path
again. We make our water last, pushing the horses on, giving them
drinks from our canteens when they need it, until we are all silent
to save our mouths from drying out. The trees are a constant, glowering presence just beyond the barrier, but I don't let my eyes stray
from the dirt road before us. It's enough that I still feel their needles
under my skin, still ache with every deep breath, still see their roots
burying me every time I close my eyes.

Still, the need for water becomes an obsession, a hyper-fixation
that drives all other rational thought from my mind. At some point
I begin to hallucinate, holding my canteen upside down above my
open mouth, vividly imagining a single drop of water rolling out,
fat and inviting, splashing against the rough surface of my tongue,
soothing the constant maddening ache. I've never known thirst like
this, like a rash that only gets worse the harder you scratch it.

When there is finally some other color save green and brown on the
distant horizon, I assume it's only a more compelling hallucination,

signaling my rapid decline. But then Vee gives a shout, pressing her heels to Thundermere, who jerks in response before breaking into a full-legged run. Rainstorm is close behind, more attuned to Vee's mount than to me, and it's all I can do to wrap her reins around my hands and press close to her mane, holding on for dear life.

The trees thin out as the path widens, their menacing stares whipping by too fast to land with any potency. And as the trees fall away, something else stretches to fill the span of empty space. Blue, a blue so deep it looks black in patches, sparkling like precious jewels in an earthly diadem, the salt smell so thick and rich it flavors the air. Vee gives an unbridled whoop of joy, throwing a fist in the air in her celebration. She looks back to me, hair whipping in every direction, mouth wide and grinning all the way to her back teeth.

"We did it!" she cries, swinging her fist again. "We made it! The Impassable Sea!"

All that water, my jaw hurts from how hard my mouth suddenly fills with longing. "Water," I croak.

"I know, it's the most gorgeous thing I've ever seen," Vee shouts.

"No. Water, Vee. *Water*."

Vee reins in Thundermere, rounding toward me. "Water, right. We can't drink from the Impassable Sea, though. It would kill us. There might be tributaries leading into it, though. I'll ride ahead."

"No, that's too long," I say, my throat rasping. I don't know how Vee manages to look so fine. It must be part of that infernal knight's training, learning to live with such deprivation. "Lyra."

Nothing happens, and I try her name again, dredging up a coughing fit from the effort. It's so much worse when I cough, but I can't help it. There's nothing to soothe my throat. I'll drink that salty water, even if it kills me.

"I wish," I manage, and then there is that strange pressure, and Lyra appears in full form before us.

"Oh no," she moans. "It's the trees again, isn't it?"

"Water," I say, and I swear on her entire fey court if Lyra makes me speak again I'll wish her into nonexistence.

Lyra looks around in surprise, her face lighting up with joy. "You made it out. You made it to the Impassable Sea! You did it!"

"Lyra, we need water," Vee says, taking over for me. "Drinkable water. That doesn't try to kill Aralyn."

"Oh, right. Of course! Two shakes of a lamb's rear."

She pops out, and I contemplate how much water might be in a fey's blood. I don't want to drink it, not really. I just can't think of anything but water, and the crash of the waves against the black sands of the beach do little to help quench that thirst. Lyra pops back in, already waving us toward something.

"I found a stream!" she says. "No water monsters, I swear it. Dove in and checked myself."

I put my heels to Rainstorm, knowing what I'm asking of her, promising something worthy in return. She seems to gather my meaning, because she throws up great sprays of black sand in her wake as we take off, outpacing even Thundermere in our pursuit. Lyra moves fast for a wingless fairy godmother, and by the time we catch up to her there's something else sparkling in the sand. Something clear and fresh. At this point it doesn't even matter to me if the water *is* possessed, I'll let it drag me down to the sea if it gives me one long, deep drink.

I half leap, half fall off Rainstorm's back as she dips her full head in the water, not bothering with my hands as I do the same. It's cold and clear, so fresh it would bring me to tears if I had any to spare. I drink until I can't breathe, until my stomach aches from the pressure, until my dress is soaked from the waist up, and then I take great scoops of it with both hands and pour it over me in a show of excess. By the time I have sated the most intense of my urges, Vee is kneeling beside me, laughing so hard that she shakes in silence.

"What?" I ask, offended.

"You are like a puppy," she says, her cheeks red from the effort to keep it in.

"I am not," I say, straightening. But I've forgotten that I was holding a handful of water, and it splashes down the front of my dress and into my lap, molding the fabric of my legs. Which only sends Vee into greater peals of laughter, wrenched out of her in surprise. Her laugh is a shock, higher-pitched than I expected, like the smaller chimes on a bell tower. It wraps me up, taking the edge off the chill of the water soaking through my clothes, inviting me to join its musicality. It must be the thirst, the sleep deprivation, the terror that accumulated in my veins over the past four days, because I can't resist the invitation. I laugh, really laugh, for possibly the first time in my life. I never knew anything could feel this good.

Lyra stands over us, the ridges over her silver eyes low and craggy, her sharp teeth gnashing in worry. "It's poisoned, isn't it. The water, it *is* enchanted. It broke the both of you. Ah, plunkers. This is my fault again! I should have known the water would have a different effect on me! I always forget how weak your mortal skins are, just letting anything through. I'll fix this, I swear it!"

"Lyra, no, no," I gasp, trying to speak around another burst of laughter threatening to erupt. I wave my hands, wheezing. "Lyra, it's not poisoned. We're just laughing."

Lyra looks to Vee suspiciously, then back at me. "No, no, I don't think so. You two don't laugh. It's the water."

"Ah, hurtful but fair," Vee says, her green eyes sparkling at me. "Perhaps it is the water after all."

There is a pause, and then Vee and I burst out laughing all over again, the strength of it doubling me over. It's a welcome pain, though, one I would take over anything else.

"They're gone," Lyra frets. "Lost. Oh, Mother won't like to hear of this. I've broken my first mortal. She'll never trust me to run the court now."

"Lyra, Lyra, we're only jesting," I say, wiping away the tears I didn't think I had. "I promise you, we are of sound mind and body. Well, as sound as they ever were. It's not the water. We are simply happy to be alive."

"Yes," Vee says in surprise. "That's it exactly."

Lyra squats before me, peering at me like I am some forest creature she has just discovered. "Are you sure? I might be able to find some herbs to purge your stomach, leech the poison out. It won't feel good, but it will save your life."

"No, no," I say hastily, sobering at the thought. "Lyra, I promise. We're fine. We made it to the Impassable Sea. We survived the Silent Forest."

"The only ones to do so since the Protector first cut that path," Vee adds. She looks at me, and I can't quite read the expression on her face. "We did it the same as we conquered the Mortel Mountains."

"Together," I say, my belly too full of water now. I clear my throat, rising to my feet and doing my best to rearrange my sopping dress. "But now we'll need to reach Sandtrap to find the next piece. Any ideas?"

Vee stands beside me, shading her eyes against the brilliance of the rising sun reflecting off the waves of the Impassable Sea, looking down the never-ending stretch of black sand. She heaves in a breath, her shoulders straightening. "There's really only one way to do it."

I lift my brows in surprise. "What way is that?"

She cuts her gaze to me, one corner of her mouth curling up in a small smile that makes my stomach quake. "We'll have to steal a boat."

TWENTY-ONE

"DOES YOUR KNIGHT'S CODE NOT PRECLUDE YOU from such activities as stealing?" I whisper as we approach several longboats dug into the sand, oars piled within or stuck into the ground beside them.

"From honest, hardworking fisherman?" Vee whispers back, snagging a pair of oars and handing them off to me. "Of course. But from rum-running, ship-sinking, treasure-hunting pirates? I believe the knight's code would consider it my sworn duty to apprehend such a boat. Now take that other end and shove it toward the water, quickly. Who knows how long it will be until they return."

I roll my eyes at her elitism against pirates but take up my position as instructed, digging my heels into the sand and shoving the boat forward. We spotted the pirate ship anchored off the shore soon after we left the stream and tracked these longboats as the crews rowed them inland. Vee left Thundermere and Rainstorm tied up behind a high patch of dunes and we lay in wait until the pirates had disappeared down the black sandy beach, hauling several large wooden chests between them.

We manage to get the boat to the waters between the two of us, and Vee snatches a second set of oars before we both leap into the longboat, instinctively centering our bodies and spreading our feet to balance the rocking motion. I nearly drop one of the oars in the water, and Vee ducks as I send the other one swinging over her head.

"Was that intentional?" she demands, raising her voice to a normal volume now that we're away from the shore. She's already set her oars in the shallow grooves on the side of the boat and dips them into the water with practiced ease, her shoulder muscles bunching as she pulls them through the water and propels us farther out into the Impassable Sea.

"I suppose this is not the most opportune time to tell you I have never been in a boat," I say, eyeing the dark waters lapping at the edge of the smooth wooden sides of the longboat. "Or on a sea. Or on any water, really. Mother always said swimming was unbecoming of properly titled young ladies."

"I swam every sun season," Vee says, launching us forward with another powerful pull. She pauses, glancing over her shoulder at me. "Though I don't guess your mother would consider anything about me proper."

"No, she would not," I say, and Vee sends me another cutting look. "This time I don't mean it as an insult, I swear."

"Put your oars in the water and copy my movements," Vee says, her breath already coming harder. "I can't row this thing by myself."

I do as she says, trying my best to emulate her strokes but coming up splashing on the first try, sending the boat tilting to the left with my second attempt. Vee grunts, pulling harder to get us back on course toward the thin line of land barely visible along the distant horizon. I wince, trying and failing several times more to aid her in rowing the boat before I finally find a rhythm and begin rowing along with her. It only takes a few strokes, though, before my back muscles are screaming in pain, begging me not to make them work one more time. Even Vee is huffing, but her strokes do not slow—no doubt thanks to that infernal knight's training she is always bragging on about. I would rather die of rowing than admit defeat before she does, though, so I keep pulling, gritting my teeth until my jaw feels locked in place, forcing myself through each movement.

The line on the horizon remains thin and distant despite my fervent wish that each stroke would be my last, and it's not long before my oars are dipping into the water in shallower and shallower pulls. The waves fight us, almost as if they are aware of our intentions. The water remains still, almost placid, until our oars dip in, and then a wave rises up, pushing us back, until it seems as if we will never make any progress. I lean over as far as I dare without tipping the boat, looking into the black depths that reflect my sweaty, frustrated expression back to me as a mirror would.

"I am beginning to suspect sabotage," I pant, slapping the flat side of my oar down on the surface and breaking up the image.

"We do seem to be making very little progress," Vee pants, even as she puts in another power pull on her oars. The wave rises up, tipping the far end of the boat up out of the water with the strength it puts into shoving us back. Vee cries out in surprise, losing her grip on her oars as she reaches out to grip both sides of the boat and keep from being thrown over the side. Something surges just under the water, and one of Vee's oars goes flying, disappearing quickly beneath the surface. She reaches out to grab the end, but I snag her sleeve.

"Don't!" I shout, watching the shape sink into the depths.

"Without that oar we're lost," Vee says.

"If you put your hand below the water, the oar won't be the only thing we lose," I say. "We weren't making enough progress anyway, with or without the oar. The sea doesn't wish us to pass."

Vee gives me a doubtful look. "It's a body of water, Aralyn. What intentions could it have?"

"Murderous ones, if I am judging by my last aquatic encounter," I say, pulling my oars clear of the water. I sigh, eyeing the black surface warily. "I think we need help."

"What help could we . . . oh. Are you quite sure?"

"Not the least bit, but we're woefully short on choices." I take a deep breath, gripping both sides of the boat. "You'll probably want to hold on. Who knows what size she'll be when she manifests this time. I wish for a way to steer this boat."

There's that curious pressure and then a pop, but we only see Lyra for a split second when she manifests, her silver eyes wide and round as coins, before she plunges under the waters of the Impassable Sea.

"Lyra!" I shout, reaching out for her, unmindful of my own recent warning. The water is cold—freezing, really—and I have horrible flashbacks of the last time I plunged my hands into such water. The waters are roiling now, filled with sleek bodies that flash and coil and writhe around Lyra. She comes up spluttering and I grab the thick ruff of her coat as Vee takes her by the arm, both of us leaning back and tipping the boat dangerously as we try to haul her up. She gets halfway up the side before something curls around her waist and tightens, dragging her down so sharply that the boat sways in the opposite direction.

"Unmanifest!" Vee shouts, letting loose of Lyra to stabilize the boat. She looks to me wildly. "Tell her to disappear!"

"I don't know how to do that!" I cry, but I release her as well. "Lyra, I wish you to return to the fey realm!"

There is a pressure, a pop, and then our boat is knocked forward by whatever just had Lyra in its grasp. It's furious now—furious enough to break the surface and latch on to the side of our boat, its arm a deep purple and slick, the underside covered in suckers. Except as it reaches another arm over the side, I see that they aren't suckers, but mouths, rimmed in teeth sharper than Lyra's. Vee screams as one of the mouths brushes against her, turning her skin red and raw.

"I wish for you to return in your smaller form!" I shout, grabbing an oar and slamming it down on the arm reaching for Vee again. The boat shudders, the wood beneath our feet bowing dangerously upward.

"I'm here!" Lyra gasps in my ear. I was so distracted by the sea creature I hardly registered her manifestation. "What do you need?"

"Wind!" I cry desperately. "The sea is fighting us, and we need to reach the land."

"You have to wish it!" Lyra cries, pulling sharply at my braid as the boat shifts violently again. The tentacles are back, climbing up both sides of the boat, and one brushes my leg, leaving behind a fiery trail of pain.

"I wish for you to blow us to that island!" I shout, bringing the edge of my oar down hard enough to sever the very tip of the tentacle.

The creature roars, rising up from the sea with a wave that drenches us, and I only have a brief moment to stare into its fathomless jaws before a powerful burst of wind shoots us out of its grasp. Vee catapults into me and I hit the back curve of the boat hard, my ears ringing from the impact. The front end of our boat lifts off the waves in response to the redistribution of weight, and were it not for Lyra's magical wind propelling us forward, I think the entire boat would have tipped end over end.

I hold on to Vee for dear life, Lyra shouting nonsense in my ear, as the thin line climbs up the horizon at an alarming rate. It sprouts buildings and masts and, most distressingly of all, enormous jagged rocks all along the coastline. Our longboat gives no signs of slowing as those rocks loom.

"Lyra, you have to stop the wind!" I shout. "We're going to crash!"

She yells something incomprehensible, her voice too tiny to hear as she whips past my ear in the wind, her grip on my braid the only thing keeping her in the boat.

"What?" I cry, grimacing at the rocks that have already doubled in size with our approach. "I can't hear you! Lyra, stop the wind!"

She yells again, and this time all I catch is *wish*. But it's enough for me to catch her meaning this time.

"I wish you to stop the wind!"

The boat stops so suddenly it throws both Vee and me into the front, and this time the blow to my head comes from the front. My ears are still ringing from the wind even though it's gone, upsetting my equilibrium. Vee recovers faster than I do, grabbing one of my oars and scrambling up to quickly row us the short distance to the nearest outcropping of rocks. When we get close enough she reaches out with the oar, dragging us forward until the side of the boat bumps against the rocks.

"Quickly," she gasps. "Before the sea or Lyra realizes we're here."

I climb out, reaching a hand down to help her out, and once we're on the rock we both lie out, chests heaving, heart rates subsiding.

"I used to think," Vee pants, staring up at the cloudless sky, "that fairy godmothers were a gift."

"Truly the worst," I agree, rolling over and forcing myself to a sitting position. I glance at my braid in alarm. "Lyra?"

"Here," Lyra says in her normal voice, manifesting before us in her full size. "Well, that was a bit of a bonker, wasn't it?"

"Could you not have conjured a gentler wind?" I ask accusingly. "You nearly smashed us on the rocks."

"Ah, sorry for that," Lyra says sheepishly, tugging at the skin along the back of her neck. "Bit discombobulated after that thing grabbed me. But here you both are, all of a piece! So not too much damage done."

"Not too much," Vee says, shaking her head, her hair spreading out along the rock. I give her a critical look and she glances at me, eyes narrowing. "What?"

I sigh. "I'd rather not tell you. You're not going to like it."

Vee lets her eyes close, turning her face toward the wan sunlight. "Could it possibly be worse than almost getting eaten by a sea creature before almost getting broken against a rocky shoreline?"

I sigh. "We don't look like pirates."

"So?" Vee says.

"So, we'll need clothes. Different clothes."

"I told you, my knight's code does not prevent me from repatriating items stolen by thieves," Vee says with a slight shrug.

"Yes, but we need to look like pirates *before* we approach the other pirates. If we show up on Sandtrap looking like this, they'll just as soon chuck us back to the sea monster as they would listen to us."

Vee cracks one eye open, looking to me in suspicion. "You're right—I don't think I like where this is going. What are you suggesting?"

I roll my eyes skyward, gathering the remaining scraps of my courage before turning to Lyra. "Lyra, I wish you to make Vee and me look like pirates."

Lyra's eyes go round and wide again. "Oh no."

TWENTY-TWO

"THIS CANNOT POSSIBLY BE RIGHT," VEE SAYS, STAND-ing with her arms outstretched, looking down at the outfit Lyra has concocted for her. "There are far too many of these silken flag materials. I look as if I've been decorated for a holiday feast at the castle, not for playing pirate."

Vee has a point about the pennants—they wrap around her waist, up over her shoulder, and across the other shoulder in an X formation. They're of varying sizes and styles, some brightly patterned and clashing, others a single deep, rich color. But they cover her plain shirt and pants, fluttering about in the wind.

"Pirates gather such pennants to represent each country or independent nation they have sailed to," I say, adjusting the strips of silk across my own waist and shoulders. "They are a point of pride. The more pennants a seafarer has gathered, the farther flung they've been and survived to return to Sandtrap and tell their tales."

"Of course they would celebrate the extent of their pirating with such flamboyancy," Vee mutters as she stashes her bundle of clothes between two large boulders, her sword and the Protector's blade camouflaged within them. "And I don't much care for leaving our only weapons behind here. What if the tide rises and washes them out to sea? Or an enterprising pirate comes along and snatches them? They'd be safer with me, regardless of whether or not they will fit the pirate look. Or at least with Lyra in the fey realm."

"It's too risky, carrying them with us. If anything happens to us, if we are captured, we can't risk the blade falling into the wrong hands. We don't know what bringing the Protector's blade into the fey realm might trigger, either. And your sword is the wrong shape. The pirates will spot you for a knight immediately. Pirates are extremely distrustful—it's imperative we look the part." Lyra had tried rather fervently to convince me to don an eye patch or let her "manifest" a few teeth out of my mouth, but I told her the pennants would do just fine. I give Vee a sly look as I tie off the thin cord binding all the pennants together. "Besides, I think you look rather dashing with all those pennants and your hair tossed about like that. Like a pirate captain already braced at the helm of your own ship."

Vee turns a bright red and swishes away from me in a flourish of silken fabric, and my laughter breaks out as she makes her stiff-legged walk up over the rocks toward the squatty, scattered collection of buildings that make up Sandtrap Island. I scramble after her, glad to be away from the sinister presence of the sea's edge washing up against the rocks. I've had no other experience with such a large body of water, but this one is unsettling in its quietude, in the silent way the waves break against the rocks, in the lack of jumping fish or swooping birds. It reminds me too much of the Silent Forest, and I have no desire to find out what lurks beneath the thin barrier of the water's surface.

There isn't much to Sandtrap Island, though I would bet those looks are meant to be deceiving. The whole of the island covers about as much ground as the castle back in Novador, and the buildings are arranged in a similar fashion, though they lack a castle to dominate their landscape. Whoever originally conceived the island betrayed their own background by laying it out in such a fashion. There were rumors that it was even founded by a runaway princess from a distant land who fled an unsatisfactory marriage match her father set up for her.

But however the buildings here began, they now house the land's most infamous seafarers, and it shows. There are hundreds of small, round wooden huts dotting the island in various locations, most likely individual residences. Some look so dilapidated that they must be abandoned, while others are cluttered with decorations gathered from far-flung travels. One hut even boasts a life-size carving of a bear—or what I believe to be a statue, until it turns its head. I quickly angle away from that section of houses.

"Do you hear that?" Vee asks, pausing beside a hut well past the bear house. She cocks her head to the side, her eyes going sharp.

My head still rings from the various bumps it's suffered on the Impassable Sea, but I do my best to listen hard. I can hear only the blow of the wind and the hard beat of my heart, rhythmic and steady. Except that, the longer I listen, the more the beat sounds as if it is coming from outside my body.

"Are those drums?" I ask, tugging at the lobe of one ear, as if that will clear the ringing.

"Sounds like it," Vee says grimly. "I hope it's not a warning of our approach."

"Only one way to find out," I say, soldiering on.

There appears only to be one road, wide and remarkably well kept, bifurcating the island. Larger wooden structures line this road, crowded together to make maximum use of the limited space, every-thing from trading posts to exchange their ill-gotten goods to saloons to a sign with a giant wooden tooth looming over the entrance that promises quick extractions. Perhaps Lyra had a point about the teeth.

"What is our play here?" Vee asks as I catch up with her on the edge of the largest buildings lining the road. The drumming is more obvious here, loud and steady as if it has always played this way. If it *is* meant as a warning of our arrival, the inhabitants seem awfully insouciant to its thrum. Out of the first door we pass a man comes flying, landing in the street with a thud. Someone within the build-ing shouts a vague threat in a language I don't know, and Vee and I hurry past before the man can collect his wits to make a retort.

"Lyra believes the second piece of the Protector's blade must be somewhere here in the Impassable Sea," I murmur, stepping around a collection of men hunched over a barrel playing with pieces of white that look disturbingly like bones. They collect them in their hands and toss them, counting up black markings along each side. They eye both of us, but once they spot all the pennants on Vee they give us a nod and return to their game.

"How do we find it?" Vee asks, standing a bit taller after the exchange. I resist the urge to roll my eyes again.

"These pirates have been all over the waters of the Impassable Sea, even to the other countries Novador no longer trades with. My theory is that the second piece must create some kind of distur-bance, like the blade atop the Mortel Mountains. A place like that would engender legends. And where the legends lead . . ."

"We'll find the second piece of the blade," Vee says, nodding. She frowns. "But how will we get any of these scum to talk? I've left my sword hidden back with the longboat. You said it would give me away as a knight."

"And so it would," I say, eyeing a shop that seems to sell nothing. Several women loiter out front, and it's not until one of the men from the bones game approaches one of the women that I realize what the shop sells. I swallow hard, averting my eyes and continuing. "It's the wrong style of blade, and it wouldn't do you much good anyhow against an island full of heavily armed pirates. These men and women have endured more than you can imagine. They are more than the legends children whisper after the candles have been blown out. Your sword would only make them laugh."

Vee's expression hardens. "I am a trained knight of the order of Novador—"

"I know all that, Vee, stop posturing," I snap quietly. "I only mean to say that these men have faced fighters more brutal than you and come out the victor. You cannot overtake them by force. If you want to beat a pirate, you have to outsmart them."

Vee snorts. "That should be easy enough. Have you got a bit of something shiny on you?"

I stop dead in the street, drawing the attention of a band of men playing some kind of hollowed wind instrument and dancing along on the other side of the street, all of the music in time to the drumbeats permeating the island. I put on my best snarl, the kind Mother would use on serving girls she thought too impertinent. The pace of their song increases.

"Do you remember when you said that you had made assumptions about me, because of my upbringing? Because of my mother?"

"Yes," Vee says cautiously. "What's that got to do with anything?"

"I made the same assumptions about you," I say, gesturing to take in her general appearance. "About you being a knight. Living in the castle. About your father, once I knew who he was."

A wave of pink creeps up her neck. "What point are you trying to make?"

"My point is that your opinion of these pirates has been formed by your father, by the nobles of the castle. By the knight's order. Men who have a financial interest in quashing piracy. Have you ever stopped to ask yourself what drove these people to piracy in the first place? What kinds of lives they must have been living, to risk the treacherous waters of the Impassable Sea to try and make their fortune? You've traveled enough of the country now to understand the true state of it. You were raised in privilege, Vee, same as me. But you do not have to be blinded by it any longer. You can be more than your father's opinions. Give these people a chance to show you who they really are."

Vee's jaw tightens, and I assume she is preparing some fresh insult to explain why these people do not deserve her consideration, much less her respect. But then she blows out a breath, softening the sharp lines of her face. "You might have a point. *Might*. Still, I do know enough about pirates to know they are distrustful of outsiders, and not likely to give up their knowledge of potential treasure without a trade. And we have nothing to trade them. So how do we learn the location of the second piece of the blade?"

"Simple," I say, giving her an arch look. "We drink."

There are plenty of establishments to choose from, but I target the largest and most raucous of them planted right in the middle of the island, towering two stories above its neighbors. The place has no written sign, just an image of a pearl nestled in an oyster shell painted across the entire front of the building. Several windows are open along the front of the building, angled to capture any meager puff of sea wind to cool their interiors, the sounds emanating from them creating a disgusting symphony of the range of humanity. Vee's expression sours as we stop before the building, the front of it littered with empty rum bottles, dozens of boots and filthy silk slippers, and shirts in various stages of deterioration.

"Do they not even employ a cleaning staff?" Vee asks. "I fear for my health just breathing the same air as these people."

I grin, clapping my hand on her shoulder as I've seen other pirates on the island do. "Remember to keep an open mind, friend."

"Friend? Why are you calling me friend?"

I lower my voice. "So we can at least make it past the entrance before someone suspects we are not the highly decorated pirates we have painted ourselves to be. Now look the part. Spit in the road or swear on someone's whore of a mother."

Vee looks horrified. "I would never."

"They're going to make us immediately," I mutter, using my hand on her shoulder to propel her through the saloon doors.

The interior is a riotous mess, the kind of scene I would assume was an all-out brawl were I to encounter it anywhere on the mainland. But here, the fistfights seem to be nothing more than scenery, the teeth littering the floor making tinkling noises as we shuffle through them. Lyra has manifested a leather tricorn hat for me and I make full use of the brim, pulling it low enough that it drops the top half of my face in shadow. I arrange the lower half into the same scowl that sent the pirates outside scurrying and shove my way through the crowd toward the bar situated along the back wall.

The first assault comes from the stench of the place alone, a violent mix of body odor, stale rum breath, and swimming through everything the filth of rotten fish. It only gets worse the farther into the room we push, so thick I have to stop breathing through my nose or risk losing my breakfast. The second assault is aural, the cacophony of music and shouting and fighting pummeling my eardrums until they start to plug themselves, muting everything into chest-thumping white noise. The final assault comes from the visuals of the place itself, a drab collection of tans and browns and grays that I am sure could never have been white. Not to mention the faces of the men themselves—wind-beaten, scarred, lost to the depths of their sea-twisted beards, eyes bloodshot and squinting.

We pass a table of men engrossed in a game of cards, a pile of dented and clipped coins loaded in a heap in the center of the table. Only then do I remember that getting a drink actually costs money, and we gave the rest of ours over to Cliod and Thana as thanks for their hospitality. I bump close to the drunkest-looking man at the table, falling off-balance and catching one hand on the edge of the table.

"Apologies, lads," I say in a low, gruff voice. I hitch a thumb over one shoulder. "This one doesn't know her own wingspan."

They look up at Vee's tall, glowering form and burst out laughing, thumping the rough wood with their fists. Vee turns a bright red, her mouth dropping open as if she is ready to unleash some scathing retort. But I don't give her the opportunity, straightening and taking her firmly by the elbow to redirect our course to the back bar once again.

"What in the starry skies was that about?" she asks, and there's a hitch in her voice. If it weren't for the clamor of the place, I might have sorted her tone into the category of "injured." Still, her mouth is doing this little pout, drawing down to one side. It's . . . adorable. I hate it.

"Relax—we needed coin," I say, holding up the hand I used to brace myself against the table and showing two copper pieces. "He's three sheets to the wind. He'll hardly notice it's missing. I needed a distraction."

"Ah," Vee says, though that pout doesn't disappear. She reaches for the coins, frowning at them. "Where are these even from? I've never seen currency like this."

"Not Novadorian, that's for sure," I say, reaching the bar. I wait for the man beside me to order his drink, then copy his movements with loud efficiency. "Two grog, and be quick about it!"

"Settle your ass, mate," says the man behind the bar, wiry and hassled. But he swipes the coins Vee lays down and replaces them with two pewter mugs of something foamy and brown and thoroughly unappetizing.

We scoop up the mugs, neither of us racing to take a drink despite our deep thirst after rowing to the island and nearly crashing into the rocks, and make our way toward the center of the saloon. There's nothing so much in the way of seating as there are crates or barrels or half-rotted trunks scattered about the place. I'm relieved that there are other women in the saloon, many of them dressed in soft blouses and loose skirts, but at least others adorned in the same colorful pennants that Vee and I wear.

"I thought pirates considered it bad luck to let a woman on their ship," Vee murmurs to me. Well, she probably says it at a normal volume, but it's so loud the words barely reach my ears.

"*Sailors* do," I correct, snatching a turned-over crate and righting it so I can sit. I put my legs far apart, planting them like tree roots, and the unexpected rush of air swirling around my ankles and upward makes me want to clamp my legs back together. But everyone else in here looks like they're braced against the railing of a ship, and I don't want to look out of place.

"Ah, another of your lectures on why we should actually respect them?" Vee asks, using her boot to tump over a drunk sleeping man off a barrel and claim the seat for herself. "I suppose they let women captain their ships as well."

"They do, actually," I say, taking a long sip of the grog and immediately regretting it. It tastes like someone's boot-washing water. For all I know, it might *be* somebody's boot-washing water. I cough my way through it, scowling, and squint through the tears at Vee. "You've never heard tales of Captain Hatchet?"

Vee's eyebrows go up. "You mean the Bloody Hatchet? Butcher of the Androian Seas? Tempest of the Titaraoh Pass? You're telling me the most famous pirate captain trolling the oceans is a *woman*?"

"A damn gorgeous one to boot," says a voice from above us, slamming a tankard on a tabletop just behind us. The curved end of a wicked blade flashes, and the place goes dead quiet. The tip is aimed just below my chin, scratching the delicate flesh of my neck. I look up at the person holding it, catching my breath and feeling the tip cut into my skin.

Glittering green eyes, like smooth sea glass, with black skin and high, flawless cheekbones, hair twisted into braids that hang down to her waist. Her lips are full and red, stained from whatever she was just eating, her waist cinched in tight with a corset fashioned of leather and metal hooks. She is more than gorgeous—she emanates power. Even her teeth are blindingly white, all of them present and organized as if they wouldn't dare to step out of line. She bares them at me; not quite a smile, not quite a growl.

"Captain Hatchet, the Bloody Hatchet, Butcher of the Androian Seas, Tempest of the Titaroah Pass, and your friend here forgot Mistress of Sandtrap Island," the captain says, her eyes cutting to slits. "And you two are trespassing."

TWENTY-THREE

"WHAT DO YOU MEAN, WE'RE TRESPASSING?" VEE sputters, her grog splashing over the side of her mug and staining the knee of her pants. Rather making the pirate captain's point, I think. "We paid our coin, same as every other fi—*man* here."

Captain Hatchet throws her head back and laughs, making me jerk away hastily to avoid a cutlass blade wedged into my jaw. There are several men behind her, flanking her like soldiers—if soldiers carried the curved blades pirates favored and wore the flags of distant nations as decoration.

"Whose coin was it you paid, now?" asks Captain Hatchet, her question aimed at Vee but her gaze holding me accountable. I swallow hard. I suppose that little trick wasn't so clever as I thought.

"We mean no harm here," I say quietly, because I can't quite seem to get my voice to operate at a normal volume. It's no matter, considering you could hear a tooth drop in the silence that Captain Hatchet's appearance has created.

"That remains to be seen," says the captain, her words lush and melodic, like everything she says is halfway to a song. She looks to Vee. "Where's your sword, soldier?"

"Not here," Vee grinds out, glaring at me. I give her a small, help-less shrug.

The captain cocks her head to one side, surveying Vee's hands. "I'd be guessing a broadsword, by the shape of those calluses. A three-pounder? That's awfully heavy for a woman, even one of your size."

I could roast a rabbit on Vee's face right now. "I will have you know I am not just *any* woman, I am a kni—"

"Night walker," I say hastily, the first thing that occurs to me. It was, possibly, the only worse thing I could have said other than just letting Vee admit she was a knight of Novador. I've just told a saloon-ful of pirates that Vee is a prostitute.

The place *explodes* in laughter, right down to the drunk man on the floor that Vee kicked off his barrel. Every single man in the place—and most of the ladies besides—laughs at Vee's expense, and I've never seen the expression that appears on her face. Burning rage and indignation, sure, but underneath it all is a deep insecurity. Shame.

Vee is ashamed that these people—these pirates, whom she looks down on so disdainfully—would laugh at the prospect of her selling her body.

And for some reason, the idea that these men—who I had con-sidered brave in their defiance of the cursed sea and the greedy crown—laughing at anything about Vee makes me want to snatch the cutlass from Captain Hatchet's hand and lay waste to the whole island. I rise to my feet, not sure what I intend to do, but knowing I intend to *do it*. Captain Hatchet holds up a hand, and the place falls immediately silent again.

"If a single one of you speaks ill against her, or so much as coughs impolitely in her direction, I'll put every single one of you in the ground myself," I say, my voice low and vibrating.

Vee startles on her barrel seat, nearly knocking herself over, her expression frozen. Captain Hatchet doesn't flinch at my proclamation, but neither do the pirates give themselves over to another round of laughter. I can't imagine my face right now, but I know the fire stirring in my chest. Whatever it would take, I would see my threat through.

"Well, aren't you two full of surprises," the captain murmurs, tucking away her cutlass and crossing her arms. "But you're trespassing, and we don't take kindly to strangers on our soil. Soil we fought and bled for. This island is our sovereign domain, not meant for your kind."

"What would you know of our kind?" I ask hotly.

Captain Hatchet chuckles. "Oh, I know plenty, princess. Or would-be princess, you look like. Used to softness, used to having your way. But fallen on hard times. I know plenty of that life."

How could she possibly know any of that just by looking at me? My face grows hot, but I don't give any ground. "I said we're not here to cause trouble, and I meant it. We're here for something. A location."

"A location of what?" asks the captain, raising one brow.

"We seek the most cursed spot on the Impassable Sea."

You would have thought I said we sought the hearts of every man on the island on a silver platter with the way the place erupts in noise. Gasps, shouts, roughly whispered conversations. Captain Hatchet ignores all of it, her sea-glass gaze cutting me.

"What would you want with such a place, if it were to exist and actually be found?" she asks.

"That's none of your concern," I say. But I hesitate, because pirates always need something to bargain for. "But if you could lead us to it, we could lift the curse of the Impassable Sea."

"Impossible!" someone shouts from the far corner of the saloon.

"No, she said Impassable," hiccups the drunk man on the floor.

Captain Hatchet rolls her eyes, shoving the man with her boot. "Get up off the floor, Henre, you skunker. Embarrassing yourself."

"Aw, just having a nap," says the man, snorting and rolling over.

"How do you plan to lift a curse that dozens of pirates before you couldn't manage?" Captain Hatchet challenges. "And who's to say we even want the curse lifted? We make our living by pirating, and only the toughest of us are willing to dare the waters of the Impassable Sea. You lift the curse, anyone could try it."

"Exactly," I say. "Anyone could traverse the sea, including merchant vessels that have been too fearful to dare them since the hundred-year storm."

Captain Hatchet glances at the man standing closest to her, a white man with the only neatly trimmed beard in the place. She says a few words in a language I don't speak, but I know it in a passing way, enough to recognize it when it's spoken.

"You're Hundilion," I say to the man.

He grunts in acknowledgment, but speaks to the captain in the same language. She presses her lips together, eyeing first me and then Vee, as if she could see our entire life stories in that single glance. And for all I know, she can; she knew my history well enough after only a look.

"Too risky," Captain Hatchet announces, waving her hand over her shoulder in a signal. The men flanking her step forward menacingly. "Put them down in the caves."

I don't know what's in the caves, but I know from the looks on the faces of the pirates around us that I don't want to find out. "I demand the Rite of Challenge!"

"What would you be knowing of the Rite of Challenge?" asks one of the pirate men advancing on me.

I stand my ground. "I know you have to grant it to anyone who requests it, by your own laws. Even an outsider. And if I win the challenge, you have to grant my request for navigation."

Captain Hatchet lets out a very human, very annoyed groan. "Why did we even make that rule?"

"It was Boemer's idea," one of the men says, looking sideways at a man with sun-darkened skin and an eye patch made of gold.

"It was a good idea!" Boemer squeaks.

"It was a stupid one, and I voted against it," Captain Hatchet retorts. "But the crew overrode me, and now here we are. Some failed princess, putting her challenge to our crew. I'll put you down in the caves myself for this if she wins her challenge, Boemer."

Boemer gives another squeak, like a mouse that's been caught by the tail. I really, very much do not want to find out what is down in those caves. I have to win my challenge. Whatever it turns out to be.

"Fine, set up on the *Windcleaver*," snaps Captain Hatchet, turning her back on us and stomping away. She pauses at the door only long enough to give me a wicked glare. "You've five minutes to prepare yourself. I hope you know what you're after, failed princess."

"As do I," I murmur, though there's no one left to hear it. All the pirates bustle out after their captain, presumably to create whatever torturous challenge awaits me.

"What is the Rite of Challenge?" Vee asks breathlessly.

"An old pirate law, and not a favored one either, apparently," I say. "Anyone can request a challenge, of the pirate crew's choosing, in order to gain a favor with the pirates. They actually have a deep sense of honor. No one has ever been denied a challenge."

"But what is the challenge?" Vee asks.

I blow out a breath, my feet already feeling like lead as I move toward the saloon door. "It can be anything. A sword fight, a race to the crow's nest, a swimming competition. I read of one man who was challenged to stand naked in the center of the island for a full day."

Vee's expression is horrified. "What happened to him?"

"A terrible sunburn is what," I say grimly. "There's no use wondering over it, they choose something new and nefarious each time. I can't possibly prepare."

"Then how can you win?" Vee asks, trailing me out of the saloon. The island has emptied in the short time we've been inside, though I hear plenty of noise over that incessant drumming coming from the docks. No doubt we'll have quite the crowd to witness my challenge.

"I don't know if I can win," I say, stomach churning. "I can only try."

"That's not very reassuring," Vee says.

"No, it isn't, is it?" I sigh. "Well, come on, then. No sense in delaying my doom."

TWENTY-FOUR

I WOULDN'T ADMIT AS MUCH TO VEE, BUT MY CALL for the Rite of Challenge had been more of a stalling tactic than anything else. I'd only read stories of challenges gone horribly wrong—men forced to swim with razor-toothed sea creatures until their skin hung from their bones in tatters, or strung up in a cage in the blistering sun until their skin boiled and peeled from their bones, or buried in a wooden chest deep in the earth until the walls rotted and gave way to the worms and beetles to tear away at their flesh. It was generally a lot of separating flesh from bone. At the time that I read it, I assumed the narratives had been sensationalized to portray pirates as a lawless, morally bereft society. But now, after having walked their island myself, and hearing the whooping cries from the docks, I am not so sure the stories were at all sensationalized.

"*Do* you know what you're doing?" Vee asks as we approach the collection of ships tucked into a large bay on the far side of the island. It seems as if the entire pirate population has turned out to witness my demise. Fantastic.

"What else would you have had me do?" I snap, far too waspishly.

I work to gentle my tone, which is not easy considering the hammering of my heart and the shakiness in my knees. "She was going to throw us in the caves besides. At least this way we have a chance."

"I should be the one to take up the challenge," Vee says, every inch the gallant, if ignorant, knight. "If it is sword fighting they wish for, I shall give them a proper show, regardless of the cut of the blade."

"I told you, sword fighting is only one of their many options," I say. "And they never choose the same challenge twice. For all I know, it could be knot-tying."

"I am well versed in the mariner's loop as well," Vee says.

I grunt in annoyance. "I am not completely useless, Vee. I do have some skill sets to my name, even if they are not of the fighting variety."

"I know that," Vee says, her voice quiet. "It is only . . ."

"Only what?" I snap. "You still don't trust me?"

"No, not at all," Vee says. "It is only that I do not wish to see you come to any harm."

"I . . ." I don't know how to respond to that, but I am saved the effort by an escort of pirates prodding me toward the largest ship in the bay. I have no idea what such a ship would be called—a flagship? A warship?—but it's impressive enough with its thirty or so cannons sticking out the sides, that were I to see her coming on the horizon, I would take my chances swimming with the creatures of the Impassable Sea. Pirates line every bare board, some hanging off the rigging above and crouched on the railings like seabirds. They bare their teeth and jeer as Vee and I pass, but I give them no mind. They are not my problem.

No, my problem is currently standing at the far end of the ship up on a higher deck, feet braced apart and arms resting on a railing overlooking the ship's wheel, braids tossed over one shoulder with a grin that would make the most fearsome Novadorian knight go weak in their prideful parts. I have envisioned all manner of torture devices or feats of prowess on my long walk down to the docks, but all the captain holds is a pewter mug.

I step onto the ship, the wood listing beneath me with the movement of the seawater and the unevenly distributed weight of the pirates occupying the ship. If Captain Hatchet sees me, she pays me no mind, casually lifting her mug to drink and leaving a thin line of white foam along her upper lip. Her second stands beside her, arms crossed over his chest, nodding along as she speaks. The rest of the pirates seem no more hurried than their captain, hanging from the rigging and chewing at wads of something brown.

"What are they doing?" Vee asks in a low, tense voice. "Why has the challenge not begun? Do you think the captain does not realize we have arrived?"

"I doubt the captain does not realize much," I murmur back. "Perhaps this is part of the challenge, waiting."

"Well, it's rude if it is." Vee sniffs. "The least they could do is make our demise timely."

"I politely disagree," I say, but I am perhaps inclined to agree. The longer I stand here, the unsturdier my legs get, and the more my stomach begins to list along with the boat. If my flesh is to be separated from my bones, let it be quick.

But the captain keeps sipping from her mug, infuriatingly sound of leg and stomach, and a steady trickle of sweat works its way from my hairline into my eyes, until they sting and burn and force me to squint. My back itches, two of my toes ache within the boots Lyra conjured for me, and the strong salt of the sea and something rotten make me want to gag. And still the captain sips, and chats, and smiles, with no indication of when she will put me out of my misery. I glance nervously at the assembled pirates, wondering if there is something I've missed, something I should have said or done, to initiate the challenge. I rack my brain for the gory lessons of diplomacy when negotiating with pirate crews that I was subjected to. But nothing comes.

"I'm going to say something," Vee mutters after what feels like hours.

"That's not necessary," I say.

"Why not?"

"Because I'm going to say something first." I take a step forward, clearing my throat of the lump that's suddenly formed there. "Excuse me, Cap—"

The captain holds up a hand to stop me, raising the other to drain her mug and slam it down on the railing. She peers up at the sky, tracking the line of the descending sun, and holds out a hand to her second. He pulls a gun from his belt and puts it in her hand, barrel first.

Vee tenses. "If this is meant as some sort of ambush—"

"Relax, lady knight," says Captain Hatchet, handing off her mug and slapping the side of the gun against her hand, catching a small metal ball as it dislodges from the barrel. "Your companion here requested the Rite of Challenge, and we pirates might be an unsavory lot, but we never go back on our word. We promised you a challenge, and so you shall have one."

She holds up the round metal ball—a bullet, I presume—with a flourish, and a hush falls over the crowd. "Today's challenge for the outsider will be to get this bullet from one side of the ship to the other."

I glance uneasily at the pirates crowding the boat. Are they all meant to attack at once? Drop on me from the rigging above? The ship is quite long, a good hundred feet from end to end, and while I'm not the needlepoint-and-nursing-type female they expect me to be, I'm not so athletic as Vee. Perhaps she was right, and I should have given over the challenge to her. I couldn't possibly fight off all these pirates.

The pirates have been putting on a good show of jeering and hollering at us, but the captain silences them again with a sharp chop of her hand. "As I said, you must get this bullet from one side of the ship to the other. *Without* touching it. It must reach the flag on the far side there in order for you to win the challenge."

"Wait," I say, shaking my head, "what—"

"Ready?" declares Captain Hatchet.

I hold up my hands. "No, wait, I don't under—"

"Good! Go!"

She drops the bullet to the deck before her, the ball bouncing once before settling into a groove and rolling toward the side of the ship. Everyone sucks in a breath as it rolls toward a scupper, an opening where a hole has been cut to drain water when it splashes on the deck. Instinctively, I run toward it and the pirates all crowd forward, the ship rocking with the movement as the ball picks up momentum as it moves toward the opening and the black waters beyond.

"Move back, you idiots!" I shout, flinging an arm toward them, all my attention on the ball. I don't even consider my words, just that pea-size bullet rolling toward my fate. But the ship rocks back as the pirates move to the other side, bringing the ball toward the center of the deck, and I breathe out a loud sigh.

But now the ball is stuck. With the ship balanced, it's at least not rolling out to the water, and I use the moment to take stock of the expanse of the ship's deck. Captain Hatchet has done me a service, I suppose, not starting up on the deck where she still stands. But there's at least another fifty feet to traverse, and the way isn't exactly easy. There are openings cut along the side of the ship every few feet, and the planks that make up the decking run from port to starboard. As if this configuration were not difficult enough to navigate, there's a large grate in the middle of the ship that presumably leads belowdecks, with square holes in it about an inch wide to allow movement of air.

And if I were to make it through that gauntlet, the ship's stern is up another set of stairs, five on each side of the deck, the red flag flapping dully in the sluggish wind barely visible from where I'm standing. I think I might have preferred a sword match or a sunburn. This challenge is tactically impossible.

Except I know that to be untrue as well, because it's another rule of the rite—the task, however impossible it *seems*, must actually be attainable. It might be the most nefarious, physically demanding, mentally breaking challenge, but it's one that's been done by some pirate before. I look back at the deck above me where Captain Hatchet still stands, arms braced on the railing, pewter mug winking in the sunlight. She doesn't watch me, but rather the deck itself, her gaze tracing meandering patterns over the wood.

But the closer I watch her, the more I think they are not, in fact, meandering. If I had a coin to bet, I'd lay it on the odds that Captain Hatchet herself has completed the very challenge she set for me. So she knows it's possible to accomplish, and she doesn't expect me to match her previous success. But I know it can be done, with the right knowledge. I don't have the captain's intimate knowledge of her deck or the movements of her ship, but I have plenty of experience with the well-worn wooden boards of Maester Edgerton's dance studio. I always knew just where the grooves were, how to run my feet through the well-polished tracks, how to find the right spot to make a perfect turn.

I check the ball before moving slowly, carefully around the deck, sweeping my feet along in just such a fashion. My boots don't make it easy to feel with my toes, and after a few fruitless swipes I'm forced to abandon them in favor of bare feet. The pirates whoop and holler like they've never seen a set of naked toes before.

"Quiet!" I snap, glaring at the nearest man with a filthy red rag tied around his neck and a patch of overgrown silvery moss sprouting from his chest. "I need to concentrate, and I cannot do so with your useless whooping and buffoonery."

I begin again, as several of the pirates whisper their guesses at what the word *buffoonery* might mean, my toes prickling as the rough wood of the ship's deck nips at the tender flesh. These boards are a far cry from Maester Edgerton's studio, my bare feet a far cry from the silken slippers I wore there, but the movements are the same. I sweep along each board, looking for the dips and grooves, learning the warp and personality of each one. The boards are rough but sturdy, weather-worn, and sealed tight. It's a beautiful ship, not that I would admit as much to Captain Hatchet. Still, by the time I reach the stairs, I've a new appreciation for her craftsmanship.

I shield my eyes against the sun, glancing up at the deck above, the red flag barely moving now. Getting the ball up the stairs will require more than one of Lyra's parlor tricks, but I'll beg for that wish when it comes to it. First, I have to get it across the lower deck.

I return to where the ball still waits, patiently caught in its groove. I run my toes once in each direction, deciding on the better path, before taking a deep breath. I believe I know the way; now all I need is a start.

"I'd hurry if I were you, failed princess," the captain says in a taunting voice.

I squint up at her. "You said nothing about a time limit to the challenge."

"No, I didn't," Captain Hatchet says, but she grins at me. Like she knows something I don't. She glances toward the sun, still well high in the sky. "But I'd hurry all the same."

"Why?" I ask, perplexed.

Something splashes up from the water, a spray misting over the decks, before it rams into the keel of the ship below the waterline. Two pirates fall backward into the water, screaming, as the bullet is flung into the air in a silvery arc. I stretch my hands out to catch it, a mindless instinct, but it sails clear of my grasp, landing toward the starboard side of the ship and rolling perilously close to one of the scuppers.

"That's why," Captain Hatchet shouts, both hands gripping the railing. "Better get a move on, princess!"

TWENTY-FIVE

"WHAT IN THE STARRY SKIES IS THAT?" I GASP, RACING across the deck toward the bullet. The ship gets rammed again, this time from the other side, sending the bullet careening in the opposite direction.

"We don't know," shouts Captain Hatchet over the frothing of the seawater around us. "But it tries to eat our ship every day at three past the high sun. Good luck!"

Luck is going to have a frightful amount to do with it, as the bullet is now rolling toward the opening that leads to the lower deck of the ship. I run toward it, the boards rocking and swaying, the wood of the hull creaking in protest as something dark and slimy wraps tentacles around it. I'm not sure the ship will survive, much less the rest of us.

I pivot, spotting the largest pirate behind me. "You there! Your name!"

"Me?" he asks, his voice surprisingly soft. "Pete. Er, ma'am."

"Pete, jump!" I command. "Hard as you can. And now, please."

Pete rises off the railing where he's been sitting, head and chest above the other pirates. He jumps as another tentacle slithers up

through a scupper, fat and purple and slick. He lands on the myste-
rious flesh with a sickening squelch, and the boat tips just enough
toward him that the bullet rolls back from the precipice of the opening. But there's no time to breathe a sigh of relief because the action
has enraged the sea creature, the injured tentacle tightening and
cracking the wood beneath it.

"You two," I shout, flinging a hand at two of the older pirates as
my eyes track the bullet's erratic new course. "Fight off that thing
before it sinks us all in the drink!"

"Yes, ma'am!" they both call enthusiastically, drawing their cut-
lasses and giving up a bellyful of a war cry before descending on
the creature.

The bullet rolls through a rut and starts toward the starboard side
of the ship as another tentacle reaches up from the deep, hugging
both sides of the boat. The pirates don't need another command
from me to know what to do, half of them going to battle with the
creature while the other half egg them on. I run ahead of the bullet,
waiting until it reaches a slight depression in the next board, before
doing my own jump and coming down hard before the ball. I might
not have Pete's size advantage or the monster's terrible timing, but
Maester Edgerton was a task-driven instructor. My turns were never
tight enough, my leaps never high enough. By the end of my lessons,
I could clear the back of a horse with enough of a running start.

And it pays off now, because the ball hits the groove and rolls
across the next board, tracking in a small arc along a whorl I found
with my toes. My neck burns and sweat blinds my eyes, but I don't
dare to do more than blink the sting away as I watch the ball's progress. The ship lists and rocks toward the bow, shuddering from the
pressure of the sea creature's enraged attacks as the pirates hack at

its exposed limbs. I reach for the bullet as it slows to a halt before reversing direction and rolling back several feet, undoing all my progress. But the ship lists again, this time toward the stern and the flag—whipping wildly now—and the ball hops along until it rolls into the short flight of steps leading to the decking there.

"Ary, you'll never clear those steps!" Vee cries from the starboard side, where she's grabbed a fallen pirate's sword and joined in the fray.

"By the fey, I will," I mutter, glancing around. More tentacles have engulfed the ship, far more than any deep water creature deserves to have. One flops on the deck beside me, landing wet and heavy on my foot and suctioning to my skin. I make a fist and slam it into the thick, rubbery flesh on instinct, and it reacts by drawing back, rocking the ship along with it and giving me an idea.

"Vee, give me that sword!" I shout, flinging out a hand.

To her credit, Vee crosses the space between us in two long strides and slaps the hilt into my open hand. I step carefully around the bullet, listing crazily along the bottom step of the raised deck, and vault up the stairs to the far end of the boat. I lean as far out as I dare, scanning the black waters below. The surface roils and rolls, throwing off whitecaps of foam that disintegrate along the edge of the boat. I can't see anything below, but I know the creature must be lurking there. At least, I pray it is. I take the sword, raising it in both hands and holding it out over the water, point down. I wait, wait for the creature to register my presence. To react. One great, milky white eye rolls up just under the surface, wide and fathomless and terrifying. I suck in one gusty breath before throwing the sword point down into that eye.

The creature has no mouth to scream, no vocal cords to fill the air with the sound of its rage, but it expresses itself all the same in the explosion of water that erupts as an enormous tentacle rises out of the water, several feet above my head, and slams down on the railing beside me. The ship rocks hard toward the water, nearly dumping me out, before the limb slithers back into the inky waters, taking its wounded eye with it.

"Ary!" Vee shouts, taking the short flight of stairs in one leap. "Aralyn, are you all right?"

"I'm fine." I nod, breathless, though I can't take my eyes off those sinking depths and the murderous creature lurking within them. But then I remember my purpose for being there and whip around to the flag, still gently flapping along with the subsiding movements of the ship. "The bullet! Where is the bullet?"

Vee and I drop to our knees, searching every warped crevice, every splintered inch of the decking. The pirates crowd the stairs and hang over the railing, trying to catch a glimpse, making the ship tilt again. Every panicked thought possible runs through my head as I search for a glint of metal among the dull browns of the ship's decking. Did the sea creature launch the ball into the waters? Could it be lost to the cursed depths below, taking my only chance of winning the challenge along with it? What will the pirates do to me if I've lost? Will they feed me to the enraged creature at tomorrow's three past the high sun?

I crawl along the space where the creature's tentacle grabbed the ship, the boards there thick with a slimy residue that sticks to my hands and blackens the skin there. I sincerely hope it's not permanent. But it has created a swath of boards that are like tree sap, and wedged in the last board of the decking just behind the flag, coated in the substance, is the bullet. My winning challenge. I grab the ball, unmindful of the residue draping like spiderwebs along my pennants and hands, and thrust it over my head with a triumphant bellow.

"By the great sea monster's beard, she did it!" shouts a pirate in my ear, and then there's a great deal of cheering and backslapping with only a minor chord of grumbling by the pirates forking over lost wagers.

"Aralyn, you genius, you did it!" Vee says, snatching me up in a hug. "You won the challenge! I should never have doubted you, I couldn't possibly have resisted the urge to snatch the darn thing up and chuck it across the decks myself. Well played."

"It was rather well played, wasn't it?" I grin, the moment carrying me away.

Captain Hatchet saunters up the short flight of stairs, her lips set firm but her eyes crinkling slightly at the corners. The pirates fall into a hushed reverence at her approach, waiting for the official decree. She lets me twist in the wind once again, her eyes gleaming like sea glass as she observes me. Perhaps I've done something wrong, touching the bullet before she had a chance to observe it. But then those crinkles around her eyes deepen as she gives me a grin, setting loose the pounding of my heart.

"Well done, failed princess," she says, giving me a nod that speaks far louder than the shouted praise of her crew. "You've won your challenge and earned your favor from the pirate crew. Name your prize."

"Take me to the cursed spot," I say, chest heaving as if I've just scaled up the riggings and leaped back down.

Captain Hatchet shakes her head, the beads worked into her braids clinking against each other. "It's your favor to ask, though I hope for your sake you know what you're doing by asking."

"I do," I say with a nod, though I'm not sure whether I mean that I know, or that I hope so, too.

TWENTY-SIX

"WHERE ARE WE GOING?" I ASK, FOLLOWING AFTER Captain Hatchet. She's left the rest of her crew back at the saloon, with drinks for the night on her. They cheer her as their leader, but I suspect her generosity has far more to do with the captain not wanting any of her men to follow us. The drumming has become a background beat to our steps, as much a facet of the island as the huts and ship masts. The sun dips low over the Impassable Sea, the dark bringing a chill edge to the sluggish wind that crosses the island. I wrap my arms around my chest, but it does little to ward off the cold when I suspect it's coming from within as well.

"This *place* you say you seek," says Captain Hatchet, moving down the road that marks the center of the island. "Why do you seek it so badly? Do you know the tales of it?"

I glance at Vee. "Not a thing."

"Exactly," says the captain. "You've never heard of it, because no one's ever returned to tell them. What treasure could be worth your unmaking?"

She turns off the road, weaving through the variously positioned huts and cottages occupied by the pirates of Sandtrap. Some have lights on within, but many lie still and cold, their owners presumably braving the Impassable Sea. Or gone after the Protector's blade and disappeared. The cold has teeth the farther away from the center of the island we travel, scratching along my bare skin and raising abrasions.

"It's not a treasure we seek," Vee says evasively.

Captain Hatchet snorts. "Knights make terrible liars."

Vee turns a deep red, proving the captain's point.

"She's right," I say. "It's not treasure we seek. It's a weapon."

Captain Hatchet tosses a look over her shoulder in surprise. We've passed the last of the cottages, and out here there seems to be nothing more than scrub and rock. The wind blows harder out here, pushing at the cliffs, sweeping the raucous sounds of the tavern and the drumming back toward meager civilization. The captain lights the lantern she's carrying, holding it up to guide our way. "A weapon? What kind of weapon?"

"The kind we hope can save our kingdom from collapse," I say. I'm not sure when I decided to trust the pirate captain, but I extend my truths as one-half of a handshake. Because I need her to return the gesture.

"Novador, you mean," says the captain.

Vee startles. "How do you know where we're from?"

Captain Hatchet gives her a judicious look. "You mean besides your skin color, your accent, and your obvious disgust for our manner of making a living? Nobody sets a foot on my island without me knowing it, and without me knowing everything about them. Why do you think my men left you that longboat to steal in the first place?"

"How could you have possibly known we were coming?" I ask in surprise. "We traveled through the Silent Forest."

Captain Hatchet gives a low whistle. "I figured the two of you were a pair, but the Silent Forest? Not even my men would let a single needle of that cursed place crunch under their boots. We spotted you on the black beaches. Never could figure out where you stole those pennants from, though."

I give a hasty cough. "We're enterprising when we need to be. So, where can we find the location we seek?"

"We're getting there, not-quite-princess," says the captain, turning down a path half-hidden by the tough little trees that dot the island. It's sandy and steep, leading down a set of bluffs we hadn't seen from our approach on the far side of the island. Captain Hatchet saunters down the narrow path as if she has traversed it a thousand times, but Vee and I are far more cautious. It's only wide enough for one person to walk at one time, no doubt designed that way to prevent invading ships from making a full assault from this direction. The rocks below are sharp, the waves throwing themselves against their harsh surfaces and exploding in foam and spray that coats our skin the lower down we get. There's something wrong with the water here, like it's too heavy and viscous. A large droplet lands on my shoulder with a sting, and as I swipe at it, I realize there was something trapped in that droplet. Something that bit me. The spot swells red and angry, and I pull my collar up to protect from any other such landings.

"Where were you before?" Captain Hatchet tosses over her shoulder at me as the path cuts a sharp switchback, the slick bottoms of my boots skidding and sending a spray of rocks over the edge. Vee catches my arm from behind, steadying me. Captain Hatchet's gaze lingers on Vee's hand at my elbow, her lips pursing.

"What do you mean, before?" I ask, the exchange making me feel odd. When Vee pulls her hand back, it feels like a rebuke.

"The Silent Forest," says the captain, turning away and continuing down as if nothing happened. "Where did you come from that you would risk such a journey? No one has traveled that route for as long as we've run Sandtrap Island."

"It wasn't as if we had much choice, and I wouldn't do it again," I say flatly. "We were traveling from the Mortel Mountains, and we couldn't risk the extra travel time going around the forest."

"The Mortel Mountains? Are the two of you on some kind of cursed excursion?"

"It does seem that way, when you say it out loud," Vee murmurs.

"Well, then, you've come to the right island," says Captain Hatchet as we reach the end of the path. There is a cave, carved out of the side of the cliff, tall and yawning and terribly forbidding. Black water rushes into the lower end of the mouth, the entrance devouring any sign of the dying rays of sunlight.

"What is this?" Vee asks, alarmed. She reaches for her hip before remembering that she's had to leave her sword behind. Still, she presses forward, shoving me behind her protectively, squaring off with the pirate captain. "If this is some kind of trick to rid yourself of us, I'll not allow it. We're not going in that cave."

"*You're* not," Captain Hatchet concedes, before nodding her head in my direction. "She is. Only one of you won the challenge, only one of you can enter the cave."

"Absolutely not," Vee says, her voice fierce.

But my gaze is drawn to the entrance. "What's in there?"

"Aralyn, you can't," Vee says.

Captain Hatchet shrugs. "No one knows. Nobody's ever returned from the depths to tell. But sometimes at night, the men, they hear a song coming from down there. Begging them to come, to seek their fortune. Too many fell prey to it. That's why we play the drums topside, to keep the song out of their ears."

Now that she's spoken of the song, I can't believe I didn't hear it before. Between the crashing of the waves and the loud beating of my own heart, I'd pushed it to the back of mind. But standing down here at the cave entrance, a high, sweet song echoes out to us. It's sad but hopeful, alluring in its promise of . . . what, I don't know. But it's strong enough that I've taken several steps toward it before I realize my feet have even moved.

"Aralyn!" Vee says sharply. She glances at the captain, moving toward me and lowering her voice. "The song is different, but the pull is the same."

I nod, catching her meaning immediately. The voices on the Mortel Mountain, the madness. I can feel the song in my mind, same as the mountain.

"It's here," I whisper. "The next piece. It must be in there."

Vee eyes the entrance warily. "Sure, but with what else?"

"You two gonna stand there and whisper all day, or you gonna go find this weapon you're seeking?" says Captain Hatchet, breaking us apart. Her expression is as hard as ever, but there's a slight tick near her jaw that betrays her. She doesn't like being down here. She gives Vee a warning look. "Only the winner."

"I don't care what she says, I'm going with you," Vee says in a low voice to me. "We only survived the mountain because we stuck together."

But that's not really true. We survived as long as we did by sticking together, but it wasn't me who made it to the summit and retrieved the blade. I failed then, but I won't fail here, now. I won the challenge, and I'll find the next piece of the Protector's blade.

"I can do this, Vee," I say, quietly but firmly. I take her hand, squeezing it as a promise. "Trust me. I'll get the next piece. I won't fail."

"I do trust you," Vee says, even though she's frowning. "But this is the Protector's weapon we're talking about. We know what it can do, when it doesn't want to be found."

"I know, but we didn't find the blade. *You* found the blade. Let me do this."

Vee sighs, squeezing my hand before stepping back. "If you need me, just shout. I won't leave until you return."

"If she returns," Captain Hatchet mutters.

Vee glares at her. "*When* you return. Be safe, Aralyn."

I nod, because I'm worried if I speak the tremble in my voice will betray me. Captain Hatchet holds up her lantern, passing it off to me.

"For all the good it will do you," she says solemnly, "good luck, not-quite-princess."

"Thank you," I say, taking the lantern and facing off with the cave.

The opening is shaped like a bowl, capturing all the roaring of the crashing waves on the rocks and drumming against my ears as I advance into the entrance. Captain Hatchet is right; the lantern she's given me does little to cut through the darkness, the walls arching up and away far overhead, but I can at least see the pebbly path that leads deeper into the cave. The way is easy enough, and it's not long until Vee and the captain are no more than distant figures behind me, swallowed by the breadth of the cave.

The entrance gives way to another chamber lower down, the path growing steep and slick with the waters rushing in from the Impassable Sea. I do my best to avoid stepping in the accumulated puddles, remembering the water droplet on my shoulder that still throbs. In the lower chamber, the rush of the sea gives way to the song, a crystalline lure that barely cuts as it sinks its hook in, tugging me farther down into the depths of the cave.

The call of the mountain had been cold, devoid of life, hopeless; but the cave is the opposite, bright and hopeful, like listening to the clink of a glittering chandelier at the greatest ball of your life. It wraps me in its warmth, warding off the chill of the cave. Always drawing me forward, down, toward its call.

Come seek your fortune, brave sailor.

Give yourself to its thrall.

Let go the trappings of your mortal self.

And follow my siren's call.

The song is so lovely, so engrossing, that I've nearly stepped off a ledge before I realize it. I gasp, flailing my arms backward, dropping hard on my backside, my feet dangling over the edge. My lantern doesn't fare as well, smashing against the ground some twenty or thirty feet below, the flame catching on something and flaring brightly. It illuminates the gruesome, half-rotted features of a sailor who made the same mistake as me and had broken his bones against the ground. It's the tattered remnants of his shirt that have caught fire, and soon his body is engulfed in the flames, the brightness revealing a collection of rocks to my right that will allow me to climb down to the next chamber safely.

I make the descent, careful of my foot placement, though I slip several times as the song becomes so distracting that I miss my footing. I crash to the bottom, my ankle smarting from the impact, but at least I've made it. Which is more than I can say for my incendiary friend.

Now I know the secret of the cave—the siren's call that lures sailors to their doom. But I have no lantern to light the hidden dangers, no Vee to keep me distracted from the song, and no way to know if the cave is leading me to the second piece of the Protector's blade or to my own certain doom.

"Well, plunkers," I mutter.

TWENTY-SEVEN

WITHOUT THE VAGUE SHAPE OF THE CAVERN IN THE lantern's light to guide me, the song quickly fills my mind. It sings of nothing and everything, of the longing that comes from a life on the sea—longing for land when there's nothing but water for miles around; longing for the water when you're drowning on so much land. The longing of missing your loved ones' faces after months or years at sea. The longing for treasure, for a way to make your name as a nobody. The longing to become somebody. I don't realize I'm crying until the tears drop on my collarbone.

I wonder how many men have been lost down here. Called by the siren, trapped in the dark, smashed against the unforgiving stones. Did they have someone waiting on a distant shore, wrapped in wool, possibly holding a small hand or nursing a mewling infant, watching the horizon for a ship that will never appear? There was no such person awaiting me if I failed. Though, the moment I think it, Vee's face appears in my mind. Vee, returning from the Mortel Mountains with the Protector's blade in hand. Vee, using that same blade to slash at the roots of the trees in the Silent Forest, diving into the frigid waters to save me. Vee, her cheeks pink and her gaze cutting away from mine. Would she miss me, if I never returned? I know she would, and it's that reminder that allows me to move again, to probe deeper into the far reaches of the cave.

Just as I did on the deck of the pirate ship, I use Maester Edgerton's training to feel my way through the cave. I slide my feet forward, checking for impediments or drop-offs, sweeping my hands in an arc around me to make sure the way is clear overhead. It's slow, torturous going, but it keeps me alive.

The song shifts the deeper into the caves I go, plucking strings from my own memory, latching on to the loneliness that has pervaded my entire existence. The loneliness of living everywhere and belonging nowhere. The brilliant, blinding spots of Mother's love and attention followed by months or years of neglect and the cruel wooden spoon of the potter's wife. My mother shunning the village girls as friends, always believing us above their station. And the village girls shunning us in turn, knowing how my mother could afford the dresses and jewels she wore. It was always, only, ever Mother, Divya, and me. But even then, it was pieces. Fragments of Mother's attention, slivers of Divya's neediness between tantrums. Crumbs of love, just enough to keep me from starving.

What would I have done, if I had been allowed to make friends? If Mother had not sent away the serving girl who asked me how I could love such a monster? What could it have meant to me, to have mattered to someone else? To have been wanted for more than a few weeks, for more than what I could do for someone?

The song shifts again, prodding these wounds I'd thought long healed over. I think of the serving girl again. Mariana. I'd forgotten her name, but the thought of it brings a pang of something. Sadness, or loss, or . . . guilt. I'd told myself that Mother sent her away because she dared to question Mother's methods. But there is another memory, older, buried far deeper. Mariana, her fingers cold, her nails half-moons of black from sweeping out the hearths in the manor. Those fingers slipping between mine, closing tight around them. Mother, finding us huddled together in the coach house. Mariana's hand on my cheek.

No, no, *no*. It had been a misunderstanding. Mariana had taken advantage of my youth and ignorance, Mother said. *We must always be careful of those who would wish to take advantage of us*, she'd said. That was why she'd been dismissed. For confusing me. Misguiding me.

But Mother hadn't seen that I had reached for Mariana's hand first.

The song is nearly unbearable now, pressing on my chest in great sobs, echoing around the cave walls until I can no longer tell which direction I've come from and which direction I've just left. I never tried to find her, Mariana. Never even asked Mother where she'd been sent. It was better that way, I had believed. I was meant to be a queen, and she was meant to sweep someone else's hearth. It never could have been a friendship. Never could have been anything else.

But there, again, is Vee, crowding my thoughts. Calling me by name on the mountainside, saving me from insanity. Vee, no doubt pacing the entrance to this very cave, barely held in check by Captain Hatchet. If I fail, she'll come after me. It's a comfort, but it's also a drive. I don't want her lost down here either, throwing herself on the mercy of the rocks.

I forge ahead, one sweep of my foot at a time, doing my best to stay oriented. It's impossible to tell where I am in the complete dark, but there is a constant rushing sound humming beneath the siren's song. The water of the Impassable Sea, pouring in from the mouth of the cave, following its own trail down into its depths. If I follow the water, I'll find where it collects in the heart of the cave.

The water, when I find it, is frigid—far too cold for an ocean. My fingers instinctively curl away from it as I dip my hand into its rushing passage. I remember the single drop that landed on my shoulder and keep clear of the water's depths, tracking along beside it instead. The loud, burbling chatter of the water at least distracts me from the siren's song.

I don't know how long I follow its downward path, listening for when it turns quiet and when it grows loud, the rushing alerting me to any approaching drops into lower chambers. Several times I lose my footing and splash into the waters, and once something slick and strong wraps around my ankle, tugging me waist-deep into the waters. I kick at it with my heel, jerking my ankle free and scrambling back onto dry land. My skin stings where the thing touched me, like icy fire.

I lose all sense of direction, all sense of time, only the rush of the waters and the siren's song leaving me any sense of direction. The song is so loud now that it vibrates in the back of my teeth, amplified through the natural curves of the cave. I must be close now, because if the sound gets any louder it will blow out my ears.

I don't realize it's getting lighter in the caves until I come to another steep drop, the water of the Impassable Sea shooting over the edge and pounding the surface several hundred feet below. I peer over the edge, wondering how I'll find a way down, when I spot something gold and glowing down in the waters.

La Sirena.

She is gorgeous, like the figurehead of a ship come to life, her hair flowing through the water like silk, her face fine and unblemished. Her body glimmers with golden scales, shifting and changing colors as she twists and turns through the pool below. Her throat vibrates as she sings her song, filling the cave below, the water shimmering around her in a cloud. My eyes fill with tears once again, overcome at the sight of her.

My gaze is so riveted to her that at first I don't notice the shores that surround the pool where she swims, their rock edges lost to the far edges of her glowing form. It's only when she makes a large circle around the pool that her light reflects off the lengths of white kindling gathered in high piles all around. Bonfires, perhaps, or driftwood caught in the sweep of the waters. But their shapes are too smooth, the ends knobbly and round.

Not driftwood. Bones. Piles and piles of them, collected around the edges, some broken and jagged, some still in the shape of the men who used to walk with them. Hundreds, thousands, an untold number of bones. Untold number of pirates who had lost their lives along La Sirena's shores.

I gasp, and the song stops immediately as the creature twists to gaze up at me. I scramble back, but it's too late. She's seen me, and now the sound is twice as loud, like a hook through my lip, dragging me back toward the edge. The waters swell and rise in waves, splashing up over the edge of rocks, landing on my skirts and soaking my feet, as if the sea itself responds to the creature's beck and call. I can't get away from it fast enough as another wave washes over me, dragging me into its current, throwing me over the edge down into the pool below.

I can't breathe, the water is so cold. I could sink forever and never find the bottom, but the blackness of the water gives way to the golden glow of the siren. There she is, nearly nose to nose with me, golden and glowing and smiling. Maybe I was wrong. Maybe she was not the cause of these men's doom; maybe she was misunderstood, same as me. She puts her hands to my cheek, colder than the water. She smiles. I smile in return.

Her tail wraps around my knees, crushing the joints together, immobilizing me as she shoots down into the depths of the pool. I am dragged down, down, down, down, down with her, too fast to even notice the pressure in my head, on my chest, in my lungs, begging to breathe. My arms fly over my head, the force of the water keeping me from even trying to beat at the creature. Not that it would do me any good. She is too strong—far stronger than I am—and we are too far from the surface for me to gather any more breath. This must be how she collects her bones, I think, as the blackness of the water invades my lungs.

There's something else, another glow, and I can make out the rocky enclosure of this deep well in its light. It eclipses the siren's glow, growing brighter and brighter until I can see every bubble escaping my nose, the last tiny gasps of air. We've slowed enough that I can look below us, down to the depths of the well, where the source of the light lies half-buried in the sandy bottom. A golden hilt, decorated in stunningly clear jewels, glowing with magic from another realm.

The second piece of the Protector's blade.

TWENTY-EIGHT

The siren drags me all the way down, wrapping her tail around my legs several times more. When she opens her mouth, her jaw is far too large, her teeth long and sharp and narrow. The delicate gills on her neck and chest flare open, and without thinking I shove my fingers into those dark gaps as hard as I can.

She screams, the force of it propelling me out of her grasp and against the rocks of the well wall. Whatever last emergency reserve of air remained in my lungs is knocked out entirely by the blow, and I suck in mouthfuls of the wickedly cold water, my body sluggish and frozen. I cannot speak, but my mouth still moves, forming a name. A plea.

A slight pressure, a pop, and then the water is churning and the sands from the bottom swirl upward as Lyra manifests in a storm of flapping arms and kicking feet. She looks at me in surprise, her silvered gaze darting toward the creature before she disappears again. I don't even have time to be surprised by her abandonment before she reappears, this time in a slightly different form, her hands and feet laced with delicate webs and her neck lined in thick ridges that open and close in a rhythm, pulling air from the water.

I wave my hands at her, the pressure overwhelming, desperately mouthing the words over and over in the hopes that she might understand me. Her gaze darts over me, shaking her head, until I am reduced to a single word.

Air! I mouth, lungs filling with water.

Lyra's expression lights up and she brings her hands together, gathering all the bubbles moving through the water until she holds a patch of air the size of her face between her palms. She presses it toward me, and for a moment the bubble breaks over me, giving me the burst of air I need in one noisy gasp.

I only get a single lungful in before the creature barrels into Lyra, driving her toward me and smashing my salvation into thousands of tiny, useless bubbles. The water is a mess now, murky from the sands and the frothing waves as Lyra twists and sets her webbed feet against the rock beside my head, her legs bunching into a powerful thrust as she shoots toward the siren, catching the creature in the chest and driving it back several feet. I can't breathe, the single gulp of air already burning in my lungs, but at least the siren is distracted by Lyra. Which leaves me free to dive for the Protector's hilt.

The sand makes it impossible to see anything, the water burning my eyes as I squint and try to keep them open. But the glow of the hilt is unmistakable, like a lighthouse fire burning in the midst of a maelstrom. I kick my way toward it, swatting at the water as if that might clear away the tiny particles obscuring my view. Lyra and the siren roil about in the enclosed space, knocking into me and driving up more sand, hiding the hilt from me once again.

"Lyra!" I shout, the silty water flooding in and lacerating my throat. "Air!"

"Busy!" she bubbles back, but she manages to capture the siren between her legs long enough to form another bubble, small and less stable, shoving it through the water toward me. It's half a breath, maybe less, but it's enough to keep the darkness from the edge of my vision. The siren screams, the rock walls vibrating and dropping stones the size of my fist down on us. The force of the call knocks Lyra back, and the siren twists toward me in the water.

I press back against the rock wall, bringing my feet up as Lyra did, waiting until the siren has launched herself at me to shove my feet off the rock wall. She smashes into the side where I just was and I dive beneath her, straight down toward the bottom of the well. I don't imagine I can swim at one tenth the speed of the creature, but still I make it no more than a single stroke before she has me by the knees again, her tail tightening until I am afraid she's broken something. I scream, the ordinary scream of an ordinary mortal, nothing more than a flurry of bubbles before my face.

But Lyra is back, shoving another air pocket in my face while she drives her fist into the siren's stomach. The creature loosens its tail enough that I can pull one leg free, the other burning in agony when I try to flex it. I can't swim now.

I grab on to Lyra's arm, pointing frantically down somewhere in the blind depths where the hilt awaits. She nods once, kicking her powerful legs and propelling both of us downward. The creature claws at my leg, adding to the burning agony, but it's no matter now. With Lyra's manifestation, we cut through the water as quick as any fish, and soon the spot of gold among the blackness alerts us to the hilt's location. Lyra kicks again, harder, and I reach one hand out toward that jeweled wink of light.

My fingers brush the cold, hard metal when Lyra is pulled back sharply, her arm wrenched from my grasp. I kick once on instinct, the pain of the effort blanking out any other sensation. If I never breathe again, at least I won't have to experience this agony anymore. But my hand brushes the metal once more, and I do not waste my chance. I close my fist tight around it, setting my good leg into the sand and pushing upward with everything I have. The hilt breaks free of the bottom, the light blinding up close.

The siren screams again, shredding my ears, cracking the rocks around us apart. The sand shifts beneath my foot, and then suddenly it's just . . . gone. The rocks pelt down on us as the world turns upside down, the sand slipping away from below as the rocks pile up from above. I can't even tell which way to move anymore, if there were anywhere to go, and then the water is pulling at my boots, dragging me down. I thought we had reached the bottom of the well, but now the water is pulling me hard somewhere else. I tumble around, head over feet, knee crashing into the walls and knocking me unconscious.

Pain is a powerful motivator, though, and when I recover my senses my knee is on fire, like someone had taken a hatchet to it, over and over. I'm moving, though, and moving fast. It takes a moment to make sense of the chaotic rush around me, but dimly I catch sight of a set of gills, opening and closing in a steady, powerful rhythm. Purple skin, the edge of a pointed ear. I lose consciousness again.

Something presses on my chest, hard and firm, a distant voice giving frantic instructions. I don't speak that language, though—or perhaps I don't speak any language at all. Words feel like a tenuous concept at best, down in the murky depths where I am. That pressure on my chest, again, and then a rushing sensation.

Water comes gushing out of my mouth, twisting from my stomach in powerful heaves as I curl to one side. I'm not in the well anymore. I'm not anywhere. At least, not anywhere I know. Everything is deep blue and black, the ground gritty under my cheek as I vomit more of the black waters of the sea, the air cool and gentle against my chin. My hand is cramping, fingers locked tight around something, and when I'm finally able to open my eyes and blink away the tears, it's there in my hand. I did it.

I found the second piece of the blade.

TWENTY-NINE

LYRA HAS TO FASHION A BANDAGE FOR MY KNEE OUT of pieces of driftwood and strips of my skirt, but she promises me nothing is actually broken. Just very badly bruised. It already feels the size of a sun melon, looks the color of the royal robes of mourning, and hurts like a thousand stab wounds whenever I put the slightest bit of pressure on it. I sling one arm over Lyra's shoulder and let her bear the brunt of my weight as we hobble our way up the shore from where the well spit us out, back to the entrance of the cave.

The sun rises as we climb, and I'm shocked to realize I've been in those caves all night. It felt both eternal and momentary, but as the tension of the battle with the siren leaches away, it leaves a bone-deep weariness that makes my shoulders hang low and my feet drag through the sands. Lyra grunts, shifting her weight beneath my arm.

"I've carried two-hundred-pound sacks of potatoes that gave me less trouble than you right now," she grunts.

"But I'll bet they weren't half so charming," I say, my words slightly slurred.

Lyra looks at me in surprise. "That goran must have given you a right good thump on the head."

"What is a goran?" I ask, frowning.

"A goran? You don't know what a goran is?"

I roll my eyes, reminding myself that she did, at least, save my life down there. "No, Lyra, I don't know what a goran is. Could you tell me, please?"

"Oh, right, well. Not used to someone asking for *my* expertise, unless they can't get their rolls to rise right."

"The goran?" I prompt.

"The goran, yes. A goran is a magical projection of an enchanted object, created as a sort of safeguard. Like an eternal sentry."

"The siren . . . that thing down there was . . . what? From the hilt itself?"

Lyra nods. "Sort of like the madness on the mountain, if you will. A way to keep treasure seekers and enterprising types away from it."

"It wasn't enough that he created a hundred-year storm and cursed all the waters of the sea around it?" I ask dryly. "It also needed this magical guard to keep anyone from finding the hilt?"

"Not anyone," Lyra huffs, adjusting my weight once again. "Just the wrong ones."

"But that's . . ." My ears are certainly still clogged with seawater, because it almost sounds as if Lyra has called me one of the *right* ones. If only by default. "Are you saying I was meant to find this hilt?"

Lyra shrugs. "I don't know. As I said, we don't speak much of the time of the Protector. But it's obvious enough that Kaung went to great lengths to make sure the pieces of his blade were kept well away from any normal mortal grasp. The fact that you were not only able to locate two pieces of it, but collect them for yourselves? Extraordinary."

"No one has ever called me extraordinary," I murmur.

Lyra looks to me in surprise, pausing to rest both of us on a large rock outcropping. "Really? My mother tells me I'm extraordinary every morning with my porridge and figs. Does your mother not do the same?"

I huff a laugh that rattles everything painfully. "Only if it's followed by something like *disappointment* or *inept*. She once told me my Ballorean waltz was passable, which was her way of saying extraordinary, I suppose."

Lyra shakes her head. "I don't understand the way of you humans."

"I don't think she is as a mother should be," I say quietly, slowly. "She never meant to be one, certainly. She made sure we knew it. As if *we* chose to come into this world."

"Oh, my mother didn't choose me, either," Lyra says offhand. "Fairy manifestations are spontaneous. Never know when a new little fey will just *pop* into the realm. Can't say I've been much of a blessing, either. Imagine, the queen of the court manifesting a halfling who can barely dig a hole, much less move a mountain. But she says a queen's worth is not in her power, but in her people. Lead them well, treat them well. Care for them and they will care for you."

"My mother told me a queen's job is to keep her subjects in line," I say.

"Your mother sounds a most unpleasant sort, if you don't take offense to my saying so," Lyra says.

"She wasn't always like this," I say, defensive. "When we were very small, she was like a third playmate. Taking us on picnics, dressing us up like dolls, throwing elaborate tea parties. It was all fun, all the time. Mother was good at fun. But the older we got, the greater a burden we were. Divya was born early and had poor lungs and was forever bringing home every sickness. And I grew too fast, always needing new dresses and shoes. Tearing holes in my stockings because my knees had grown too knobby. No one wants a seven-year-old and a five-year-old at their feasts. By the time she married Ci— Ellarose's father, we were destitute. He was meant to be our salvation, all of us, but he grew ill in their first year of marriage. The estate suffered for it. And then Mother had three children, a failing manor, and a year of isolation in mourning. I think it broke her. She was never the same after. She became obsessed with making me queen. Something that would mean she never had to scrabble ever again."

"That's a great burden to place on you," Lyra says, and I know she means it to be supportive. But it rankles, because she's right. It was a terrible, unbearable burden. One I never complained about, not once. But I was never asked what I wanted, who I wanted to be.

But I have a choice now, don't I?

"We'll have to part ways here," I say, wincing as I rise from the rock. I squint at the cliff above, spotting the lip of the cave entrance. Captain Hatchet and Vee wait there, the latter pacing and shaking her head furiously, the former half-asleep against a rock wall. "We can't let the captain see you. If she thinks I've had help retrieving the hilt, she might consider that a breach of the terms of the Rite of Challenge."

Lyra eyes my knee with concern. "Are you sure you can make it up there?"

"Not even a little bit," I say. "But I can't shout for them to come and get me with you still here."

"Ah, got it." Lyra carefully unwinds my arm from around her shoulder, helping me rest against a rock before stepping back. She still eyes me with concern. "Are you sure you don't need my help anymore? My roast has already burned back at court, I'm sure of it. There'll be smoke everywhere, they'll have to call in the water fairies to deal with it. They won't need me."

"I'm sure," I say. "Lyra. I couldn't have retrieved the Protector's hilt without you. Thank you for your help. And sorry. About your roast."

"Oh," Lyra says, her silver eyes round and wide. "I don't think I've ever been a help to anyone before. I was surprised you called for me, after that 'boat nearly crashing into the rocks' business. I figured you . . . I figured you didn't need a fairy godmother."

"I figured as much myself, once upon a time," I say, tucking the hilt into my belt so I can better grip the rocks. "But I figured wrong."

Lyra breaks out in a grin that shows all her needle-sharp teeth, oddly reminiscent of the siren down in the caves. Amazing that I didn't notice the similarity before. Of course it was fey-crafted. The Protector had created the goran in the likeness of his own kind. Lyra disappears with a pop, and I take a moment to gaze over the waves before gathering my strength to make the final ascent to the cave entrance above.

The sun sits low on the horizon, staining the sky a variety of oranges and reds and golds. It could just be my vantage point down here, but the water seems brighter this morning, sparkling and blue with tidy whitecaps forming across the top of the incoming waves. Even the air smells fresher, like salt and wind and opportunity. Standing here, with my face raised to the sea winds and my eyes closed, letting the sun kiss my cheeks, I can imagine why someone would trust their life to the wooden boards of a ship's deck.

"Aralyn!" Vee cries from above me, shattering the stillness of the morning. I open my eyes and lift my gaze, and there she is, already leaping down the rocks without bothering to check whether or not her landings are safe. She crashes to the dirt before me and takes me by the shoulders, her green eyes searching every cut and scrape across my face.

"You are alive," she says, and the words are an agony.

I soothe them with a smile. "Yes, I am. And I come bearing gifts."

I pull the Protector's hilt from my belt and raise it with a grin, laughter bubbling up out of me at the sheer ludicrous nature of the situation. Vee doesn't even bother with the hilt, just drags me forward and hugs me so tight my ribs creak. I don't complain.

"You were gone the entire night," Vee says. "I imagined the worst possible things. I tried to go after you so many times, but Hatchet caught me every time."

"I was busy," I say, prodding her stomach with one edge of the hilt. I can't keep the foolish grin off my face. "I made it back, though. I succeeded, Vee. I found the second piece of the blade."

"It's exquisite," Vee says, sparks of gold reflecting in her gaze as she surveys it. "Wait until Lyra sees it."

"Oh, she has," I say, but then Captain Hatchet is there behind Vee, her gaze filled with the sight of the Protector's blade. Her feet land silently, but to Vee's credit she's spun and faced the pirate captain with the blade gripped in both hands, their steps wary as they circle each other.

"So, you found it, did you?" Captain Hatchet says in a soft, curious voice. But it belies the hunger in her gaze. "The curse of the Impassable Sea."

"Not impassable any longer," I say, sweeping an arm out to the crystalline waters below. "The curse is lifted, Captain Hatchet. Your men no longer need to fear the sea."

"Spoken like a landlubber," Captain Hatchet says, lifting a brow at me. "Do you know how many men have given their lives in search of what you hold in your hands there? How many of *my* men disappeared hunting after it? Do you know what a thing like that would be worth to the proper buyers?"

"Don't even think about it," Vee growls, her grip on the hilt tightening. "Aralyn won the challenge. It's ours by rights."

Captain Hatchet scoffs. "And what would you know about using it? Huh? In my hands, a piece like that could make my career. It could feed my men and their families for life. It could turn this island from a scrubby little outpost into a damn fortress. Your Novadorian soldiers would never cut us down or burn us out again."

"You have no idea what that blade can do, or where it's from," I say quietly. "You think of what it can do *for* your men. You should consider what it can do *to* your men. I believe you're a good captain, Hatchet. And a fair one. You gave me the Rite of Challenge when you could have thrown me to the mercy of the sea. You care for your crew, and you would never intentionally see harm done to them. And now you never will. The curse of the siren is gone, and the seas are sailable once again. Make your fortunes out there. Let us go."

Captain Hatchet's gaze is shrewd, calculating. She knows I speak true, but I know there are a dozen things I haven't said. We need her to let us off this island, and we'll never make it to land if she decides she doesn't want us to. We square off in tense silence, Vee braced for battle, me angling for peace, Captain Hatchet running the risks and rewards in her mind. I can only wait, begging her to do the right thing for all of us.

"Get yourselves gone before the sun leaves the water's edge," she says, still watching the sword, her body tightly wound. "And don't let my men see you, besides. One look at that blade, and I won't be able to hold them back."

Vee carefully tucks the blade into the holder she's fashioned across her shoulder, adjusting the collar of her shirt so it mostly covers the jeweled hilt. "We'll be gone by the time you make it back to the mainland. Set your men in pursuit of us, and I'll be forced to cut them down."

"I've no doubt you would," says Captain Hatchet, her tone straightforward. "Be careful once you reach the land, though, girls. There's plenty greater dangers than me and my kind between here and your capital."

"We're prepared to face them," I say, hobbling toward Vee and taking her proffered arm for support. My knee is a wretched agony, but I don't let it show on my face. Vee's grip on my arm is strong and sure, and I realize I expected it to be no less.

"Captain Hatchet," I say as she prepares to climb back up the rocks. "If you ever find yourself on land long enough to make it to the Novadorian capital, I promise the queen will have a special dispensation for you and your men to sail the Impassable Sea unmolested. You'll only have to promise to leave Novadorian vessels be."

"Leave all that treasure to the Novadorians?" Captain Hatchet calls back from above, tossing me another raised eyebrow. "What kind of pirate captain would that make me?"

I smile and nod in concession. "Fair point. Good luck to you on whatever your future journeys may be, Captain."

"And to you two as well," the captain says, pulling on the edge of her leather tricorn. She lets her gaze drift out to the sea, the sun dusting her skin in gold. "Time's almost up, failed princess. Better get a move on."

"Aye, aye, Captain," I say, leading Vee in the opposite direction toward where we left our stolen longboat only just a day before.

"Odds that she won't send her crew to hunt us down?" Vee mutters as she helps me hobble along.

"Let's not stick around and find out they aren't in our favor," I mutter back.

THIRTY

IT TURNS OUT, ALL THE MOTIVATION WE NEED TO row the short expanse of sea between Sandtrap Island and the main shore is the potential threat of a horde of pirates chasing us down. Vee works double time despite her fatigue, the longboat fairly skipping over the water's surface as she pulls hard around the island to retrieve her sword and the Protector's blade before steering us toward the shore. It helps that whatever creatures haunted the waters have retreated to the depths, leaving the deep blue waters blissfully tentacle-free.

"You would think they would be grateful," Vee huffs, dipping her oars in and shooting us forward several feet. "You ended the curse of the Impassable Sea. No more siren to lure them to their death in the caves. No more raging storms. Clear sailing for all ships."

"I think that might be what they object to," I say wryly from my position at the far end of the boat where I huddle with the Protector's blade, unable to row due to the strain on my knee. I've had to prop it up on the seat, as it won't even bend anymore. "They've learned how to navigate the treacherous waters and bring back black-market goods. With the curse lifted, nations can resume trade for them-selves, putting the pirates out of business."

"I hadn't considered that," Vee concedes. She frowns before putting her oars in the water and pulling even harder. "In that case, we'd better hurry."

"Yes, I think we'd better," I say, gazing behind me toward the island. There doesn't seem to be much movement yet, but the sun has nearly left the horizon and taken our head start along with it. "I don't believe I trust Captain Hatchet to let such a treasure slip out of her grasp without at least trying to retrieve it."

"I don't trust her to take a breath unless it's stolen from someone else's lungs," Vee says. She tilts her head to the side thoughtfully. "Although she did respect the Rite of Challenge, which showed more honor than I would have guessed any of those pirates possessed."

"I meant what I told her, Vee," I say, turning to face her again. "I intend to ask Cind . . . Princess Ellarose to grant the pirates of Sandtrap Island special dispensation to sail the waters and join the trade. It's the least they deserve, and they know these waters better than any Novadorian sailor by now."

Vee raises her brows skeptically at me, but she puts her oars in the water and pulls hard. We reach the shore, the lurch of the bottom of the longboat hitting shallow sand, knocking my head against the back of the boat. Vee leaps out and drags it the rest of the way, putting it behind a high dune and using her boot to sweep away the evidence of our landing. I can barely walk now, but Vee simply ducks under my arm and puts hers behind my back, half carrying me along as we search for our horses.

"I see why you became a knight," I say, wincing from the slightest pressure on my leg.

Vee glances at me suspiciously. "Because Princess Ellarose's father took pity on me?"

"No," I say in surprise. "Because you never quit. He might have done you a favor, recommending you for a squire position, but I have no doubt you earned your spurs all on your own."

Vee glances at me again, her lips twisting. "I am trying to find the buried insult."

I roll my eyes. "Take the compliment as it was intended, Vee. When I insult you, I'll be sure you know it."

Her cheeks stain a light pink. "Well, thank you, then. I am proud of who I am, and what I have become. But it can be difficult to carry that pride alone."

"You don't carry it alone," I say. "Not anymore."

Vee pauses, twisting so that she faces me. My arm still drapes over her shoulder, now wrapped around her neck. The movement has brought us close, her face only a few inches from mine. Her eyes glow like the Protector's treasure, her hair tousled in the sea wind. She smells of salt and sea, wind and worry. She smells like Vee, and I breathe it deep.

"Aralyn," she says softly, hesitantly. A question.

"It was you," I whisper. "When I was lost in the caves, it was you who brought me out. You were the reason I kept going. I couldn't let you down, or leave you behind."

She reaches up with her free hand, her fingers brushing my cheek, brushing away the guilt and shame of the last time someone touched my face like this. When Vee's strong, callused fingers touch my skin, it feels as if they were always meant to be there. My fingers curl against the back of her neck, the skin there soft with downy hair, nicked with small scars that tell a story of her life. A story I want to read with my fingertips.

A pressure, a pop.

"We did it!" Lyra crows, blasting us apart. She holds up two enormous wooden mugs, thrusting them toward us. "Go on, then, my own recipe. You'll see colors you never imagined!"

Vee's face is a color I've never imagined, a red so deep it borders on purple. I can only imagine what mine looks like, but I could shove Lyra in the sea right now. She looks between us, her grin falling.

"What? Why aren't we celebrating? Did something happen?"

"Nothing," I say acidly, taking the proffered tankard and draining half of it in one go. If I weren't furious at Lyra's interruption right now, I would admit that it tastes absolutely delicious. Like honeyed wine from some undiscovered fruit, tart and sweet and fresh. The long draft does loosen the knot in my gut, though, and I take a deep breath and let it out with a sigh.

"Where to next, Lyra?" I ask, taking another long drink. It really is delicious. I wonder if I could ask for a second serving. Vee takes her tankard more warily, eyeing the contents with suspicion. Which, given our history with Lyra's magical interventions, I don't blame her.

"What do you mean?" Lyra asks, magically producing a third tankard and taking a long drink of her own. Purple foam crests over her lip.

"I mean, where is the final piece of the blade?" I ask, holding up the hilt.

"Oooh," Lyra says instead of answering me, tossing her tankard to take the hilt from me and pulling the blade from Vee's holster on her back. The runes carved across the blade's sharp edges seem to glow like fire in the rising sunlight as the blade slides into the hilt with a click that I feel down in my toes. There's a brief flash of light as the two pieces of ancient magic are joined once more. Lyra coos over the sword, turning it carefully in her hands. She taps one of the jewels in the hilt, a cheery yellow one. "Look at this, karacite! I haven't seen karacite in ages. I wonder if it works."

"If what works?" I ask as Lyra puts her hand over the stone and hums a single note.

The air around us vibrates, and then suddenly Vee and I are thrown a good thirty feet away from where Lyra stands. We land in the soft sand with a hard thud, kicking up a spray of glittering black that momentarily blinds us. I throw my hands over my head with a groan.

"Whoops, sorry!" Lyra calls. "Should have warned you."

"What was that?" I croak, trying to stand before remembering my knee. Vee has to help me up, but she quickly removes her hands as soon as I am stable. I'm not sure how to feel about it, but Lyra proves once again to be a distraction.

"Karacite, a fey mineral from the Court of Icein," Lyra says, holding the hilt close to her face. "Bury me in the fields of Silveritl, I think this is soothspar."

"Don't touch it!" Vee and I exclaim simultaneously.

"Why not?" Lyra asks. "It won't do anything. At least, I don't think it will. I'm pretty sure the legends about its power are exaggerated."

"I don't wish to find out," I say, hobbling toward her and taking back the weapon, careful not to touch any of the minerals. But I can't help eyeing some of the stones in a new light. "Do all of these have powers like the first one?"

"Oh sure," says Lyra, reaching for it.

I hold it out of reach. "Just tell us about them. Please."

"Bit fidgety, aren't you?" Lyra says, but she pulls her hand back. "The Court of Icein was once the official jewelry makers for the fey realm. They lived in the lowest caves and mined the minerals there. According to fey legend, the minerals were born from the bones of our ancestors who had returned to the earth, and were imbued with their magics. Each mineral had its own property, like karacite. A musical mineral. Find the right tone and it can amplify it a thousandfold."

"We've seen that one at work," I say. "What are these other ones?"

"That gray one there, that's moonwater," says Lyra. "It's said that it can darken the sun for short periods of time. And this red one here, that's mountrite. Prized among the fire fey, though there's precious little of it left in the realm. Mostly they use it to amplify their manifestations. You know, turn a little flame into a big bonfire."

"I'll bet that one was popular when the Protector was cutting his path through the Silent Forest," Vee says.

"And this purple stone, that's soothspar. Allegedly. I've never actually seen such a specimen before."

I raise my brows. "And what can soothspar do?"

Lyra chews at one corner of her lip, a rare show of hesitation in my willful fairy godmother. "According to legend? It can unravel a fairy's manifestation in the mortal realm."

Vee and I both draw back in surprise. "That sounds . . . painful."

"Oh, I'd assume it would be," Lyra says, nodding along. "Fey live a long time and they're not nearly so sensitive as mortals to things like fire or drowning, but unraveling a manifestation? They wouldn't be able to put themselves back together in our realm."

"Why would anyone mine a mineral like that?" Vee asks in horror.

"Why do you carry a sword?" Lyra asks, looking pointedly at the weapon in question strapped to Vee's thigh. "As a weapon. The courts don't get along any better than your human equivalents. The ability to end another fey would be too great an advantage to pass up. But all of the known quantity of soothspar was destroyed when the Protectors were stripped of their powers. Part of the Peace Accords. There used to be a small sample of it in the archives for the scholars to study, but there was an accident and a young historian lost an arm and half of a leg, so it was also disposed of. And anyway . . ."

"What a relief," I say dryly. "Now that we've established that we won't be letting this sword fall into any other fey hands, there's the small matter of finding the third piece of the blade. Do you have any idea where it might be?"

Lyra blows out a breath, shaking her head. "I've been looking, but no such luck. With the Mortel Mountains and the Impassable Sea, there were the legends to follow. There are no other such places I can find in the kingdom with such a cursed history. But the fey libraries are admittedly out of date when it comes to the mortal realm. We don't manifest here as much as we did in the days of the Protector."

"Then there is only one place we can go that might have more knowledge than your fey libraries," I say, dreading the journey back. Already I can feel myself stiffening and shrinking, lessening who I am to fit in with everyone else's expectations of me. Even when I was fighting for my life out here—which was frightfully often—I've never felt more like myself. My true self.

But there's no other resolution for it. We need to find that third and final piece of the Protector's blade.

"We'll have to return to the castle and the king's library there."

THIRTY-ONE

SOMETHING IS NOT RIGHT.

We've been riding as hard as the horses can allow for the better part of a week to make it back to the capital, and in all that time we haven't passed a single occupied village. The first few abandoned outposts we pass on our way back from the Impassable Sea we chalk up to the pirates' presence nearby. No doubt the villagers have been driven out by their raucous passage. But the closer to the capital we draw, the eerier and more undeniable the quiet becomes.

There is no sign of violence, no burned buildings or belongings strung throughout the town centers. On several of the houses, doors stand wide open, and we even pass a few where the tables are set with full plates of food, buzzing with flies and gnats. But the villagers themselves are nowhere to be found—not even as corpses.

"Something is amiss," Vee says, her grip tight on the hilt of the sword strapped to her waist. The Protector's blade sits across her back, wrapped in my traveling cloak to protect it from what we thought would be prying eyes along the way. She glances at me warily, and even Thundermere gives a sniffle of discomfort. "These villagers should be harvesting their crops by now. Look at the fields. Where have they all gone?"

"And more importantly, what made them leave?" I ask, my voice sounding far too loud in the quiet. A soft wind blows through, rustling the crops in eerie susurrations. Rainstorm jerks at the reins with a sidestep that bangs my knee against her flank, sending a dagger of pain up my side. The swelling has gone down enough that I can flex it, but the skin is still as mottled as a rotten apple.

"Could it be something to do with the Protector's blade?" Vee wonders, leading Thundermere around a cart loaded with goods, abandoned in the roadway. "Some kind of, I don't know, magical repellent? Like what Lyra did when she touched that one stone?"

"If it were, you would think we would see more damage to the villages themselves," I say, glancing into the cart. Cooking pots and ladles. A traveling tinker, then. "I've met these tinkers; they'd sooner sell their children than abandon their wares. What could have possibly made this man flee?"

"There's something in the fields up there," Vee says, covering her eyes against the sun and pointing toward the far end of the village where their crops stretch on. "It looks as if they had started the harvest, at least. That field is barren."

"Perhaps it was fallow," I say, though I set my heels to Rainstorm's side to nudge her toward the field in question. Vee is right—it's been cut down low, unlike the others, the green stalks trampled or torn up in places. "Whoever harvested these crops did a poor job of it, not to mention a rushed one."

"These crops weren't harvested," Vee says, swinging off Thundermere to walk into the field. She kneels down, picking up a broken stalk. "They were cut down, with no regard for their value. Someone used this field for something else."

I slide off Rainstorm's back, still clumsy with my bandaged knee, and limp over to her. "What else could they possibly need this field for? The country is starving as it is; we can't afford for anyone to cut down essential crops."

Vee pulls something out of the ground and rises to her feet, her expression grim as she holds it up. It's a simple wooden stake with a bit of rope knotted around it, the ends frayed as if they've been cut. "This is from a tent. Someone cut down the crops to accommodate an encampment."

My heart beats harder, yet everything else feels slower. "What kind of encampment?"

Vee's expression is set in stone. "Most likely a military one."

The breath slides from my lungs, thin and slow. "Valley Banomal. She's really done it."

"Who has done what?" Vee asks.

Vee and I have shared so much over the past few weeks, enough to bring us as close as I've ever felt to another person. And I was so focused on the Protector's blade that I shut out what came before. I didn't want it to be real. I assumed she would fail. But now I have one more great secret from Vee, one I didn't mean to keep. But certainly one that could break the bonds we've built.

Still, I am not my mother. I don't want to become her. If anything is to survive between Vee and me, it will be woven from truth and honesty.

"My mother," I sigh.

"What has the crone done now?" Vee groans.

"Betrothed my sister to the prince of Valley Banomal," I say. "She said she would have revenge on Ellarose, but I thought she meant she'd make Divya a better match."

Vee is so tense I'm afraid she'll crack a tooth. "And you only thought to mention this just now? When you know my sworn duty is to protect the kingdom? To protect Princess Ellarose?"

"I never imagined she would . . . Mother is a schemer, not a military strategist. If Banomal is marching on Novador, those plans were set in motion long before she got involved." *I hope.*

But Vee is shaking her head. "I'll need to ride with all haste to try and outpace their army. The capital will be taken completely by surprise. The castle will need to be fortified. We'll need to send messengers to call up the soldiers on our eastern borders. My father's private retinue will need to be redirected. There's not enough time. Thundermere, my friend, you'll have to ride harder than you've ever ridden before. Are you prepared?"

She lays her hand on the horse's nose, and he dips it once in assent, as if he can actually understand her. For all I know, he can. She said he'd known no other rider besides her. But as she swings up into the saddle, taking the reins firmly in one hand without a backward glance at me, my gut twists in anticipation. I know what it looks like to be abandoned, and Vee is planning just such an escape.

"Vee, wait," I say, ignoring the pain in my knee to limp before Thundermere, opening my hands wide. "Please. I know you must be furious with me, but I swear I did not keep this information from you intentionally. Please, give me a chance to explain."

"What?" Vee says, distracted. "Aralyn, move. I need to get back to the castle as quickly as I can."

"Please, don't be angry." I can't understand why I'm so desperate for her to wait, to give me a chance. To look at me again as she did on the beach, when she touched my cheek. I can't explain why my heart feels as if it might beat so hard that it will stop altogether if she rides off without me right now. "Vee, please, let me fix this."

"Aralyn, I am not—" Vee huffs out an impatient breath. "I am not *happy* that you said nothing before now, but I am not angry at you. I am sworn to defend the crown. Sworn to my oath. I have to protect the princess, and I cannot do that with you standing in my way. I've got to return to the castle as soon as possible, to warn the royal guard."

"But what about me?" I ask, absolutely hating how small and insignificant I sound. "What will I do?"

"You can't return to the castle, not if Banomal marches on it." Vee reaches over her shoulder, pulling the Protector's blade loose of its covering and holding it out to me. "You'll have to find another way to locate the third piece of the blade and complete the weapon. It may be the only thing that can save Novador now."

I reach for the blade, my fingers closing around hers. "I can't do it without you."

Vee's expression relaxes enough that she gives me a small smile, like the sun emerging after a long rainstorm. Blessing the lands. "Aralyn, you've survived everything the Protector has thrown at you. It was you who secured the second piece of the blade. You are the strongest, bravest, most stubborn person I know. Besides me, of course. You can do this. You have to."

She pulls her hands away and straightens up, every inch the knight as she looks down at me. And for all of my life—however long or short it proves to be—I will never forget how she looks, clad in her armor, sun illuminating her hair like a crown of gold. I don't believe in myself, but I believe in her. I want to be what she believes in me.

"You are Aralyn of House Teramina," Vee says, her words quietly intense. "And you will not be bested by a pile of rocks, or a vengeful forest, or a magical siren."

"And you are Sir Vee-Lira of House Doerr," I say, my throat closing around the words. "The only knight worth a damn in the entire order."

"I will see you soon," Vee says. From anyone else, it would sound like an empty promise. A trite gesture you make at any parting. But from Vee, I know it for what it is. A solemn vow.

"Be careful, Vee," I say, clutching the blade to my chest as she sets her heels to Thundermere, the two of them riding off at a speed that makes it obvious how much of their power and strength they'd been holding back on my account. Vee could have left me at any point, ridden off in search of the next piece of the blade without me dragging her down. She stayed because she trusted me.

And now she's entrusted me with the Protector's blade, and the impossible task of locating the third piece. Alone.

Well, not entirely alone. There is that familiar pressure, and then a pop. I groan without turning around, rolling my eyes heavenward as Vee disappears over the horizon.

"You honestly have the worst timing," I groan at Lyra.

"Do I?" asks an unfamiliar voice. "I thought my timing rather perfect."

I whirl around, clutching the blade tighter, to face a tall, willowy figure. Same purple skin, same pointed ears, same ridged brows as Lyra. But this fey is older, the lines around his eyes and mouth deeper, a set of horns curving out from his hairline. When he smiles at me, it's all teeth and no eyes.

"Finally, a chance for us to meet," the fey says, crossing his arms. "I am Fornax."

THIRTY-TWO

"Divya's fairy godfather?" I ask in surprise, glancing around. "Is she here? Is Divya all right?"

"Ah, I see my great reputation precedes me, as it should," Fornax says, his voice deep and smooth. Hypnotic. Already I feel my grip loosening on the Protector's blade, though I don't remember telling my fingers to do so. "I am afraid your dear sister is engaged in other matters at the moment. But she sent me in her stead to greet you."

I will my fingers to hold tighter, though it seems to take far more concentration than usual. "Was this you, convincing her to tell the prince of Banomal to march on Novador? If you've hurt my sister . . ."

Fornax's ridged brow rises up. "Playing at concern for your sister now, after all this time? When she finally has all *you* wanted? How convenient."

I narrow my gaze at him. "I never wanted any of this, for me or for Divya. And she would know that, were she not so blinded by Mother's attention and your magic. They are but parlor tricks, your antics, trying to turn Divya and me against each other."

"You little fool, I never had to turn your sister against you. The poison was already in the well when she called for me."

I shake my head. "Divya may be . . . selfish, but she's not a . . . a warmonger." The words are sluggish, my thoughts cloudy. "This has to be you, starting a war between human courts."

"Is that what you think is happening? War is such a bloody, unnecessary business. So many lives lost. Who would want such a thing?"

I frown. "Why else would there be a military encampment here? What other intentions could Banomal have, bringing soldiers unannounced onto Novador's terrain?"

"Stupid girl, it's not a declaration of war. It's an offering of peaceful capitulation."

His tone is incredibly condescending, as if he needs to explain to me why the sky is blue or why snow falls during the winter moons. I see why Lyra hates him.

"Novador would never capitulate," I say, letting the edge of the Protector's blade bite into my skin just the tiniest bit. The pain seems to help focus my attention away from the flow of his voice. "Certainly not peacefully."

"Mmmm, we shall see," Fornax says musingly. "But I am not here to debate the finer points of diplomatic negotiation with you. I am here for that sword."

He puts out a hand, his fingers curling, and I take a half step toward him involuntarily. I can't understand it. How is he doing this? I am not some element of nature to be so easily manipulated. I squeeze until a thin line of blood runs down the blade, shaking my head free of the fog that has descended.

"No," I say, but even the single word is slow and slurred. "How are you doing this?"

He raises his brow again. "Doing what? Foolish mortal, you *want* to give me that blade. It's so terribly heavy, such an unnecessary burden. You never wanted it in the first place. You always meant to give it over to me, to your mother and sister. To their greater wisdom."

I did mean to give it to my mother, but how could he know that?

"That's not . . . no, I don't . . ." I can't find the words in this fog, my arms shaking from the effort of keeping the sword in my hands. The tip drops into the earth, digging a small trench. I wish I could lie down beside it, make a soft, cozy trench for myself. Close my eyes, maybe never open them again.

"Give me the Protector's blade," says Fornax, his voice the only clear thing through the fog. "You wouldn't know what to do with it anyway. Let me take such an unwieldy burden off your hands."

It is so impossibly unwieldy. Why did Cinderella force me on this path? I lost everything because of her—the prince's hand, my mother's favor, my very home. I've almost died several times over, and for what? To give her the blade, to make *her* queen? I was the one meant for the throne, not that simpering, ungrateful—

"No," I snap, looking up at Fornax. I realize I've dropped to one knee, still holding the blade. "No, those are not my words. That's not my voice. You're doing this to me, somehow."

Fornax's silver eyes narrow until they're nothing but tiny daggers. "Give me the Protector's blade."

My hand shoots out, offering him the blade, and I have to grab it with my free hand and struggle to bring it back toward me. I can't do this on my own. I should never have let Vee leave. I should have gone with her. Or made her stay. She's wrong, I'm not strong enough. I'm not enough of anything. Whatever Fornax is doing—however he's doing it—I don't have the power to hold out against it much longer.

"Vee," I gasp, desperate, dropping to one knee again.

"Your little companion is long gone, right where I sent her," Fornax snarls. "And so shall you join her shortly, as soon as you *give over that blade.*"

"No," I sob, on my hands and knees, crawling toward him. The sword scrapes through the mud, but I haven't let it go yet. "I won't. You can't . . . the blade . . . you can't."

"I can and I will," Fornax says. "You have held out far longer than your insipid fool of a sister, I will give you that. But you are still nothing more than a flesh bag, a fly's life-span and consciousness. You cannot withstand me. You are completely alone. No one is coming for you, because no one cares for you. I didn't even have to burn any maternal love from your mother's mind."

That should have landed like a gut punch, but instead it shines a light like a ray of sun through dark clouds. Fornax might have been right several weeks ago, but he's not right now.

"Lyra," I whisper.

"Don't you dare," he thunders.

"I wish for Lyra."

"I don't mean to tell you your mortal business," Lyra says, after a pop, "but you really do have the most inconvenient timing. I was just pulling— Wait, Fornax? What in Elvnar's graces are you doing here? And, Aralyn, why are you on the ground? What's going on?"

"This is none of your concern, halfling," Fornax says in his most imperious tone yet. "Manifest yourself back to the lower caves where you belong."

Lyra stands before me, feet set wide apart, fists balled at her side. If Fornax meant to cow her with his insults, I believe he's done quite the opposite.

"Don't lecture to me, pretender," Lyra shoots back. "I don't see your mortal anywhere abouts, which means you're breaking fey law, interfering with my charge."

"I'm not interfering, I am resetting the balance," Fornax retorts. "That meat bag has no business with a fey article of such power and history. It belongs in our court, among those who can actually wield it. Not you and your pathetic manifestation of power."

"The Protector's blade? That's what this is about?" Lyra glances back at me with surprise. "Aralyn, did he harm you? If he so much as puffed a breath of wind in your face, I swear by the gong of Threpnar I will—"

"He's done something," I say, shaking my head. The mists clear, but only slightly. I concentrate all my attention on Lyra. "Something to my mind. He's . . . controlling me."

I might as well have said that he put his hand up my backside and made me his puppet, for the look of horror that crosses Lyra's face. "That's impossible," she whispers.

"The stupid girl lies," Fornax says simply. "She is mistaken. She is only weak and seeks a reason outside of her own failing courage to blame."

"Aralyn is a lot of things," Lyra says, pivoting toward Fornax. "But she is *not* weak. What have you done, Fornax?"

"How dare you, halfling," Fornax sneers, his expression turning vicious. "To question *me*, after all this—"

"What have you *done*, Fornax?" Lyra shouts.

"What needed to be done!" Fornax shouts. "The courts were crumbling! The veil was thickening. The mortals were willful and impatient, always wishing for asinine possessions, love potions or livestock or gold coins. Useless bits and bobbles, foolish dreams.

Should we really subjugate our superior strength to their whims? This way, we all prosper. You could prosper the same, if you did not share your mother's archaic views on our magic."

"It is not archaic to respect life," Lyra retorts. "Seeking to manipulate mortals! What you are doing is dark magic. The kind of magic that nearly tore the courts asunder all those millennia ago. That magic is the reason the Protectors were formed in the first place! How are you even . . . Where are you getting these abilities?"

"That is none of your concern," Fornax sniffs. "And I am quite through explaining myself to your kind. Now hand over Kaung's blade and let this little farce be done with."

"You are not fit to speak the Protector's name, much less wield his blade," Lyra says, holding out a hand. I'm not sure what she means to do, but she throws a look over her shoulder at me. "The sword?"

"Oh, right," I mutter, pressing the blade into her hand.

She swings it around, holding it before her, pointed directly at Fornax. "Now you will leave my charge alone and manifest your own sorry hide back to the upper caves. Or else."

"Or else what?" Fornax sneers. "You are sorely outnumbered, you and your pathetic meat bag."

Fornax waves a hand, and out of the fields comes a line of Banomalian soldiers, their expressions blank, their weapons glinting in the light. I don't even know how long they've been standing there among the crops, still and silent, undetected. They march as a single unit, their feet lifting and landing at exactly the same time, creating an ominous rhythm as they fall in behind Fornax. I count at least twenty, but who knows how many more he might have hidden away in the fields.

"There is nowhere for you to run, halfling," Fornax taunts her. "Now give me what is rightfully mine."

"The blade is not yours," Lyra says, her grip tightening on the hilt. "Aralyn and Vee found it. The Protector chose them, as prophesied."

"Prophesied," Fornax snorts. "That prophecy is as useful as your magic—half-formed nonsense. As if a disappointment such as yourself could truly understand the complexities of soothsaying. And with the Protector's weapon incomplete, you cannot even wield it. Not that you would be able to, with your pathetic magic."

"Maybe, but I still know a few things you don't," Lyra says, glancing back at me once again. She lowers her voice so that only I can hear her. "Aralyn, get down."

"What?" I whisper. "Why?"

"Get *down*."

I only have time to press my face close to the mud before Lyra cups her hand over the sword hilt, humming that same note she did on the black sands of the Impassable Sea. The impact is no less impressive as it blows through Fornax and his mind-controlled soldiers, throwing them all several feet away. Even down in the mud, with my hands over my ears, I'm driven several feet back, my head thrumming. I don't even have a chance to recover before someone is hauling me up, dragging me at a run.

"We need to go!" Lyra shouts in my ear over the ringing. The soldiers look about them in confusion, as if coming out of a fog, and Fornax is struggling to get on his knees. "Quickly! Where is your horse?"

"Rainstorm!" I call, giving a sharp whistle like I've seen Vee do so many times. Rainstorm, the fairy godmothers bless her, comes galloping out of a nearby field where she has presumably wandered off to chew up the crops to her stomach's content. Lyra lifts me like I'm a bag of flour and tosses me over her saddle, slapping her rump.

"Run, fair beast!" Lyra says, a blur beside us.

"I didn't know you could run so fast!" I shout as Rainstorm's hooves thunder against the packed dirt road.

"Me either," Lyra huffs, brow furrowed low. "I guess I can with the proper motivation."

I look in the other direction to check on our motivation, but a powerful burst of wind blows dust in my eyes and blinds me. Rainstorm screams, rearing up and tumbling me sideways out of the saddle.

"You will come to regret that," says Fornax, only it's not quite his voice anymore. It's like a frigid wind blowing just before a storm, like the thunder that announces a burst of lightning. Even the sky seems to dim as his form condenses and solidifies on the road before us. His eyes spark, but there is a hollowness to his cheeks, his skin a shade grayer than before. The effort is costing him.

"How?" Lyra gasps from where she's landed on the road, a few feet away from me. The sword has fallen just a few feet behind her, and Fornax's gaze lands on it at the same time as mine.

"How are you doing this?"

"Soothspar," Fornax says, his voice an ominous rumble. His eyes spark lightning again. "A full stone can unravel us, but do you know what you can do with the tiniest dusting inhaled by a fey? You can loosen the bonds between body and magic. Just enough that someone else can take that magic. Do you know what happens when you take another fey's magic? You gain their power. Their skill. Their knowledge. And eventually, we learned, their very essence. It cost me an arm and a leg, literally, gaining that knowledge. And all our supply of soothspar at the time. But look at that lovely, robust specimen you have there. Enough to take the magic of the entire court of Eventide."

"No," Lyra whispers, eyes wide and round in terror. "Tell me that's not how you've done this. How you're able to control the mortals."

"It tastes of starlight, their magic," Fornax says, raising his gaze upward. "Of night mists and endless fields. Like drinking in the mysteries that lie between the veils."

"Fornax, you can't," Lyra gasps. "Our own kind!"

His gaze comes down on her with a crack. "They deserve it, those who are not willing to adapt. Those who would rather magic silken dresses and glass slippers than use their magic in the interest of their own court."

It is my turn to gasp. "Cinderella's fairy godmother. You killed her fairy godmother. That was why she couldn't call on her. Why she was so upset when I told her about Lyra."

"Not Galandrel," Lyra says, halfway to a sob. "Oh, Fornax, no. When my mother hears of this—"

"Your mother will never hear anything of the kind, because there will be no one left to tell her," Fornax says, baring his teeth. And even as I watch him, his form seems to shift and change, elongating and lightening until I can see the road through his legs, the sunlight piercing through his chest. Lyra makes a strangled noise.

"It was you," she says, scooting back several feet until she bumps into the Protector's blade once more. "You were in the Silent Forest. You were the thing that dragged Aralyn under."

"Wasn't I," Fornax said, shifting and changing once again until the quester from the Mortel Mountains stands before us, the one who ran Vee off the cliff. He shifts again, his hand the exact shape and color of the creature that tried to upend our boat in the Impassable Sea. " I thought to do us all a favor and end your pathetic existences before the magic of the Protector's blade obliterated you. But it turned out you had quite the knack for collecting the lost pieces. And holding on to them, despite my efforts. I suppose I should thank you for doing so much of the difficult work for me. But I can no longer afford your irritating interferences. And so, your usefulness comes to an end."

Lyra reaches for me, her grip tight on my arm. "Aralyn, I'm so sorry."

I shake my head, my vision blurring. "Don't be, Lyra. You couldn't have known. But Novador, the blade—"

"No, I mean I'm sorry for what I'm about to do."

I frown as Lyra takes hold of the Protector's blade, her silver gaze boring into mine. I open my mouth to ask what she means to do, but I don't have a mouth anymore. I've been shredded apart, scattered across existence. Unmade.

Lyra has manifested out of the mortal realm and taken me along with her.

THIRTY-THREE

I HAVE BEEN DRIVEN MAD BY A MOUNTAIN, BURIED BY a vengeful forest, drowned by a siren, and attacked by an evil fairy godfather. And yet I would happily relive all of those near-death experiences before ever experiencing a manifestation between realms. It is *agony*. It is beyond agony. To be unmade, to be shredded down to single cells, to be reconstructed by a bumbling fairy god-mother holding a bloody ancient sword—I can't describe it. A single cell out of place, and I'll have fingers growing out of my eyeballs, or bones on the outside and skin on the inside. A tooth in the center of my hard palate. I am nothing but a cosmic scream.

"Aralyn? Oh, plunkers, Aralyn, did I kill you? I should have gone to the court first, asked for Mother's help. She could have put you back together right."

I know that voice, which means my ears are working. Or, I'm dead. Either of which would be a blessing at this point, honestly. But someone lays a cool hand against my forehead, which means I also have a forehead. A forehead that pounds with a blinding head-ache. Something like a groan shifts in my chest.

"Oh no, I've put her lungs back wrong," Lyra frets. "Or her throat. She can't speak."

"That's normal," says Cinderella's voice, slightly amused. How dare she. "She always sounds like that when she's waking up. Terribly unladylike, isn't it?"

"I hope you prick your thumb on a sharp tack," I growl, my throat feeling new and raw.

"There she is," Cinderella says happily. "You must be her fairy godmother. I'm Ellarose, what a pleasure to finally meet you."

When I open my eyes, I'm almost shocked at how normal everything looks. We're back in the castle, in Novador, in Cinderella's personal quarters. It seems both five minutes and five lifetimes since we were last here, plotting our journey. When Vee still hated me, and I still planned to betray them all. I sit upright, the movement making the room spin.

"Vee," I gasp, like this is the first time I have tasted air. "Where is Vee?"

"I don't know," Cinderella says, stepping back and shaking her head. "I was reading about the bylaws when the two of you just sort of appeared here. How did you do that, by the way?"

"Lyra, you have to find Vee," I croak. "Fornax set a trap for her. You have to find her and get her here. Safe."

Lyra nods, her ridges furrowing in worry. "I'll find her and bring her back."

"Not like this!" I manage. "Don't manifest."

"No, no, I'll find another way," Lyra says.

"The blade," I say, looking around wildly. "Where is the Protector's blade?"

"I don't know," Lyra says, as if she's just suddenly remembered a roast she had in the oven. She glances around wildly. "I was so focused on putting you back together right that I didn't think about where I manifested it. I just had it, I swear I did, but I don't know where it—"

"Is this what you seek?" asked Cinderella, pointing to a blade stuck halfway through the stone wall of her chamber.

"Oh, plunkers," Lyra mutters.

"Just find Vee, quickly," I say, standing and testing out my legs. My knee doesn't hurt anymore, which I suppose is an unintended blessing of passing through the realms. "Cin— Ellarose and I will find a way to get the sword loose. We don't have time to waste."

"Just a moment," Lyra says, holding her hands over my head and speaking a few words in a deep, guttural language that I assume is the language of the fey. It's harsher than I expected, full of grunts and growling, and as Lyra speaks her expression transforms, becoming something more ethereal, more ancient. More primal. I don't know what she's said, but it settles on my bones like Vee's armor clinking into place. When she opens her eyes, the silver gleams. "That should do it. Hopefully."

"What did you do?" I ask.

"Put a protection spell on you. My Feyrish isn't the best, but hopefully it will keep Fornax from locking on your location and manifesting when I'm not around. I don't know how long the protection will last. I never was the greatest student at these kinds of protections. But it's better than nothing."

"Thank you," I say, and I mean it. "You need to find Vee now."

Lyra nods before disappearing with a pop, and I can't help but shudder at the sound. I don't know how the fey can stand it, being pulled apart and stitched back together by their own consciousness like that. I hobble over to the sword, giving the hilt a test pull. It doesn't budge, and all I can hope is that the blade is still intact within the solid stone.

"You wouldn't happen to have a blacksmith on call, would you?" I ask, peering at the stone to check whether or not the metal has fused with the rock.

"No, though I could call for someone to go down to the stables and see if the town blacksmith is here reshoeing the horses," Cinderella says.

"No time for that," I mutter, wrapping one hand around the hilt and placing the other over the yellow stone set in it. "I'm going to try something. I'm not sure it will work, but if it does, you'll want to lie flat on the ground."

"Should I get beneath the bed?" Cinderella asks, always so patient. She hasn't even asked a single question since we arrived, besides asking how we got there.

"It's probably not a bad idea," I say, waiting until she fits herself beneath the heavy mahogany frame before searching my memory for the specific note Lyra used to engage the stone. It takes me a few sliding tries, but eventually I hit the right note and the sound reverberates through the stone, blasting me backward with the sword still in hand. I land hard on the soft mattress, and Cinderella gives a small groan from beneath. But the sword is free, a fist-size hole in the thick rock wall the only evidence remaining.

"Sorry," I grunt, rolling off the bed and reaching under to help her climb back out.

"You really did it," Cinderella says, eyeing the blade in wonder. "You found the Protector's blade."

"Not all of it," I say sadly. "There is still the third and final piece we haven't been able to locate. But we were put off our course. Ellarose, there's something else."

Her brows lift at my use of her name. "I'm not sure I've ever heard you call me by my given name."

I resist the urge to follow up that comment with some sort of slight. That is what my mother would do. I'm not her ward any longer. "There is a great deal I have to make amends for, including the cruelty with which I have treated you these past years. But right now we have a much greater problem. Valley Banomal troops are marching on Novador as we speak. They are not far from the castle, a day at the most."

"What?" Ellarose says in shock. "How is that possible? We've not had a single scout report from the borders."

"It's a very long story, but I believe Divya's fairy godfather, Fornax, has been using dark magic to hypnotize people into doing his bidding. Including Novadorians. He used an ancient stone to siphon off the magic of other fey. Ellarose, he . . . he used your fairy godmother. He killed her."

Ellarose clamps a hand over her mouth, her eyes filling with tears as she shakes her head. "Please say it's not so. I knew something was wrong, because she hasn't come when I called for her, but I thought I'd been doing something wrong. I never imagined . . ."

I put both hands on her shoulders, forcing her to catch my gaze. "Whatever has become of your fairy godmother, I swear to you we will find out and we will make sure justice is done. But right now, the capital is under threat. We need to gather the troops, warn the council, and prepare for war. They believe they can take the country without a fight, but I intend to prove them wrong. And I need to return to the library and search for any records of the time of the

Protector here in Novador. We have yet to locate the third piece, and the weapon's power remains incomplete until we do."

It's a lot for Ellarose to absorb, but she pivots with surprising alacrity, dashing away her tears as she pulls a velvet cord near her door. A young girl with tawny braids and pale skin appears, bobbing in a curtsy.

"There's no time for that, Kiara," Ellarose says, lifting the girl up. "I need your swift feet and your courageous heart now. We believe there is a threat marching on Novador, soldiers from the Valley Banomal."

The little girl gasps, tugging at one long braid. "Could it be so, Your Royal Highness? What can I do?"

Ellarose crouches to look the girl in the eye. "You can run, fast as your feet will carry you, to the king's quarters and alert his personal guard. Then I need you to carry on to the great hall, where Prince Fael is holding council with the king's advisors. Speak only to the prince, not High Chancellor Cordo or any of the other advisors. This is a great deal to ask you, I know, but you are my most trusted handmaiden. I know you can handle it."

"'Course I can, Your Royal Highness," says Kiara, rising on her tiptoes with pride. "I outrun the stable boys so bad, they won't let me in their races no more. I'll be back before they serve your tea."

"That is my good girl," Ellarose says, chucking the girl's chin. "Now off with you, swift as the wind."

The girl goes running and Ellarose straightens up, shaking out her skirts. "We'll need to alert the townspeople immediately, get as many of them inside the castle gates as possible. We'll need food, and water, and sleeping pallets and blankets. Will you be able to handle the library on your own?"

I nod, looking at her in a new light. She might not be the ruler I would have been, or the ruler I thought Novador needed, but as always her first thought is of everyone else. Perhaps she is the ruler we needed after all. With a little bit of help.

"The first two pieces were in obvious locations," I say, "places of legend and infamy. The Mortel Mountains, the Impassable Sea. Each place cursed by the Protector's blade hiding itself away. But where else is there such a place in Novador?"

"May I see the blade?" Ellarose asks, holding out her hands to me.

A moon's time ago, I would have scoffed at such a request. Turned the blade on her instead, or used the stones in the hilt to force her to give up the throne to me. Now I hand it over without a second thought, except to marvel at the changes that the past month has wrought in me.

She takes the weapon and sits in a nearby chair, running the flat of her palm over the surface of the blade. "These markings look so familiar."

"I don't know why they would," I say, crossing my arms and leaning against the nearby table. There's a letter there, half-written. A plea from Ellarose to one of the king's ministers for Prince Fael to lead the king's council. "Lyra says the markings are from an ancient fey language that they don't even speak in the courts anymore. It was outlawed when the Protectors were stripped of their powers."

But Ellarose traces one of the symbols absently, shaking her head. "I swear I have seen this symbol before. Perhaps in my readings in the library."

I raise my brows. "Would you know which book it came from? It could have a clue to the location of the third piece of the blade."

"I remember it, etched in leather," she muses, mostly to herself.

"Perhaps a book cover? But no, the shape is all wrong. I've seen it somewhere else. Maybe the relics room, or the great hall."

She closes her eyes and presses her fingers to the bridge of her nose, as if that might help her remember. I don't want to rush her along, but we don't exactly have time for leisurely trips down memory lane, either. I tap one foot against the soft rug, waiting as patiently as I can until I can stand it no more.

"What if we went to the library?" I suggest. "If we browse the stacks, it might jog your memory. Or we could walk through the relics room and see if—"

"No!" Ellarose exclaims, jumping up so quickly that I have to lunge to catch the Protector's blade before it tumbles from her lap to the floor. "I know where I've seen this symbol! Follow me!"

"Wait, don't we need to—"

But she is out her door and running down the corridor as if she were some common serving girl and not the future queen of the realm. I sigh, setting the Protector's blade against my shoulder.

"At least I no longer have to limp," I mutter, before hurrying after her.

THIRTY-FOUR

I EXPECT ELLAROSE TO VEER OFF FOR THE LIBRARY as we leave the south wing of the castle, but instead she heads in the opposite direction, toward the stable doors where she led me into the castle when she first asked for my help. We startle plenty of servants on the way out, the princess running full speed and her disgraced stepsister wielding an enormous battle sword chasing after her. I catch a few shouts of warning, but I blow right past them before anyone can think to stop me. I can't imagine what scene they think they're watching play out.

"Where are we going?" I shout at Ellarose as we come bursting out of the stable door. I've caught up with her, but just barely, and my passage from one realm to the other and back has left me weak and shaking. "Ellarose, please, slow down. You can't imagine how many times and ways I've almost died in the past moon."

"Apologies," Ellarose huffs, slowing down but still walking at a brisk pace. "I got excited. I know where I've seen those symbols. I think I might know where to find the third piece."

"Truly?" I ask in shock. But why not? After all the trouble we faced finding the blade and the hilt, *of course* she would just conveniently know where to find the third piece.

"Yes," she says, coming to a stop so suddenly I almost lop off a piece of ear running into the back of her. She holds her hands up, smiling serenely. "Here."

We stand at the entrance to the castle gardens, the entrance arch twined with greenery and lush purple blossoms and white-and-green striped leaves. It's gorgeous and enchanting, even to someone like me, who can't tell their gooseberries from poisoned berries. Still, I have no idea how or why Ellarose would think the final piece of the Protector's blade would be here.

"You'll see," she says, as if she can hear my thoughts. She glances behind us furtively, taking my hand and dragging me along. "Quickly, before anyone sees us."

"Ellarose, I don't mean to doubt your remembrance, but if the third piece of the Protector's blade were here, we would know it," I say, even though I follow her through the winding paths. The plants are well maintained, and I remember what Vee said about Ella's father. "Did your father plant all of these?"

"Yes," she says, with a smile so proud it stabs me clean through. I've never even asked about her father before now. I wonder what it would feel like, to have such pride in a parent even long after they're gone. "Some of these are from neighboring kingdoms, but many of them he cultivated himself. He taught me how, before he died. The garden had fallen into terrible disrepair in his absence. No one cared for the plants as Father could, but Fael gave me free rein to do as I wanted here after we were married. There are still parts of the gardens that need care, but we've brought a great many of the vines back to life. I spend most of my time out here when the weather is good, which is how I found this."

We stop on the path before a great, twisted tree with sharp needles and thick bark. I know that type of tree, I would know it by smell alone. It will haunt my nightmares for the rest of my life. Ellarose approaches the tree with a hand out, and I have to grab her by the arm and jerk her away before she can come within its reach.

"Don't touch that tree!" I say sharply, drawing us to the far side of the path. "That tree is from the Silent Forest."

Ellarose raises her brows in surprise at me. "How do you know that?"

I point the tip of the Protector's blade at the tree. "Because I was almost buried alive by one that looked exactly like that."

The tree's limbs shake as if a strong wind has come rushing through, even though the air is dead and the rest of the plants around us are still. Needles stab into the ground, just inches from the toes of our boots.

"See? I told you," I say. "That thing will uproot itself and squeeze you until your bones crack. You can't trust it."

"Of course I can," Ellarose says simply. "It's only a tree, Ary."

I roll my eyes, reminding myself to be patient. "You weren't there, Ellarose. You don't know what these things are capable of."

"We're all capable of terrible actions when we've been wounded," she says, so simply and directly that I have a suspicion that she is not speaking only of the tree. "You scared it with that sword of yours."

"*I* scared *it*?" I echo incredulously. "It's a bloody tree, Ella. What am I going to do to it with a sword?"

"Look at it, Ary," Ellarose says, nudging me forward. "Put the sword down and just look at it. Try to understand."

I would rather light myself on fire and run straight at it screaming, but I don't have a flint and I don't suppose that will make whatever point Ellarose is trying to make. Reluctantly—more reluctantly than I've done anything in my life—I set the Protector's sword down on the ground and put my hands up, to show the tree I am unarmed.

"This is ridiculous," I mutter. "It's a *tree*. What am I doing?"

"It's a living thing, like any other," Ellarose says. "And it's been hurt. Can't you see?"

Once I get close enough to distinguish the rough ridges on the bark, I see what she means. There are thick cuts along the trunk of the tree, black and bubbled over like tar, some of them so deep I can see the rings of the tree within. Whatever blade made those marks must have been wielded hundreds of years ago.

"By the fey," I whisper, stepping closer to examine one of the cuts along the root. "The Protector's blade. He cut the path through the Silent Forest with his blade. That's why they reacted the way they did when we came riding along the route. They remembered."

"I remember when my father brought this tree to the castle grounds, not much more than a sapling," Ellarose says quietly, stepping up beside me and laying a hand on the bark. "It was so badly torn up, its root system almost completely hacked away. It shouldn't have survived. But Father always had a magic touch with even the most wounded creatures. He planted it here, and it has thrived. But he remarked that there was something buried in its trunk, and he never could remove it. And that's when I remembered."

She points upward, to the heart of the tree, where an object is lodged deep within the wood. It's nearly the same color as the surrounding bark, but the texture is all wrong. It's too smooth, narrow and long, with golden etchings that have faded over time.

"A scabbard," I breathe, climbing up the tree's roots and grabbing the exposed top without thinking.

The tree reacts instantly, limbs bending and cracking as they swoop toward me, wrapping around my arms and pressing me hard into the trunk until the bark scratches at my face and neck. Needles stab into my skin, tearing away strips of my clothes and imbedding deep into my arms. Ellarose cries out, tumbling backward onto the path, as the tree squeezes harder.

"Ella, run!" I scream, before a falling needle rips at the corner of my lip. "Take the sword and run!"

"I can't leave you, Ary!" she cries.

"You don't understand these trees!" I shout, but my words are muffled by the bark and the hissing of the tree's leaves.

"Please, wait!" Ellarose cries, and at first I think she is speaking to me. But then her voice draws closer, and I can see just out of the corner of my eye as she approaches the tree. She kneels before the tree, placing a hand on an exposed root.

"Ella, don't!"

"It's okay, Ary," Ellarose says in the same voice she would use to talk to the kitchen mice and the fledgling birds in spring. Gentle, soothing. Melodic. "I know what it is to be alone. To be torn from your loved ones, raised among strangers, to bear the wounds of loss. You don't belong here. You belong back in the forest, among your own brethren. And I swear to you, on my honor as princess of Novador, that I will see you returned to the Silent Forest. But first, I need my sister released. Please. She means as much to me as your lost brethren mean to you."

The tree hesitates, not yet letting go but not squeezing any tighter. I hold as still as I can, praying that Ellarose's peculiar brand of magic with living things works on this cursed tree. I've seen her charm a mouse into giving up a hunk of cheese and a bird into gifting her their tail feathers for a decoration. If anyone can keep this tree from murdering me, it's Cinderella.

"No one will ever hurt you again," Ellarose says. "You don't need to hold on to the pain any longer. Let it go, and let yourself be free."

Branches creak and scrape across my shoulders as the tree loosens its hold, chunks of bark falling away as it releases the scabbard at the same time. I draw it out from the heart of the tree as gently as I can, as much to save the tree any more pain as to keep the sacred object intact. By the time the tree has moved its branches back into place and I tumble down the roots onto the path, I hold the scabbard in both hands.

"You did it," I say, shaking my head. "You convinced a bloody tree to let me go."

"I spoke only the truth," Ellarose says simply. She takes the sword from the path, careful to hide it behind her skirts where it won't spook the tree again. She gives a deep curtsy to the tree. "I will make plans for your return to the Silent Forest as soon as our kingdom is secure. Thank you."

The tree shakes its limbs in an approximation of a bow in return.

"Unbelievable," I murmur.

"All living things deserve respect," Ellarose replies. "This tree has suffered a traumatic fate. It's natural that it would lash out with the same anger. If you want peace, you must first offer it yourself."

"I don't think an offering of peace will work on Fornax and the Valley Banomal," I say as we make our way back down the garden path. Ellarose hands me the sword, but I don't yet slide it into the scabbard. "But now we have the three pieces of the Protector's weapon, they can't stop us."

A rider comes thundering into the stable yard as soon as we exit the garden, and the dust has barely settled before Vee is off Thundermere, heading toward us at a dead run.

"Vee, you're safe!" I call out.

But she doesn't look safe, not by a long shot. She holds her shoulder, red leaking through her fingers.

"What happened?" Ellarose cries.

"Where is Lyra?" I ask.

"Holding them off, for now," Vee gasps, dropping to one knee. "Valley Banomal soldiers. Closer than we thought. They'll be on the city within the hour."

THIRTY-FIVE

"WE NEED TO GET YOU TO THE INFIRMARY," ELLAROSE says, taking Vee's good arm and swinging it over her shoulders.

"There's no time," Vee says, though she winces as she says it. "We need to organize the castle forces."

"We will make time," Ellarose says in a voice I've never heard before. One that brooks no argument. She looks fierce as she gazes up at Vee. "I will need you by my side, whatever comes our way in the next hour. You are *my* knight."

Vee's cheeks turn a light pink, and a sharp spear of jealousy cleaves me in two. She dips her head in assent, allowing Ellarose to guide her toward the castle door.

"I guess I'll just wait here, then," I mutter to myself.

"Don't be a fool," Ellarose says over her shoulder. "I was talking to both of you when I said I needed you by my side."

Vee risks injuring her shoulder further just to throw a smirk over at me.

"I find the both of you intolerable," I say, though I follow their path into the castle.

Vee must not have been the only Novadorian soldier to have

beaten the army to the castle, because inside is chaos. Servants rush through the halls, their arms loaded with all manner of goods as if they mean to abandon the place entirely. Ellarose does her best to calm them, or direct them to more useful tasks, but it's clear they've been given different orders by someone higher up than her.

"The infirmary will have to wait," Vee says, turning resolutely toward the main hall. "Something is going on, and we need to find out what."

Still, I snag a linen sheet from a passing servant, tearing strips from it and tying them into a knot to make a sling for Vee's arm. I help fit it over her shoulder as we reach the massive oak doors of the hall, and she gives me a grateful smile.

"Does it hurt?" I ask quietly.

"Like the dickens," she says, grinning. "Don't worry, I gave better than I got."

"I have no doubt you did," I say.

"We request an immediate audience with the king's council," Ellarose says to the line of guards standing before the door. Her voice warbles, but she draws herself up to her full height, chin tilted at a regal angle.

"We have orders not to let anyone in," says one of the soldiers, sounding apologetic about it.

"This is an emergency," Ellarose says. "Soldiers from Valley Banomal are marching on the castle now. We need to prepare for the attack immediately."

The soldiers exchange a glance. "We know, Your Royal Highness," says the same soldier. "That's why we have our orders."

Vee's gaze narrows. "What does that mean? What's going on in there?"

There's a bang from within, followed by a shout, and Vee lurches forward, already pulling her sword from her scabbard. The soldiers close ranks, though, and there are far too many of them for Vee to cut through.

"Let us pass," Vee grinds out.

"Please, I must see my husband," Ellarose adds. "I must see the prince."

"He's not the prince no more," mutters one of the soldiers.

"What?" Vee exclaims.

I growl impatiently, holding up the Protector's blade. "We don't have time for this," I say, cupping a hand over the karacite. "Ella, you know what to do."

"Oh dear," Ellarose mutters, grabbing Vee by her good arm and dragging her to the ground.

The soldiers look at us like we've lost our minds. "What kind of bloody—"

This time I get the note right on the first try, the pulse of energy throwing the door open and tossing the soldiers into the great hall like sacks of dried beans. I manage to keep my feet this time, planted wide like a pirate at a ship's helm.

"I think I'm getting the hang of this," I say.

The round table of old men tug at their white beards in shock within the great hall, obviously interrupted in the midst of what looks like an attempted coup. Prince Fael is held back by two soldiers, with a third pointing a sword at his throat. Vee's father, High Chancellor Cordo, stands imperiously at the head of the table, his face red with fury as he takes in our arrival. His gaze falls to his daughter, rising from the floor with Ellarose's help, and his expression further sours.

"What is the meaning of this?" he snaps in his most imperious tone. "What do you think you are doing, child?"

"What are *you* doing, Father?" Vee counters, and I could cheer the core of iron in her reply. She glances at Prince Fael. "Are you hurt, cousin?"

"Not yet," Prince Fael says, throwing a worried glance at Ellarose. "You shouldn't be here, my love. My uncle seeks to usurp my father's throne."

"I seek to protect the people of Novador," High Chancellor Cordo counters acidly. "Something you would know nothing about, boy. We have neither the men nor the resources to battle the forces Valley Banomal has sent across our borders. The only way to protect our people is to negotiate a surrender to them and avoid bloodshed."

"Surrender?" Vee cries. "We cannot surrender to them, Father. They mean to subjugate us!"

"I have seen what they can accomplish with their own people," Cordo says. "Novador would do well to learn a similar humility and sense of pride in their work."

"Father," Vee says, her voice thin and hollow. "Did you do this? Did you *arrange* this attack with Valley Banomal?"

Cordo leans his hands on the table, piercing Vee with a glare I recognize from my own overbearing parent. It is a look that is meant to still the tongue and shrink the soul. "Do not presume to think you could understand what choices I make, or why I make them. I would never explain myself to a lowly soldier, and do not think because you are my progeny that I would consider you any differently. You wanted to play about with swords and armor like the boys, so you will fall in line like them as well. If you fail to do so, you will suffer the same fate as the other knights who thought to defy me."

Vee crumples against Ellarose's shoulder, looking utterly defeated.

"Well, you are exactly as I expected you to be," I say. "Pompous, hideous, and idiotic."

Cordo's eyes bulge so wide it seems to be a magic trick. "I will have you hung up in the stocks—"

"You will do no such thing," Vee says, her back snapping straight.

"Your daughter and I have done what a tableful of decrepit old men could not," I say, ignoring Cordo's sputtering. "We have found a way to *actually* save Novador. Right here."

I hold up the Protector's blade in one hand and the scabbard in the other, my arms trembling from the weight of both. But I don't dare let them dip when the king's council is looking right at me.

"A decorated sword?" Cordo scoffs. "What do you plan to do with that? Cut a wheel of cheese as an offering to the Banomal delegation?"

"No, I am going to use it to restore strength and prosperity to the kingdom," I say, before holding both over my head and sliding the sword into the scabbard. I squeeze my eyes shut tight against the impending magic, bracing myself for its power.

"Very dramatic," says High Chancellor Cordo dryly several moments later. "But if you are quite through with your empty promises and pathetic threats, perhaps you will let the adults in the room finish our business?"

I crack one eye open, looking up at the sword to be sure I actually managed to fit it into the scabbard. It's there, all three pieces together, but it's doing . . . nothing.

"Is it supposed to do something?" Ellarose whispers.

"I don't know," I whisper back. "I thought once the three pieces were united . . . Maybe it needs one of its own kind to engage it. Lyra, I wish for you to wield this sword."

A pressure, a pop, and then Lyra comes flying through the room and crashes onto the center of the table, smoke rising from her leathers and fur. There's a cut running down the side of her face and her hair tufts out in all directions. She looks dazed as she climbs up off the table, ignoring the scoffing and protesting of the old men seated around the table in favor of focusing on me.

"What in Elvnar's graces took you so long?" she fairly bellows, slapping out a tongue of flame licking up near her ear. "I've been waiting for you to wish me out of that conflagration for a good twenty minutes now. Nearly lost my eye to one of their arrows."

"Where did you come from?" I ask in surprise.

"Just outside the city gates," Lyra says grimly, tugging her leathers into place. "Where Fornax and his brainwashed army are advancing. Well, tickle me tinsel, is that it? You did it?"

I grin, holding the Protector's blade out to her. "We did it." My smile falters. "But we can't get it to work. We thought you could help."

"This is the most ridiculous, asinine thing I have ever been forced to be a party to," Cordo interrupts, his tone turned nasally and thin. "We will have no more interruptions to our preparations for making peace with Valley Banomal. Guards, remove these women."

"Father, you cannot—"

"I will deal with *you* later," Cordo says, piercing Vee with a look. "For now, you will remove yourself from this chamber and from my presence. We have real work to do."

"You will not get away with this, Uncle," says Prince Fael, struggling against the soldiers holding him. "The people of Novador will not so easily accept defeat, nor will they bow to a usurper. You've kept my father locked away for ten years, running his council as if it were your own. No more. The people of Novador will rise up against you!"

"The people of Novador will do exactly as I tell them," Cordo sniffs. "As soon as Valley Banomal shares the secrets of their magic."

"You can't do that," Ellarose gasps. "High Chancellor, you don't understand what they're doing, how they're doing it. Aralyn says—"

"I don't care what the disgraced daughter of an impoverished social climber says, and frankly the fact that you *would* only confirms for me what manner of princess you truly are. Now I shall do what should have been done years ago, when my brother could no longer fulfill his duties. I will take his throne for the good of Novador and send his son, along with the rest of you, to the dungeons."

THIRTY-SIX

Silence falls in the great hall, sliced in two by the sound of a sword sliding out of its scabbard. I assume it's Lyra, drawing the Protector's blade, but Vee has the tip of her sword pointed at her father's throat, the blade steady and unwavering.

"Release the prince," she says, her voice deadly calm. "Now."

Cordo's eyes bulge. "You wouldn't *dare*—"

"I would dare a great many things at the moment, High Chancellor, and all in the name of the very people you seek to disgrace in this room. You will keep me silent no more. You will keep me aside no more. I earned my spurs the same as every other squire, and if you don't order my cousin released right this instant, I will show you how I did."

Cordo opens his mouth to no doubt spew some greater insult, but Vee tips up the edge of her blade, effectively shutting his jaw. She cuts her eyes to the soldiers holding Fael.

"Release the prince."

They don't wait for Cordo's assent, instead standing back and letting go of his arms. He leaps away from them, grabbing a rusted sword from a wall display and standing shoulder to shoulder with Vee. I raise my brows at him.

"What is that for?"

"In case we need to fight our way out," Fael says.

"What is your plan of attack? Lockjaw? I do believe Vee has you covered."

"This treason will not go unpunished, daughter," Cordo says through gritted teeth, glaring death at his own progeny.

"No, it will not," I say, stepping up beside Vee. I glance around the chamber at these feeble, weak-minded old men. "Some king's council you are. Coin is the only crown you lot would take the knee for. I've been from one end of Novador to the other and back in the past few weeks. I have seen the conditions you've left your people in while you cower up here in your great hall planning your revolt. The king may be infirm and his son naive, but that does not mean you are any better for Novador than they are. You would wring the blood from Novadorian bones just to slake your greedy thirst. You don't deserve the council."

"You know not of what you speak, girl," says one of the council members, his voice so creaky it needs a good dose of oil. "Manners of state are far above such coiffed heads as yours. I'll not be spoken to in such a manner."

"But she is right," Ellarose says, surprising the room. Her voice, usually so demure and kind, is bright and loud. She steps forward, focusing her attention not on the council, but on the soldiers guarding the room. "You have been lied to. We have all been lied to for a great many years, but that ends today. We have no time for polite debate or musty bylaws. Right now, as we speak, forces from Valley Banomal are marching on our capital, intent on subjugating all of

Novador to their will. This will be no ordinary battle, no ordinary capitulation."

She steps closer and their eyes follow her, riveted. "They have magic on their side. Not the magic of fairy godmothers like Lyra here, but corrupted magic. Dark magic. The kind of magic that will bend you to their will and never let you go. Is that what you truly want? To serve these men and their insatiable hungers? To lose your power of choice? To be a puppet, your strings pulled by someone else? Because that is not the Novador that Prince Fael and I envision. We envision a country of prosperity, of equality. A country where everyone has a say, not just a locked room of privileged old men who have never toiled in the fields or held a sword in their lives. Are these the people you want to die for? Or do you have family out there, beyond the castle walls? Family who will be the first to fall to Valley Banomal if we don't get them inside the castle walls immediately. High Chancellor Cordo and the king's council would see them cut down before the Valley Banomal's soldiers. But if you pledge your loyalty to Prince Fael, we will see that they are brought inside the castle walls and sheltered from the advancing troops as we plan our own counterattack. Are you with us, or will you let these men continue to rule you and use you as nothing more than a body between them and what they fear?"

"What utterly preposterous claptrap," Cordo sneers, wincing as the edge of Vee's blade bites into the soft skin under his jaw. "I have had enough! Remove your sword this instant, daughter. Guards, take all of these children to the dungeons immediately. That is an order from your sovereign."

"You are not their sovereign," Fael says, looking surprisingly intimidating despite the flakes of rust raining down from his makeshift weapon. "My father is, and I in his stead. We have all been prey to your hunger, Uncle, but no more. Ellarose is right. We have a duty of care to our people that begins with bringing as many townsfolk under protection of the castle walls as possible."

"Commoners? Here in the castle?" says one of the council members, and I cannot even tell if it was the one who spoke before or a new man. I swear they are interchangeable.

Prince Fael points his sword in the man's direction. "Is that really whose orders you wish to follow?"

One of the soldiers, a young man with sandy-blond hair, puts his sword in his scabbard and steps forward, bending one knee to the ground. "I am with you, Prince Fael and Princess Ellarose."

The others follow suit, one after the other sheathing their swords and bowing their heads in deference to Fael and Ellarose. There's a great deal of spluttering and outrage from the ousted king's council, but no one pays them any mind. Fael gives instructions for the lot of them to be removed and sequestered somewhere in the castle while the servants prepare the great hall to accommodate as many townspeople as we can get through the gates before the forces from Valley Banomal arrive. High Chancellor Cordo struggles the most of all the council members, shouting threats at every person in the room before his malevolent gaze lands on Vee.

"I always knew you had too much of your despicable mother in you," he sneers. "I should have told the midwife to leave the cord around your neck when you emerged, so that you would have departed along with her and saved me this disgrace."

Vee sucks in a breath, her face gone white, and I am across the room before I even know what I'm about. My fist connects squarely with the High Chancellor's jaw, cracking his head to the side and toppling him back into the soldiers escorting him out. He looks up at me, dazed, a red blotch already decorating his jawline.

"You never deserved her," I hiss.

He speaks no more as the soldiers half escort, half carry him out of the great hall, but I am still trembling with rage and have to stop myself from chasing after them to deliver him another blow.

"Aralyn," Vee says from behind me, softly.

"You deserve so much greater than a disgusting wretch like him, Vee," I say, shaking my head, gritting my teeth. "You deserve love, and kindness, and basic human decency. You deserve to see him strung up and all his fingernails pulled out."

"Aralyn," Vee says, more directly, forcing me to turn and look at her. I can't decipher the expression on her face, and now I wonder if I've gone too far, striking her father like that. But then she gives me the most beautiful, most perfect smile. "Thank you."

Lyra comes barging in, as she is wont to do, slinging an arm around my shoulder. "So, shall we charge up this Protector's blade or what? Put down Fornax and his puppet army?"

"You know how to make the blade work?" I ask, my knees weak from the relief that floods through my system.

"Not a clue!" Lyra says, giving me a shake. "But let's try it anyway!"

We leave Prince Fael to organize the castle's defenses and start moving the townspeople into the castle walls, Vee leading us to the upper reaches of the castle where we'll have more privacy. I assume Ellarose will stay behind with her husband, but as we reach the second floor of the castle she comes running up the stairs after us, waving a hand.

"Wait!" she gasps, pausing at the top of the stairs and holding the railing as she catches her breath. "I used to spend entire days, sunup to sundown, scrubbing floors and hauling cooking pots, and now I cannot manage a flight of stairs."

"You should be with the prince," Vee says. "He'll need your help. My cousin means well, but he's a terrible organizer."

Ellarose smiles fondly. "He truly is, but I've left my most trusted lady in waiting, Kiara, to help him. I'm coming with you."

"That's really not necessary," I say, frowning. "We can manage. We found the Protector's blade in the first place, we can figure out how to activate it."

"Ah, but you only found two of the three pieces," Ellarose counters, holding up a finger. "I was the one who found the third piece. You might need me again."

A month ago, I would have put Cinderella in her place. I would have told her how utterly useless she was, or how the only thing we would need her for is polishing the blade. But now she is the princess, and I am . . . I don't know what. Something less than before, but also more. And she's right; we can use all the help we can get right now, as I'm pretty sure Lyra has no better idea than the rest of us what to do with the weapon.

"Where can we go for some privacy?" I ask. "Lead the way."

Ellarose grins, her fatigue forgotten as she zips off down the hall toward another set of stairs. We do our best to keep up with her as she leads us higher and higher, through corridors coated in motes of dust, doors so long unused their locks have rusted shut. I don't know this section of the castle, and it seems Vee doesn't, either. Still Cinderella climbs, higher and higher, until we reach a set of stairs so narrow we can only pass one at a time. Lyra's broad shoulders scrape the stones on each side, her hair brushing the ceiling. She looks so powerful with the Protector's blade over her shoulder, like she was always born to wield it. Or manifested, however the fey come into being. But maybe this will work after all. Maybe we really can save the kingdom.

"Ta-da!" Ellarose announces as she throws open a heavy wooden door with a flourish.

"Is this . . . a war room?" Vee asks, looking around the chamber in wonder. "I didn't even know we had such a thing in the castle."

"That's because it's long since fallen out of use," Cinderella says. "I read about it in the archives when I was researching the king's council by-laws. This used to be the true seat of power of the castle, far more useful than the throne room."

The chamber is large and round, with windows covered in heavy velvet drapes that block most of the sunlight. But even in the meager lighting, I can make out maps hung on every spare inch of wall. Maps of Novador, maps of Valley Banomal, even a map of Sandtrap Island. I wonder if Captain Hatchet knows of its existence.

There is also a massive wooden table that dominates the middle of the room, the top carved into valleys and ridges and wide plains. There are small figurines collected on the edge of the table, and as Vee moves one across the tabletop I realize their use.

"Those are armies," I say, nodding to the figurines. "Soldiers, knights, war machines."

"This is a planning table," Vee says admiringly. "I've never seen its like. I wonder if Sir Kenna ever stood around this table and planned any campaigns."

"Did you see him?" I ask, waving a hand toward the veiled windows. "When you were fighting?"

Vee gives a small smile. "Front of the ranks, as if he'd never left them."

"Why is it so high up?" Lyra asks. "Seems like a lot of work for those decrepit mortals down there to try and climb all those stairs."

"Ah, this is why," Ellarose says with a sly grin, stepping up to one of the windows and ripping the curtain back.

We all catch our breaths, approaching the windows in awe. We can see everything. For miles. All of the surrounding township and into the fields beyond. We can see far enough that we can see the thin line approaching on the horizon, deceptively short from this great distance. But they are there. Valley Banomal.

"It is a perfect vantage point," Ellarose says quietly. "You can see everything, all around the castle. No one could ever attack in surprise. But we are so high up, these windows are unreachable. It is a perfect war room."

"Then let's win a war," I say, turning away from the window. "Lyra, what do you need?"

"I'm not sure," Lyra says sheepishly. She pulls the sword from the scabbard once again, examining the interior. "Maybe it requires some kind of spell? Or maybe you have to read these inscriptions here. I told you, all our records of the time of the Protectors are rumors."

"Can you read the inscription on the sword?" Ellarose asks, twisting her fingers together.

Lyra shakes her head. "Maybe my mother could. But she's got her hands full right now in the Court of Eventide. Fornax has stirred up a full-on rebellion and she and the loyal fey are trying to fight them off. He's sided with the Court of Vespers."

"Well, we need *something*," I say, an edge to my voice. "I nearly died three times for that bloody blade, four if you count Fornax's little stunt in the Silent Forest. It has to work. We've got no other way to stop Valley Banomal."

"All right, all right, untwist your petticoats," Lyra says, her pointed teeth working the corner of her lip. "I know some very basic things about written magic like this. I can't read these specific inscriptions, but sometimes it's enough to get close. Let me try something."

"You're going to want to stand back, Your Royal Highness," Vee murmurs, taking Ellarose by the arm and moving her to the far end of the room as Lyra climbs onto the planning table.

Lyra takes the blade in one hand and the scabbard in the other, holding them out before her as she intones something in Feyrish. The blade takes on a soft blue sheen, and at first I attribute it to a ray of sunlight or a reflection of the wider sky. But the glow brightens until the individual inscriptions along the blade shine in a bright gold. Ellarose gasps and Vee reaches for my hand, her grip tight around my fingers. I can't stand to take a breath, too afraid to break whatever spell Lyra is working. The light becomes so bright that we're forced to look away right as a burst of energy blows through the room, pressing all of us back against the wall. Smoke fills the room, stinging our eyes and choking us.

"Lyra?" I call. "Are you all right?"

"No," Lyra says as the wind through the windows blows away the smoke. She kneels in the center of the table, holding the separate pieces of the blade cradled in her lap. When she looks up at me, her silver eyes glimmer. "I broke it. The Protector's blade. It's ruined."

THIRTY-SEVEN

"How is that possible?" Vee asks, rushing across the room toward her.

Lyra holds up the pieces helplessly, the blade as black and blue as if it has been dipped in a blacksmith's fire. "I don't know. I thought it was working, but now . . ."

Ellarose steps up beside Vee, frowning. "Perhaps it only needs a good cleaning? Or a different incantation? We could try again, couldn't we?"

"Or we might make it worse," Vee says, also frowning. "Lyra, do you think we could call your mother? Just for a moment, just to ask?"

"She has her hands full with the dissenters Fornax has stirred up, trying to cover what he's been up to over at the Court of Vespers. Maybe I could manifest the blade into Eventide, though. I know a few of the older fey who might still remember a bit of the old High Feyrish."

"But if Fornax has a presence in the court, he could steal the blade while it's there," Vee says, shaking her head. "Too risky."

They continue discussing their options, hardly noticing that I haven't moved from the wall where the blade blew me back. I am still tensed against the impact, my fingers curled into fists, my breath short and fast.

"Parlor tricks," I say softly. "That's all your kind are. Parlor tricks."

"What?" Lyra asks, looking over at me in confusion. "What's that supposed to mean?"

"It means that we—I—sacrificed *everything*, and for what? For this useless hunk of metal? For a lie that your people could do *anything* to save my people. What a joke. What a damn bloody joke!"

"Ary, go easy on her," Ellarose says, always the peacemaker. "This isn't her fault."

"It's exactly her fault!" I shout. "All of this is her fault! From the very beginning, she's done nothing but create chaos and cause problems for me. For all I know, she has been working with Fornax all along."

"Don't you dare," Lyra says. "I wouldn't align myself with that blighted bartoad if he offered me all the flour in the land."

"We have nothing, Lyra! Nothing! You can pop off to wherever and go about your bizarre fey business; meanwhile we'll all be subjugated to Fornax's blood magic. We'll be pawns, puppets. Enslaved. This is the end for us."

"Surely this can't be the end," Ellarose says, though her expression doesn't hold her usually sunny optimism. "There must be something we can do."

"We did what we could, and it wasn't enough," I say bitterly. "We're doomed."

"Aralyn," Vee says, but I can't stand to hear whatever she'll say next. I storm out of the room, knowing I'm acting like a child throwing a tantrum. I can't think to do anything else. I tried, I really *tried*, for once in my life, to do the right thing. The selfless thing, the thing my mother could never imagine. I tried to be something more than her pawn, her progeny. I tried to be myself. And it wasn't enough, not by a long shot. Now everything is ruined.

By the time I find a door that leads out to a walkway I am gasping for breath, a scream clawing up my throat. We're still so far up here that I let it loose, startling a passing flock of birds. But it doesn't feel any better; it doesn't change anything. We failed, utterly failed.

"Aralyn," Vee says from behind me.

"If you've come to strong-arm me into returning to the war room, save yourself the battle," I say without turning around. "I won't go back. I can't help."

"I'm not here to convince you to return," Vee says, her voice unusually gentle. "I only wanted to check on you."

Somehow the comfort only makes me feel worse. I don't deserve it. "I am not a feverish child or an ailing invalid like the king, Vee. I don't require checking on."

"I know," she says in that same infuriatingly gentle tone. I didn't know she was capable of such a subtle volume. "You know that none of this is your fault, Aralyn."

"Of course it's my fault!" I burst out, throwing my arms wide. "I was the only one among us with the knowledge, the training, the mind to stop this. To see it coming, to maneuver it to my own gain. And what did I do instead? I let myself go soft. I left the future of our kingdom in the hands of your fool cousin, your corrupt father, and my naive stepsister. And worst of all, I let myself believe in that bumbling, sorry excuse for a fairy godmother back there."

"That is your mother talking," Vee says.

"And she's right," I hiss. "We have nothing, Vee. Nothing! The kingdom will fall to Valley Banomal and Fornax, my mother will finally get everything she wants, and I will spend the rest of my life scrubbing fireplaces. If she allows me to live after the defiance I have shown toward her. No doubt she will have me publicly humiliated and have me cast out of the kingdom instead."

Vee's expression turns strange. "She would do that to her own child?"

I turn on Vee. "You have no idea of what she would do to her own child."

Vee looks at me for so long it makes my skin feel raw and my eyes burn. "Has anyone ever truly loved you?"

The question lands harder than a punch to the gut, knocking all the air and the fight out of me. "I am far beyond tolerating this game of insults any longer," I say hoarsely.

She shakes her head. "You misunderstand me."

She steps forward, taking my face so gently in her hands that it makes me jump back. She keeps her hands up, though, a strange light in her eyes. Almost like an uncertainty.

"May I?" she asks.

I'm not entirely sure what she's even asking, but I cannot deny her. I jerk my head in assent, and she steps forward once more, cupping my face. She gives me a delicate smile, ripping my heart clean in two and sewing it back together again as she leans down and presses her lips to mine. They're soft, the antithesis of her callused fingers against my cheek, tasting like the sweetest dessert wine. When she pulls back, the air tastes different. It tastes like her. I can't breathe it in enough.

"You are worthy of love, Aralyn," she says, echoing the words I spoke earlier after striking her father. "True love. Not the misleading manipulations of your mother."

And then, because her lips have knocked every other thought clean out of my head, her words form a new one.

"Manipulations," I whisper. I grasp her hands so tightly in mine that she gives a startled gasp, holding them to my cheeks like I might drift off to sea without their anchor. "Why now?"

"Why *what* now?" Vee asks, confused.

"Why would Banomal invade now? We have been enemies for centuries. What would drive them to cross our borders, to risk war, now?"

Vee shakes her head. "I couldn't say. My father might know, since he seems to have been in contact with them. Not that he would help us. Perhaps they believe our kingdom weak, and they see an opportunity to capitalize on it."

I shake my head. "I think it's more than that. Fornax said he sent Lyra searching for the Protector's blade. Think of how much power it must take for him to keep the people of Valley Banomal under his manipulations. I saw how much it cost him to retain control when Lyra confronted him with the power of the karacite. He's been drinking the blood of other fey to steal their power, but that can't be a limitless supply. Certainly not now that Lyra and her mother know what he's been up to. He *needs* the power of the blade. Think of it. An object imbued with the power of all the fey, meant to protect their human kingdom? He doesn't want Novador, he wants the blade."

"But it doesn't work," Vee says. "Does it?"

I shrug. "I have no idea. Lyra has admitted herself that she's not the most powerful of her kind. Maybe she just doesn't know how to wield it. But if we can convince Fornax that she does, maybe we can call his bluff."

"How are you going to do that?"

I grin. "Through misleading manipulations."

Now it's my turn to sprint through the castle halls and up the narrow staircase until I burst through the war room door, Vee lagging behind as she tries to keep up with me. Lyra and Ellarose startle at my appearance, Lyra's silvery eyes immediately squinty and distrustful.

"I have an idea," I say, breathless from my run. "About the Protector's blade. It's a long shot, but it's the only shot we've got."

Ellarose gives a delicate cough before raising her brows meaningfully at me and tilting her head toward Lyra. My fairy godmother refuses to make eye contact, choosing instead to study a nearby tapestry of the slaughter of the War of the Valley. The urge to roll my eyes, to snap at the lot of them for their childish insistence on expressing their feelings, is so strong I have to bite my lip to keep the insulting words from tumbling loose. Because Vee is right; it *is* my mother talking. She is every first thought I have, every instinct. Built on survival. But if I am to form my own thoughts, I must build them out of something new. Something far more delicate, but potentially far stronger. I sigh, approaching the table and sitting on the edge beside Lyra.

"I shouldn't have said what I did, Lyra. I was upset, and I let my temper get the best of me. You are not just parlor tricks."

"But that's just it," Lyra says, her voice unusually subdued. "That *is* all I am. Parlor tricks. And not even very good ones, at that. I have none of the skill with elemental manipulations that most of the fey have. I can't lead like my mother. I can't change my shape like Fornax. That's why he calls me *halfling*, because I have half the power I should. You were right, what you said on the Mortel Mountains. I am the worst fairy godmother you could have asked for."

I cringe, because while I don't remember saying any such thing, it sounds exactly like something I *would* say. Even now, some casual barb sits on the tip of my tongue, ready to strike. But I already know what it will feel like to unleash it, how hollow and petty and small it will sound without Mother around to hear it and praise it. Though if I am honest with myself, perhaps the barbs had always felt so hollow, and it was only the fleeting approval of Mother's laughter that had filled me up.

"I am not good at these types of relationships," I say to Lyra, trying to unsnarl a lifetime's worth of emotional repression. "Friendships, family bonds, whatever it is that exists between us. I was taught they were weaknesses, that such connections would only be used against me. And I let myself believe that for far too long, even when I knew what I was doing was wrong. The way my mother would treat Ella, the way she taught us and encouraged us to do the same, it was disgraceful. I can't change that overnight. I can't magically be someone else like your kind can."

"It doesn't change who you are on the inside," Lyra says. "Fornax is proof enough of that. Magic cannot make you a better person."

"The truth is, you are the perfect fairy godmother for me. We are both a bit lost, trying to live up to our mothers, trying our best and failing more often than we succeed. But we don't stop trying, either of us. We are fighters. Survivors. You saved my life, more than once. I would take you and your spells that backfire over Fornax and his rotten core any day of the week. I truly am sorry, Lyra."

Her eyes shine like a mystical morning dew, and suddenly she tackles me into a hug that steals my breath and makes my ribs pop.

"I can't stay mad at you," she says, squeezing me even harder. When she pulls back, she wipes one of her silvery tears and it splashes on the table. "But if you ever compare my mother to your mother again, I'll manifest you into the lower caves of Eventide."

I shudder and laugh at the same time. "Your warning is duly noted."

She slaps her hands on her thighs. "Right, so what's this plan of yours?"

I give her a sly smile. "We're going to use your parlor tricks to make the Protector's blade work again."

THIRTY-EIGHT

VEE RIDES ACROSS THE BROAD, GRASSY FIELD FAR outside the castle walls where we have chosen to meet the forces of Valley Banomal head-on. Fael sent a messenger ahead to Prince Pever requesting a diplomatic meeting to discuss terms, as I instructed him. The wording of the message did not specifically indicate surrender, but it was just groveling enough that Mother's greed and Pever's arrogance will assume we have capitulated.

"Is Sir Kenna in position?" I ask as she approaches and dismounts.

Vee nods, scanning the empty—for now—horizon to the west. "He is, along with the guards who pledged their loyalty to Fael. They'll be ready when I give the signal. There aren't as many of them as I'd like, though. And it's awfully open out here. No high ground, no natural shelter, and nowhere to retreat."

"Exactly," I say, following her line of sight across the horizon. "Fornax will want to make a show of strength here, to avoid the prospect of an actual war. He knows he's caught us on the back foot, advancing as swiftly and quietly as he has. He expects to find us underdefended and outmatched. He will bring as many soldiers as he can possibly control, to try and scare us into surrender."

"Which will put all of his resources on the line," Vee says, nodding. "I know. Still, I don't like it. And the princess shouldn't be here. If Fornax or your mother try anything, I'll be hard-pressed to defend her."

"I am just fine where I am, Vee," Ellarose says from her position beside me. "I am the princess, soon to be queen. I will not cower while my people are threatened."

"And that is why I married you," the prince says, taking her hand.

Ellarose graces him with a smile as she squeezes his hand tight. I'm not sure who is giving comfort to whom just now, for the prince looks a bit green around the gills. Still, he's gone along with our plan so far, despite how it must have sounded to him when we first arrived at the main hall to share it.

"Are you sure about your fairy godmother?" Fael asks me, for what must be the hundredth time since we left the castle walls. His gaze shifts across the horizon in a continuous motion, one hand on the sword buckled at his waist. At least he managed to find one that wasn't rusty this time around.

"I am as sure of Lyra as I have ever been," I say, which isn't the endorsement he thinks it is. But in order for this plan to work, I have to trust all its moving parts. And that includes my flighty fairy godmother. "Besides which, she will have her mother to help if she needs it, along with the loyal fey of Eventide. While Sir Kenna mounts the physical attack, they will mount a magical one."

Prince Fael goes even greener. "What will that mean for us non-magical sort if we get caught in the cross fire?"

"We must put our trust in Aralyn and her fairy godmother, darling," Ellarose says, patting his hand. I don't miss the hitch in her voice when she mentions Lyra, the grief of her own recent loss still fresh. I have the ridiculous urge to take her free hand, to comfort her, and then I realize the urge is not ridiculous at all. Only the pressure to fight it is. So I take her hand and squeeze it. When she smiles at me, tears sparkling on her lashes, I know I've done right.

"Aralyn," Vee says in a low voice beside me. Her gaze flicks to me before sweeping back out to the horizon, every line of her alert. "If this does not go our way—"

"It must go our way," I say firmly.

Vee pauses. "I never thought there would come a time where you would be the headstrong optimistic one and I would be the naysayer. But still, we must face the possibility that we will not come out of this situation the victors. And if that is the case, if the tides turn against us, I want you to take Ellarose and flee for your lives. Have Lyra manifest you to the fey courts, or to the highest regions of the Mortel Mountains. Perhaps you can find refuge on Sandtrap Island, given enough monetary incentive. Whatever it takes, you must escape. You must survive."

"And what will you be doing while I flee?" I ask, my voice surprisingly steady given how hard my heart is hammering.

Vee's nostrils flare on an inhale. "I will be making sure you can flee safely."

I raise a brow at her. "You mean you will stay here and fight? And yet you expect me to run away?"

"Don't argue with me, Aralyn," Vee says, her voice low and vibrating. "Get the princess safe. And you. I can face whatever comes my way, but not if the two of you are . . ."

"The only way you're getting Ellarose out of here is if you knock her unconscious and drag her out," I say. "And the only way you're getting me out of here is if you knock me out first so I won't know it's coming. We're staying, Vee. All of us, together. We are only here now because we have stuck together, and together is the only way we're getting out."

Vee watches the horizon a few moments longer, her jaw twitching like she wishes to argue with me but doesn't have the right words to do so. I expect another assault when she finally unlocks her jaw to speak, but she surprises me yet again.

"If we do survive the day, perhaps we should discuss . . . earlier. You and I, on the terrace."

I lift my brows. "What is there to discuss?"

"I thought . . ." Her cheeks flame a deep red and she turns her head away from me. "Perhaps there is nothing to discuss after all."

I slip my hand into hers, threading our fingers together and clenching her fingers tight. "Exactly. Nothing to discuss."

She looks to me, cheeks still red and eyes gleaming, and I can't imagine how I ever thought her stiff or wretched. She's the loveliest person I've ever seen.

"They're coming," Ellarose says beside me, her fingers squeezing mine. We are a chain, unbroken.

Time to put my slapdash plan to the test.

A line of soldiers rises up from the horizon, changing the shape of the land as wave after wave crests the tall grass and tramples it underneath the singularity of their bootfalls. I had assumed Fornax would make a show of the extent of his influence, but the bodies stretching out across the field defy even my expectations. There are hundreds, thousands of men, far too many to count even if I had the time and luxury to do so. They move as one, same as the soldiers Fornax used to attack me in the village, their footfalls making the ground quake beneath our feet as they approach. Fornax no doubt meant this as his great show of force, and it takes all my years of training to not let it show how effective it really is.

The approaching army carries the golden banner of Valley Banomal at their head, the color meant to represent their prosperity. But now that I know how they came about such wealth, the brilliant color shines too brightly, too garishly. Vee's fingers grip mine so tight I feel the bones grind, and Ellarose's have a tremble in them I expect is an echo of the prince's on her other side. We are four against four thousand, all of us barely more than children, none of us with the experience to face an entire invading army. Maybe the Protector was wrong about choosing us, or maybe he was exactly right. Maybe this was his final revenge on the court that betrayed him, to leave their future in the hands of those bound to destroy it.

"You are Aralyn, first of her name, the only one worthy of bearing it," Vee says to me softly. "And you will not be bested by a callous mother, a scheming sister, or a greedy fairy godfather."

I blow out a harsh breath, raising my chin and straightening my shoulders as the tension I'd been holding there uncoils just the slightest bit. "And you are Sir Vee-Lira, the only knight of Novador worth a damn. Well, besides Sir Kenna, I suppose. But certainly my favorite by a long shot. Let's save a kingdom, shall we?"

The soldiers come to a sudden halt, still several hundred feet away, and their flanks open to spit out a smaller group on horseback. They take their leisurely time approaching us, as if their day is already set, and the gall of it is all I need to shake the rest of my nerves loose. I would rather die on this field today than spend a single minute under their rule.

"Have you negotiated the terms of surrender with your uncle already, Prince Fael?" calls out Prince Pever of Valley Banomal. It has been a great many years since he was welcome in Novador, not since Divya and I were barely out of short dresses, but that time has not improved my opinion of the young prince. He might have been considered handsome under other circumstances, but as he draws closer I can see the cruel set of his mouth, the haughty arch of his brow. The face of a sovereign who sold out his people for his own prosperity.

"I am afraid my uncle is indisposed," Prince Fael says mildly. But I don't miss the iron in his voice when he tacks on, "Permanently. You'll be dealing with me today."

"Is the king still unwell?" asks a voice so familiar it could have come from my own head. I can't help it, even though I've told myself to stay strong, I jump slightly at the sound of my mother's voice. She nudges her horse out from behind the prince, clearly displeased to have been forced to go second. Divya is right behind her. "Such a pity. It's been so long since he was able to hold court. A kingdom suffers without its leader."

"Sometimes a kingdom suffers *because* of its leader," Prince Fael says, his gaze cutting to Prince Pever.

Pever gives him a wan smile. "Yes, we've seen the destitution on the way here."

The barb cuts right to the quick of the prince, the wound so clean I am sure it was sharpened by my mother. Prince Fael's mouth opens and shuts, and Valley Banomal has won their first strike.

"Novador has suffered, it's true," says Ellarose, her voice soft yet confident. "And we have suffered along with our people. Trapped by men who thought they knew better than their own people. Something I believe Valley Banomal could sympathize with, but their suffering ends here, today. Right now."

"Ah, good, so you *have* brought terms of surrender," says Prince Pever, clapping his hands together like a small child. Divya winces and something old and instinctive rises up within me.

Prince Fael clears his throat, glancing at Ellarose. "We have not brought—"

"I wish to speak with my sister," I blurt out, foolishly undermining my own plan. "Alone."

"Darling, what are you on about now?" Mother asks in that tone she uses to let us know we're boring her. "You're embarrassing yourself, interrupting negotiations like this. Honestly, it's no wonder you failed to catch a prince's eye with a loose tongue like that. Recognize your betters and acquiesce to them."

A month ago, such a rebuke would have sent me cowering to the farthest reaches of the manor in shame. Now it only makes me prickle with annoyance that she would interrupt me. I turn to Ellarose, hoping she can read my intentions in the words I cannot say.

"May I have a moment with my sister?" I ask.

She nods. "Of course."

Divya looks not to her new husband, but to my mother for confirmation. Mother gives a small sigh, waving a hand in the air. "If she really must."

Divya dismounts from her horse, and I lead her off just far enough that I can be sure Pever and Mother won't overhear us. Divya crosses her arms, her mouth set in that permanently petulant expression even Mother could not rid her of.

"What do you want?" she asks, and in her tone I am reminded that she is still only fifteen years old, a pawn of more experienced players. I know the exact feeling.

"There is still time to stop this," I say, low and urgent. "To get you free of Mother and Fornax's meddling influence. I know you think they are only doing what is best for you, but they don't care a whit about you. They care only about power, and feeding their own greed. You don't have to be a party to this. There is still time to save yourself, as I have."

Divya bites her lower lip, her tell when she is nervous, and flicks a glance back at the small party waiting on us. A month ago, I couldn't have imagined two princes, my stepsister, a lady knight, and the full force of Valley Banomal's troops waiting on a conversation between Divya and me.

"It's too late," Divya says, but her voice wavers. "I am already betrothed to Pever. No matter what you have planned, Cinderella and her prince will know what side I chose."

"You had no choice, and they will know it," I insist. "We know what Fornax and the Court of Vespers have done to the people of Valley Banomal. We know how he controls them."

"You do?" Divya says in surprise.

"He admitted as much to me when he attacked me to get the Protector's blade. But we have the blade now, Divya. We can stop him. And you can help us."

Divya's gaze bounces wildly over the brainwashed soldiers, Mother's growing impatience, and Pever's slit-eyed irritation. "I couldn't. I couldn't possibly."

I take both her hands, willing her terrified gaze away from the others and onto me. "You can, I will protect you, same as I always have. I promise."

She bites that bottom lip, her teeth sharp and glinting, but she gives me a discreet nod. "Tell me what I need to do."

I could cry with relief, but I don't let the feeling show. Not when I know Mother's eyes are still on me. "We have forces hidden in the grass, ready to attack and overwhelm Fornax's control of the Banomal soldiers. While he is distracted, I will call for Lyra and she will appear with the Protector's blade to force him into submission. When that time comes, I want you to wish for Fornax to surrender. I don't know if your bond will be strong enough to make him submit, but it's worth a try. Can you do it?"

"I think so," Divya says, her eyebrows drawing together in a frown.

"I know you can," I say, giving her hands a squeeze before dropping them. "Just wait for my signal, all right? I promise to keep you safe."

"Are you quite finished?" Mother snaps as we approach. "Or shall Cinderella call for tea while the two of you chitchat?"

"That won't be necessary," I say, giving Divya one last final look of encouragement before I return to Vee's side. "We have reached an understanding."

"We have," Divya says, nodding solemnly. She looks to Prince Pever, her gaze hard, and in that moment I've never been more proud of her. "Your Royal Highness, there is something you must know."

"Get on with it," Pever growls.

Divya gives me one final, haughty smile as my only warning. "My sister has informed me that Novador has forces hiding in the grass waiting to spring a surprise attack. Tell your men to fight *now*."

THIRTY-NINE

"DIVYA, NO!" I SHOUT AS THE SOLDIERS OF VALLEY Banomal let out a battle cry in a single voice, the slice of their swords leaving their scabbards ringing out across the plain. Vee puts her fingers to her mouth and lets out a sharp whistle, the signal for Sir Kenna and his men to attack. The high grasses shake and suddenly there are skirmishes breaking out everywhere as pockets of Novadorian fighters spring up among the Banomal ranks.

"Divya, what have you done!" I shout as Vee draws her sword and forces me back along with Ellarose and Prince Fael.

"What I had to do," Divya says defiantly, glaring at me. "You really can't stand it, can you? That I bested you."

Fael draws his sword as well, stepping up beside Vee as if Prince Pever will fall on them immediately. But the prince seems far too engaged in the skirmishes taking place within his ranks, his men unable to adequately fight the varied attacks of Sir Kenna and his men. Fornax's control is costing them precious time on the battlefield, and Pever knows it. His forehead breaks out in a sweat, coating his face in an ugly gray sheen as he watches whole swaths of his men fall before our swords.

"Divya, it was never about besting you!" I say, but my words are drowned in clashes of steel and grunts of pain.

"How dare you try to turn my daughter against me," Mother snaps, her eyes like fire.

"*I* am your daughter," I say.

"You are no daughter of mine," Mother hisses, and I don't need to hear the words to feel them. I don't know what I expected, but the pain of Divya's betrayal and Mother's abandonment—even now, after all these years, after all I have done for her—are like a punch to the gut. It takes the wind right out of me.

"The plan, Ary, we need to stick to the plan!" Ellarose shouts in my ear, her eyes wide with concern.

I nod, trying to marshal my thoughts and emotions. There will be time enough to feel betrayed later, when we are sure Novador is safe. Sir Kenna and his men are doing their job, attacking the Banomal soldiers in swiftly changing, unpredictable patterns. But they are still no match for the sheer number of soldiers present, and Fornax—wherever he is—has learned to simply hack and slash in any direction, unmindful of cutting down Banomal's own soldiers. After all, what is a human life to him?

"Where is he?" I shout to Vee, unable to see through the melee. "Can you see him?"

"We need to draw him out," Vee calls back, swinging her sword at a Banomal soldier who has drawn too close to us. "You need to call on Lyra."

"It's not time yet!" I say. "We need to find Fornax before Lyra brings the blade."

"They have the blade!" Divya cries, flinging a hand at me. "She told me herself, her fairy godmother is hiding it!"

Pever rounds on me, his eyes watery, his face twisted in a grimace. "Give me the blade!"

"What do you know of the blade?" I ask, stumbling back as Vee steps between us with her sword raised.

"Don't try it," she growls. "Prince or not, I'll cut you down."

"You lot don't deserve a fey treasure like the Protector's blade," Pever snarls at us. "Fornax told me all about it. About how your pathetic fairy godmother could never hope to wield a weapon of such power. It belongs in the Valley Banomal, where it can prosper as our people have prospered under the guidance of our fairy court."

"Your people have not prospered!" Ellarose says. "They have been manipulated! Subjugated to a corrupt fey court that uses horrible, forbidden magic to power itself."

Pever's expression turns ugly. "What could you possibly know about the power of the fey courts?"

"I know that they've had to resort to murder to get their way," Ellarose says, her voice clear and bright, her eyes shining. "Any court, mortal or fey, that has to kill to keep their power is never one we should respect."

"We don't want your respect, you stupid girl," Pever says, closing his eyes, his face contorted with effort. His skin has turned a sickly gray, his muscles stretching and lengthening in impossible ways. "We want your complete capitulation."

"Ellarose, watch out!" I cry, grabbing her and diving to the ground as Pever's form wavers and shifts and dissipates entirely, leaving Fornax standing in his place. He drives Pever's sword forward, right where Ellarose would have been. Vee catches his downward slash before he can strike again, sweeping his sword aside.

"You *useless* mortals," Fornax sneers, baring his pointed teeth at us.

"I should have driven you off the side of the mountain and drowned you when I had the chance."

"You tried," Vee says dryly. "And you failed. Just as you will fail here today. You were so busy fighting us, you forgot to fight your men."

Fornax's silver eyes go wide and he spins around to face the battlefield he'd forgotten. Without his direction, his men have stood helpless while Sir Kenna and his loyal soldiers disarmed them and rounded them up. I help Ellarose to her feet, Fael standing before us at the ready. Fornax lets loose another snarl at the sky, speaking a language whose guttural syllables I recognize. The edges of the grass field shimmer, and suddenly there are dozens of fey surrounding our men.

These fey are nothing like Lyra, so hearty and robust and full of life, and it shows in the gauntness of their cheeks and the long, lean lines of their arms and legs. Their skin is a washed-out gray, not the deep purple of Lyra, and I realize with a start that Fornax must have once looked like Lyra as well. The blood magic, the hunger of it, has eaten them from the inside out. Even the magic that radiates out from them feels wrong, like a nauseating stench hanging in the air. Several of the soldiers closest to them, Banomal and Novador, drop to their knees and retch.

"Did you think your pathetic attempts at rebellion would work?" Fornax asks, his eyes so bright, his skin so wan. "We are the Court of Vespers, oldest bloodlines among the fey. We built the human realm with our magic. We taught you foolish mortals how to make your fires, how to tend your livestock, how to make the most of your pathetically short lives. Did you really think we would let you emerge victorious today?"

"Did you really think we would show up unprepared to face you?"

I counter. I raise my voice to match his. "Queen Sagitta of the Court of Eventide, I call forth your army!"

The air shimmers once again, and suddenly there are twice as many fey as there were before. For each member of the Court of Vespers, there is a fey from the Court of Eventide, armed to the teeth and ready to do magical battle. The air is heavy with the weight of their powers, already clashing in ways we can't see. A strong wind blows through, driving back the fetid stench of rotted magic and filling the field with the relief of fresh grass and spring flowers. A female fey who looks like an older, fiercer version of Lyra shimmers into being before us. She towers over all of us, even Fornax, who now looks like a spoiled child standing before her.

"Fornax the betrayer," says Queen Sagitta, and her tone could put Mother's most disapproving moments to shame. "Or should I call you Fornax the murderer? Fornax the coward? Fornax the fool? It won't matter as your existence will be stricken from the hall of records. Permanently."

"I don't wish to be in Eventide's paltry records," Fornax sneers in an eerie echo of Divya's petulant expression. "I will write my own future, correct my own past."

"As what, that princely form you took on?" Sagitta asks, looking him up and down. "Were you no longer content with manipulating the mortals, now you wish to wear their skin?"

"I did the prince a favor, taking on those responsibilities at which he balked."

"Responsibilities like starting a war with his neighboring kingdom?" Ellarose challenges.

"Responsibilities like expanding our seat of power in the Court of Vespers," Fornax snarls.

"Yes, the court of the magic stealers," Queen Sagitta says, making it evident what she thinks of them. "Once the other courts know of your transgressions, Vespers will be cut off from the Fount forever."

"You wouldn't have the audacity," Fornax says, his eyes narrowing.

"Do not presume to tell me what I have the audacity to do," says Queen Sagitta, making the lesser fey shrink even further into himself. "I am queen of Eventide, keeper of her secrets, mother of Lyra, who protects of this realm and the humans who occupy it. And you are trespassing. Aralyn?"

"Lyra," I say, loud and clear, my gaze fixed on Mother and Divya. "I wish for you to bring forth the Protector's blade."

"No!" Fornax cries, lurching toward me as Lyra manifests between us, blocking his path. She holds the Protector's blade in one hand, the scabbard in the other. "Give me that weapon, halfling!"

Queen Sagitta flicks her wrist and the earth lurches beneath us, startling the horses and knocking Divya to the ground. Mother manages to keep her seat through sheer willpower, but even she blanches at the power that radiates from the queen as the earth crumbles and surges around Fornax, rocks pinning him to the ground.

"Call my daughter, the future queen of Eventide, a halfling once more, and I will sever your ties to the fey realm myself," Queen Sagitta says, her voice menacing. Another strong wind blows through, gusting hard enough to knock the rest of us down even as it does not disturb a hair on the queen's head.

Lyra, to her credit, holds her ground as well as she stares down Fornax and raises the blade and scabbard above her head. "You were never worthy to hold such a weapon, Fornax. No amount of dark magic will ever change that."

"Don't you dare!" Fornax warns, but he's too late.

Lyra slides the blade into the scabbard, the weapon exploding in light as the power ripples out from her, tumbling the rocks away from Fornax and knocking over the front line of Valley Banomal soldiers like the figurines on the planning table in the war room. Many of them stay down, Fornax's attention riveted to the blade and no longer commanding them. Lyra draws the blade out of the scabbard once again, now glowing with a soft blue light.

"In the name of Kaung, Protector of Novador, and Queen Sagitta, leader of the Court of Eventide, I banish you from these lands," Lyra says, her voice amplified.

FORTY

"Impossible," Fornax hisses, his silver eyes reflecting the blue of the blade.

"Well, don't just stand there!" Divya says, her voice plaintive. She scrambles to her feet, her hair sticking out at all angles and her skirts in disarray as she tries to wrangle her horse. "I order you to stop them, Fornax! Do *something*."

"You do not command me, flesh bag," Fornax hisses at her.

"Trouble in the marriage already?" I say. "Doesn't bode well for the honeymoon, now does it?"

"Shut up," Divya snaps at me. "Fornax could wipe the floors and scrub the chimney with your little fairy godmother. The worst fey in the court of Eventide. Perfectly suited for the worst sister in this realm."

Lyra opens her mouth to defend me, but I put a hand on her arm. This is not a battle anyone can fight for me. "All my life, I tried to shield you from the worst of what Mother put us through. The years she would abandon us while she chased her next paramour. The months-long parties where she was more interested in wine and dancing than she was in bedtime stories and protecting us from the kind of men who attended."

"How dare—" Mother begins, but I cut her off with a look.

"I am not speaking to you yet," I say, waiting until she has snapped her mouth shut in shock to continue. I look back to Divya. "I tried to protect you, even when Mother made me the target of her ambitions. But I couldn't overcome your envy, your selfishness, the ties you share with Mother. Always wanting more, never appreciating what you have. Mother let it ruin her marriage, her family, her whole world. And you, Divya? We could have been sisters, you and I. We could have been friends. But instead, you let Mother make us enemies."

"I don't need friends," Divya sneers.

"Don't you? Tell me, Divya, who here will put their lives before yours? Not Mother, certainly. Not your corrupted fairy godfather husband. Not the people of Valley Banomal once we free them from their enchanted bonds. Who will be left to care for you? To defend you? I would lay my life down for any of these people here, and they would do the same for me. Who would do the same for you?"

"You have grown weak and indolent, daughter," Mother says, her tone dripping disappointment. "You always were too hardheaded for your own good. You abandoned my lessons."

"They weren't lessons, Mother," I say, surprised at the strength in my own tone. "They were the bitter failings of a small-hearted, mean-spirited woman who had been spurned one too many times. All I ever was to you was an opportunity to reclaim the glory you lost. You never loved me the way I deserved to be loved. You abandoned me the moment I could no longer fulfill that promise. But in that same moment, you set me free. Free of your poison, free of your expectations. Free of the manipulations."

"After all I have done for you," Mother says, her voice trembling with rage. There was a time that tone would have brought me to my knees in fear and desperation, but now it only makes my heart ache for her. For how small she is. How petty. How unloved.

I sigh. "Vee, Ellarose, and Lyra have done more for me in the past moon than you have ever done for me in my entire life. I found my true family here, in them. And I won't let you, or Divya, or Fornax bring them any harm. And neither will the Protector's blade."

"The little half—fool doesn't even know what to do with it," Fornax says, eyeing the blade with pure envy.

"Don't I?" Lyra says, swinging the sword in an arc toward the soldiers behind Fornax. A line of fire springs up, forming a high wall as the blaze drives the men apart, isolating Mother and Divya beside Fornax. I glance at Vee, who has subtly given the signal to Sir Kenna to drop a stick of fire along the line of fuel we laid down in a hidden trench along the ground. She gives me a wink, her expression remaining stern.

"Impossible!" Fornax shouts, though he cringes away from the wall of fire. The fey of the Court of Vespers look transfixed, drawn to the power of the flame like moths. "Only a fire fey can use mountrite."

"If you think that is impossible, you're not going to like what's next," Lyra says. She swings the blade again and the sky turns dark, a shadow passing over the sun. Divya screams, swooning into Mother. Mother shoves her upright with disgust.

"Moonwater," Fornax gasps, eyeing the sword with a healthy fear now.

Queen Sagitta makes a discreet motion with her hand, scuttling along the little cloud she called forth with a wind so high in the sky we couldn't feel it down here. When she catches me looking, she gives me a wink.

"That's right, Fornax," Lyra says, holding the blade before her. "I think you know which element is left."

She hovers her hand ominously over the soft gray stone and Fornax physically recoils. "You wouldn't dare!"

"Free the people of Valley Banomal from your spell," Lyra commands, every inch the Protector. "And leave the land of Novador, never to return. All of you."

Divya gasps. "But Novador is our home! We belong here!"

"Not anymore you don't," I say gravely. "You chose your side, now stay on it."

"You ungrateful, spiteful, useless child," Mother hisses. "I should have abandoned you the moment you left my body. I would have been better off."

"I would have, too," I say, though it hurts me to do so.

"Release the people of Valley Banomal," Lyra says again, pointing the blade directly at Fornax. "Or I will use the soothspar."

"This will never be over," Fornax says to Lyra, the gleam of a promise in his eye. "You have no idea of the power of the Court of Vespers."

"A power that will soon be no more, once these prisoners are brought before the High Court," says Queen Sagitta, waving a hand at the fey surrounding them. "Vespers will be no more, and you will spend the rest of your existence trapped here, with no access to your magic. Now release the mortals."

Fornax simmers with rage, but he waves his hand before him in a complicated pattern, and there is a pressure and a pop in the atmosphere. The soldiers of Valley Banomal, still trapped behind the wall of fire, shake themselves as if rising out of a long sleep. They look about in shock, and I feel something like pity for them. They had no idea of the extent to which they were being manipulated, and I think it will take them some time to come to terms with it. I can certainly sympathize with being under such an influence.

"You are banished from the land of Novador for the rest of your days," Lyra says, her voice still echoing from the supernatural effect she's used to amplify it. "Never again will you walk the soil of this country, for as long as the Protector's blade resides within the court of Eventide."

"We'll see about that," Formax says.

Lyra gives an impatient huff. "You lost, Fornax. Just accept it."

Fornax's only response is a scowl.

"Some all-powerful fairy godfather you turned out to be," Divya mutters petulantly.

"Shut up, flesh bag," Fornax snaps.

"You two are banished as well," Prince Fael says, looking at my mother and sister. "I should have banished you the moment I asked for Ellarose's hand in marriage, but she begged clemency. She thought you could be redeemed. I think you have proven otherwise now."

"High Chancellor Cordo will not be pleased with such a decision," Mother sniffs.

"Cordo is no longer high chancellor," Ellarose says with relish. "Prince Fael has replaced him as head of the king's council. A new council, made up of members loyal to the prince."

"For now," Mother sneers, but I finally see her threats for what they are. Empty.

"Leave, Mother," I say, suddenly terribly weary. "And pray that Valley Banomal and the actual prince take mercy on you. Though I won't be surprised if they don't."

"You would abandon your own mother like this?" Mother asks. "To starvation, or homelessness, or worse?"

"You're right, Mother," I say, reaching into a pocket of my dress and drawing out a coin. "I should leave you with the same provisions as you left me. A single copper piece. Spend it wisely."

"You are no daughter of mine," Mother says, all venom.

"I think that's rather a blessing, don't you?" I say, but my heart is not in it. She is still my mother, the only one I will ever have. Severing my ties to her is like cutting out some rotten piece of my heart. It might be rotten, but it was still a piece of my heart. I turn away, because I can't stand to look at her any longer. "Sir Kenna, if you and your men would escort Lady Teramina and Divya to the border to be sure they don't try to slink back in, I would appreciate it. Ellarose, Vee? Let us return to the castle and begin the real work of rebuilding Novador."

"Yes, let's," Ellarose says, linking one arm through mine and the other through Vee's. Together we form an unbreakable chain, united in our dedication to one another and our country. Divya's plaintive cries and Mother's barbs of fury fade into the background, receding as they are led away by Sir Kenna and his men.

"Ooo, I can order cake!"

"Lemon and blueberry would be an absolute dream right now," I say, glancing back at Lyra. "Are you—"

But the air before her shimmers, and only too late do I realize that Fornax is no longer standing behind us. Lyra doesn't even have time to raise the Protector's blade before Fornax solidifies in front of her, something long and sharp gripped in his hand. He thrusts it forward, right for Lyra's stomach, and a scream erupts halfway out of my throat before a blinding light and a loud boom throw us all to the ground.

FORTY-ONE

"Lyra," I cough, the air smoky and thick around us as if there has been a fire. Maybe it is the wall of flames gone out of control, or we spilled some fuel while making the line. But I can't see a thing, much less find my way to my fairy godmother. I crawl forward a few feet as the smoky air starts to settle, filled with nothing but shapes and shouts as others around us start to recover from the blast.

"Lyra!" I croak, my throat thick with smoke. I stumble into someone, grabbing on, but it's one of our soldiers. "Where is she? My fairy godmother, have you seen her?"

"Your what?" the soldier asks, clearly still dazed.

I shake my head. "Never mind. Find the princess and Vee and make sure they're safe."

I stumble on as light filters through the heavier parts of the smoke, checking every prone body I find, the dread squeezing my stomach into a fist and closing up my airways. I can't stop seeing the flash of that blade in Fornax's hand, Lyra's silvered eyes wide and round and guileless. I should have known he would try something. Maybe Divya put him up to it, wished him to it. Maybe Lyra was able to defend herself, even though the memory playing on repeat in my mind tells me otherwise. I can't accept it. I won't. Lyra will be fine, if I have to wish for it myself. And then I'll deal with my mother and sister and her fairy godfather.

"Lyra!" I cry, tripping over something on the ground. I grunt as I stumble, and the thing grunts back. An arm, purpled skin, the fingers more like claws. I gasp and grab it. "Lyra!"

"Hello," Lyra says in a funny singsong voice. Her eyes aren't open, and she's lying flat on her back with her arms spread out on either side. Her hand barely squeezes mine back.

"Oh, Lyra, no, you're going to be fine. I promise. I swear it. We'll find Vee and Ellarose and get you to the infirmary right away. Or do we need to get you back across the veil? Your mother! Where is your mother? She'll know what to do. Queen Sagitta! Queen!"

"Aralyn," Lyra says softly, her fingers twitching in mine.

I shake my head, my vision wavering and blurring. "No, Lyra. No. No speeches, or declarations of love or apologies or whatever claptrap people subscribe to on their deathbeds. You will keep quiet and we will get you to the infirmary and you will be *fine*. I won't accept any other outcome."

Lyra's chest spasms as she coughs. "Aralyn, please—"

"No," I whisper fiercely. "You are not dying. Not here, not now. Possibly not ever, I don't fully understand the life-span of your kind. But definitely not today."

"Ary!" Ellarose comes hurrying through the fog, Vee right behind her, and drops to her knees on the other side of Lyra. "Oh, Lyra, oh no."

"Princess, it's—"

"We will save you, Lyra," Ellarose says, taking up Lyra's other hand.

Lyra shakes her head. "No, you don't—"

"Don't speak," Vee says, kneeling beside Ellarose. She glances at me over Lyra's prone form, eyes shining in a reflection of mine. "What do we need to do?"

"We need to find Queen Sagitta," I say. "She can take Lyra across the veil; I'm sure the fey have some kind of cure for whatever has happened to Lyra. Or maybe they can perform some kind of healing ritual here, I don't—"

"Everyone!" Lyra says, her voice surprisingly hearty. "I'm fine!"

"Of course you are, dear," Ellarose says, patting her hand. "You will be."

"No, I mean . . ." Lyra grunts, pulling her hands out of both of our grips to roll over and push herself upright. She towers over us, shrouded in the final remnants of smoke. "I'm fine. See? No wound."

"Wait, but how . . ." I rise beside her, patting her stomach where I swear I saw the blade go in. "How is this possible? I saw Fornax, I *saw* him stab you. How are you all right?"

"I don't entirely know, to be honest," Lyra says, her voice recovering some of her normal sensibility. "He manifested, I was sure I was a goner, and then there was this blast, and when I came to you were telling me I wasn't going to die."

"The Protector's blade," Vee says suddenly, looking around. "Where is the blade?"

"Here" comes Queen Sagitta's voice from some distance away. She stands in the tall grass holding up the blackened, twisted remains of what was once the Protector's blade. It looks far worse for the wear, pieces of it breaking off and disintegrating in her hands as she holds it. Another fey from the court of Eventide holds up a shriveled hunk of leather—the scabbard—and Vee catches sight of something glinting in the grass a few feet from us and holds it up. The hilt, the gold turned to a dull gray pewter, pockmarked and black where the stones have gone missing.

"What happened?" I ask, bewildered.

"Fornax must have struck the blade," Lyra says, shaking her head. "I can't fathom it. Maybe he activated the karacite and it just exploded."

"But the weapon is ruined," Ellarose says, frowning. "How will we hold off Fornax and the court of Vespers now?"

"I don't think we will have to worry about Fornax or Vespers anymore," says Queen Sagitta as she joins us, her expression grave. "Daughter, I don't think he struck the karacite. I believe Kaung's blade did its duty and protected you. When Fornax tried to attack you, the sword used the last of its magic to protect its bearer."

"Oh, but why would it do that?" Lyra asks, her voice faint.

"Because that's what it was crafted to do," her mother says gently. "To protect. The soothspar unraveled Fornax. And without his ties to the mortal realm through Aralyn's sister, the rest of the Court of Vespers disappeared. The High Court will vote to sever their access to the Fount, I am sure of it. They are done."

"Oh." Lyra grimaces. "What a fate. I mean, he did try to kill me. But still, to be shredded apart like that?"

"What will we do now?" Ellarose asks. "Without the Protector's blade, even without Fornax, Valley Banomal will know we are vulnerable. And we have no way of restoring the prosperity of the kingdom anymore."

"Yes, we do," I say, taking her hand and helping her up. I take Vee's hand as well, and together we form a tight circle. "We have you, and Vee, and the prince. We have a new sovereign who will actually care about the well-being of the people and not just throw lavish parties. This is a new era for Novador, and if we can't have the magic of the Protector's blade, then we will forge our own magic. Out of your benevolence, and Vee's strength, and—"

"And your brilliant strategy," Ellarose adds. She squeezes my hand. "Don't think I won't be doing this without my family. My entire family."

Is that what I am now? Finally, after all this time? *Family.* The word tastes so luxurious, and yet so familiar. A dream I had always woken up too early to remember, until now. I squeeze both of their hands until the bond feels unbreakable, giving them both a nod.

"Together, then. We restore Novador to her full glory together."

"It's you," Lyra says in wonder, standing just over my shoulder.

"What?" I ask.

"It's you. It's all of you."

"What are you talking about?" I ask, frowning.

Lyra's silver eyes pop wider in delight. "Oh, did I figure out something before you? Finally!"

"Lyra," I say, an edge of irritation in my voice. But she waves me off.

"Hang on, let me just bask in this particular moment. I get so very few of them."

"Lyra!" the three of us say together, exasperated.

"Fine, fine," Lyra grumbles. "I mean it's the three of you. You, Ellarose, Vee—you three are the Protector's weapon. That's what the prophecy was meant to bring together. Not that old hunk of junk. You."

"How is that possible?" Ellarose asks in wonder. "How would it even know we existed?"

"Oh, prophecies are always like that," Lyra says. "Cryptic, confusing, causing more wars than they ever end. People always seeking their destinies. But the three of you, together, you're the true Protectors of Novador. Just think of it! If it weren't for the quest for the pieces of the blade, you three wouldn't be here now, working together. No doubt the fortune of the kingdom was meant to turn around the moment you all were born under the same moon, but your terrible parents stifled your gifts."

"But now that we have thrown off their influence and chosen one another instead," I say slowly, "we have fulfilled our destinies."

"Exactly!" Lyra says with a grin. "Novador's true Protectors."

"That's quite a lot to live up to," Ellarose says.

"Do you doubt we can do it?" I ask.

She looks to me, then Vee, her furrowed brow smoothing out and stretching as she gives us a smile of pure trust. "I don't, no. I don't doubt us at all."

I look to Vee, my eyes full of so much more than just hope. "And you? Are you up to the task?"

Vee returns the look a hundredfold. "With you by my side? I'll battle mountains and forests."

"Oh, forests," Ellarose says suddenly, breaking our circle to clap her hands together. "I nearly forgot. I made a promise. You don't suppose you could make one more trip?"

Vee sighs, nodding to her future queen. "Can we at least have a slice of cake before we go?"

EPILOGUE

"ARE YOU SURE YOU WANT TO DO THIS?" VEE ASKS me, crossing her arms over the pommel of her saddle and leaning forward to give Thundermere a scratch behind the ears. "You can always wait out here until we're done."

I shake my head, mimicking her motions to calm Rainstorm. She's grown skittish the closer to the forest we've drawn, and now she snuffles and dances sideways at the first scattering of tree needles along the path. "I'll be all right, Vee, I promise. I need to do this."

"Very well, but no drinking from any conveniently located streams," Vee says, the faintest hint of laughter in her voice.

"Why would you even say such a thing?" I ask, but she's already put her heels to Thundermere, edging him forward and leading Ellarose's carriage along the Protector's path into the Silent Forest. Behind the carriage, one of Fael's newly minted personal guards drives a cart with the tree from the castle gardens in it, its roots bundled into a rough burlap sack. The guard eyes it warily over his shoulder, his face sporting several fresh scratches from the long journey.

The forest is as silent as ever as we ride along the path, though the leaves give an occasional hiss when one of their own passes onto the Protector's road. We don't go far, just enough that we can be sure the eyes of the forest are watching. Vee calls for a halt, swinging down off Thundermere and giving him a few murmured words before approaching Ellarose's carriage and pulling the door open for her. Vee hands down the new queen, still in her mourning blacks for her recently departed father-in-law, her crown heavy and glinting in the late afternoon sunlight.

"Are you sure about this?" Vee asks for at least the hundredth time on this journey, glancing at each side of the barrier holding the Silent Forest back. "There is still time to change your mind."

"I made a promise, Vee," Ellarose says, putting up an unconscious hand to stop her crown from tumbling. "I always keep my promises, even those I make to sentient trees. Come along, bring the cart forward. Where is my shovel?"

"Ella, you've made your point, you don't really have to do the digging," I say, though I pull one of the shovels from my pack that I've brought along with two others and hand one down to her. "You're a queen now—that's what servants are for."

"No, servants are for seeing to the castle's needs," Ellarose counters. "Not to do labor. I prefer to do it myself, anyhow. Besides, Fael is not here to see me, and neither of you are going to tell him, right?"

I roll my eyes, but Vee has the dignity to nod in acquiescence. "As Your Royal Highness wishes."

"Oh, don't start on that title nonsense with me, Vee-Lira," Ellarose says. "I'll have you demoted."

"You wouldn't." Vee frowns.

"Well, no, I wouldn't. I can't get rid of the head of the castle guard and the queen's new champion. But I will make you wear a dress to the next castle ball if you tell your cousin anything."

"Duly warned," Vee says, lifting her brows in amusement at me. "Shall we?"

I hand the second shovel to her, taking the third and dismounting as gracefully as I've ever managed to do from Rainstorm. We find a spot near the center of the path and begin our digging, the three of us making quick work of the dirt there. The trees watch us silently, the eyes along their trunks wide and unblinking in the most unnerving way. I know Ellarose is right, and we are doing what we must, but I'll never feel at ease surrounded by forest ever again.

When the hole is deep enough, Ellarose calls for the guard to bring forth the tree from the castle gardens. She holds up a pair of shears, giving soft murmurs of encouragement to the tree as she cuts through the burlap wrapping its roots. Among the four of us, we manage to maneuver the tree into the hole we've dug for it, shoveling the dirt back into place and lightly tamping it down. Ellarose takes a deep breath, turning toward the trees on one side of the border and spreading her hands wide.

"To the inhabitants of the Silent Forest, we bring what we hope will be seen as an apology and an attempt at recompense. A great misdeed was done to you in our name many lifetimes ago, but we seek to rectify that misdeed here, today. We return one of your own to your embrace, and we hope that in this gesture you can begin your healing. As queen of Novador, I apologize for the past damages done, and pledge to protect the borders of the Silent Forest from any such harm again, for as long as my descendants hold the throne."

She turns to me expectantly, and only now does my stomach turn. "Are you sure we need to do this?" I ask, echoing Vee's attempts at reason the past few weeks. "We have no idea how the trees will react. We should at least get out of here first."

But Ellarose shakes her head, sure and stubborn as ever. "If the forest is ever to trust us again, we must first demonstrate our trust for it. I would do it myself, but as you know . . ."

I sigh. "I know, Ella. I know. All right. Lyra?"

The air shimmers, and then Lyra and Queen Sagitta stand beside me on the path.

"Bet you're none too happy to be back here," Lyra says to me with a good-natured grin.

"Yes, thank you for the reminder," I say dryly. "We're ready. Are you?"

Lyra looks to her mother, who gives a short nod. "We're ready."

I take a deep breath, bracing myself for whatever might come next. "Very well. Lyra, Queen Sagitta, I wish for you to remove the barriers put in place by Kaung, the Protector of Novador."

Lyra and her mother join hands, speaking a few words in a language I don't recognize, but that feel oddly reminiscent of the inscriptions on the Protector's former blade. I suppose they would, considering they were forged from the same magic. There is a rush of air down the path, one that doesn't touch the leaves of the Silent Forest, and then nothing.

"Is that . . . it?" Ellarose asks.

"It is done," says Queen Sagitta, her voice deep and melodious. She presses a hand to her chest, giving a deep bow to the trees on either side. "The deepest apologies of the court of Eventide to the trees of the Silent Forest for keeping the barriers up for so long. We have pledged to never work our magic against your borders again."

I brace for any kind of impact, branch or trunk or otherwise, but the trees don't move. They don't blink; they don't do anything. Only the tree in the center of the path moves, shimmying its branches, the needles along them tinkling like chimes in the wind.

Soon the trees along the edge of the former barrier respond, stretching and reaching their limbs out where they had been denied for so long. The earth cracks and moves as they press their roots outward, already beginning the process of healing the scar so long held open through their territory.

Ellarose kneels before the tree we've just returned to the earth, taking a small satchel she's worn around her waist and unbuttoning it to pull out a small glass slipper from within. She sets it gently at the base of the tree, the ground sparkling and distorted through the bluish glass.

"Goodbye, old friends, and thank you for all you have done for us," she whispers, placing one hand on the trunk of the tree. "If Galandrel were here, she would festoon you with flowers, or tinsel, or something grand and elegant. But it's only me now, and this last token left to me. Do take care of it, will you? I shall miss you, but I'm glad to see you returned home."

Ellarose stands and wipes at her eyes, bowing to the trees. Several clustered around us bend their trunks in return.

"Shall we do the same and return home?" Vee asks, eyeing the nearest swipe of branches. They don't reach for her—yet—but I am of the same mind. I don't want to overstay our welcome.

"Back to the castle," Ellarose agrees, letting Vee hand her up to the carriage.

"Back home," I say, mounting Rainstorm. Vee places a hand on my leg, comfortable and intimate.

"Back home," she echoes, smiling up at me. "There is still work to be done, Ary."

I place my hand over hers, linking our fingers. "So long as we do it together."

ACKNOWLEDGMENTS

Some books leak out of you slowly like a tap that won't close, and some books gush like a broken water main. I was so blessed that this book was the latter for me, and that these girls and their wounds and their need for love resonated so soundly with me. I'm so grateful I had the opportunity to steward their stories into the world.

To my editor, Kieran Viola, thank you for taking a chance on me and thinking of me for this book. To my editor, Kelsey Sullivan, thank you for the enthusiasm, the support, and jumping in exactly where you were needed. You were an absolute joy to work with.

To my agent, Elizabeth Bewley, thank you as always for being my advocate, and for always being only a phone call away. You truly are a rockstar.

Thank you to Jen Malone for her insight and expertise, and to Shannon Doleski for putting us in touch.

To the entire team at Disney Hyperion, thank you for the support, the insight, and the dedication to projects like these.

To my family—Joe, Max, Lily, Mom, Matt—thank you for putting up with the mood swings, the foggy brain always half existing in another realm, and for listening to me go on and on and ON about story. Sorry I ruined movies for you.

And to you, reader, if you're still hanging around—thank you for continuing on this journey with me. I hope you found a piece of yourself in this story the same way I did, and I hope you never look at a tree the same way again (they're watching you right now). And if you're here simply because this is a Jenny Elder Moke book—you're my favorite, and don't ever let anyone tell you otherwise.